Christie Barlow is the autho romantic comedies including th series, *A Home at Honeysuckle F Boat Dream*. She lives in a ramsha~~ckle~~ cottage in a quaint village in the heart of Staffordshire with her four children and two dogs.

Her writing career came as a lovely surprise when she decided to write a book to teach her children a valuable life lesson and show them that they are capable of achieving their dreams. Christie's dream was to become a writer and the book she wrote to prove a point went on to become a #1 bestseller in the UK, USA, Canada, and Australia.

When Christie isn't writing she enjoys playing the piano, is a keen gardener, and loves to paint and upcycle furniture.

Christie loves to hear from her readers and you can get in touch via Twitter, Facebook, and Instagram.

facebook.com/ChristieJBarlow
twitter.com/ChristieJBarlow
bookbub.com/authors/christie-barlow
instagram.com/christie_barlow

Also by Christie Barlow

The Love Heart Lane Series

Love Heart Lane

Foxglove Farm

Clover Cottage

Starcross Manor

The Lake House

Standalones

The Cosy Canal Boat Dream

A Home at Honeysuckle Farm

PRIMROSE PARK

CHRISTIE BARLOW

One More Chapter
a division of HarperCollins*Publishers* Ltd
1 London Bridge Street
London SE1 9GF
www.harpercollins.co.uk
HarperCollins*Publishers*
1st Floor, Watermarque Building, Ringsend Road
Dublin 4, Ireland

This paperback edition 2021
First published in Great Britain in ebook format
by HarperCollins*Publishers* 2021
Copyright © Christie Barlow 2021
Christie Barlow asserts the moral right to
be identified as the author of this work
A catalogue record of this book is available from the British Library

ISBN: 978-0-00-841309-5

Printed and bound in Great Britain by
CPI Group (UK) Ltd, Croydon CR0 4YY

For Mum and Dad,
With much love.

Chapter One

The hot summer sun was shining in the cloudless sky as Molly McKendrick indicated right and turned her convertible Beetle into the magnificent driveway of the most exquisite hotel she'd ever set eyes on. She smiled to herself; this was home for the next few days and even though she was attending a work conference she was wholeheartedly looking forward to throwing herself into her time away from her busy daily routine.

Driving around the car park she saw the hotel was busier than she'd imagined, and after finally noticing a parking space under a weeping willow tree at the side of the lake she pulled in and closed the roof of her racing-red car before cutting the engine. The day was glorious, and she had the next few hours free to herself before she attended an introductory meeting for the course ahead.

Molly was a qualified vet with her own practice and animal hospital over in the town of Glensheil. For as long as she could remember, her career had been her life, striving to be the best in her field and working ridiculously long hours. But lately, after a number of misbehaved dogs had come through her surgery doors, she'd decided to add another string to her bow and offer a service that benefited herself and her clients: dog behavioural classes. That was why she was at the hotel today, to learn from some of the best in the field.

Before climbing out of the car Molly took a quick look in the mirror. She pushed her sunglasses to the top of her head and dabbed on a little lipgloss. She looked different today; there were no green scrubs to be seen or white clogs on her feet. Her hair wasn't scraped back off her face; instead, her glossy auburn curls fell loose past her shoulders. She'd applied a little make-up and her skin glowed and her eyes sparkled. With a quick squirt of perfume she declared herself ready and stepped out into the fresh air.

As well as the new business venture, Molly had also begun to give a little more thought to her personal life. The majority of her friends were married with children and she had to admit she'd begun thinking about her own future more and more. It wasn't as though she was unhappy with life; she had everything going for her – her own home, a car she loved, a successful business and just the best friends. But she couldn't help feeling that she was missing that special someone in her life to curl up with on cold winter nights or amble along to the pub with in the summer, but she just never seemed to meet the right person.

Tilting her face up to the sun, Molly murmured to herself, 'This is the life.' She couldn't wait to get checked in and hopefully within the next twenty minutes she'd be enjoying a chilled glass of wine, sitting in the sunshine admiring the magnificent grounds of this spectacular hotel. Just as she was about to close the car door, she heard her phone ringing from inside her bag. It was her friend Isla, no doubt checking whether she'd arrived safely. She'd call back once she'd settled in, Molly thought as she stuffed the phone back in her bag and stepped backwards.

'Woah! Steady!'

Molly spun around and apologised profusely. 'Oh my God, sorry! I wasn't looking where I was going.'

The man standing in front of her was looking down at the ground. Molly had knocked his holdall clean out of his hands. There, scattered on the ground from his open bag, was a pair of pristine white Calvin Klein boxer shorts. How bloody embarrassing for them both.

Without thinking, Molly bent down to pick them up and so did he.

Bang!

Their heads bumped, and Molly made a noise like a punctured balloon. 'Shit, sorry again,' she said, instantly feeling the red blush in her cheeks. Standing up straight, she rubbed her head, feeling absolutely mortified. Then she met the dark eyes of the handsome stranger standing in front of her, the warmest of smiles lifting the corner of his mouth.

'I never thought coming away for a few days would involve losing my pants and concussion before I'd even checked in,' the guy said, with a spark of humour and a glint in his eye.

Molly swallowed, then her mouth dropped open. She knew she was catching flies but couldn't help it. She was too busy getting lost inside his deep hazel eyes that were staring back at her. There was only one word to describe the man standing in front of her: hot!

Dear God, you have answered all my prayers. Molly was praying those words were just whirling around her head and hadn't actually left her mouth. She blinked slowly. She wasn't sure if she even believed in love at first sight … until now. Taken by surprise, she lost herself for a moment. His features were perfect: slim and muscular. Molly had already glimpsed his strong arms that fitted into his tight white shirt very nicely. His tousled brown hair was thick and lustrous and he had an almost perfectly symmetrical face that stopped you in your tracks. This encounter felt like a scene from a movie. Any minute now, Molly thought, he was going to sweep her off her feet and kiss her like she'd never been kissed.

'Are you okay?' he asked, staring straight at her. 'You seem a little dazed.'

'Lovestruck' is what Molly wanted to reply, but thankfully her brain was working quicker than her lips. 'Yes, why wouldn't I be okay?'

He pointed to her head. 'We bumped heads.'

She flapped her hand in front of her. 'That was nothing.'

He was grinning at her. 'Glad to hear it.'

Their eyes diverted back to the boxer shorts once again.

He stretched out his hand. 'I'll get them this time. I wouldn't want any more injuries on my account.'

Molly watched as the handsome stranger bent down once more, quickly scooped up his possessions and stuffed them back in the top of his holdall. 'That'll teach me to fasten up my bag.'

'And it will teach me to look where I'm going.' Even though Molly was extremely glad she hadn't been looking where she was going.

'I hope there are no lasting effects …' He nodded towards her head.

Already knowing there *were* lasting effects, Molly realised she was going to think about this stranger for a long time. She bit down on her lip to try and suppress her smile and knew she was acting like a schoolgirl with a crush. What the hell was happening here?

Taking the bull by the horns – 'Maybe…' She was about to say, 'Maybe we could grab a drink together?'

'Maybe,' he interrupted, his dark eyes glistening and locked on hers.

But she didn't finish her sentence, and he turned and walked away, leaving a burst of adrenalin electrifying her heart, which was racing at a pace she hadn't experienced in a long while. Shit, what was happening to her?

For a split second, she closed her eyes and inhaled his woody masculine smell then breathed out, only to discover, when she opened her eyes, he was looking back over his shoulder smiling. Molly was mesmerised – surely he must have felt that too? The attraction between them was off the scale. The last time Molly had felt that instant connection was when she discovered David Beckham's Instagram and she'd lost a whole night's sleep scrolling through every image he'd ever posted. David was hot but of course she was never going to pull him in this lifetime or the next and it didn't help that he was married to someone equally famous and beautiful.

Molly knew she wanted to know more about the mystery man. In fact, she wanted to know everything about the man who had just disappeared inside the hotel.

'Damn, I didn't even get his name,' she muttered under her breath.

Chapter Two

Molly was still smiling, with an added spring in her step, as she ambled towards the hotel reception with her long floating summer dress bouncing just above her ankles. Talking to herself only confirmed one thing for her: the stranger in the car park had stirred up feelings in her and she was intrigued by him. Casting her mind back, she couldn't remember the last time she'd been on a date.

As she wheeled her suitcase through the revolving door she saw the hotel reception was busy. She waited patiently in line and looked around. The foyer was lavish, with a crystal chandelier hanging from the ceiling; the marble floor stretched towards a regally arching stairway, and an oak balcony circled the entrance hall. The place was dotted with people going about their day, including large groups of business-type people wandering through the lobby, chatting on their phones or lounging on the large chesterfields tapping away on their laptops. Molly noticed a cluster of guests sitting at the bar and drinking from champagne flutes, visible through the double doors, and an army of staff circulating with trays of hors d'oeuvres. There were three gigantic windows that ran floor to ceiling at the far end of the reception that looked out over freshly cut lawns and a fountain. That's when she saw him again, the stranger from the car park. She couldn't help but stare. His skinny blue jeans improved his strong thighs, and his tight white T-shirt complemented his tan.

What I'd do to have those arms wrapped around me for one night only, thought Molly, as her mouth slipped back into a smile. The handsome stranger must have got the feeling he was being watched, because he glanced over his shoulder. Molly caught his eye and coyly lowered hers, then looked back up slowly. Biting her lip, she tried to hide her smile but that was proving difficult as inside it felt like hundreds of fireflies were fluttering around her stomach. With a glint in his eye, he gave her a look and held her gaze for a second longer before taking a sip of his drink. She was watching him, and he was watching her.

'Can I help you?' The receptionist's voice was bright and cheery, causing Molly to jump. Whilst watching the handsome stranger she had been oblivious to the queue disappearing in front of her and now the receptionist was smiling up at her from behind the desk.

'I'd like to check in, please,' answered Molly, still looking in his direction. 'Molly McKendrick.'

The receptionist tapped away on the computer in front of her then pulled open a drawer at the side of her desk. 'Have you stayed with us before?'

Molly shook her head. 'No, it's my first time.'

'And I can see you are booked in for a course whilst you are here. They are meeting this afternoon in the Swallowtail suite, which is just down that corridor on the right, at 2 p.m. for an introductory meeting.' The receptionist resembled an airhostess as she used her hands to point in the right direction.

'Thank you,' replied Molly, taking a swift glance in that direction.

'Your room is through those double doors on the ground floor, one of our best deluxe rooms overlooking the gardens,' the receptionist continued. 'We do hope you enjoy your stay with us.'

'Thank you, I'm sure I will.' Molly picked up the key and took one last look over her shoulder at the handsome stranger, who was in conversation with a group of people and had moved over towards the bar. She set off through a maze of corridors on the ground floor until she found herself hovering outside her room. For a second she struggled with the keycard but thankfully, after hearing a click and seeing the green light flicker, she pushed open the door and was finally inside.

The room was breathtaking; olde worlde, with old-fashioned cottage lights and a huge four-poster bed dressed in crisp white ruffled linen. There was an open fire which would be perfect in the winter months and a leather armchair, a coffee table with a bottle of wine, two glasses, and a welcome pack. Molly poked her head into the bathroom, which was a good size, with cream and stone-coloured tiles and equipped with a large bath, power shower, and a basket of luxurious bath products. It had been a long time since Molly had stayed in a place like this. After taking in the aroma of the gorgeous handwash, she pushed opened the door to the balcony and discovered her own piece of heaven for the next few days. With a sunken hot tub, bistro table, and chairs, Molly decided she was going to enjoy her getaway starting right now. After pouring herself a drink and placing her book on the bed, she hung up her clothes and picked up her phone. With her legs swung over the arm of one of the wrought-iron chairs, Molly actually felt herself grinning as she rang Isla back.

For the next five minutes, with a glass of wine in hand, Molly caught up on gossip with her friend.

'Just a heads-up, in a couple of weeks Allie has got the weekend off and apparently Dr Taylor is having retirement drinks in the pub and the new doctor is arriving,' Isla's voice trilled out. 'Make sure you're free.'

Molly was absolutely in. A night out with the girls was just what she needed after throwing herself into work for as long as she could remember. She'd decided it was about time she made more time for herself.

'And what's all this I hear from Rory? A new business venture in Primrose Park?' prompted Isla. 'It sounds like you are going to have your hands full.'

Molly emanated a tranquillity all around and when Rory, the local vet in Heartcross, had suggested that she would be brilliant at training the out-of-hand rascals that came into both their surgeries, making them into the best dogs they could be, she'd started to think about the idea seriously. How difficult could it be to run dog behaviour classes? She had great patience, and usually dealing with the dog owners proved to be more difficult than the actual out-of-hand hounds.

'That's why I'm here, learning about the psychology of dogs and their owners for the next few days before starting dog behavioural classes in Primrose Park. There's an introduction meeting this afternoon and after we hang up, I'm on the lookout for the gorgeous mystery man whose underpants I knocked clean out of his hands in the car park on arrival.'

Isla was spluttering with laughter. 'What have you been up to now?'

'Isla, he was hot, and I mean hot. You know when you just know.'

'Behave! How much have you had to drink?'

'I'm being serious,' replied Molly. 'There was something there. The sparks were flying. I knew I was staring at him, but I couldn't help it. He's my happy-ever-after, but there's only one problem with that: he just doesn't know it yet.' Molly chuckled, knowing that there was no way on this earth that the handsome stranger wasn't already married or in a relationship.

Peals of laughter were ringing down the phone, 'It looks like you are in for an interesting few days. At least if you find a real man there's no need for any more talk of this sperm-donor rubbish.'

Two months ago, on a night out and after copious amounts of gin in the Grouse and Haggis, Molly had shared with her friend that she was feeling a little broody. She was envious of her friends who were settled in families and she was beginning to think more and more about having children. There was just one problem with that: her body clock was ticking. Molly knew she'd make an excellent mother; she was a strong independent woman, financially secure in her own house and business with so much love to give, but as her friends pointed out there was only one thing missing: the man.

'Who needs a man?' Molly had blurted, and to her friend's astonishment had shared the thought that it would be simple to cut out all the love and romance and just go straight to the source.

'It's simple, honestly, Isla, there's internet sites …'

'Stop right there,' Isla had interrupted, sounding absolutely mortified, but Molly had carried on.

'Two hundred pounds for the sample and turkey baster but for the grand total of two hundred and fifty pounds the man has sex with you – he basically does the deed and leaves straight after. Obviously I'd have to vet the person, check out their background, intelligence levels, looks as well …'

'Isn't that actually prostitution?' Isla had thrown in, sounding outraged.

'I think we could interview a few men; it would be fun.'

'No! We can't! You absolutely crease me up. We can't go around interviewing men for their sperm – and don't drag me into this. Drew would have a fit!'

'Oh, you can! I'll have to. I want good genes, professional doctor's genes, good-looking genes … They have to be a decent height, same colour hair and eyes. It's the way of the world. I'm a modern woman and these men make a proper living out of it. Could you imagine three samples a day, seven days a week? That's a decent income.' Molly had been enjoying winding Isla up but the more she thought about it, the more it was beginning to make sense. Why couldn't she do this? She didn't need to be in a long-term relationship to have a child, did she?

'This donor stuff isn't rubbish,' Molly objected, trying to sound hurt yet wearing a huge grin on her face.

'You are bonkers, Molly McKendrick!'

'It's okay for you to say that, you have a beautiful family, gorgeous children. I can't remember the last time I even fancied anyone,' stated Molly, racking her brains.

'Do you know what I think? I think it's about time you let your hair down. All work and no play makes Molly a dull girl. Go and pour yourself a glass of wine…'

'Already done,' chuckled Molly, holding up her glass, but obviously Isla couldn't see it.

'I reckon you go and get your mystery man. Did you get his name?'

'No, but I'm going to have a wander down to the bar in a minute and that is the first thing on my to-do list.'

'Good, and no more talk of turkey basters. Things are not that bad … just yet, anyway.'

Taking a sip of her wine, Molly gazed at the magnificent hundred acres of parkland, comprising formal gardens with ornamental ponds, a Victorian walled vegetable garden and a woodland trail. There was a group of guests playing croquet on the freshly mown striped lawns and Molly noticed a couple walking hand in hand before sharing a kiss at the side of the fountain. For a second, she had romantic notions of running across the lawn barefooted and diving straight into the arms of the mystery man next time she saw him. He'd sweep her off her feet and from that moment on they'd become inseparable. There would be no need to even think about turkey basters.

Her thoughts were interrupted by the pinging of her phone – a text message from Isla.

Stop surfing the internet and go and find your man!

Sometimes it felt like Isla could actually read her mind.

I will, in a minute!

Molly replied before pulling out the course information pack and quickly scanning what the next few days would entail.

Molly had left her surgery and boarding kennels in good hands. She had an army of staff who were reliable and she worked closely with Rory, who had his work cut out manning his brand-new practice up at Clover Cottage, which had been up and running for approximately six months. They had a good working relationship and after his father Stuart retired, Rory'd been hinting to Molly that they should join forces. She was tempted.

In the last few months Molly had trialled a dog walking sideline from her practice, which had led to her employing two full-time staff. She'd never anticipated that within forty-eight hours of advertising the demand would be so great. But what was plain to see was that there was another gap in the market. Most of these dogs were naughty, the frazzled owners at their wits' end, and when Rory bumped into her walking through Primrose Park and suggested she was the dog whisperer after a naughty cockapoo had slipped his lead and was running from the owner, the idea was born. But for Molly it was all or nothing; she wanted to be the best at everything she did and had visions of herself taking it to another level – being the best dog trainer at Crufts perhaps. Of course that might be pushing it a little but you had to believe in yourself and that's what made her successful in everything she did.

Her early childhood wasn't one she'd wish on her worst enemy. Her biological mum and dad had married young, just turning seventeen. As much as they had tried to do the right thing to keep their family together, they hadn't been ready to play happy families. They'd lived in a tiny, damp flat above a row of shops. Molly remembered she didn't even have her own room, but slept on a mattress in a cramped space in the corner of the living room. Her father was hot-headed, drank way too much and was the kind of person you would dread meeting down a dark alley. From what Molly could remember her mum was timid, cried a lot, and spent many hours walking whilst pushing Molly in a pram. At the age of four Molly could vaguely remember a tall, slim woman with a kind smiling face taking her by her hand and her mum handing over a bag alongside her cherished cuddly toy. The tears were coming down her mum's face and that was the last time she'd ever seen her.

Molly had been adopted by Di and Doug and their family dog Willow, who was a little ball of energy. Her life had changed overnight. Those two people had brought so much love and happiness to her that she could never thank them enough for choosing her to be their daughter. And Primrose Park had been a special place to them, too. This was where Molly had enjoyed her time with her adoptive father walking their family dog, and one afternoon, after Willow had cut his paw on a piece of broken glass, Molly announced, at the age of eight, that she was going to become a vet as well as be the best mother in the world, just like Di.

Primrose Park was a beautiful park situated just off the main high street which backed onto Starcross Manor, with Heartcross Mountain towering in the distance. Wrought-iron gates framed the entrance, and oak trees flanked the main gravel path leading towards the duck pond surrounded by its pea-green grass. The creation of Primrose Meadow was breathtaking, with a grand pergola alongside the fountain, and during the summer months it attracted hundreds of butterflies feeding off the wildflowers. In winter the trees and shrubs provided rich habitats for robins and squirrels. Over at the far end there was a small lake for fishing, and it provided a perfect feeding ground for bats, as well as an octagonal roofed bandstand. There was a fantastic calm and beauty about the place, and it was a favourite with dog walkers.

Molly checked the time. She had a couple of hours before she needed to head to the introductory meeting and, as she pushed the course information to one side, visions of the mystery man began to seep through her mind again. She felt a little flutter in her stomach at the thought of seeing him again and leapt to her feet. There was no point sitting around her room when there was a whole hotel to enjoy and people to meet. Swigging back the rest of the wine in her glass, she grabbed her bag and headed towards the hotel bar.

When she got there, the bar was extremely busy, and after ordering a gin and slimline tonic she found a table on the outside terrace, overlooking the gardens, and pulled her book from her bag. Everyone seemed to be in small groups or couples but soon Molly would be introduced to people on the course and hopefully would be able to share dinner with someone tonight. Taking a glance around, she couldn't spot her mystery man or the people he was chatting to earlier. She felt a little disappointed but wasn't going to let it dampen her spirits; she was sure she'd bump into him again at some point. Lowering her sunglasses, she opened her book and began to read. This was the life: the sunshine, a gin, and a few days away from her usual hectic lifestyle.

'So you're a romantic comedy kind of girl?'

A dark shadow had crept over Molly and blocked out the sun. Immediately she lifted her head and found her mystery man looking down at her with the most kissable smile she'd ever laid eyes on.

'I am. Are you?'

He gave her a smile, 'I'm not a girl, but I can be partial to the odd romcom.'

Jesus Christ, her hormones were on fire. How did he do that? That look, that smile had such intensity.

'Glad to see you are in touch with your feminine side.' With his eyes still locked on her, her heart pounded – it was now or never. She wanted to know his name, who he was, where he lived, his occupation – everything! In a flirtatious act, she lifted her hair off her neck and twisted it into a bun, then let it cascade back over her shoulders.

'We meet again.' He gave her a lopsided grin.

He was a vision of total gorgeousness and Molly had to remind herself to breathe in, out, in, out. The words were whirling in her mind. 'We do, and this time your underpants aren't on the floor.'

A couple walking past the table picked up on the conversation and raised an eyebrow. Molly laughed and extended her hand towards him. 'I'm Molly McKendrick, and you are?'

'I'm Cam, pleased to meet you.'

Even with just a slight touch of his hand, the skin on the back of her neck prickled. Molly's heart was racing.

'Do you fancy a walk?' Cam nodded towards the fountain in the far distance.

'Perfect,' replied Molly, slipping her book back in her bag and standing up.

They walked side by side, Cam's arm lightly brushing her elbow, as Molly stepped down the grey stone steps towards the garden.

'What brings you here, Molly?' he asked, taking a sip of his drink but keeping his eyes well and truly on her.

'Work. I'm here for the conference. I have my own vet practice over in Glensheil.'

Cam narrowed his eyes? 'Glensheil?'

'A smallish town on the other side of the bridge that is linked to Heartcross? The village was in the news when its bridge collapsed leaving the residents stranded.'

Cam nodded and didn't hesitate. 'Ah, and the supervet who was in the news report, Rory…'

'Scott,' Molly finished his sentence. 'He's a great friend of mine. And what do you do, Cam?'

'Underwear model.' Cam's face was deadpan before it broke out into a smile.

'You had me there for a moment.' Molly laughed.

'I'm a dentist,' Cam replied.

'Well, my dentist doesn't look like you. Maybe I need to come to your practice.' Molly knew she was flirting, and that her statement sounded so cringeworthy.

'Maybe you do.'

'You really do have a winning smile.' As soon as the words left her mouth, she knew exactly how uncool she sounded and shook her head whilst rolling her eyes. 'And you're here because...'

'It was written in the stars that I'd meet a girl called Molly from Glensheil...' He was teasing her. 'I'm having a night away, meeting up with my cousin, a game of golf and some old university mates... You know how it is.'

'And how long are you around for?' asked Molly, hoping the answer was for at least the next couple of days.

'I'm going home tomorrow.'

Disappointed, Molly felt a tiny slump in her mood, but watched in amusement as Cam raced ahead with a huge grin on his face. He looked back over his shoulder, 'Come on!' he said, with a sparkle in his eye.

'What are you doing?' she asked, puzzled, watching him kick off his loafers before sitting on the wall of the fountain and swinging his legs over the stone edge, his feet now dangling in the water.

'You are crazy! Everyone is watching you!' said Molly, admiring his carefree attitude.

'Who cares? Let them watch! The sun is shining, I have a drink in my hand and a beautiful girl by my side. Come on!'

Molly's heart gave a flip at his words.

'Come on,' he urged again, balancing his drink on the edge of the fountain and holding his hand towards her.

'Daredevil you!' Molly laughed, enjoying the sunshine and feeling carefree as she reached for Cam's hand.

'Jump!' he said, his strong hand pulling her upwards. Her fingertips tingled with adrenalin.

Molly giggled as she sat on the edge of the fountain. At the shock of the cold water touching her feet, she quickly lifted them up, exclaiming, 'It's freezing!'

'It isn't!' He grinned, lightly bumping shoulders with her.

Molly watched as Cam slid off the edge of the fountain, cupped his hands in the water and playfully threw it in Molly's direction, making her raise her legs to shield herself. 'Stop!' she giggled, secretly enjoying every second.

Cam's eyes were playful, and there was a sense of fun about him. Molly felt like she'd known him for years. She was so comfortable in his company.

The sunlight glittered off the hundreds of water droplets as a frothy cascade of water fell into the circle of stone, water spraying as it hit the pool of multi-coloured pebbles splattered with coins.

'Here, make a wish,' Cam said, reaching inside his pocket and pulling out a coin. He handed it to Molly.

She held the coin in her hand for a couple of seconds

before closing her eyes and throwing it towards the centre of the fountain.

'Well, what did you wish for?' asked Cam, sitting back down, his fingers right next to hers on the edge of the fountain.

'I can't possibly say! Otherwise, my wish won't come true!' She held his gaze and widened her eyes, making them both laugh. 'So, do you normally jump into fountains with girls you've only just met?'

'It wasn't on my to-do list today.' He grinned. 'Do you normally jump into fountains with men you've only just met?'

Molly pretended to think. 'It wasn't on my to-do list either today!'

'See, we've got something in common already!' exclaimed Cam, taking a sip of his drink and not taking his eyes off her.

'What else have we got in common, do you think?' asked Molly, knowing she had a silly grin on her face that she couldn't tame.

'Tea or coffee?' he asked.

'Tea,' replied Molly.

'Good choice! Pizza or curry?'

'Curry every day of the week!'

'Again, good choice! Dogs or cats?'

Molly let out a loud peal of laughter. 'I'm a vet! I can't choose.'

'Fair point.' He grinned. 'A night at a nightclub or a

romantic walk along the river eating fish and chips wrapped in newspaper followed by a bottle of wine and Netflix?'

'The absolute latter, how about you?' she asked, wondering if he was a party animal.

'The latter too.' He nudged her arm playfully, sending an electric shockwave through the whole of her body.

'See, me and you, Molly McKendrick, veterinary surgeon from Glensheil, have so much in common.'

Hearing Cam's name being called from the stone steps near the bar they both swung around. A man was looking over in their direction and tapping his watch.

'My cousin. Golf calls ... unfortunately,' said Cam, standing up, much to Molly's disappointment. She really wished he could stay around for a little longer. He slipped his wet feet back inside his loafers and put out his hand to turn Molly round to face him.

'One last question,' he said.

'Go on...'

'Boyfriend? Husband?' he asked, still holding her hand. The question took her completely by surprise.

For a split second the question hung in the air.

'Neither,' replied Molly, and watched the smile grow on Cam's face.

He nodded. 'Well, it was lovely meeting you, Molly McKendrick.' He stared at the coins in the bottom of the fountain. 'And I hope your wish comes true.'

He held her gaze a second longer before he turned and walked away.

'Just one more question,' she shouted after him.

He glanced back over his shoulder and stopped walking.

'Will I see you again?' Molly secretly had her fingers crossed behind her back.

'I absolutely hope so,' came the reply.

Molly swung her legs back and forth like an excited child as he carried on walking towards the steps. She couldn't take her eyes off him. Just as he was about to disappear through the door of the bar, he looked towards her and gave Molly one last smile, causing a flurry of goosebumps across her body.

'Damn golf,' she chuckled, slipping her feet back into her shoes and ignoring strange looks from a couple walking by. 'I've never liked golf.' What was the point of it, walking for miles whilst hitting a ball?

Picking up her drink, she ambled back across the grass and thought about Cam's answer. He wanted to see her again and Molly had everything crossed that it might happen tonight. All she could do was hang around the bar area looking her absolute best and hopefully bump into him again before he went home tomorrow. Yes, that's what she would do. She pulled out her phone from her bag and pinged a text to Isla.

My mystery man is called Cam!

Almost immediately she received a reply.

Very nice name, and where is Cam from?

Molly looked at the text. Bugger, she'd forgotten to ask him that.

Eek! I never asked, but I do know he's a dentist who plays golf.

She quickly typed back.

Well, if push comes to shove there can't be too many dentists in Scotland called Cam! Get googling! Is he the one?

Molly laughed. In her mind she could see Isla already having them married off and their first baby on the way, but the funny thing was, so could Molly. Never on this earth had she ever had such an instant connection with anyone. She had every intention of finding out as much as she could about him.

Sitting back down at a vacant table, Molly opened up Google and began to search the web but all that came up was several dentist practices called Cam Dentist Practice. There wasn't a thing she could find out about him. Molly could have kicked herself. She hadn't even asked him where home was.

Chapter Three

Molly had been sitting in the introductory meeting for nearly an hour and for most of that time her mind had been elsewhere. Usually, she was on top of her game, always paying attention, making notes and listening intently, but on this occasion she had been well and truly distracted by her thoughts of Cam.

Suddenly, she became aware the whole room had fallen silent. Everyone sitting around the large circular table in the Swallowtail Suite was looking in her direction. Molly felt the crimson blush rise up her neck, heading swiftly towards her cheeks. She wanted the ground to swallow her up as the woman sitting next to her – Sally, according to the large white sticker on her blouse – nudged her elbow. 'It's your turn,' she whispered. 'You need to introduce yourself and tell everyone why you are here, business or pleasure.'

Molly was mortified. How had she let her mind wander that much that she had no clue what was going on in the room? Luckily the trainer came to her rescue. 'Molly, isn't it?' she said, taking a quick look at her name sticker. 'We were just talking about what brings you here for the next few days. Is it part of your business to understand the behaviour of dogs or are you here for personal reasons? Maybe you've got yourself a puppy or a rescue dog.'

Still aware that all eyes were looking in her direction, Molly swallowed. 'Hi, I'm Molly and I'm a vet. I'm here because I offered a dog walking service which took off immediately and I'm here to learn more about it.'

Even though Molly knew she hadn't been listening for most of the time since they arrived, the trainer looked very impressed.

'I think there is a huge gap in the market for this type of service. Just think how many people welcome a new puppy into their home and never train it properly. There's the saying "you can't teach an old dog new tricks", but I disagree.' The trainer switched on the TV screen mounted on the wall. 'This will give you food for thought for the first session tomorrow. Once it's finished, you can sign out and I'll look forward to seeing you all in the morning.' The trainer turned towards the screen and pressed a button on the remote control, and everyone sat back in their seats and watched.

'You can go back to sleep now,' whispered Sally with a chuckle.

'How embarrassing. I wanted the ground to swallow me up,' Molly mumbled.

'There's a few of us who've already arranged to eat together tonight if you fancy joining us?' shared Sally, taking a sideways glance at her.

'Perfect,' replied Molly, thinking at least she had some company for tonight even if she didn't see Cam again.

Twenty minutes later, after the video had finished, they filtered out into the lobby. Molly and Sally looked at each other and burst out laughing. Molly couldn't believe she'd been caught out like a naughty schoolgirl not listening to her lecture.

'You were off with the fairies,' giggled Sally, walking towards the bar. 'Do you fancy grabbing a quick drink? And then we can book the restaurant for this evening's meal.'

As they walked into the bar area, instantly Molly was looking around the room, but there was no sign of Cam. 'How long does a game of golf normally take?' Molly was thinking aloud.

'Golf? I've no idea.' Sally raised an eyebrow. 'Where did that come from? Are you going to train your dogs to play golf?'

Molly laughed as the bartender handed over their drinks and they grabbed a table outside on the veranda overlooking the beautiful fountain. Molly smiled at the earlier memory of Cam kicking off his shoes without a care in the world and splashing her with water.

'Now there's an idea… So what do you do?' asked Molly, turning towards Sally, who was filing one of her long manicured nails like her life depended on it. Thinking about it, Sally didn't look like an animal person at all. She looked more like a supermodel. Molly couldn't at all imagine Sally walking dogs in the rain or looking bedraggled in any way. Even her heels looked expensive.

'I'm actually a beauty therapist with my own salon,' said Sally with a smile, 'but my daughter has just opened up a dog training centre and has asked me to cover her reception one day a week until she finds a suitable employee. That's why I'm here, so if anyone asks me any questions at least I can give an educated answer. And to be honest, a few days away in a luxury hotel is right up my street.' Sally looked down at Molly's nails and pointed. 'Do you make much time for yourself?'

Molly looked at her own not-so-manicured nails.

'I think I need to – I don't seem to have much spare time,' she confessed.

Sally looked at her watch. 'There's plenty of time before dinner – shall we go and see if they have any spare treatment slots over in the spa? I like to check out the competition.'

Molly didn't waver. 'You know what, let's do it!' She couldn't remember the last time she had been pampered; relaxing wasn't something she did naturally. She had never in her life had her nails painted or had a massage, but she'd told herself she was going to make the most of these next three days and that's exactly what she was going to do.

Two hours later, Molly felt like a million dollars as she strolled back along the hallway towards her room, swinging her bag at her side. Her afternoon had consisted of one too many glasses of Prosecco, and a back massage, and she'd been plucked to within an inch of her life. Never in a million years could she have imagined a couple of beauty treatments would leave her feeling so stress-free.

There was an hour until the evening meal was booked. Molly hovered outside her room and rummaged in her bag for the room key. 'I really do need to stop carrying so much crap in my bag,' she mumbled, and waved the keycard in front of the keypad on the door.

'Why do you never work for me?' Molly was still muttering under her breath. She quickly glanced up at the number on the door to check she was standing outside the right room. She tried again, her expression knotting with concentration.

'Are you having trouble there?' a voice filtered down the corridor.

Molly spun round to see Cam strolling towards her with a huge beam on his face. Her heart gave a little leap.

'I'm a little bit useless at trying to make this keycard

thingy work.' She waved it again in front of the keypad but still nothing.

'Here, let me try.' Cam took the keycard from her and as his fingers brushed against hers Molly felt that electrifying feeling again, shooting through her whole body.

'You're staring at me,' he said, with a look of amusement on his face.

Molly knew she was, but she couldn't help it. 'I'm not,' she protested, thanking God that was all she'd said and no verbal vomit had slipped out of her mouth.

He grinned. 'I think you are and you'—he narrowed his eyes at her—'kind of look different, glowing.'

'I've just had a couple of hours of pampering and a few glasses of Prosecco.'

'And you look good for it.'

Molly was suitably flattered by his flirtatious smile. 'How was the golf?' she asked, watching Cam waggle the keycard in front of the keypad.

'Between you and me, I'm rubbish at it, but it's exercise and there is always a pint at the end of it.'

Hearing a click and seeing the green light on the keypad, Cam pushed open the door. 'You're in. There's a bit of a knack to it.' He had an air of confidence and a twinkle in his eye. As she took the keycard from his hand, Molly knew the attraction between them was strong.

'Thank you,' she said, beaming. She stepped in front

of him and paused in the doorway of her room. 'Will you be around any time tonight?'

'I'm sure I won't be too far away.' He took one sideways step and waggled another keycard in the air. Molly watched in astonishment as he held the keycard against the door of the room right next to hers. By the time she heard the door click, her jaw had fallen somewhere below her knees. Christ on a bike, he was in the room next door and there was no denying she was secretly pleased. After spending just a little while in his company she knew she wanted to know everything about him.

They grinned foolishly at each other as he stepped inside his room and shut the door behind him. Molly did the same then turned and launched herself at the bed and belly-flopped on top of the covers before lying on her back, silently screaming and waggling her legs in the air. As she sat up and pushed her hair out of her face, she spotted something in front of her that she hadn't noticed before – an adjoining door between the two bedrooms. 'OMG,' she mumbled, her heart pounding nineteen to the dozen. Quickly reaching for her phone, Molly punched a text to Isla.

The vision of gorgeousness IS IN THE ROOM NEXT DOOR! Sorry for the shouty capitals but I'm a tad excited.

No way! This was meant to be!

Came Isla's instant reply.

Typing furiously:

And there's an adjoining door!

You may not need a turkey baster after all!

Molly threw her head back and laughed heartily before stamping her feet on the bed one last time, then sat up. She leant across to the bedside table and put her phone on charge. She knew time was ticking and she needed to get ready for tonight's dinner, but how she wished she was going to dinner with Cam. 'Slowly, slowly, catchy monkey,' she murmured to herself, looking through the clothes she'd brought with her and suddenly feeling disappointed in her choices.

Damn, there was nothing that looked drop-dead gorgeous; she hadn't been anticipating that she might need to dress to impress. This was exactly the reason that Molly liked to wear her scrubs for work, because it was very rare that she had to think about what to wear. The last time she dressed up to the nines was at the Scotts's Christmas party last year.

She looked down at the underwear she'd brought with her too – Bridget Jones pants and her old favourite grey worn-out bra which had been white once upon a time... The sheer embarrassment of it! With everything laid out on the bed, Molly plumped for her skinny blue jeans and a tight white T-shirt, and it was going to have to be the black jacket on top. She looked at herself in the mirror. It really wasn't screaming sexy at all but what choice did she have? The jacket was on and off umpteen times before she took it off one last time and sighed. When she'd packed the case she'd never given a thought to the possibility that she might bump into a gorgeous guy she didn't know from Adam. Yet she wanted him to want her as much as she wanted him, and wasn't sure this was the outfit to entice him for a nightcap. But there wasn't anything she could do. She pulled the jacket on a final time and slipped her feet into her ballet pumps.

Curiously – Molly didn't know what possessed her – she quietly tiptoed over to the adjoining door, then placed her hand on the handle. Dare she twist it to see if it was unlocked? There was no denying she was tempted. She had the scenario all planned out in her head: the door would swing open and she would apologise that she thought it was a cupboard and hadn't realised it was a door and he'd invite her in for a drink and they would spend the rest of night in each other's company.

'What are you doing, you absolute loon? You are throwing yourself at a complete stranger with no shame.' Molly let go of the handle and took a step back then reached for it again and pressed her ear against the door. She was beginning to feel obsessed by the man behind it. She could hear the sound of the TV and then a phone ring. Molly heard Cam's voice quite clearly answer the call but was unable to make out any of the conversation. What the hell was she doing listening in on conversations through closed doors? This really wasn't a good look. She was about to walk away when she was sure she heard Cam's voice rise in what was obviously a heated exchange of words. The only words she could make out clearly were, 'I am not talking about this anymore. I've come away for a few days to get away from this. NO!' Cam's voice was now clear. He must have moved closer to the door. Molly stepped backwards, feeling a pang of guilt for listening in.

'I am hanging up now. I don't want to talk about this anymore.'

Then there was silence, except for the background noise from the TV.

Yikes, thought Molly, and wondered what that conversation had been about. Cam sounded rattled. She was still listening when she heard the TV go silent then a door slam. He must have left the room.

Within seconds, there was a knock on Molly's door and she froze. Was that Cam? She quickly checked her reflection in the mirror, puffed up her hair and gave herself a quick squirt of perfume, then she took a deep breath and opened the door – only to find Sally standing there tapping her watch.

'You were meant to meet us in the lobby ten minutes ago.'

Molly had lost all track of time. 'So sorry, I'm just

coming,' she said, quickly grabbing her bag, her phone, and the keycard before joining Sally in the hallway.

'Everyone else from the course is already in the restaurant. Did you know you've got a dishy neighbour staying in the room next door to you?'

'Have I? I've not noticed.' Molly smiled to herself.

'He didn't look like he was with anyone. Striding down the hallway he was leaving behind an attractive aroma.' Sally inhaled. 'I love a good aftershave, don't you?'

'Absolutely.' The second she'd met Cam in the car park his scent had made Molly go weak at the knees.

'I think we should hang around your hot tub later; we might get another glimpse of him!'

Molly wasn't sure whether that was a serious suggestion but there was no way anyone was gatecrashing her room later. She already had hopeful plans and they didn't involve Sally.

'That would be lovely but I'm thinking more of an early night for me.'

'Really?' Sally raised an eyebrow.

'I want to be fresh as a daisy for the course tomorrow. I think I showed myself up enough today and that cannot happen twice.'

'Fair point,' replied Sally with a smile. 'You were really funny.'

'But maybe tomorrow night,' she said, knowing full

well Cam would have left the building by then and returned home.

'Sounds like a plan to me,' answered Sally, holding open the lobby door for her.

As they walked towards the restaurant Molly heard her phone ping. It was Isla.

Have a good night and don't do anything I wouldn't do!

Molly grinned and quickly typed back:

I'm having dinner with some of the course members and even if I get the chance there is no way on this earth I can scare anyone with the sight of my Bridget Jones big knickers!

After receiving a handful of laughing emojis back from Isla, Molly followed Sally into the restaurant. She quickly scanned the area for Cam but he was nowhere to be seen. But Molly wasn't worried, because she knew from the look on his face when he closed his bedroom door that she would be seeing him sometime tonight. It couldn't come soon enough.

Chapter Four

M olly had looked out for Cam and his cousin all night but, much to her disappointment, they never appeared. She'd strolled through to the bar countless times throughout the evening but still there was no sign of them. Just after 10.30 p.m., a little disappointed, she made her excuses and retired to her room.

The room next door lay in complete silence as Molly poured herself a drink and wandered out onto the balcony. She sipped her wine and took in the view, thinking how much she'd enjoyed her night; the food had been delicious and it had been good getting to know the others on the course. But she had been distracted, with one eye always on the bar, waiting and watching to see if Cam would walk in.

After a few moments, she sighed, turned around and walked back towards the door.

'You took your time; why the huge sigh?'

Molly jumped out of her skin and brought her hand up to her chest. There was Cam sitting outside on his decking with a glass of red in his hand. His eyes sparkled and his stubble glistened from the spotlights shining up from the floor of the decking.

'Moon or stars?' he said.

Molly looked up to the sky. 'Definitely the stars.'

'Good choice. Would you like a glass?' He waggled the bottle in the air.

She held up her own glass. 'I've just poured one.'

They looked at each other for a second.

'Are you coming here or am I coming over there?' His tone was soft and inviting.

Molly felt her heart race. She bit her lip then answered, 'How about you come over here?'

Cam didn't need asking again but immediately stood up. Molly opened the adjoining door with a trembling hand. As he stepped inside her room he said, 'We meet again,' before dipping his head and placing a soft kiss on her cheek. Then he lingered, his lips centimetres from hers. Feeling brave, Molly leant up and placed a kiss on his lips. 'Do you normally go around kissing complete strangers?' she murmured.

'Not usually, but there's something about you, Molly McKendrick.' He smiled at her then took the glass of wine from her hand and placed it on the dressing table.

'And there's something about you, Cam...' Molly whispered, hoping he'd fill the gap between them and kiss her again.

But Cam didn't. Instead he whispered, 'Dentist or doctor?' still playing their game.

'Absolutely dentist,' Molly replied, not faltering from his gaze.

'Dark or light?' she asked, watching him narrowing his eyes as she leant across and switched off the light. Their eyes locked as shadows passed across the contours of their faces. He tilted Molly's face towards his and placed his lips on hers again.

Molly's heart was thumping; never in her life had she been attracted to anyone in this way, and she forced herself to breathe calmly even though her whole body was trembling. She hadn't felt longing like this for ages. In complete darkness, she pressed her body against his and gasped with desire. She grabbed at his hair then kissed him hard. The electricity sparked between them. Molly pushed him towards the bed, wanting to be closer. Still kissing him, she felt an immense tingle through her body and she didn't want it to stop. As they started to pull at each other's clothes, Molly ran her hands over Cam's body, his strong arms, his toned torso – it had been a while since she'd touched a man's body and it felt so good touching Cam. His face was in her hair, kissing her neck, his hands tugging at her clothes and exploring her body. Every nerve tingled as he lifted off her top and unhooked her bra.

'Are you sure, Molly?'

Molly felt dizzy, her eyes locking with his. Never in her life had she done anything like this before, or wanted to. She felt scared yet excited – Cam had knocked her off feet so fast. He was looking at her with such adoration that she had to remind herself to breathe. Molly knew it was out of character for her: she was the sensible one, the one who weighed up both sides and the consequences, but not tonight. With an overwhelming desire to spend this night with him, she embraced the tingling pleasure flooding her body. Molly wanted him right now and she didn't want to think about anything else except him.

'I'm sure.' And with those words Cam kissed her again, stealing what was left of her breath.

_____

An hour later, lying in bed wrapped in Cam's arms, Molly felt an overwhelming happiness surge through her body. She tilted her head up and kissed him lightly on the lips. She noticed his face was flushed and he smiled at her, before kissing her on top of her head.

Molly couldn't help but smile back. This night with Cam had been perfect. One she would never forget.

Chapter Five

When Molly woke up the next morning it seemed like she'd been sleeping for hours. She felt like the happiest girl on the planet when she opened her eyes, and she turned over with a huge smile on her face and reached out – only to find the covers pulled back and the space next to her empty. Sitting up in bed, she stared at the empty space and listened. There was absolute silence except for the dawn chorus filtering from the balcony outside. Her eyes scanned the floor, but all of Cam's clothes were gone; the only trace left of him was the half-drunk glass of wine abandoned on the bedside cabinet.

'Cam?' she called out, but there was no answer.

Quickly, Molly pushed back the duvet, looked down at her underwear in disarray, and felt embarrassed. It had been an amazing night but now she was having a quiet internal wobble. Surely he couldn't have just up and left without saying a word? They hadn't even said goodbye, swapped numbers, or anything. Swinging her legs to the floor she hurriedly checked the bathroom then listened at the adjoining door but there was only silence. Rapping lightly on the door she waited but still nothing. Taking the plunge, she turned the handle and looked inside. His room was empty, the bed made and his suitcase gone.

Molly exhaled. Cam had gone – upped and left and never said goodbye. Last night had been amazing, one of the best nights of her life, and she'd thought their connection had been off the scale. But now what had happened? Never in a million years did she think he'd just disappear. Feeling confused, Molly frantically searched her room, looking for a note or anything from him, but there was nothing. With a sigh, she sat back down on the bed.

'Charming.' With a crushed, anxious feeling swirling in the pit of her stomach, she picked up her phone. It had only just gone 7 a.m. She quickly pinged a text to Isla.

Are you up?

Immediately she received a reply.

Of course I'm up, I'm married to a farmer!

Molly pressed her number and after only one ring Isla picked up. 'What's up?'

'I think I've just become a modern woman.' Molly just didn't know what to make of it all.

'Come again?'

Molly spilt the beans about what had happened between her and Cam. 'But I've woken up and he's gone,' she added.

'You are a dark horse, Molly McKendrick. They always say the quiet ones are the worst.'

'It's not funny! Honestly, it was amazing, just the best night, and now he's gone. Why would he do that?' Molly could feel her bottom lip trembling. 'I just don't get it. We connected emotionally and physically.' Molly couldn't help but wonder if she'd done something wrong.

'Surely you must have found out his surname, where he lives? Anything to go on?'

Molly was shaking her head. 'No, I didn't.'

'You didn't get any more personal information from him at all?'

Molly was sitting cross-legged on the bed, fiddling with the laced hem on the duvet cover. 'We kind of skipped the talking part altogether.'

'Well, in that case, there's only one thing you can you do. Take it for what it was – an amazing night.'

Molly knew that's all she could do but a part of her felt humiliating disappointment. Last night she'd felt something she hadn't felt in a long time: sexy and desired. She thought they would be waking up wrapped in each other's arms and maybe meeting up again in a few days after they'd swapped numbers and stalked each other on social media. There was no way he hadn't felt what she had.

'I just can't believe he's left no trace. It was like last night never happened.' Molly heard her voice crack.

'Don't dwell. Just remember how last night felt. How he put a smile on your face and today is a new day. You just have to roll with the good times.' Isla was trying to smooth the way, but it wasn't making Molly feel any better. In fact, she was beginning to feel like she'd let herself down. The swirling feeling of lust and excitement from last night had now turned into one of shame and embarrassment.

Molly knew Isla was right, that she had no choice but to take the memory of last night and smile about it, but of course she felt blind-sided. Surely Cam could have told her he was leaving and said goodbye? Even a *thank you for a great night*, scribbled on the hotel notepad, would have been better than absolutely nothing.

Chapter Six

Three months later

Molly stood on the pavement and checked the address on her phone; she was definitely in the right place. The tiny thatched cottage in front of her was set back from the road. The low stone wall beside it was packed with tiny blue flowers that hung over the edges, adding to the beauty of the place. As she pushed open the rickety wooden gate, Molly stepped onto a gravel path that crunched under her feet and meandered through an overgrown lawn with wild pink foxgloves standing tall from the flowerbeds. Molly admired the pale pink roses twisting themselves around the oak porch that flanked the heavy duck-egg-blue wooden front door. Littered all over the step were several plant pots of red geraniums and window boxes full of colourful pansies dancing in the light breeze. Bumblebee Cottage, according to the name on the sign that hung above her head, oozed beauty and was obviously a very well-loved home.

Molly hadn't even known this place existed. It was tucked away just up the lane from Clover Cottage next to The Old Bakehouse and she hadn't really paid that much attention to the place before. She knocked on the door and waited. There was commotion inside, a dog barking, a woman's voice shooing the dog, followed by the sound of a door banging. Footsteps echoed up the hallway before the door swung open and Molly was greeted by a rosy-cheeked woman whose hair was pulled back in a tight bun. Her tight olive-green cardigan was buttoned up around her bosom and a grey tweed A-line skirt clashed with a pair of bright blue Hunter wellington boots on her feet. She held a jar of honey in one hand, a sticky spoon in the other.

'Good morning,' she sang, thrusting her hand forward before realising she was holding the jar of honey, which she quickly placed on a dresser in the hallway that was overloaded with china plates and framed photographs. 'You must be Molly. Come in, come in... I can't begin to tell you how pleased I am to see you. I'm Birdie. We usually deal with Rory but he's recommended you, spoke very highly of you ... claiming you are the dog whisperer.'

'You can't believe everything Rory tells you,' Molly

joked, stepping onto the red flagstone floor inside Bumblebee Cottage, but she was secretly quite pleased Rory had spoken highly of her.

Inside, the cottage ceilings were low and the hallway was cramped; the coatstand was overflowing with battered old green wax jackets, scarfs, and hats. Underneath was an array of wellingtons and walking boots and sticks toppled sideways. There was an old-fashioned cream telephone on a small circular oak table with a pad bound together by elastic bands. As Molly followed Birdie she glanced at the walls, which were lined with paintings of horses and foxes and a photograph of a man dressed in a white beekeeper's suit.

'This is an interesting place,' said Molly, taking in her surroundings.

'It is indeed, full of character and memories.' Birdie smiled warmly and led Molly down a step and through an archway leading to the kitchen.

Numerous pans hung from the wooden rack on the ceiling, alongside bunches of dried lavender. There was an impressive stone alcove that housed a racing-green Aga that stood proudly and kicked out a lovely warmth into the room. Shelves lined one wall and were crammed with plates and floral china cups. Molly imagined some great Christmases sat around the old farmhouse table in the centre of the room, which was now cluttered with post, catalogues, and old newspapers. Jam jars lined the worktops, cookbooks piled up on the shelves, and the old Belfast sink, positioned under a window that looked out across a most magnificent garden, was crammed full of dirty plates. There was stuff everywhere.

'It's a bit of a mess, isn't it?' Birdie spoke the exact words that Molly was thinking. 'I'm just in the middle of clearing it out. Mum was a hoarder, wouldn't throw anything away. All this junk has been the bane of my life and I knew one day it would be left to me to clear it all out.' For a second Birdie sounded a little brusque but then she softened. 'But Mum's become very forgetful lately and even a little … let's say aggressive. It's been a very difficult time, especially when Mum doesn't remember that she's lashed out. So she's finally gone into a care home. At least now I can get a decent night's sleep without worrying, knowing Mum is in safe hands.'

'Dementia?' asked Molly.

Birdie nodded.

'It must be very difficult for you at the moment,' replied Molly, pulling out a chair and removing the stack of letters on the seat and balancing them on top of another toppling pile on the table before she sat down. 'Do you live here?'

Birdie shook her head. 'I live next door, at The Old Bakehouse.' She sat down at the table with Molly. 'My nephew is renting this place from Mum for a while, arriving sometime in the next few days I believe.' She raised her eyebrows and scanned the room. 'He doesn't know what he's letting himself in for. It may look picturesque but the boiler is temperamental, the water pressure nonexistent, leaking taps, pipes that clang all night and then there's the bees ... plus overgrown greenhouses, the summerhouse is in need of some TLC... He's going to have his work cut out.'

'Bees?'

'It's not called Bumblebee Cottage for nothing.' She held up another jar of honey. 'Honestly, those hives out there are like busy cities ruled by the queen. Many moons ago my father used to supply to all the local delicatessen and farm shops. He made a good income from a hobby that turned into a full-time job. Now I have Gabe, a local beekeeper, coming in to help me out. Anyway, I'm babbling. I've not even offered you a drink.'

'A cup of tea would be lovely, thank you,' replied Molly.

'You may need a stiff drink once you meet my mother's dog. Brace yourself,' declared Birdie. She let out a breath. 'I'm really hoping you *are* the dog whisperer.'

Birdie's wellington boots clomped over the tiles in the kitchen and she looked over towards a faded red tartan dog bed that had seen better days. Birdie swung open the door and Molly heard a tiny yelp before spotting something sliding towards her on the tiled floor. It was the cutest ball of chocolate brown fluff she'd ever laid eyes on.

'Oh, my life.' Molly was up from the chair and on her

knees as she scooped up the potbellied puppy in her hands. 'He's absolutely gorgeous!'

'He is, isn't he. Meet Hendricks, named after my favourite gin, and I've gone through a fair few bottles of that in the last twelve months, believe me.'

Molly settled on the floor with the energetic whirlwind and chuckled as Hendricks tugged at the cuffs of her jogging pants with surprising force. His bum waggled in the air as he growled softly then rolled over onto his back waving his paws in the air. Molly tapped his wet, glossy black nose and ruffled his tummy.

'And what's the problem with Hendricks?' asked Molly. 'Is it training classes you need for him?'

Birdie blew out a breath. 'I didn't call you about Hendricks; he belongs to me.'

Molly looked up, surprised. 'Oh.'

'I need help with my mum's dog. Let me put the kettle on.' After lifting up the chrome lid of the hotplate and placing the kettle on the Aga, Birdie turned back towards Molly. 'Mum has only had her a few months but she needs rehoming and I've tried – believe me, I've tried – and now I just don't know what to do. That's why I need your help. Rory mentioned you boarded dogs too?'

'Yes, I have boarding kennels over at my practice,' replied Molly, taking a mug of tea from Birdie and noticing Hendricks had literally crashed on the red tartan bed whilst Birdie walked towards another door.

'Follow me,' instructed Birdie.

Standing up, Molly followed Birdie down another dinky hallway towards the front of the cottage into a sitting room. Here, the bookshelf was spilling over with books and every inch of wall was covered in framed photographs. A little two-seater settee in worn green velvet was covered by a cosy multi-coloured crochet blanket with tapestry cushions and faced an impressive open fire with logs stacked either side. On the coffee table there was a stack of magazines alongside a knitting basket with yarn and a half-completed project. Another dresser, looking a little too big for the room, housed even more books and a shelf packed with knick-knacks and scented candles. From nowhere Molly saw a movement from behind the curtain, and she jumped out of her skin when a Jack Russell bounded onto the arm of the armchair. Immediately, it began barking, followed by a growl that was far from welcoming. The dog never took its eyes off Molly.

'Meet Darling. She likes to sit in the window. I think she's waiting for Mum,' bellowed Birdie, projecting her voice over the dog's bark. They were both standing in the doorway and Molly had to admit she really didn't want to take another step closer as she didn't fancy her chances against the tiny creature, who didn't look happy in the slightest to see her. Molly couldn't quite believe all that noise was coming from such a small body.

'Darling?' Molly raised an eyebrow.

'I know. Her name isn't very fitting, is it? But it's better than my son's name for her ... Effin.'

'Effin?' Molly looked perplexed.

'Will that effin dog ever shut up!'

Molly couldn't help but smile. 'I think that name suits her.' Molly braved a step closer only to find herself shuffling backwards quickly. Darling was having none of it. The tan and white dog was down on her front paws growling, and she wasn't for stopping anytime soon. In all of her years of being a vet, Molly hadn't quite come across a character like this. 'How did your mum cope with her?'

Birdie shut the sitting-room door behind them. 'Let's go back to the kitchen. At least we can hear each other talk in there.'

It was evident from the long shuddering sigh that escaped from Birdie that she had no clue what to do or how to control Darling.

'Like I said, she's only had her a few months and would you believe, she doesn't bark or growl at Mum at all?'

'Really?' Molly was taken by surprise.

'She only behaves like this with everyone else. Why she couldn't get a nice, easygoing cocker spaniel or something I'll never know but that would have been too simple. I promised Mum I would look after her but if I'm being honest with you, I really couldn't cope. Hendricks shakes with fright if they are even in the same room – and so do I.'

Molly glanced over at Hendricks who was still curled up on the bed, snoring lightly.

'To be honest, Jack Russells, with their compact size and happy-go-lucky temperament, usually make the perfect family pet, but Darling seems to have lost her sparkle a little,' observed Molly.

'That's a good way to put it.' Birdie attempted a smile. 'But also, since Darling has been separated from Mum, she leaves a trail of destruction everywhere she goes. She's chewed the skirting boards, several pairs of shoes, armchairs, rugs. In the garden she's dug up a lot of plants. I've tried everything, chews, new toys … but nothing seems to work. She even nips at people's ankles whenever anyone walks near her, which is why I'm wearing my wellington boots indoors.' Birdie looked at her wits' end. 'I've placed adverts in the local shop and newspapers to try and rehome her, had a couple of takers in fact, but once they came to visit, their enthusiasm dwindled then became non-existent.'

Molly could see why.

'So I was wondering…' Birdie was looking straight at Molly, who had a feeling she knew exactly what was coming next. 'Could you take her?'

Silence.

Molly felt her eyes widen. 'Take her?'

'Rory said there might be a chance she could board with you.'

Molly made a mental note to thank Rory next time she set eyes on him. 'But I can't board her for ever, it would cost you a fortune. It's twenty pounds a night and I think what's happening here is Darling is pining for your mum. There's some sort of separation anxiety going on.'

'So surely that can be fixed?' Birdie was now pleading.

'It's not going to do Darling any good being confined to a kennel. What she needs is someone who can invest some time in her, someone that can be with her most of the time, just like your mum.'

Birdie was quiet for a second. 'Provide her a forever home then. She'd be the perfect candidate for your new dog behavioural classes. If anyone can turn her around, you can.'

Molly blew out a breath. 'Flattery…'

'I'm really stuck. I can't leave her here and I'd rather she go to a new home with someone we know. At least I can still see her then. Please help me.'

Molly was torn. She could hear the desperation in Birdie's voice. 'And there's no way your nephew can take her?'

Birdie shook her head. 'He doesn't even know of Darling. He's been busy with work and he's got an old dog of his own. I'm afraid Mum will go downhill even more if I can't provide her with regular updates... I suppose the only other option is to ... you know...'

Molly's eyes widened. 'You can't go putting down a perfectly healthy dog.'

'What choice do I have?'

Molly knew that this was emotional blackmail, but she would never let any animal be put down unless they were suffering, and Darling was only suffering from a broken heart. Maybe she could turn her around – after all, they didn't call her the dog whisperer for nothing – but Molly knew this was going to take a lot of work. She thought about it for a moment. How was Darling going to fit in with her life? Of course, she could take her to her behavioural classes and possibly to the surgery with her, but only if she'd stop barking and settle down. This was going to be a challenge and Molly was fully aware of that. She exhaled.

'Okay, Birdie, you've caught me in a good mood.' Molly had always found it difficult to say no and sometimes she wished that one-syllable word would come out of her mouth, but she always put herself out for anyone, especially when there was an animal involved.

'You'll take her?' Birdie interrupted before Molly could finish her sentence.

'I'll take her but there are conditions.' Molly's voice was firm. 'I will give her a temporary home for a few months, but you still need to be looking for a permanent home for her. However, I will try my best to make her calmer and a little friendlier. This will ease the pressure for a few months at least.'

The look of relief spread across Birdie's face like wildfire. 'You are simply the best!'

Molly wasn't feeling simply the best. She couldn't help wondering what she had let herself in for. The next biggest challenge was transporting Darling back to her house in her van without somehow being mauled to death. But Birdie was up and out of her seat and disappeared inside a pantry. After some clanging about she reappeared holding a shopping bag full of dog bowls, food, and Darling's lead. Birdie was taking no chances: she intended to get Darling shipped out of Bumblebee Cottage before Molly changed her mind.

'Now? You want me to take her now?' Molly had her rounds to do, not to mention she'd had a lovely couple of hours to herself planned this afternoon, which didn't include being barked at by a Jack Russell. 'Birdie, I can't take her this second. I've got my rounds to finish first. I can't just abandon her in a strange place. It would be too stressful for her ... and me,' admitted Molly.

Birdie looked disappointed and placed the bag on the floor. 'Oh.'

'I'll be back just after five o'clock. And we need to think about how we are going to transport her.'

'I've just the thing.' Birdie was back rummaging around in the pantry and bought out an old wicker cat carrier. 'This will work just fine.' Birdie had thought of everything.

'And have you any ideas about how we are going to entice Darling into the basket?' Molly really didn't fancy her chances at picking up Darling just yet. She valued having five fingers on each hand.

'We could drug her?' By the look on Birdie's face she was serious.

Molly raised an eyebrow, 'We? Are you telling me you have a stash of drugs stored in the cottage?' Molly was playing with her, but Birdie looked alarmed and brought her hands up to her chest.

Molly laughed. 'I'm teasing you.'

'I just thought you could inject her with a sedative or something.'

'That would be the last resort. Did Dixie have a special blanket or cushion or anything with her scent on?' asked Molly, taking a look around the room.

'Mum always put a soft woollen grey blanket over her knees at night and Darling used to curl up on top of it. It's thrown over the bannister in the hallway.'

'That might do the trick.' Molly was up on her feet, grabbing the wicker basket in one hand and retrieving the blanket from the stairs before heading back towards the living room with Birdie following close behind her. For a second, Molly paused outside the door and took a deep breath. As soon as she stepped into the sitting room Darling was up on her feet, barking and growling.

Taking her life in her hands Molly slowly stepped towards the armchair and began talking in a calm low tone, just as if she was talking to a baby. 'Now, now, Darling, look what we have here, it's Dixie's blanket.' Slowly stretching her arm towards Darling she held the blanket in her hand towards her. 'Here you go.'

Darling was having none of it. She crouched down on her front paws still barking.

Thinking she would have to purchase some earplugs before Darling arrived tonight, Molly placed the cat carrier on the floor near the armchair, laid the blanket over the seat of the chair, then stepped back. With one beady eye still on Molly, Darling stopped barking and took a sniff of the blanket.

'She's thinking about it.' Molly looked over her shoulder at Birdie, who gave an encouraging smile. 'What we need to do is put the blanket inside the cat carrier with the door open and hopefully Darling will venture inside to lie on the blanket… Fingers crossed.'

'You really are the dog whisperer, aren't you?'

'Don't go singing my praises just yet until we have her safely inside.'

'I've every faith,' said Birdie flatteringly. 'At least she's stopped yapping.'

Molly slowly moved the blanket and draped it half inside the cat carrier then turned around and nodded towards the door. Pulling the door almost to, they stood in the hallway and watched Darling in silence through the crack in the door.

'She's jumped down,' whispered Birdie. 'She's going over to the blanket.'

They watched as Darling began to scuff up the blanket under her paws before she circled it a couple of times then lay down on top of it.

Birdie grabbed Molly's arm in excitement. 'That was a master plan.'

Molly smiled and pulled the door shut. 'Leave her there for now and I'll be back later to pick her up.'

Birdie nodded, the relief written all over her face. 'I'll be waiting.'

Molly shut the cottage door behind her and for a second felt a little light-headed. Taking a breather, she sat down on the stone wall, putting the dizzy feeling down to skipping breakfast. She took some deep breaths whilst she checked her phone and noticed she had three missed calls from Isla. Hoping there was nothing wrong up at the farm, she rang her back and Isla answered after just a couple of rings.

'Good morning!' she chirped. 'How's life treating you today?'

'I'm not quite sure. I've just adopted a Jack Russell that I don't think likes me very much.'

'That wouldn't be Dixie's Jack Russell, would it?' quizzed Isla, letting out a strangled laugh.

'That'll be the one. How do you know? I know village gossip travels fast but that is ridiculous, I'm still outside the cottage.'

'Oh, Molly, good luck with that! Birdie popped into the farm at her wits' end wanting to find a new home for the dog. Drew nipped into the cottage to see if we could help out but let's just say he came back petrified. Apparently Darling wouldn't stop snarling at him.'

'And Drew would be right; that's exactly what she did to me.'

'You, Molly McKendrick, need to learn to say no!'

Molly knew that Isla was right, and she really wasn't a hundred per cent sure how much she was looking forward to her new house guest, but if anyone could turn Darling around it was going to be her. Her new dog behavioural classes were starting on Monday in Primrose Park, so she was going to have to practise what she preached and take Darling along with her. Goodness knows how that was going to end up but surely it couldn't be that disastrous.

'I couldn't say no – Birdie was really stuck and apparently her nephew is arriving next week, renting out the cottage, and has an elderly dog with him. He's not up for taking Darling on too.'

'I bet he isn't. He's got sense.'

'Everyone keeps calling me the dog whisperer so it's about time I lived up to my reputation.'

'Good luck with that,' chuckled Isla. 'I called because I was thinking of having a girly get-together tonight up at the farm. Drew's out with Fergus and Rory so I thought we could take advantage.'

Molly was quiet for a second, every one of her dog whispering instincts screaming at her. She was never going to calm Darling on the first night. Already in her mind she pictured carnage, chewed skirting boards, torn sofas... She really couldn't risk leaving Darling all by herself, even if it was just for a couple of hours. She could leave her in one of the kennels but if she continued to bark all night the staff and other dogs would be a little disgruntled.

'You know that word you've just insisted I should say more...'

'No, you can't say no,' exclaimed Isla, 'the whole gang is coming.'

Molly sighed. She could really do with a night with the girls. 'There's only one solution. You'll all have to come to me and wear protective gear.'

Isla laughed heartily. 'She's a Jack Russell, not a lion!'

'And she's no darling yet either. Is Martha around to babysit for you?'

'I'm sure she will be.'

'I'll pick up some cakes from Bonnie's teashop.'

'Felicity has already sorted the nibbles, just text her

and let her know the change of venue, and I'll bring a few bottles – it sounds like you need it. Don't worry, I'm sure you'll charm her.'

'Who, Felicity?' quizzed Molly, losing the thread of the conversation for a second.

'No, Darling, you idiot!'

Molly hung up the phone then swigged from the warm bottle of water that was in her bag. She was feeling ravenous. Up on her feet she clicked the central locking and opened the door of her van. There was time before her next house call to take a trip to the teashop. All she had on her mind was a freshly baked cheese and onion pasty. She couldn't remember the last time she'd eaten one of those but as she started the engine that was all she was craving.

As she put the van in first gear Molly looked back towards Bumblebee Cottage. Birdie was in the top window wafting a feather duster and when she saw Molly she waved. She certainly looked happier then when Molly first arrived. All Molly could hope for was that Birdie kept her side of the bargain and continued to look for Darling's forever home. Waving back at her, Molly wondered what the hell she'd let herself in for.

Chapter Seven

Hearing a taxi pull up outside, Molly looked through the upstairs window to see the gang piling out armed with bottles of wine and nibbles. They were laughing and joking and as Molly hurried downstairs, she was greeted by Darling's snarl followed by a volley of barks. Molly was already at her wits' end after the trauma of bringing Darling home and had poured herself a large glass of gin.

Earlier, when Molly arrived at Bumblebee Cottage, Birdie had greeted her wearing a pair of high heels, her wellington boots cast aside. Darling was ready and waiting, locked up in the cat basket by the front door alongside her food and bowls.

65

'Here she is, all ready for you and very excited about her new home,' chirped Birdie.

Molly had bent down to take a look in the basket and been greeted by a low-level growl that quickly turned into a bark. 'She doesn't look very excited,' murmured Molly, thankful she'd stopped off at the pharmacy on the way here and stocked up on earplugs. She was sure she was going to be in for a noisy and sleepless night.

'Straight in the basket she went; she loves that blanket. You really do know your stuff, don't you?' Birdie was looking impressed.

Already Molly was beginning to doubt herself. Three months had already passed since she'd attended the dog behavioural course and not one information session had prepared her for a dog like Darling.

'Oh, I'll miss you so much, Darling,' claimed Birdie, sounding all gooey as she picked up the basket and handed her over to Molly, who was not at all convinced that Birdie was going to miss her in the slightest. Molly took the basket from her hand and immediately Birdie picked up the other bags loaded with Darling's belongings. 'I'll take these to the van.' Obviously Birdie was keen to get Darling loaded up before Molly could change her mind.

'That's very kind of you.' Molly hoped the sarcasm in her voice wasn't too obvious.

With Darling's basket placed on the front seat and her belongings stowed in the boot, Birdie shut the car door and stood back on the pavement outside Bumblebee Cottage. She was already waving before Molly had even put the key in the ignition. After she started the engine, she lowered the window. 'Don't forget, Birdie, you need to be looking for a home for Darling. Three months max.'

Birdie was nodding, 'Yes, yes, yes, of course. Oh, and Mum says her favourite walk is in Primrose Park... Catch up soon.'

Molly closed the window and put the van in gear. She had a feeling that Birdie had no intention of looking for a permanent home and she had just become the brand-new owner of a Jack Russell that didn't seem to like her that much.

———————————

As Molly flung open the front door, the gang held up their carrier bags filled with wine and goodies before their eyes diverted towards Molly's feet.

Isla pointed. 'Are we expecting another flood or something? Why in God's name are you wearing wellington boots indoors?'

'She's finally lost the plot,' chuckled Felicity, stepping into the hallway.

'Oh, you lot may laugh but you won't be in a minute. Come on in and meet Darling.'

After kicking off their shoes they cautiously followed Molly into the living room. As soon as the living-room door opened Darling was up on the arm of the chair snarling and growling. Everyone took a step back.

'She is a darling, isn't she?' claimed Allie, peeping around the door. 'Are you sure it's safe?'

'She's only a Jack Russell,' said Isla with a laugh, taking the plunge and being the first to walk into the room. She placed the carrier bag full of wine on the table then gave a little shriek as Darling jumped down onto the carpet and began snapping at her ankles.

Molly pointed to her feet. 'And that is the very reason I am wearing wellington boots, because every time I walk near her, she nips my ankles.'

All eyes were on Darling. 'I don't suppose you have any more boots, do you?' asked Felicity. With Darling's beady eye watching her she guardedly side-stepped towards the settee then quickly tucked her legs underneath her as the others followed suit.

'You're wearing the boots, so you'll have to pour the wine. We are not moving. I need my ankles; they kind of hold my feet to my legs,' exclaimed Isla, trying to make a joke but not taking her eyes off Darling.

With Darling following closely behind, Molly walked into the kitchen. Darling wasn't giving up for a second and continued to dive at her boots. With full wine glasses in her hand, Molly returned to the living room, where the girls hadn't moved a muscle.

'Hopefully, she'll settle in a second,' said Molly, handing out the glasses.

The girls watched as Molly took Dixie's blanket and laid it out in front of the cat box on the other side of the coffee table. Darling was watching Molly closely as she patted the blanket then moved away. As soon as Molly had sat on the chair Darling sniffed her way towards the blanket, circled three times, stretched out her front legs and lay down. She rested her head on her front legs but still had a watchful eye on the girls.

'Thank God for that. Fingers crossed she stays quiet, but if anyone moves you do so at your own risk.' Molly couldn't help but notice everyone looked petrified. 'Honestly, her bark is worse than her bite.'

'And that's the reason you're wearing wellies,' said Allie, slowly swinging her legs to the floor.

Darling sat up and growled and immediately Allie tucked her legs back underneath her, causing everyone to laugh.

'And are you going to sleep in your wellies?' teased Isla. 'And with one eye open?'

'Don't jest. I've not quite worked out the sleeping arrangements yet, but we will not be in the same room,' replied Molly, taking a sip of her wine. 'And goodness knows if she's going to settle or not, but I'm prepared.' She held up a packet of earplugs.

Much to everyone's relief, Darling settled back down on Dixie's blanket and finally closed her eyes.

'So come on, what's the gossip in the village? I feel

like we've not had a catch-up for ages,' asked Molly, looking around them all.

'Gran has become a hypochondriac,' giggled Isla. 'Since the new doctor has arrived in the village. She's put him right up there with Zach Hudson – heartthrob material.'

'Got to love Martha!' Allie grinned.

Molly sat up. 'I'm not sure how I've not bumped into him yet. So he's good-looking, great profession, and single?'

'Apparently so and he's moved into the flat above Peony Practice,' confirmed Allie.

'It must be strange retiring, don't you think?' said Molly, thinking about Dr Taylor, who had been a part of the community for as long as she could remember. 'Imagine doing the same job, day in and day out, and being a huge part of this community, and then that routine is no longer there anymore.'

'Very strange,' agreed Isla. 'The key is to keep busy, but I really do need structure and routine in my life,' she added.

'Talking of young, hot professionals'—Allie held up her wine glass towards Molly and she knew exactly what was coming next—'are we any closer to finding your mystery man?'

It had been over three months since Molly had spent the night with Cam at the hotel and he'd crossed her mind every day since. Of course she'd tried to search for him but hadn't quite decided what she was going to do if she found him.

'No.' Molly shook her head. 'All of my searches have thrown up absolutely nothing.'

'Surely it can't be that difficult in this day and age?' joined in Felicity.

'It's a little tricky with no surname to go on,' admitted Molly, 'but I've googled every dental practice I could possibly find within a ten-mile radius of the hotel, then searched through the list of the names of staff.' She shrugged. 'He's a hard man to find.'

'That's a lot of searching.' Isla raised an eyebrow.

'What else can we do?' asked Felicity. 'People can't just disappear.'

'Well, he did, right that very morning. I wouldn't mind. I'm such a light sleeper; I can't believe that I didn't wake up. Usually when a leaf blows across the grass I'm up, and this one morning...' She sighed.

'And we don't even have a picture to go on?' continued Felicity.

Molly shook her head. 'I even tried to blag the receptionist at the hotel for more information, but I didn't manage to get a surname out of her either... Damn data protection. She was way too good at her job.'

Everyone laughed.

'So all we have is a first name and occupation. Next time we need more!' teased Allie.

'I'm not sure there is going to be a next time. I know this is going to sound mental so don't judge me...'

All eyes were on Molly.

'I keep driving back to the hotel and looking for his car in the car park. Doesn't that make me sound crazy? He was only there for a weekend playing golf. Why would he even go back there? I know I'm being ridiculous, but I keep getting this romantic notion that he'll park his car in exactly the same spot and be looking for me too.' Molly was shaking her head, knowing exactly how that sounded. Normally she wouldn't have even entertained the idea of such a thing but there was something inside driving her. Cam was different; she just knew it. A feeling that had not been ignited inside Molly for so long was well and truly lit and still burning nearly three months after the night they'd spent together. Molly couldn't envisage that feeling going away anytime soon.

'And what are you going to say if you see him?' tested Allie.

Molly blew out a breath. 'I've not quite got that far... Maybe I was just going to accidentally bump into him and say, "OMG, how are you?"' Her voice rose an octave and straightaway Darling was up on her feet, looking at Molly and growling. She reached over and took a treat from the bag on the table. 'And this goes against everything I will be reinforcing at my dog behavioural classes,' she said as she tossed the treat towards Darling, who swallowed it in one gulp. 'All I have done there is reinforce the fact that if Darling growls she gets rewarded.'

'And this is Birdie's dog?' asked Felicity.

'No, it's Dixie's and I think this behaviour is just a severe case of separation anxiety.'

'Which is exactly what Molly has had for three months,' teased Allie, causing everyone to hoot with laughter.

'Never mind the dog, we want to get back to Cam,' said Isla, attempting to steer the conversation back on track.

'What more is there to say? He's disappeared off the face of the earth and although I'm a hopeless romantic I'm not sure there's much more we can do… He's the one that got away. I just can't believe he upped and left when the emotional and physical connection was off the scale.' Molly shrugged. She was still clearly very smitten with him after all this time but really she needed to put the mystery man out of her mind.

She leant over and topped up the glasses. Darling gave yet another growl. 'And do you really think Birdie is going to keep searching for a home for her?'

'No!' chorused everyone.

'You have been well and truly stitched up.' Allie gave her a knowing look. 'That dog is going nowhere.'

'It looks like it's down to me to teach her how to behave, which is a bit of a bugger if she doesn't comply with my instructions at my very own classes, because I'm going to look a bit of a fraud.' Molly placed her wine glass on the table next to her and gazed at Darling.

'And it's tomorrow your behavioural classes start?' asked Isla, taking a handful of crisps from the bowl beside her.

'Primrose Park, 9 a.m., just left of the bandstand. Eight dogs in total, eight owners, and an hour of chaos.' Molly flicked on her phone. 'And tomorrow the weather is a little cloudy but thankfully no rain.'

'Eight dogs and eight stressed owners yapping around your feet first thing in the morning. You are a braver woman than me; I'm not sure I'd have the patience,' admitted Felicity. 'But you will be the best.'

'Is that the dogs or the owners yapping?' joked Molly, who knew that sometimes the owners were more highly strung than their dogs.

Allie looked towards Darling. 'She's so cute though … when she's quiet!'

'She would be if she didn't go around baring her teeth every two minutes, but we will get there, won't we, Darling?' Molly sounded more optimistic than she felt.

'Pass me those over please.' Felicity gestured towards the bowl beside Molly, who picked it up. The smell of salt and vinegar crisps caught her by surprise.

'Gosh, those smell strong.' She passed the bowl towards Felicity, who wrinkled her nose.

'What, these? I can barely smell them,' replied Felicity. 'And you've only had a couple of sips of your wine. You're lagging behind. Don't think we haven't noticed.'

Molly looked at her glass. 'This is exactly what I needed – a girls' night in, all the gossip. But you know when you're willing the wine to go down and it just isn't? I just feel exhausted. Work has been full-on and I feel like I'm coming down with something.'

'That's not like you. You're usually superhuman and manage to dodge every cold or flu bug possible,' pointed out Isla.

'And I feel bloated and goodness knows what's going on with my chest.'

'What do you mean, going on with your chest?' asked Isla, sitting up straight and looking at the other girls.

'My breasts feel, like, really tender. I just don't feel right at all.'

They were all staring at Molly, the pause like the silence after a gunshot.

'Why are you all staring at me like that?' Molly looked around her friends and then down at Darling, who had thankfully settled again.

'You, my girl, are pregnant.' Isla pointed at Molly then laughed. 'But obviously you needed a man for that unless you have been interviewing sperm donors and not telling us,' she teased.

'Please tell me you aren't still hung up on that idea, even though it could be fun interviewing donors,' quipped Allie.

But now it was Molly's turn to stay silent. She felt the colour drain from her cheeks and she quickly stood up, leaving Darling floundering and giving a belated growl. All eyes were on Molly as she walked over to the desk in the corner of the room and flicked back through the pages of her diary for the last couple of months.

'Shit. Shit. Double shit.' Molly tapped the diary. 'I'm late.'

'How late?' queried Felicity. 'A couple of days?'

Molly's heart was racing. 'Very bloody late,' she replied, letting out a long shuddering breath. 'In fact, my period should have started two weeks after my encounter with Cam.' She started to panic, her mind tripping over her own thoughts. Could she possibly be pregnant? Of course she couldn't; they'd used protection. Her thoughts were batting to and fro in her head like a fast game of tennis. The uncertainty now engulfed her as shock waves shot through her body. Taking deep controlled breaths, she looked at the faces of her startled friends sitting in front of her.

'I'm shaking.' Molly held out her hand. 'Oh my God, what if I am pregnant? What am I going to do? I can't be...' Her thoughts were all over the place. She didn't know what to think or feel.

'Jeez, Mol, did you...?'

Molly knew exactly what Isla was going to ask. Molly hadn't taken birth control for over a year; she had no need to. After her relationship had ended with her last boyfriend she didn't see the point in taking the pill anymore but she and Cam had definitely used a condom. 'Yes, a condom,' she shared with her friends. 'So I can't be, can I?'

Molly was feeling panicky. She didn't know what to think.

'Let's not panic,' declared Felicity, 'There could be a hundred and one reasons why your period hasn't started.'

'There's only one way to put your mind at ease, though.' Isla looked down at her watch. 'The late-night pharmacy is open, isn't it? The one on the corner.'

'You're not suggesting we go and buy a test now?' Molly wasn't exactly sure how she felt about that.

'What's the point in waiting? At least we'll know,' reassured Isla, 'and you have us all here, holding your hand.'

In all honesty, Molly was feeling a whole dollop of nervousness. Why hadn't she even clocked her period was so late? And what was she going to do if the test was positive? She knew financially she could support herself, but what about mentally and physically? How would she be able to run a business and go out to work with a small baby? She knew she'd talked about bringing up a child on her own, but now that idea seemed to be getting more real by the second.

Allie and Isla were already fastening up their coats while Darling was attempting to nip their ankles. 'Relax, have a drink… In fact, don't have a drink,' said Allie, moving Molly's wine glass away and gesturing towards Felicity to get her a glass of water. 'We won't be long.' Before Molly could object, they were up and out of the door.

'Well, it looks like it's just us three,' said Molly, looking between Felicity and Darling.

'Or four.' Felicity dipped her head towards Molly's stomach. 'And you didn't even give it a second thought?'

Molly shook her head. 'Why would I? It wasn't as though we were irresponsible. I just don't know what to think.'

'Mmm, but think about it this way…' said Felicity. 'You've talked about having a baby all by yourself. How are you feeling about that idea now?'

That was a very good question. 'Scared. Nervous. How the hell will I do this on my own?' Molly knew she had teased her friends about hiring a man to get herself pregnant but that was only because the right person hadn't crossed her path yet. She'd always imagined herself happily married with a husband to support her, a partnership – but that's not what she had at all right now. She had herself and a dog that didn't like her and there was no way Darling was going to welcome a baby into the fold any time soon.

'If you are pregnant, you can do this. If anyone can do this, it's you. Look at this place and your business. You have an army of staff to support you at work and more drive than all of us put together, and we are always here. I know that's not the same as having someone here all the time, but we are only over the bridge – a phone call away,' reassured Felicity. 'And also a little disappointed we aren't interviewing potential sperm donors sometime in the near future, I might add. And just think, if this Cam is handsome and a dentist he's got some intelligence going on,' added Felicity, trying to smooth the worries away. 'The baby will have perfect genes.'

Molly gulped down a breath to stay quiet. The word *baby* was pounding inside her head. She knew the second she took that test her whole life was going to change one way or another and even though she'd talked about doing this on her own before, this was the here and now.

'A mother – there's a possibility I'm actually going to be a mother.' Molly was thinking out loud.

'And you'll make a good one at that,' replied Felicity, pointing to Isla and Allie, who had just walked past the window. 'They're back.'

As the front door opened, Darling went into full throttle. Molly felt dizzy as she stood up to coax Darling back to her bed and threw her another chew.

Isla was holding up a white paper bag. 'Ta-dah! It was buy one, get one free.' She waggled the bag in the air before handing it over to Molly.

'Why would I need two? I'm either pregnant or I'm not,' replied Molly, having a peep inside the bag. She pulled out a long rectangular box and stared at it before turning it over and reading the instructions. 'This is going to change my life one way or another.'

'And what do you want it to be?' asked Allie, which was exactly the same question that Molly was asking herself at this very second.

In shock, Molly perched on the arm of the chair, still staring at the box. 'Surely this won't be positive? But if it is, I have been thinking about this for a while. I just thought I'd have more control over the timing.' It wasn't planned but sometimes things happened for a reason and deep down maybe this was a blessing in disguise? Maybe she was ready to be a mother.

'You know what,' Molly said, standing up and looking at all her friends, 'I'm not getting any younger and if this is positive I'm going to grasp it with both hands. This is my turn and meant to be... Fate. Even though I'm scared out of my mind how I'm going to manage everything, I will. I know I can do this.' Molly gave a nervous smile. Darling jumped up onto the chair next to Molly and for a second took a sniff at the box before lying down without making a sound.

'It's like she knows something is going on,' remarked Isla.

'As long as she's quiet, that's all I ask,' replied Molly. 'Okay, there's no time like the present. Here goes.'

Molly walked into the bathroom, closed the door behind her, sat down on the edge of the bath and took a deep breath. She heard movement outside the bathroom.

'Do you lot know how difficult it is to pee when you're all waiting on the other side of the door? The pressure?'

'Sorry, sorry, we'll be waiting in the living room. We just didn't want you to be on your own,' claimed Isla, hushing them back into the living room. Molly kicked off her wellington boots and sat down on the toilet. 'Bloody hell, this wasn't on my list of things to do today,' she muttered, taking the pregnancy test out of the wrapper with a shaky hand and holding the plastic white stick underneath her. Molly thought this was going to be the longest two minutes of her life but in her case it wasn't. There was no need to hold the wand up to the light or even wait the two minutes; there was no mistaking the dark blue text that was screaming *PREGNANT* right back at her. It was too bold and blue to even think there was any kind of mistake.

Molly perched on the edge of the bath, her hands visibly shaking while she still stared at the no-question-about-it-I-am-pregnant stick. Her emotions were mixed: she was shocked yet excited, and didn't know whether to laugh or cry. She had never envisaged when she got up this morning that this was how her day was going to end. 'I'm going to be a mum,' she said out loud, a nervous smile spreading across her face. 'I'm going to be a mum,' she repeated, still trying to take it in. But deep down Molly felt a sense of sadness tinged with a little guilt. This was big news, big, big, big news, and Cam was in the forefront of her mind. She wanted to share it with him, let him know about the pregnancy. But how was that even going to happen? Molly knew she was very much on her own on this journey and just hoped she was going to be good enough.

'Looks like we're in this together, kiddo,' she said, rubbing her stomach, still not fully believing there was a baby growing inside her and she was going to be responsible for someone else all by herself.

'Come on,' urged Allie, 'we've timed five minutes already.'

Molly knew her friends were waiting not so patiently in the living room, but she wanted to take just another moment to herself. This was a huge turning point in her life; it wasn't every day she found out she was going to be a mum. What happened next? Molly knew she would have to make an appointment with the doctor, and, given the stage she was at, it wasn't going to be long until her first scan, which in fact could already be overdue.

When Molly opened the door, still clutching the wand, all eyes were on her. They were all sitting on the edge of their seats, wide-eyed, in silence.

'Well?' asked Isla.

Molly's face broke out into a nervous smile.

'Oh my God, you are, aren't you?' Allie was up on her feet peering at the test in Molly's hand. 'She bloody is!'

'I'm going to be a mother,' confirmed Molly, biting her lip, looking around at her friends.

Isla was the first one to congratulate her, pulling Molly in for a hug. 'This is amazing news!'

'Thanks, I think! It's just all such a shock.'

'But you're smiling so that's a good sign.' Allie mirrored Isla's actions and wrapped her arms around her friend. 'Huge congratulations!'

'I'll tip your wine away, right into my glass,' giggled Felicity. 'We don't want it to be wasted now.'

'You'll be wasted,' joked Isla, then turned her attention back to Molly. 'Sit down, take the weight off your feet. You've got to start looking after yourself and taking it easy.'

'How am I going to take it easy? My life, my job is full-on and I have to work.'

'Well, you have to pretend to take it easy then.'

Molly's head was in a whirl. She had no one around to help. If she ran out of milk then she was the one who had to go and get it. If she forgot to load the washing machine then there was no one else to do it. 'How hard is this going to be?' she asked, feeling panicky, staring straight at Isla.

'It's going to be the hardest thing you've ever done but believe me, the most rewarding. When that little baby smiles at you for the first time, and walks, and talks, you will be the proudest mum on this earth. But being by yourself, there's no break. The sleep deprivation is the worst, feeding in the night, but I'm sure the girls will agree, we will support you as much as we can. You're going to need your friends around you. Honestly, we can take care of the shopping and washing, and I can cook extra meals, et cetera, but you'll soon get into a routine and find your own way. You've got this!'

Molly was taking all this in, and feeling scared out of her wits. 'I can do this, can't I? People do this all the time, don't they, single parenting?' She was looking for a little reassurance.

'There's no denying, Mol, this is huge, and it's not going to be a walk in the park. But please don't think I'm interfering when I say this'—Isla looked towards Darling —'you don't need any extra stresses.'

'It's all happening today, isn't it? New dog, new baby – hindsight is a wonderful thing but surely when my news is out, Birdie will have to take note. We did agree she would carry on looking for her forever home.'

'Let's hope so,' added Felicity, raising an eyebrow and not looking at all convinced.

They all looked down at Darling, who thankfully had settled by Molly's feet. She'd pulled out Dixie's blanket from her bed and was now snuggled up in it looking like butter wouldn't melt.

'Maybe she's going to settle, who knows?' said Molly. 'I'll see how she handles being around other dogs in the morning. Fingers crossed she comes good.'

'I've got everything crossed,' chipped in Allie. 'Anyway, here's the question – boy or girl?'

'Eek! I don't know! When I got up this morning I

never thought in a million years anyone would be asking me that question today. Girl… Boy… I don't mind at all and I don't suppose I have a choice.'

'It might be one of each, you never know,' suggested Felicity with a straight face, leaving Molly looking horrified.

'Could you imagine? Twins! How would I cope with two babies and one pair of hands?' Molly was seriously giving this some thought. 'I've only ever held your children a couple of times.' Molly looked towards Isla.

'Surely babies can't be that different from puppies,' teased Allie. 'And you never know, Cam might have twins in his family, or triplets … who knows?'

'Stop right there. You lot are going to give me a heart attack.' But Molly was thinking that she didn't know anything about Cam or his background. What if there were health problems in his family? Was that even important? 'This would have been something I would have researched with a donor,' she admitted.

'And they could have lied; you would never know. This way you know the baby is going to be gorgeous because there was a strong attraction between you two,' pointed out Allie.

'But what about the baby when they start asking about their father?' Molly knew she was getting ahead of herself but this was going to happen one day. What exactly would she say?

'When the time is right, you will know exactly what

to do and say.' Isla had always been the sensible one. 'There's no point worrying about things in advance.'

'And what are you going to do about Cam?' asked Felicity.

'There's nothing I can do. Without a surname or a photo, it'll be like finding a needle in a haystack.'

'Golf, you said he played golf? So we're on the hunt for a golfing dentist that goes by the name of Cam,' chipped in Allie.

'Like I said, it's like finding a needle in a haystack,' reiterated Molly.

'Sometimes things are just meant to be and this is just meant to be. I am chuffed for you, Molly, and with three aunties all willing to chip in, this baby will be so loved and looked after.'

Molly came over all emotional, her eyes brimming with tears. She had just the best friends, and they always looked out for each other. She flapped a hand in front of her face. 'Look at me crying. You are all just the best. This is it, isn't it? I'm not dreaming; I'm actually going to be a mum.' She stared at the wand one last time before standing up and placing it in the kitchen bin.

'And you'd better get used to the crying lark,' said Isla. 'Honestly, the tears never stop. Your hormones will be all over the place, and even worse when the baby arrives. I can remember when I was eight months pregnant because Drew had used the last of the milk in the fridge and the carton was empty and all I wanted to do was have a glass of milk to try and curb my heartburn. I was beside myself crying, sobbing out of control… How could he do this to me? I remember Drew looked at me like I was absolutely mental. "We own a bloody dairy farm," he said. "Stop crying. There's always milk."'

Everyone laughed.

'And that's the difference. At least you had someone to cry at. I'm going to be all by myself.'

'Molly, thousands of woman have done this, brought up children without a man – the difference being that you have us. Aggie and Martha are always up for going for walks with a baby in a pram but what you need to remember is, don't struggle by yourself; ask for help and your little army of aunties will be right by your side.'

'Don't, you'll make me cry again!' Molly managed a grateful smile through her tears. Isla was right; she was fortunate to have them and a good support network within the community. 'Thank you, guys. I suppose there's only one question left that needs answering…'

'And that is?' asked Allie.

Molly raised her eyebrows. 'Which one of you is going to be my birthing partner?'

'Woah! Not me, I was no good when Isla went into labour. I sent Felicity… I'd be useless. I faint at anything, I do,' confirmed Allie.

'And I'll be waiting with the champagne and chocolates,' said Felicity with a grin.

'Good job you've got me; these two are useless,' said Isla. 'It would be an honour to be your birthing partner. I'm a dab hand at delivering alpacas so babies are going to be easy! But you need to book an appointment at the practice to get the ball rolling. You'll need a scan. In fact, it can't be long before your first scan is due. This is exciting! A new baby!'

'Pregnant after a one-night stand,' Molly said out loud. 'What does that make me?'

'A modern woman, who knows her own mind and can do this all by herself,' chipped in Allie.

'Think yourself lucky there isn't a man involved, because they just get in the way and you will have your baby's love all to yourself,' added Felicity, sipping her wine.

'It makes you one of the strongest women on this planet,' confirmed Isla.

Molly smiled at her friends, 'It does, doesn't it!' Molly was thankful for all the support of her friends and even though she had mixed emotions, excitement with dollops of trepidation, she was feeling optimistic about the journey ahead. A tiny part of her wished Cam had never disappeared the way he did, but there was nothing she could do about that now.

Chapter Eight

Early the next morning, as the alarm began to beep, Molly stretched out her arm towards her clock radio and pressed the snooze button. Thankfully she had another ten minutes before she needed to get up. She had had the worst night's sleep in a very long time. After the girls had left, Darling had spent a couple of hours barking at the front door – pining for Dixie, Molly assumed. She knew it must be strange for Darling, being away from home, and she had tried everything to settle her down, but in the end Molly had done exactly what she would be telling everyone not to do at the first dog behavioural class in the morning: she'd given her a treat. Which literally shut up Darling for a couple of minutes, giving Molly enough time to do – again – exactly what she'd promised herself she wouldn't do: move Darling's

89

bed into her own bedroom. By the time Molly had brushed her teeth and changed into her pyjamas, Darling had pulled Dixie's blanket up onto Molly's bed and was snuggled up on top of it. Molly weighed up her options: she could either wrestle with Darling, which would result in stress and no doubt further barking, or she could leave her where she was and slide into the bed alongside her. Feeling exhausted, and against her better judgement, Molly went for the latter and could have sworn Darling was smirking at her in her sleep.

She'd lain awake for hours, thoughts of being a mum very much on her mind, and wondering why the hell Cam had done a runner without even a goodbye. Molly assumed she knew the answer to that question: it was more than likely that he was already in a relationship and had taken a chance while he could. The only hope was that he remembered the night like she did; she would never forget it, especially now that she would have a permanent reminder. Already she was trying to imagine what the baby would look like. A little bit of him and a little bit of her. What would their personality be like? Molly knew she wouldn't have to wait long for the answers.

Swinging her legs to the floor, Molly stood up – and sat right back down. She felt dizzy, worse than she'd felt before. Closing her eyes, she took a few deep breaths. She knew during the past weeks she'd felt exhausted, but she'd put it down to the long shifts at the surgery and lack of food. Thinking of food, she began to retch. 'Oh my,' she blurted, running to the bathroom and throwing up the toilet lid. Darling trotted after her and watched intently as Molly reached up to the windowsill and fumbled for a hair band. Once her hair was tied back out of her face, Molly retched again, nausea gripping her as she threw up bile.

'Urgh.' She wiped her mouth with a piece of toilet tissue.

All Molly wanted to do was to crawl back into bed and pull the duvet over her head, but she had no chance. In the next few hours she would be standing in Primrose Park educating dog owners how to train their dogs But if she didn't feel better soon, it was going to be a struggle to get through the day. With her hands gripping each side of the toilet, Molly couldn't move. She retched and retched until there was nothing left inside her.

'Rally yourself,' she murmured, splashing cold water on her face. 'You are pregnant, not sick. Come on, girl, you can do this,' she continued, looking towards Darling, who was sitting on the bathmat staring up at her. 'And you are being ridiculously quiet all of a sudden.' Darling cocked her head to one side, looking like she was actually paying attention.

There was nothing else for it. Molly slipped back into bed. 'Five more minutes and I'll try again.' She reached for her phone and pinged a message over to Isla and immediately her phone rang.

'Ginger biscuits is what you need. It worked for me and takes the edge off it. I'm literally out on an early morning delivery for Drew over your way so I'll drop some off. Give me five minutes and ring the surgery. You need to book an appointment and get the ball rolling.'

'Thank you and I will,' replied Molly, hanging up the phone and praying ginger biscuits really were the answer. She exhaled and searched for the doctor's number on her phone.

'Good morning, Peony Practice, Retta speaking, how may I help you?'

Retta was sounding way too cheery for Molly's liking. She could feel the surge of nausea again and closed her eyes for a moment.

'Hi, I need to make an appointment to see the doctor as soon as possible, thank you.'

'We have a spare appointment with Dr Sanders at 8.30 a.m.? Can you make that?'

Molly glanced at the clock. She had no choice but to make it. 'Perfect,' she replied, giving her details over the phone before hanging up.

'Men really do have it easy,' she murmured, hearing the doorbell and pulling on her dressing gown. Immediately Darling bounded down the stairs and was barking at the front door before Molly had even left the bedroom. 'Darling, it's only Isla.' Molly scooped up the dog, leaving her stunned for a moment, before she swung open the door and Isla stepped inside.

'Woah! You look white,' said Isla, holding up the packet of biscuits. 'And kind of green. And absolutely exhausted too. Welcome to pregnancy!'

'I've felt awful over the past few weeks, and I just thought I was working too hard, but today I can't even think about having a cup of tea without retching.' Molly put Darling down on the floor and she ran into the living room, jumped straight up on the armchair, and began a low growl.

'You poor thing, I won't offer to put the kettle on then.' Isla touched her arm. 'Nibble on one of these. I swore by them.'

Immediately Molly opened the packet and took a bite. 'I've got an hour to get to the doctor's, then it's my first day dog training, and all I want to do is curl up in bed and avoid hanging my head over the toilet.'

'Mind over matter,' encouraged Isla, sitting on the settee, as far away as possible from Darling.

'How long does this last for?' asked Molly, finishing the first biscuit and straightaway tucking into the next one.

'Usually they say the first three months, but not for me – I was sick all day, every day until the day I gave birth, and the moment that baby left my stomach was the first time I felt human again.'

'You are really not selling this to me.'

Isla grinned. 'When you read all these books, telling you how women bloom in pregnancy… I did not bloom; I was blooming awful from start to finish, but it will soon be over, and when you hold your bundle of joy in your arms it will all be worth it, I promise you. But then that's when the real fun starts.'

'Yesterday I was beginning to feel excited and now I'm thinking, how am I going to do this? I can't just go taking time off work because I feel sick.'

'Yes, you can – you're the boss and have wonderful staff! It's difficult, I know, especially when you're feeling sick, but don't eat all of those biscuits as your waistline will be expanding more than ever.'

Molly smiled. 'Actually, these might have worked,' she said, feeling the sickness ebb away a little.

'The key is to try not to think about it. If you focus on the sickness you will feel worse. Lots of fresh air and deep breaths.'

'I've got an appointment with the new doctor in'— Molly glanced at the clock—'forty-five minutes and I don't even want to shower.'

'So don't; who's going to know?'

'But look at my hair. It needs washing.'

'Tie it up. Just get through the morning and you'll feel better later, then have a soak in the bath.'

Molly nodded. 'I'll ring work and let them know they need to cover me this morning.'

'Good idea, and let me know how you get on at the

doctor's. If you need me to come to your first scan I will – in fact I'd love to. You are not on your own.' Isla stood up and Darling followed, nipping at her ankles. 'And get on to Birdie, make sure she's doing everything possible to find that one a new home.'

After Molly watched Isla drive off, she shut the door and looked down at Darling, who was now dragging her blanket onto the sofa. In a funny kind of way Molly was glad she was here as she didn't feel alone and was already becoming attached to Darling's misbehaving ways. 'You are definitely what they call a character.'

Darling wagged her tail.

'Oh my God, did you actually wag your tail?' Molly smiled at her. Darling's eyes were wide as she watched Molly. 'I'll take that. Let's have more wagging and less barking and you and I will get on just fine.'

Forty minutes later, still feeling nauseous, Molly was waiting in the reception queue at Peony Practice. After she checked in, she sat down in a red wingback chair and thumbed through a magazine that had seen better days. Dr Taylor's name had been replaced by 'Dr Ben Sanders' on the plaque above the door. When Molly heard her name being called over the tannoy she followed the burgundy carpet along the corridor towards Room 2.

Knocking on the door, Molly waited until she heard the sound of the doctor's voice. 'Come in.'

She didn't know why she was feeling nervous as she pushed open the door. Immediately, Dr Ben Sanders stood up and introduced himself and gestured for Molly to take a seat at the side of his desk.

'Good morning,' he said, softly but with a smile. 'How are you? Actually I shouldn't be asking you that if you are here.' He was still smiling.

'You're not from around these parts,' observed Molly.

'Does the Irish accent give that away?' He grinned.

'Maybe,' she said, sitting down, glancing at the doctor, who was really very handsome. His shaggy curls were midnight black, his deep chocolate-brown eyes framed by graceful brows, his face strong and defined. Dr Sanders was tall, around six foot, and manly. He was slim but muscular, as Molly could tell by the way his crisp white shirt clung to his abs. He was going to be a welcome addition to the village, and they were going to be swooning all over him.

'So what's the problem?'

'No problem except I'm pregnant.' Molly felt the grin spread across her face. She was proud to be announcing her pregnancy, as if no woman had gone through it ever before.

'Congratulations! Is it your first?' asked Dr Sanders.

'It is and I only found out last night.' Molly bent

down, whipped the test – which she'd rescued from her kitchen bin – out of her bag and placed it proudly on the desk in front of him. 'Pregnant.' She pointed at the word.

Dr Sanders was smiling. 'It's okay, Molly, I don't need to see the test. I'd probably suggest placing it in the bin now.'

'Oh yes, sorry, I was just a little … well, you know,' she said, taking the test back and looking at it one last time.

'I need to take a few details and then we will get your blood pressure taken. Is Dad chuffed?' asked the doctor as he began typing on the keyboard.

The question completely threw Molly. Dr Sanders stopped typing and glanced towards her.

'There isn't a father,' she blurted. Then, realising how stupid that sounded, she added, 'Well, obviously there was at some point, at the time, but not now.'

Dr Sanders cocked an eyebrow.

'Too much information. I'll just confirm there is no father present in our lives and now I'll shut up. I'm completely on my own... Single mother and very capable.' Molly noticed that Dr Sanders was biting his lip to suppress a smile as her mouth was still running away with her.

'I'm sure you are. How are you feeling in general?'

'Excited,' she replied.

'I meant healthwise,' he said, looking amused.

'Oh yes, sorry. This morning a little sick. In fact that's a lie – so sick my head was stuck down the toilet for a while and I'm exhausted beyond belief. I just thought I was working too hard but now I know the reason why.'

'Date of your last period,' he asked, his hands poised at the keyboard of the computer.

'Over three months ago,' she confirmed, handing over a piece of paper with the date written down on it like it was top secret.

'Looking at this, Molly, your first scan is already due. I'll book you in over at the hospital as soon as possible and they will take everything from there,' he said, taking Molly's blood pressure. 'And this is a little on the low side. Are you feeling dizzy?'

Molly nodded. 'It seems to be worse in the morning but this morning I discovered ginger biscuits!'

'I believe they do the trick,' he said with a smile.

After the doctor had taken down a few more details, Molly left the surgery and headed towards her van. She had enough time to pick up Darling and head over to Primrose Park for her very first dog behavioural session.

'Molly! Molly!'

Molly spun round to see Birdie waving madly and hurrying across the car park towards her.

'I'm sure Darling is settling in well and you two are getting on like a house on fire.'

Birdie had a knack of asking questions in such a way that your answer was exactly what she wanted to hear.

She didn't let Molly reply. 'My mum is asking after her and I've told her how wonderful you are and that you've given her a very good home on Rory's recommendation.' Birdie was indeed throwing out the compliments left, right, and centre.

'Birdie, we agreed a temporary home...'

Birdie waved her hand, 'Don't worry about that but Mum is asking to meet you – just to put her mind at rest. Early evening tonight would be great. Are you free?'

It looked like she had no choice. Molly knew if she didn't agree to go tonight Birdie would suggest another night so it would be easier to get it over and done with. Birdie was tilting her head to the side whilst waiting for an answer.

'I would love to go and visit Dixie tonight. Would 6.30 p.m. suit?' replied Molly, thinking she would finish evening surgery at 6 p.m. and she might as well go straight from work, which hopefully meant home by 7 p.m. with her feet up and PJs on by 8 p.m.

For a second Birdie paused. She was looking back at the surgery and then towards Molly. 'Are you well?'

Now it was Molly's turn to hesitate. Even though the girls knew about her pregnancy she wanted to keep it under wraps from the rest of the world until her first scan.

'Just dropping off some leaflets regarding my new dog behavioural classes before I start work. And now I'm off to pick up Darling before heading over to Primrose

Park. You enjoy your day, Birdie, and I'll look forward to meeting with Dixie tonight.'

'Just one thing, remember I said Mum is very forgetful et cetera. She will try and tell you we've tricked her into going into the home and she shouldn't be in there. Sometimes Mum can be a little full-on.'

'Ah, don't worry, I understand,' replied Molly.

As soon as Molly sat in the car, her stomach began to churn again. This nausea was not going away. She reached for another biscuit from her bag. She could see Birdie in her rear-view mirror as she pulled out of the car park and headed towards home; she thought about how hard it must be watching a loved one deteriorate before your very eyes. She really must have a lot on her plate and maybe taking Darling would help her out a little.

Twenty minutes later, Molly arrived at Primrose Park. Darling refused to get out of the cat carrier, and Molly felt a fool. There was only one thing for it: if she couldn't coax her out of the basket she'd have to carry it over to the bandstand, where there was already a group of dog owners, looking slightly harassed, holding the leads of their unruly dogs.

'Good morning!' Molly chirped, sounding brighter than she felt.

Already the owners were wrestling with their dogs, who were jumping on their hind legs trying to launch themselves at each other. Molly was beginning to question her own state of mind. When had she ever thought this was going to be a good idea? One unruly dog was bad enough, never mind eight. 'You are beginning to look like a saint, Darling,' she whispered towards the cat carrier as she placed it carefully on the ground and introduced herself to everyone who was waiting.

'Okay,' said Molly, 'I would like you all to form a circle over there on the grass, keeping a couple of metres apart.'

Whilst everyone made their way over towards the grass, she pulled Darling's lead from her pocket and opened the cat carrier. At first Darling refused to step outside – until she saw the group of dogs, and then Molly had to do everything in her power to hold onto her. Barking continuously, Darling was up on her back legs, bouncing along the ground, pulling Molly towards the rest of the group.

'And you lot thought you had dogs that were misbehaving,' she joked, as all eyes were on her. 'You've not seen anything yet.'

Once everyone was standing in a circle Molly instructed them to keep their dogs on a short lead whilst everyone took it in turns to introduce themselves, their dogs, and the reason they were here.

Now it was Molly's turn. 'I'm Molly and this is Darling and Darling really doesn't seem to like much in life at the moment. I think she's sad and I'm hoping to make her happy again. First, I want us to walk around the circle. I want to see how each dog walks on their lead. If they continue to jump and pull, what I want you to do is change direction. They are trying to express dominance but you need to remember you are the boss. The key is to keep them on their toes and distracted at all times. As we walk I will continue to talk…' They set off walking in a clockwise direction. Molly led the way and as soon as Darling pulled on her lead or barked, Molly would immediately change direction.

'Dogs usually misbehave through boredom or a lack of physical and mental stimulation, and many problems such as barking and biting stem from a lack of communication. Simply put, your dog is not aware of what is expected of him or her. Right, I want you all to change direction again…'

Molly was getting in her stride and thankfully the sickness had eased a little. She really did feel better being out in the fresh air. The key was mind over matter: keep yourself busy and, if all else fails, eat ginger biscuits. She glanced over at Iris opposite her, who was holding on to her greyhound's lead like her life depended on it. Molly knew if she let go of that lead it was unlikely they would get the dog back anytime soon.

'It's all about setting boundaries and sticking to them. Make it clear to your dog what is acceptable and unacceptable behaviour every time… Change direction!'

Molly looked down at Darling, who was still growling and she quickly changed direction again. 'Even though at times it may seem like your dog is behaving poorly to spite you, this is not the case. There will be a trigger that sparks that behaviour, and we are here to identity those triggers, which is our first crucial step in solving the problem. Okay, I want you all to stand still and face inwards and tell your dog to sit. As soon as they sit, reward them with a treat.'

As the group listened to what Molly was saying, Darling had other ideas. Molly was instructing her to sit but Darling had turned her attention towards the woodlands just past the lake. She was stretched on the ground growling. Something had spooked her. Molly glanced over towards the trees but couldn't see anything out of the ordinary. There was nobody in sight.

'Darling, sit,' repeated Molly in a firm voice, but Darling wasn't listening. With one almighty launch forward her lead was tugged straight out of Molly's hand and she was running as fast as she could towards the trees. 'Just what I needed,' muttered Molly under her breath. It really wasn't looking good that on her first session she couldn't even keep control of her own dog.

'Sorry, sorry, just keep walking around and changing direction!' Molly flapped her hand at the dog owners before taking off after Darling. 'Get back here now.' Molly's voice was fraught as she watched the tip of Darling's tail disappear into the woodland. 'Damn you, pesky dog.' She stumbled and tripped as her feet snagged the nettles and she brushed past the bushes. Still hearing Darling's barks, she ran along the side of the fishing pond and lost her footing.

THUD. She landed on her backside and slid down the bank into the not so inviting algae-covered pond.

'Urgh … how do bloody fish live in here? Double damn you, Darling,' she muttered crossly. Her arms were cut from the brambles, her legs stinging from the nettles, and now she had the most stinking green algae dripping from her backside and her feet were submerged in the worse brown sludge, which stank to high heaven. An angry Molly blew out her breath, pushed herself back on her feet and like a trouper carried on after Darling with her feet squelching inside her trainers. There she was, just up in front. Darling had stopped dead in her tracks. 'Don't you dare move,' Molly muttered, slowly and carefully creeping up on her. Like a dog-snatching ninja she swooped down and successfully grabbed Darling with both hands, but the success was short-lived as Darling launched herself into the air and ran across the clearing to a man who was walking an Old English Sheepdog and very much minding his own business.

Embarrassingly, Darling's selective hearing meant she was still totally ignoring Molly, who was mortified to witness the walker visibly trying to shake Darling from the bottom of his jeans. She was snarling and hanging on for dear life.

'Get control of your bloody dog,' the man snapped.

Quickly Molly grabbed Darling's lead and wrapped it

around her wrist twice. 'I'm so sorry, I don't know what's come over her.' She obviously knew exactly what had come over her. Darling was being a disobedient pain in the arse and causing her a lot of embarrassment.

The disgruntled man continued gruffly, 'That dog should be muzzled. Here we are enjoying a gentle walk in the park and I'm savaged by—'

Immediately, Molly recognised that voice and locked her eyes on his. Her jaw fell open and with her heart beating nineteen to the dozen, she couldn't quite believe her eyes. Standing in front of her was Cam – but something had changed. He had a dark, stony look in his eyes, not the warm, sexy smile she remembered. In fact, he looked angry and was staring straight at her. Had he not recognised her?

'Cam, it's me, Molly – the hotel.' She touched his arm, but Cam took a step back. Molly already knew if she had to explain who she was this really wasn't going well. She was expecting his dark, brooding look to break out into a smile, but it didn't seem likely.

He stared at her. 'You need to keep that dog under control.'

Flustered, Molly felt herself blush. 'She's just a little temperamental at the moment after being rehomed.'

'And that's not my problem. Maverick is a little long in the tooth and the last thing he needs is some scrappy dog—'

'Darling,' interrupted Molly.

Cam raised an eyebrow. 'Are you calling me darling?'

'No, it's not a term of endearment; it's the dog's name.'

'I could think of a better name.' He gave her an icy cold stare.

Molly watched in bewilderment as Cam turned and walked off without giving her a second glance. What the hell had just happened here? Coldness was growing in her stomach. She'd hankered after this man for nearly three months and now it seemed he was nothing like she remembered at all. What had happened to the guy with the twinkle in his eye, the guy who gave her goosebumps with the touch of his lips on hers and the magical night they'd shared together? Now he seemed more like a distant stranger. Molly had fantasised about them bumping into each other again, throwing themselves into each other's arms, and now how stupid did she feel? All that wasted time giving her energy to someone who'd immediately dismissed her, leaving her feeling hurt and empty. He hadn't even given her the time of day and was rude. Her heartrate was up, but this time for all the wrong reasons. 'Damn you, Cam whatever-your-name-is.'

Molly watched him all the way to the entrance of Primrose Park until he disappeared. 'And what the hell are you doing in Heartcross?' she shouted after him but of course he was long gone.

Feeling like a complete fool, she rubbed her stomach.

She was standing there carrying his baby and now she felt like she'd imagined the whole night. He'd just acted like a jerk. She wished he'd never crossed her path again, as it seemed her memory of the night they'd spent together was playing tricks on her.

Chapter Nine

The last thing Molly wanted to do was go and visit Dixie after work, but she'd promised Birdie and although she'd had a bad day she knew that Dixie would be looking forward to her visit and wanting to hear only good things about Darling. Molly knew she would have to exaggerate – a lot. That morning Molly had attempted to take the rest of her class in her stride, but she'd been completely distracted by seeing Cam again. In fact, she felt like an emotional wreck and had to do everything in her power to hold back the tears that threatened to spill.

She just didn't understand why he'd been so cold and had acted like she didn't matter. He never even passed the time of day or asked her how she was. Confusion was at the top of her emotions, quickly followed by upset. What had happened to the man she'd met in the car park at the hotel, the warm, smiley, handsome guy who'd splashed her in the fountain, and the hot man who had appeared in her bedroom? Maybe this was the real him and he'd shown his true colours. After all, she didn't know him at all. He'd upped and left the next day without saying a word – who would do that?

Once the class had finished and Darling was safely back in the car, Molly had let the tears fall. She was finding it hard to control her emotions as it was, and they were yo-yoing all over the place. Of all the places to bump into Cam again, what was he doing in Primrose Park? Why was he in Heartcross? She'd never seen him around these parts before and she had no clue whether she was ever going to see him again.

On the way to visit Dixie, Molly stopped off at the newsagent and picked up some wine gums, a wordsearch book and a pack of playing cards. She wasn't sure if Dixie had things to occupy her in the care home but she didn't want to turn up empty-handed. After parking her van, she pressed the button on the intercom and the door to the care home automatically swung open.

Molly stepped inside and the fresh smell of bleach hit her instantly. There was a hallway off the main reception area that was wide enough for wheelchairs and had handles on the walls too. A special events board hung on the wall and next to the reception area was a gigantic fish tank. She noticed residents sitting in a nearby room just staring into space.

Walking over to the reception desk, Molly was greeted by a member of staff who showed her to Dixie's room, which was situated on the ground floor. After walking past a dining room with large central tables and a TV room dotted with comfy-looking chairs Molly arrived outside Dixie's door, which was ajar.

Dixie was sitting in an armchair with a small table at her side, looking out over a very small garden with a bench placed under a tree. The room was narrow, painted cream, and very plainly furnished. The adjustable bed had side rails and plain white sheets. There was one wardrobe, behind the door, and a linen basket with Dixie's name on it. The sterile setting must be an enormous change for Dixie, Molly thought, after living in Bumblebee Cottage all those years.

'Hello, Dixie, I'm Molly. I think you're expecting me?'

Dixie turned around and squinted at Molly 'You're the girl looking after my Darling, is that right?'

Molly nodded. 'Yes, isn't she an absolute dream,' she lied.

Dixie flapped her hand and looked towards the door. 'I need to get out of here. I shouldn't be in here. I'm not going mad or forgetful. They are trying to take my home.' Looking stricken, Dixie continued, 'You have to help me; no one believes me. They all think I'm forgetful and I'm really not... I just don't remember the things they are saying I'm doing.' Dixie's eyes were wide, looking earnestly towards Molly.

'Who are *they*?' enquired Molly curiously, knowing she shouldn't be encouraging this conversation. This was exactly what Birdie had predicted would happen when Molly arrived in Dixie's company but the look on Dixie's face was extremely convincing.

'That daughter of mine, she thinks the world owes her a living. Unlike my other daughter who lives in New Zealand – she'd help me. Birdie couldn't even look after Darling, that was too much trouble for her, yet she'd swipe my home from underneath me. Why won't anyone listen to me?'

Molly leant across and touched Dixie's hand. 'I'll chat to the manager here,' she said soothingly, trying to calm Dixie down. 'If anyone can help, surely they can.'

'I've tried; they won't listen either. My grandson is arriving today. He's staying at Bumblebee Cottage. You need to go and talk to him. Tell him what they're doing to me. Promise me you'll get me out of here?'

'I'm sure he'll come and visit, and you can talk to him them.' Molly didn't know what to say for the best.

Dixie was small-framed. Her hair was scraped back in a bun and pink blusher striped her cheeks. She sported a large sparkly brooch on her black jumper with a long gypsy skirt that touched the floor and a pair of bright pink slipper boots poked out from underneath. She was just on the acceptable side of eccentric.

'No one bothers with me except my grandson who's coming to stay, but recently he's been very busy and I've not seen him for a few months. My other grandson is just as bad as his mother. The apple doesn't fall far from the tree. I barely see Birdie and she only lives next door. She only visits if she wants something. That's why I got Darling for company. She is a darling, isn't she?' Dixie's face softened at the mention of Darling and Molly held back from bursting Dixie's bubble even more. Darling was a work in progress and not in the slightest a darling.

'An absolute darling. We've been to the park today,' Molly confided, making herself comfortable on the chair opposite Dixie.

'Primrose Park?' Dixie's eyes widened. 'That's our favourite park. I met my husband there, you know, married for a lifetime.' Dixie's voice faltered a little. 'Handsome bugger George was. We met at the bandstand, but over the years he put on a bit of weight. He used to pretend he was going for a walk, but he'd sneak off for a cheeky pint and a packet of pork scratchings – no good for his waistline.'

Molly gave a little chuckle. Dixie wasn't holding back – she just said it how it was. 'It's a lovely garden out there.' Molly looked out of the window and placed the carrier bag down on the table in front of her.

Dixie didn't agree. 'The size of a postage stamp. How is Darling? Is she missing me?'

'Of course she's missing you. She snuggles on your blanket and drags it around the house with her.'

A smile lit up Dixie's face. 'That's my girl, such a

loving character. Loves a bit of ham, she does, in her tea too, and a little bit of steak.'

'Don't we all,' said Molly, laughing and feeling her stomach rumble at the thought of food. 'I've bought you a word search and a pack of cards. There's some sweets too.' Molly pushed the carrier bag across the table.

'You've bought me presents?' Dixie looked surprised as she reached over towards the bag, pulled out the pack of cards, and turned them over in her hands. 'Cards! My favourite!'

Molly witnessed the twinkle in Dixie's eye.

'Never lost a game in my life. I used to play cards with my George on a Saturday night; he was always a sore loser. Thank you.' Dixie's eyes glistened at her memories. 'There's not much going on here. We have bingo on a Monday and knitting club, but I think I'll get a card club going with a little bit of gambling on the side, otherwise what's the point?' She gave Molly a mischievous look.

'That sounds like a plan to me, and here, I've printed you off a photo of Darling and put it in an old frame of mine. Sorry I've not had time to go to the shop, but I thought you might—'

'I love it. There she is – my girl,' interrupted Dixie, taking the photograph from Molly and clutching it with both hands to her chest. 'Thank you.'

Molly watched as Dixie got up from her chair and propped up the photograph on her bedside table next to a photo of a young Dixie and a man. 'My George, he wouldn't have let Birdie get away with putting me in here. I've tried to escape but I can't climb that wall and the front door is always manned.' Dixie became tearful again. 'Hopefully my grandson will come and visit soon.'

'I'm sure he will,' reassured Molly.

'George'—she pointed at the photo—'there was no one like him. He passed away a couple of years ago. He loved his bees, you know. Talked to them like they were children.' Dixie sat back down. 'Our little honey business became quite famous. George started it on a whim, supplying the pub, local village shop, and the farmers' market, then all of a sudden people couldn't get enough and we couldn't make it quick enough. He joined forces with The Old Bakehouse next door. His brother owned the bakery and the sky was the limit. Before we knew it there were jars of honey everywhere and I branched out into jams and chutneys made with the fruit from the orchard.' Dixie gave a little chuckle. 'Not once in all those years was George ever stung either. Bloody lucky beggar, I say.'

'Very lucky,' agreed Molly. 'And what happened to the business?'

'It wound up when George passed away. I'm a little sad about that, end of an era, but none of the family were interested in keeping it going. Birdie wants rid of the bees and the cottage... It's her inheritance, you see, but that place is my life and I've told her I'm not parting with it until I'm six foot under.' She took a breath.

'Tell me about The Old Bakehouse. That's the gorgeous building next to the cottage, isn't it?'

'There were two ends to the village with the pub in the middle. Love Heart Lane was the furthest lane in the village, leading to the path to Heartcross Mountain, and Bonnie, my friend, opened up the teashop all those years ago. Right at the other end was The Old Bakehouse, which did exactly what it says on the tin – the shelves were packed with every type of bread that you could ever imagine, baked fresh on the premises.'

'The smell of fresh bread is one of my favourites,' said Molly, wafting her nose in the air and closing her eyes.

'Mine too, but once Ted, George's brother, passed away, there was no one to carry on and the bakery was closed. Birdie moved into it even though Ted had left it to us in his will.'

'And wouldn't it be lovely to see it up and running again, a proper bakery.' Molly loved history. When she'd arrived in Glensheil, she'd looked to buy a house in the village but there was nothing for sale.

'It would, and I have a plan that Birdie isn't going to like.' Dixie tapped her nose. 'That grandson of mine that's coming to stay, he's having a hard time, needs a change of scenery, and he would make the perfect baker. I know once Heartcross gets its teeth into you there's no getting away. Mark my words, he's going nowhere.'

Molly couldn't help but smile. Dixie had everything worked out whether her grandson liked it or not. 'And does he have any say in the matter?'

'Like with any man, you convince them it's their idea and he needs a fresh start.' Dixie paused. 'I just want to be at home.'

Molly couldn't imagine being Dixie right now, moving from her gorgeous cottage and having to hand over her dog. Her whole life and routine had changed in a blink of an eye.

'Do you have any great-grandchildren?' asked Molly, looking up as the carer appeared at the door carrying a tray with a teapot and a couple of biscuits.

'Here, I've bought you and your guest a drink,' she said with a smile, placing the tray on the table.

'This is Jan, she's the new manager and looks after me.' Dixie patted her hand. 'I've told her I shouldn't be in here and Jan is looking into it. She also sneaks me the odd gin in a tin to keep me going.' Dixie gave Jan a look of approval.

'I think your memory is playing up again; I don't do any such thing.' Jan winked. 'Cards – I love a game of cards. What do you play?' She was looking towards the deck of cards of the table.

'Gin rummy.'

'Excellent, I'll be back for a game on my break.' Jan left the room and Dixie turned back towards Molly.

'That one is lovely, but others are rather short with me

sometimes. They try to give me drugs to calm me down when they say I lose my temper. I just shouldn't be in here. You can hear them whispering about me in the hallway but that one has a heart of gold.'

'I'm glad you have a friend,' said Molly, pouring them both a cup of tea.

'Do you have any great-children?' Molly asked again, returning to the conversation before Jan had appeared.

Dixie shook her head. 'I have two children, two grandchildren and no great-grandchildren. I would love great-grandchildren but I can't see that happening anytime soon. But that's another story. In fact...' Dixie bent down, picked up her bag, and put it on her knee. After rummaging inside for a second she pulled out a set of keys. 'My grandson should be arriving today. Would you be able to drop these off at Bumblebee Cottage? These are my keys; he may as well have a spare set.'

'Of course I can, but it might be first thing in the morning before I do my rounds, if that's okay?' Molly was feeling exhausted. After the day she'd had all she wanted to do was go home and put on her PJs.

'More than okay, thank you.'

After ten more minutes of chatting, Molly glanced at the clock and decided to make her move. She placed her cup and saucer back on the tray and grabbed her handbag off the floor and the keys that Dixie had given her. 'I've got to make a move. I've not had my dinner yet.'

Dixie looked a little disappointed. 'You will come back and visit soon, won't you?'

'Of course I will,' replied Molly. 'I'll brush up on my card skills too and I might even bring you a few gins in a tin.' Despite feeling exhausted, she had enjoyed chatting to Dixie. 'I promise I'll see you soon.'

As Molly reached the door, Dixie called her name. 'Molly, you will keep hold of my Darling? I like you. She'll like you. Just give her time.'

Emotional blackmail must run in the family, thought Molly, remembering how Birdie sang her praises too. Looking at Dixie's face, Molly knew she had to say what Dixie wanted to hear. She didn't want her worrying, and at the moment there was nothing to worry about.

'Don't you worry about Darling. I'll be back to give you regular updates. Oh and Dixie'—Molly held up the keys—'what's your grandson's name?'

'Cameron. Tell him he must come and visit me straightaway.'

Chapter Ten

Pulling open the van door, Molly could barely breathe. She sat down on the seat and stared at herself in the mirror. Cameron. Dixie's grandson was called Cameron. Surely it couldn't be the same person? But Molly had a niggling feeling it was exactly the same person and there was only one way to find out.

Twenty-four hours ago, Molly's life had been simple. Not anymore. She'd wished with all her heart that Cam would walk back into her life – but now... She took a huge gulp of air and tried to steady her breathing. Cameron was the father of her baby, which meant Dixie was the great-grandmother and there was a whole extended family out there, living up the road. Molly didn't know what the hell she was going to do about any of it. 'Christ on a bike.' She leant her head back on the seat and exhaled.

The more she thought about the situation, the angrier Molly began to feel. What was Cam's problem with her? Why had he completely ignored her? Actually, how dare he? Who did he think he was? Right there and then she made the nerve-wracking decision to go and hand over the keys to him at this very moment. It was just a little after 8 p.m. and she was dead on her feet, but she wanted to know what he had to say for himself. Molly couldn't shake off the way he'd treated her. To him it seemed like the whole evening never happened. With a pounding heart she started the engine and began to drive towards Bumblebee Cottage.

Within ten minutes she found herself nervously standing on the doorstep with her fist poised in the air, about to knock on the door and with no clue how this was going to pan out. Obviously, Cam could be rude again but surely not. Maybe it was all down to Darling being a pain this morning and catching him off-guard? But now she was just making excuses – he really hadn't been happy to cross her path again.

Molly took the plunge and knocked on the door with no clue what she was going to say, no conversation rehearsed in her head.

Rap, rap, rap.

As she waited, she smoothed down her scrubs. She'd at least managed to change her clothes from this morning after landing in the algae but hadn't managed to pull a brush through her hair since. There was no point worrying what she looked like now. She shuffled from side to side with her hands stuffed in her pockets and waited.

She knocked again, but still no answer.

Taking a quick glimpse through the living-room window she could see no one, but then she heard Cam's voice filtering from the garden. She stood still and she could hear him shouting for Maverick.

Quickly, she needed to make a decision. Was she bold enough to walk around the back of the cottage or was that being too intrusive? She hesitated for a split second but then, realising she had a legitimate reason for being there, she plucked up her courage and followed the path around the back of the cottage. The garden was beautiful, with everything pruned to perfection, the array of colours simply stunning. The freshly mowed grass opened out into an orchard, trees set out in orderly rows with fallen fruit dotted on the ground. Molly could immediately picture Dixie picking the fruit from the trees for all the jams and chutneys she made. There was an array of wheelbarrows, pruning tools, bushels and baskets, and a wooden ladder leaning against the trunk of a tree. To the left of the orchard there was a sectioned-off area which housed numerous beehives. Bushes hemmed the meandering flow of the stream trickling through the bottom of the garden. No wonder Dixie didn't want to leave this place; it had a sense of beauty and calm about it. It was simply stunning.

As soon as Maverick spotted Molly he gave a friendly bark – nothing as annoying as Darling. Molly could tell he was an old dog; he didn't even bother to come bounding over. Cam was sitting at a wrought-iron table, reading a newspaper and enjoying the evening sun. In front of him was an open bottle of wine and he was sipping from a glass. Hearing Maverick bark, he looked over and met Molly's gaze.

Her whole body reacted the way it had the very first time she'd set eyes on him in the car park at the hotel: tingling in his presence. No matter how he'd treated her that morning, he was still ridiculously handsome and he looked like he'd just stepped out of the shower. His hair was wet, slicked back and his lounge pants looked super sexy clinging to his toned waistline.

'Sorry, I knocked on the door but there was no answer.' Molly made her apologies quickly. 'Hello ... again.' Her voice sounded uncertain and cautious. She had no clue how Cam was going to react to her.

'That's because I'm sitting here, enjoying a glass of wine, minding my own business.' His manner was still as abrupt as this morning. She noticed him immediately silence his phone, which seemed to be ringing off the hook; he turned it face-down and pushed it across the table.

Molly didn't want to point out that he didn't look like he was enjoying anything. Cameron was miserable. He looked like he had the weight of the world on his shoulders. It was obvious to anyone he didn't want her there, but she wasn't going to let that deter her.

'And what a gorgeous garden to be sitting in,' she chirped, trying to jolly the conversation along a little. 'Dixie was telling me all about your grandfather's honey business and your great-uncle Ted the baker. Look at those hives; there's a lot of history in this place.'

Cameron eyed her. 'Can I help you with anything?'

Molly took a deep breath. At least she had his attention for a moment. 'I'm sorry about this morning. Darling can be a little bit of a handful. In fact, she's only been with me a day or so; she was … is your grandmother's dog.'

Cameron raised an eyebrow. 'I'm glad I didn't agree to take her on then if that's how she behaves.'

There was silence as Molly bent down to stroke Maverick. 'What a beautiful dog. How old is he? Twelve, thirteen?' guessed Molly, trying to keep the conversation light.

'Thirteen, and he doesn't need any out-of-control dogs barking at him in the park.'

Molly stood up. She noticed Cam hadn't even asked her to take a seat. 'About this morning, I think we were kind of caught off-guard,' she offered softly. 'After that night, I did try and look for you, you know, but I didn't have a clue about your surname, where you lived…' Molly knew she was beginning to ramble. 'Can we talk?'

Cam stood up and picked up his wine. 'I'm sorry, I've

literally only arrived today and had a hell of a day. I'm just looking forward to a quiet evening on my own and I'm sorry if that sounds a little abrupt.' Cameron dismissed the conversation almost immediately, leaving Molly feeling crushed to the core. It wasn't the reaction she'd expected or wanted. Of course there was something to talk about; even though he didn't know it, she was carrying his baby.

He began to walk towards the back door and suddenly Molly couldn't believe he was behaving this way. She'd had a hell of a day too but that didn't mean she was going to be rude about it, and here he was walking away from her. She was confused by the whole situation. He'd made her feel like she wasn't worth talking to, yet he'd thought differently the night in the hotel. Molly couldn't understand the change in him. Had she done something wrong the night they were together? Because it was starting to feel that way.

'Wait, these are for you.' She held out the keys towards him. 'That's why I'm here. From Dixie, a spare set and a reminder to go and visit her. She's not happy in the home. She thinks your auntie has forced her there. She's very upset about it all.'

Cam cocked an eyebrow as he took the keys from her fingers, his brushing against hers. He lingered for a second then grasped the keys in his hands. 'Thank you.'

At least he remembered his manners and said thank you, thought Molly. Taking the bull by the horns, 'And just for the record, I have no idea where the lovely, gorgeous Cam has disappeared to from that night, but I'm not liking this Cam.' Molly felt herself trembling inside. 'And I'd answer that phone. Someone obviously wants to get hold of you.' Cam's phone was continuously vibrating on the table.

He didn't say another word but picked up his phone and disappeared inside the cottage, shutting the door behind him.

'How bloody rude,' bellowed Molly towards the closed door. 'What an absolute jerk,' she muttered. She'd never expected him to fall straight into her arms and declare his undying love but she'd expected more than this.

Feeling her heart thumping against her chest, Molly headed back towards her van and squeezed her eyes shut. Her eyes teemed with tears as she started the engine and clutched her stomach, her heart sinking to a new depth. She rang Isla's number on her handsfree kit then began to drive.

Isla picked up after three rings. 'How did this morning go? Have you survived?'

Molly swallowed down a lump. 'Isla…'

'What's the matter?' urged Isla, instantly recognising that Molly was upset.

'He's here, in Heartcross, and he's not the man I remembered.'

'Who's here? Do you mean Cam?'

Molly took a breath as she drove home over the bridge towards Glensheil.

'Yes.'

'Where? How?'

'He turned up in Primrose Park this morning. Darling wasn't being a darling and neither was he, and to top it all off he's staying here for a while. It turns out he's Dixie's grandson.' The words died in Molly's throat. 'I just don't know what happened.'

'Cameron is back in town and that Cameron is your Cameron?'

Molly was stunned. 'You know him?' she quizzed, surprised at first but then, thinking about it, why wouldn't they know him? Dixie had been part of the village and living at Bumblebee Cottage for a lifetime.

'Of course we know him. As a kid he used to come to Heartcross for the summer holidays and stay with Dixie and George. He worked at the bakery in his teenage years; that was his—'

'His uncle's bakery,' interrupted Molly. 'Well, it's a complete disaster, Isla. I honestly feel like I've been hit by a truck. I just don't know what to do or think.' Molly couldn't help the tears rolling down her face. Her emotions were up and down like the worst rollercoaster ride she'd ever been on. 'He's an absolute... I would have been better off with a sperm donor. At least I wouldn't have had my heart broken.'

'I'm coming over,' announced Isla. 'Drew's home, and the kids are in bed.'

'I've not even eaten yet, even though I've no clue what I'm eating. I'm so exhausted. I've had enough today.'

'I'll bring you food – we have leftovers. Get your PJs on and I'll see you in twenty minutes.'

Before Molly could object, Isla had hung up. As Molly pulled onto her drive she could see Darling was already dancing about on the windowsill and barking. Molly sighed. She was hungry and tired. All she wanted was peace and quiet – just what Cam had asked for moments ago.

'What an absolute day,' she said, slamming the van door shut and heading towards the front door. 'Of all the parks in all the towns, he had to be walking in our park.'

Fuming inside, she was thankful Isla was on her way over. Maybe she could help her make sense of it all.

The second she walked through the door, Molly spoke to Darling in a calm voice. She felt far from calm, but the last thing she needed was Darling snapping at her ankles. 'Go and get your toy.'

Much to Molly's surprise, Darling stopped barking and ran off and returned with a well-loved cuddly toy in her mouth. She sat in front of an amazed Molly and dropped the bear. 'Well, look at you. At least something is going right today. Good girl. Did you actually just wag your tail? Let's get you fed.' Darling trotted behind Molly into the kitchen and sat patiently by her bowl. 'I think you are just misunderstood, but please, please, no more barking at Old English Sheepdogs in the park. We keep our cool, okay?' But Darling wasn't listening; she was already tucking into her food.

Waiting for Isla to arrive, Molly kicked off her boots and switched on the kettle, then immediately switched it off again. She didn't feel like a cup of tea. In fact, she didn't know what she felt like; she had a funny metal taste in her mouth and was suddenly consumed with tiredness. She really wasn't feeling herself but that wasn't surprising after the hell of the day she'd had. Fingers crossed, it couldn't get any worse.

Taking a swift glance at the clock, Molly had time to pull on her PJs before Isla arrived. She padded up the stairs. She risked a tentative look in the mirror then wished she hadn't. Her hair was knotted, her mascara smudged under her eyes – it wasn't the most attractive look and she sighed as she took a make-up wipe and rubbed it across her face.

Five minutes later, hearing the sound of a car engine outside, Molly looked out of the window to see Isla waving back at her and juggling a casserole dish with a smile on her face. Molly was beaten to the front door by Darling, who was already growling.

Molly tried the same tactic as before. 'Go and get your toy,' she ordered in a soothing, calm voice and to her amazement, just like before, Darling disappeared back into the living room whilst Molly opened the door.

'The cavalry has arrived. What a day you've had, by the sounds of it,' said Isla as she stepped into the hallway.

'You know what, Isla, you should be bottled. I know you've got enough on your plate without traipsing over here with food for me.'

'Don't be daft, Drew and Fergus are out in the garden enjoying a beer and I'm here looking after a friend in need. That's what we do...' Isla handed over the casserole dish. 'Lasagne and salad.'

'Perfect – and yes, what a day indeed. I don't even know where to begin. I went to visit Dixie, who believes they are drugging her and tricked her to go into the home so Birdie can get her hands on all her money; then to top that she informs me her grandson has arrived in the village and it turns out her grandson is the father of my child. And then this morning Darling attacks him in the park. Can my life get any worse?'

'Woah! Slow down, take a breath. I can't believe your Cam is Cameron Bird.'

'He's not my Cam, he was very clear about that. Nice to learn his surname at last,' replied Molly, tipping the salad onto a plate before bunging the lasagne into the microwave.

'It's been a fair few years since he's been back in Heartcross... Very good-looking though so I'm assuming he's still as handsome,' said Isla, pulling out a chair and sitting down in the kitchen opposite Molly.

'Very blooming handsome – more than handsome. Off the bloody scale handsome.' Molly let out the biggest sigh. 'What am I going to do, Isla? He couldn't even look at me and was so very rude.'

'Exactly what you were going to do before he walked back into your life this morning: get on with yours. This baby is your baby, and you were fully prepared to go it alone before he arrived and nothing has changed.'

'But the father is only a few miles up the road. Do I even tell him? What would be the point? He can't even be civil to me.' It wasn't sitting right with Molly. 'It just doesn't make sense. What do you know about him?'

The microwave pinged and Molly stood up and slid the lasagne onto a plate next to the salad.

'Like you said, Cameron is Dixie's grandson. His mum took off to New Zealand, if I remember rightly. Birdie is his auntie and he has a cousin called Albie.' Isla rolled her eyes. 'He's nothing like Cam – a bit of a rogue. There was something about him that unnerves me. Anyway, whatever my opinion of him is he is a very successful businessman. Albie owns the very famous chain of Birdvale – the garden centres.'

Molly raised an eyebrow. 'Bird being their surname.'

'Exactly that. I don't think Birdie ever married. Her real name's Marjorie, but people always called her by her nickname,' confirmed Isla. 'In fact, if I remember rightly, I think Cam went into business first with his cousin – gardening. They opened their first plant nursery behind The Old Bakehouse; it was just small. And then the next I heard, Cam had left the business to go and study dentistry, but he doesn't sound like the man you are describing today. He was always good fun and polite.'

'There was nothing good fun or polite about him today,' confirmed Molly.

'So you're thinking you want to tell Cam about the baby?'

Molly blew out a breath. 'It's a little bit awkward, isn't it? But don't you think I have to?'

'These things happen, and you're not the first. Is telling him going to change anything? Do you think he's going to welcome the news with open arms?'

Molly shrugged, 'From the way he's acting I very much doubt it, but this is huge. I can't keep it from him – he deserves to know, even if he decides he doesn't want anything to do with the baby. But surely he isn't going to cast aside his own flesh and blood?'

'I'm past second guessing what anyone is going to do or think these days, but you know we're here to support you.' Isla looked down at Darling, who was sitting next to Molly's chair. 'And has she been tranquilised? I know you're a vet and everything but surely that's not ethical.'

Molly laughed. 'She seems to be a little more settled tonight. Either that or she senses I can't take much more today.'

Isla reached over the table and squeezed her friend's arm. 'This is a life-changing event you're going through and it's not easy, but you can do it. If Cam wants to be a part of your life and the baby's then that's brilliant but if not, you are going to be just brilliant by yourself.'

Molly nodded. She knew from the moment she discovered she was pregnant that she would give it everything she had. That was before she even bumped into Cam again. But him being in Heartcross had changed everything. She had an extended family out there and even if he didn't want to know her or the baby, surely there was nothing stopping her from having a relationship with Dixie?

'And thanks for this. This is just what I needed.' Molly had devoured the lasagne and pushed the empty plate away from her while she took a sip of her drink. 'From the moment I opened my eyes this morning I've felt rough and not myself. Now I think about it, I've actually been dizzy and nauseous for weeks but I kept putting it down to skipping meals as I was so busy at the surgery.'

'Did you see the doctor?'

'Oh, I did, and he's going to be a welcome addition to the village, isn't he?' Molly blew out a breath and fanned her face with her hand.

'I believe so.' Isla smiled. 'He's moved into the flat above Peony Practice.'

'He doesn't have far to go to work then, does he? He

said my blood pressure is low and that's why I feel a little dizzy. And my first scan is imminent.'

'That's the time when it all becomes so real. It's such a magical moment seeing your baby for the first time,' gushed Isla, bringing her hands up to her heart.

Molly stood up and stared out of the kitchen window. She looked towards the enormous cherry trees that flanked the edges of the garden. Tears were pricking her eyes as she turned back round towards Isla. 'And wouldn't it just be ideal if I could share that moment with Cam? But my efforts to try and hold a conversation with him failed. One minute he's kissing me like I've never been kissed before and the next he can't get away from me quick enough. I just don't understand what I did wrong.' The sheer frustration of the situation was playing with her emotions.

'You haven't done anything wrong. We don't know what's going on with Cam. Why's he back here? Did Dixie give any more away?'

Molly shook her head and sat back down.

'I don't know why he's back,' Isla continued, 'but I'm telling you this because you are my friend…'

'Go on, what is it?' Molly folded her arms on the table and leant forward.

'And this might have changed, I don't know, but as far as I know, Cam is married.'

The words hung in the air and Molly scrunched up her eyes. 'You are kidding me?' With a sharp intake of breath she turned the words over in her mind and gave a slow, disbelieving shake of the head. Married? She would never have spent the night with him if she'd known he was married. Molly felt humiliated and betrayed, which was daft really because Cam had never promised anything. If she had known all the facts, Molly knew that night would never have happened. 'I didn't see a ring but that would explain why he doesn't want anything to do with me. Can this situation get any worse? What am I going to do now?'

'What you are going to do is not stress about anything. You and that baby have to come first.'

Molly nodded, but she *was* stressing. If Cam was married that changed everything.

'Was he at Dixie's alone?' quizzed Isla.

'As far as I know. Dixie didn't mention anyone else being there and I only saw the dog.'

'There you go then – why has he turned back up in Heartcross on his own? We need to discover all the facts first before we jump to any conclusions and get in a tizz.' Isla was the voice of reason and Molly knew she was right, but it was going to prove difficult if Cam ran away every time she attempted to make conversation with him.

'And let's face it, if he is sticking around it won't be long before he puts two and two together. Give it another few weeks and you, my girl, are going to get rounder and rounder.' Isla gave her a knowing look and glanced towards her stomach.

'Oh God. And isn't that something to look forward to.' Molly cupped her stomach with both hands. 'Why can't life just be simple?'

'Because it would be boring. Honestly, Molly, I know this is all extremely daunting but what will be will be. That baby comes first.'

Molly nodded. 'Received and understood and thanks for coming over … again.'

'That's what friends are for – and just in case you chomped through the whole packet of ginger biscuits, I picked you up these from Hamish's store on the way.' Isla reached in her bag and pulled out not one but three packets of ginger biscuits. 'These will keep you going!'

'No kidding! And that's the reason I'm going to get rounder and rounder, not because I'm pregnant.'

'This is your only excuse to eat as much as you want. I embraced it!'

Molly smiled at her friend. No matter how emotional she felt, Isla always stepped up to the mark and helped her put things into perspective. This was exactly what she needed tonight after the day she'd had.

'And promise me not to get stressed. See how the land lies with Cam over the next few days. Like I said, we have no clue why he's here or what's going on for him so in the meantime you get up, put a smile on that face, and when you get the date for your scan through, we will take it from there.'

Molly nodded. 'I promise,' she replied, but Cam was firmly fixed on her mind. Isla was right, she didn't know what was going on his life, but deep down Molly knew she wanted to tell him what was going on in hers – technically theirs. She wanted to give him the chance to redeem himself, apologise for the way he'd acted. She wanted him to hold her hand at the very first baby scan, but the truth of the matter was she didn't know him at all. She'd spent so little time in his company then for the last few months she'd put him high up on a pedestal and fallen in love with the idea of being in love. Cameron was just not who he had been on that night they'd shared. In her eyes he'd now clearly knocked himself off his own pedestal, and the hurtful thing to her was that it seemed he hadn't given her a second thought in all that time. Maybe she'd fantasised about their time together being more than it was.

She washed the casserole dish and passed it back to Isla. 'Food always tastes better when it's made by someone else. I really need to get myself into a routine and make some meals for the freezer because if it hadn't been for you tonight...'

'That you must. I can always make a bit extra and get you started. Now, if you don't mind me saying, you look exhausted.'

Molly glanced up at the clock. It was just before 9

p.m. and she had an early start tomorrow. There was the second session of dog training before morning surgery and if today was anything to go by she'd be going non-stop. 'I'm just going to curl up and have an early night.'

'Good idea.' Isla stood up and gave Molly a hug. 'And I'm always here, day or night, just ring me.'

'Thank you, that's exactly what I needed right now.'

Darling was hot on Isla's heels as she walked towards the front door. 'And don't rush into any decisions,' Isla added. 'You have plenty of time to talk to Cam. Wait until the scan time comes through and then make a decision. Who knows what each day is going to bring?'

'The joy of life,' said Molly, even though she wasn't feeling very joyous. 'And if he's got a wife?' she asked, engulfed in anguish. 'How does that make me look?'

'You aren't at fault here. What will be will be.'

Molly nodded and shut the door behind Isla then held on to the banister. For a second the dizzy feeling engulfed her again and she took some deep breaths. Feeling like some fresh air, she headed out towards the garden and grabbed her laptop on the way. She knew exactly what she was searching for when she opened up the lid but wasn't sure whether she was ready for the answers. Darling followed Molly outside then scuttled off down to the bottom of the garden, sniffing amongst the hedgerows as Molly logged on to Facebook. Searching for Cameron Bird, she hit enter and there he was, staring straight back at her on the screen with his arm wrapped around a woman and Maverick by their side – one happy family.

Immediately, Molly shut the lid. She couldn't bear to see any more. Why was she doing this to herself? It felt like torture. What exactly was she going to do now? Her dilemma was growing by the second. It looked like Isla was right; Cam was married, and she couldn't go breaking up a family, but she couldn't keep the baby a secret either, because soon the whole of Heartcross was going to know.

'Right, you can do this,' Molly said out loud, causing Darling to stop in her tracks and look straight at her. She barked before running the length of the garden and sitting down in front of Molly.

'And if only you would behave like this in the morning it would make my life a lot easier.'

Wearily heading back inside, Molly locked up and climbed up the stairs. She knew she needed to make plans for herself and the business as soon as possible because, even though it seemed like a lifetime away, the baby would be here before she knew it. She hovered at the door of the junk room, which was cluttered with boxes, old clothes, and goodness knows what. There was that much stuff Molly couldn't even see the spare bed, which of course would have to be dismantled and put into the garage. This room was going to have to be transformed into a nursery in the next few months and that wasn't going to be an easy task. Walking over to the window, Molly glanced out at the glorious River Heart glistening in the distance and the traffic driving over the bridge into Heartcross.

'Blue or pink, I wonder?' she said, taking one last look around the room before she noticed Darling dragging Dixie's old blanket up the stairs. She couldn't help but smile; Darling was definitely a character and Molly was too tired to argue with her.

'My bed again then, is it?' she said, watching Darling launch herself onto the duvet before settling on her own blanket. She knew she was making a rod for her own back; after all, she would preach just the opposite at the dog behavioural class in the morning, but anything for an easy life. She brushed her teeth then slipped under her covers. Her head was in a spin. Never in her dreams had she thought that Cam was going to turn up in Heartcross out of the blue. 'What are we going to do, Darling?' But Darling wasn't listening; her eyes were already firmly closed.

'Well, at least we've got each other, and we are not going to stumble at the first hurdle,' she murmured, rubbing her stomach gently, 'and that's all that matters.'

An exhausted Molly closed her eyes. All she could do was try and get some sleep and see what tomorrow brought.

Chapter Eleven

The sun was shining and there wasn't a cloud in the sky as Molly drove over the bridge into Heartcross. She was beginning to be thankful that her third trimester of pregnancy was going to be in the cooler months because already she was feeling hot and sticky. This morning she'd noticed that her trousers were snug around her waist and her stomach was looking a little bloated, but that could be down to the fact that she was already on her third ginger biscuit of the morning.

Hamish waved at her as she drove past the village shop and she beeped her horn. Already the village was a hive of activity with tourists walking along the high street and heading down to the river. This was perfect weather to enjoy all the water sports the boathouse had to offer or catch a ride with Flynn Carter's boats. The multi-award-winning businessman, owner of Starcross

Manor and the Lake House, was now operating tourist excursions up and down the water.

Molly didn't know what possessed her but this morning she took the longer route to Primrose Park, which meant driving past Bumblebee Cottage. She was curious to see if there was another car parked on the drive; whether Cam had company. She knew this wasn't classed as normal behaviour but bordered on stalking, and her only defence was that she was trying to make sense of it all. With a thumping heart she glanced towards the cottage, but the curtains were still drawn, there was no sign of life, and the same car was on the drive as yesterday. Molly assumed it was his. She carried on driving, not knowing what she was going to do anyway. After all, he had his own life and it really was nothing to do with her.

Within minutes, Primrose Park was in sight and Molly observed some sort of commotion going on up ahead. She squinted. There were people gathered everywhere, spilling out on to the road. Up ahead there were police cars, a fire engine, and a news reporter. Carefully manoeuvring the van into a space, Molly climbed out, leaving Darling inside in her basket for a moment. Noticing Felicity and Isla standing further up on the road, Molly hurried towards them, then stopped by their side and stared.

'Jesus!' The sight in front of her was not one she was expecting. Beautiful Primrose Park was a blaze of charcoaled trees, churned-up shrubs and flowers, and a bandstand burnt to the ground.

'What the hell has happened here?' Molly was aghast. The beautiful park was no more.

'Vandals, and they seem to have got way out of hand. Drew caught them up at the farm last night; they set fire to the hay bales but thankfully we only lost a handful. They left the gates open and vandalised some of the fences, and the alpacas were spilling out onto the lane but luckily they are all safe and back in the top field.'

'And why would people do that?' Molly was mystified. 'Why exactly would anyone want to destroy something for no reason? This park means so much to so many people and look at it now.'

'Maybe destructive youths with time on their hands,' Isla was shaking her head. 'God knows what goes through the minds of these types of people.'

The scene was one of pure devastation. The wrought-iron fences looked like they had been driven into, bent and hanging off the posts, the pea-green grass was black and scorched, the meadow had been churned up and the flowers destroyed. Molly pointed towards the grand pergola that had been vandalised with spray paints. The top of the fountain had been pushed over.

Everyone stood and watched as the police secured tape around the fences of the park. The smoke from the burning trees was still billowing up into the sky as the firefighters battled to put the flames out at the far end of the park.

'You will not be able to use the park. Please can everyone move away,' shouted a police constable, securing everyone's attention. 'Primrose Park will be closed until further notice.'

'And how long will that be?' came a voice from the back of the crowd.

'Indefinite. The park is not safe; the fire is still burning.' Another policeman slapped a huge sign on the damaged gate – DO NOT ENTER.

'And if anyone saw anything in the early hours of the morning, please can you contact the police station immediately,' the police constable continued.

As the crowd began to disperse, Molly hung back with Felicity and Isla.

'This seems so unusual,' remarked Felicity. 'Nothing like this has ever happened in our village before. Is it something we should be worried about?' Felicity directed her question towards the police constable.

'There's been a spate of similar incidents across the villages on the other side of Glensheil. Parks, buildings et cetera. We are hoping it's just adolescent teenagers who need to find a less destructive hobby, so we are sure there's nothing to worry about, but we would still like to catch the culprits.'

'Mindless vandalism, spoiling the park for everyone else. I was bringing the boys here later for a picnic and to feed the ducks,' commented Isla, still looking towards the burnt-down bandstand. 'Can you imagine the cost of putting all this back to normal?'

'It's never going to be back to normal,' said Molly. 'That bandstand has history. It's been there for a lifetime. Many romances have started listening to bands over there on a Saturday night.' Molly immediately thought of Dixie, who she knew would be devastated at hearing the news.

'And what does anyone gain from spray painting fountains and churning up flowerbeds?' added Felicity. 'I know Mum will be devastated to hear this news. That place holds special memories for her too.'

'And Martha – in fact everyone,' added Isla.

They watched as the firemen continued to hose down the trees then Molly heard Darling's bark coming from the van and suddenly panicked. 'And where am I going to do my morning classes now?' Molly was looking towards her clients who were now trundling up the road with their pooches, looking in alarm over at the park. 'I need to think fast.'

'You've got the small green opposite Bumblebee Cottage, or you can borrow one of the fields up at the farm, but just not today, as the cattle are in the spare field because these idiots vandalised our fences too.'

'Looks like there's only one option.' Molly rolled her eyes and exhaled. 'The small green opposite Bumblebee Cottage it is.' Molly wasn't quite sure how she was feeling about that but now, with a number of owners and their dogs standing in front of her, she couldn't think of another answer fast enough. She made an announcement. 'Unfortunately, due to the vandalism at Primrose Park, the class is unable to take place here this morning. So my suggestion is we all head over to the small green. Is everyone okay with that? It's a five-minute walk away.'

Everyone was in agreement, and as Molly freed Darling from the cat carrier inside the van and placed her down on the pavement, she became light-headed for a second. 'Whoa,' she murmured, holding onto the door handle whilst taking some deep breaths. The queasiness was beginning to rise again as she tried with all her might to think about anything else except feeling this way. Felicity must have noticed and was holding onto her arm. 'You okay?'

Molly shook her head. 'All the snippets about pregnancy I've read in the last forty-eight hours… You are not ill, you are pregnant. Well, I feel awful. This dizziness just consumes me.'

'Sit down on the wall for a second,' suggested Isla. 'Take in some more deep breaths.'

'I've got a vile taste in my mouth and honestly I want to retch, but I can't.' Molly had lowered her voice. 'I need to try and act normal otherwise people will start guessing what's up with me and then the gossip will spread like wildfire.'

'And it'll be no one's business except yours,' replied Isla defiantly.

'Right, well, I best try and look lively; there's morning surgery after this.'

'You need to reconsider that. You have staff to cover for you. That's what they are there for. Low blood pressure is no laughing matter. You need to rest, Molly.' Isla was forceful.

Molly nodded. 'I do and I will, but I'd best go and sort out these unruly dogs first.' She kissed both of her friends on the cheek and headed down the road with Darling pulling on her lead, constantly barking and trying to keep up with the other dogs in front of her. 'This is going to be another long day,' murmured Molly, already counting the hours until she could curl back up in bed and shut her eyes.

Within five minutes, they'd all arrived at the green. Darling had turned into the devil dog once more and Molly was beginning to regret bringing her along. Today, they were working on recall training. Molly organised everyone into a circle and from her rucksack took out extra-long leads and handed one to each owner. 'For the rest of the week you are going to be working closely on bonding with your dog. For those dogs that run away as soon as you let them off the lead, the situation isn't going to be fixed overnight.' While she addressed the group, Molly had positioned herself so she was facing

Bumblebee Cottage. She could see that all the curtains were still firmly closed.

'To bond closely with your dog, games of fetch, Frisbee, and walks on these long leads are perfect. Not only are these games much-needed physical and mental stimulation, this is all part of demonstrating to your dog that they are a much-loved and valued member of the family.' Molly looked down towards Darling, who was sniffing about in the bag of toys that she had brought along.

'Unfortunately, with the change of venue we can't shield ourselves under the shade of the trees, so we need to make sure the dogs have regular drinks. Did we all bring a bowl and some water?'

Everyone nodded.

Just as they started the first training exercise, Molly took another quick look up towards the cottage window and was taken a little by surprise as she locked eyes with Cam. The upstairs curtains were wide open, and he was standing in the window looking straight back at her. Feeling a blush on her cheeks, Molly looked away first. A couple of minutes later she dared to look up again, but now he was gone.

After forty minutes of intensive training the session was over, and everyone agreed to meet at the same place tomorrow. As the dog owners began to disperse in different directions, Molly sat down on the wooden bench on the edge of the green to catch her breath before she walked back to her van, which was still parked at Primrose Park. She closed her eyes and took a deep breath, knowing she needed to make a move. Morning surgery started in thirty minutes' time and she was already cutting it fine.

The second she stood up, Molly felt light-headed again but walked across the road towards the pavement.

'This low blood pressure is no fun. You are putting me through the wringer,' she whispered to her stomach as she passed the cottage, not daring to glance in that direction.

Out of nowhere, the sound of Maverick's bark could be heard filtering from the cottage garden. Taking Molly completely by surprise, Darling slipped her lead and hurtled over the low stone wall. Molly watched in dismay as she disappeared around the side of the cottage.

'Shit! Double shit! Get back here,' she ordered. The last thing Molly needed was a run-in with Cam just before morning surgery.

Reluctantly Molly followed Darling, hoping she would manage to escape the wrath of Cam, but luck, it seemed, was not on her side this morning.

'Recall training going well then?' Cam was looking straight at her from over the garden gate.

Molly felt an absolute fool and frustrated. Here she was trying to teach other owners how to handle their dogs when she couldn't even control her own.

'Obviously not,' she replied, adopting the same tone as him.

'Is there any particular reason you keep bringing your dog to terrorise mine?'

Darling was spinning round in circles and still barking at Maverick, who was sitting down as good as gold next to Cam.

'It's not by choice, believe me.' Molly felt like throwing her arms up in the air and walking away, leaving them all to it, but of course she couldn't. Darling was definitely showing Molly exactly who was boss, and Molly tried to adopt a firm approach, but the situation was incredibly embarrassing.

'Darling, here.' Molly dared to glance towards Cam. Was he really smiling? She shook her head in disbelief and reached down to grab Darling's collar. Molly's vision blurred, and she felt sickness like she'd never felt before. Stumbling forward she grabbed the gate then slumped against the wall, sliding to the ground. Everything became a whirl as she closed her eyes and willed the dizziness to stop. Losing time for a few seconds, Molly felt herself being lifted, then carried, until Cam placed her gently down on the sun lounger under the shade of the parasol.

'Do not move. Stay still. I'm just going to get you some water,' he said softly, his voice gentle.

Molly didn't move because she was trying with all her might to hold on to the contents of her stomach.

Within seconds Cam returned with an ice-cold glass of water and handed her a damp cloth. 'Drink this and wipe your brow.'

'Thank you,' murmured Molly, bringing the glass to her lips.

'Have you eaten?' he asked. 'It's already hot out here and you haven't got a hat on. Maybe you've had too much sun and you're dehydrated.'

Molly knew exactly why she was feeling this way but she wasn't going to share those details at this point. She wiped her brow.

'Here, let me,' he said, giving her a genuinely warm smile.

Their hands hovered against each other's as Molly placed the cloth in the palm of his hand. She felt an instant pull towards him and summoned up enough courage to meet his gaze. He was staring straight at her, and his eyes dropped for a split second towards her lips. There it was again, that electrical jolt, the crackling in the air that she felt every time in his presence. Cam didn't break eye contact as he gently dabbed the cloth across Molly's forehead. Her heartbeat quickened, her mouth dry as she never faltered from his gaze. She felt an overwhelming desire for him and surely, by that deep longing in his eyes, he felt it too. Molly knew there was an attraction between them whether he liked it or not.

'There,' he said, placing the cloth down.

'Where's Darling?' remembered Molly, suddenly

panicking as the gate was open. She couldn't see her or hear her and Maverick had taken himself off and was lying down under the shade of the trees.

Cam touched her knee. 'Don't worry, she's fine,' he reassured her.

'Her recall skills aren't the best.'

'You don't say.' He smiled. 'She's actually in the kitchen lying in the old dog basket. She's made herself at home.'

'Maybe because this was her home.' Molly noticed Cam was staring at her from under those long lashes, with those same eyes that she was instantly attracted to the very first time she'd seen him. He'd gone from brooding, abrupt Cam to being genuinely caring and comforting. Molly liked this Cam best.

'Keep taking small sips of the water,' he instructed.

Molly sat up straighter. 'Cam, I feel sick.'

'Okay.' Cam looked around quickly and reached for a nearby plant pot and placed it between her knees. 'Here,' he said, taking Molly by surprise as he leant forward and gently tucked an escaped strand of hair behind her ear. 'I'm going to ring for the doctor. Don't move. We need to get you checked out.'

'I've no intention of going anywhere,' she replied, retching into the plant pot as Cam stood up and hurried indoors before quickly reappearing at the back door.

'Who is your doctor?'

'Peony Practice, Dr Ben Sanders,' she managed to shout before throwing up in the plant pot.

Within seconds Molly could hear muffled conversation and her name being mentioned. 'Molly, her name is Molly.' Cam's voice became clearer as he was now standing at the back door. 'Her surname's McKendrick.'

Molly was impressed. He'd even remembered her surname after all this time.

'I think she must have sunstroke or something. She's dizzy and has just vomited,' he said, giving the details. 'She's at Bumblebee Cottage, next to The Old Bakehouse.'

Molly was absolutely mortified when Cam returned and sat back down next to her. Her body had gone into full retch mode and she just couldn't stop.

'Are you sure it's not a hangover?' He gently rubbed her back as she retched again. 'The doctor is about five minutes away.'

'Thank you,' replied Molly, not daring to look up and make eye contact. 'And definitely not a hangover. But how embarrassing is this?'

'Try and take some deep breaths,' Cam suggested. 'The doctor shouldn't be too much longer.'

For the next few minutes Molly sat still with her head in the plant pot before looking up. 'Maybe I should faint and be sick more often in your company, as that way you seem to be nice to me.' This time she dared to look him in his eye to see his reaction. She noticed him take a deep breath and look like he was just about to stay something when they heard the car pull up outside then the sound of hurried footsteps.

Immediately Darling shot out of the back door and forced Dr Sanders against the wall as she went for his ankles.

Molly attempted to get up to rescue the doctor but, feeling light-headed, she sat immediately back down. 'Cam, you'll have to grab her and put her inside.'

Cam took control and called her name firmly, and immediately Darling was by his side.

'Well, I never,' exclaimed Molly, not believing her eyes. She watched Cam swoop her up in his arms, place her inside the kitchen, and shut the back door behind her.

'It seems you've either got it or you haven't,' teased Cam, grinning at Molly, who rolled her eyes, shaking her head in happy disbelief. Cam's joking attempt to belittle her dog whisperer skills made for playful banter – a positive shift in his behaviour towards her.

'I'm just glad someone's got it,' joked Dr Sanders, walking over towards Molly, 'because giving myself a tetanus injection was not on my list of things to do this morning.' He offered a smile and pulled up a garden chair next to Molly.

'How are you feeling?' he asked.

Molly took a swift look inside the plant pot and wriggled her nose, 'Not great if I'm honest.'

'Dizzy?' asked Dr Sanders, reaching inside his bag, 'I'm just going to take your blood pressure.'

Molly looked from the doctor to Cam, who was watching, and hoped with all her might that Dr Sanders didn't mention the pregnancy word. Cam caught her eye and must have realised she was looking a little uncomfortable.

'I'll give you some privacy and go and check on Darling,' he said, quickly disappearing inside the cottage, much to Molly's relief.

'Okay, I need you to sit upright and place your feet flat on the ground and'—Dr Sanders pulled the garden table over to Molly's side—'and rest your arm on the table.'

Molly did exactly that. 'I don't want anyone knowing I'm pregnant … just yet,' she said quietly, looking towards the back door, but thankfully Cam was out of sight.

'Your health is confidential,' confirmed the doctor. 'Now tell me exactly what you've done this morning – have you eaten?'

Molly went through her morning routine. 'Is this normal? Because honestly I really don't know how I'm going to get through morning surgery feeling like this.'

'I don't think you are. I need you to go home and rest.

Have you got anyone to cover for you?' asked Dr Sanders.

'Yes, there's plenty of staff on the rota. This low blood pressure, will It affect the baby in any way?' Molly had no clue about pregnancy. This was the first time she'd ever been pregnant in her life and, judging by the way she was feeling, the last.

'Low blood pressure tends to link to dehydration, and when your fluids aren't being replaced, it drastically affects the way that blood flows within the body. The hot sun won't be helping. Generally, low blood pressure during pregnancy isn't cause for concern but a huge drop may indicate there's something more going on, so I want to err on the side of caution to put your mind at rest as well as mine. I'll chase up your scan appointment and see if we can get an earlier date.' Dr Sanders took a breath. 'Low blood pressure may also be a sign of an ectopic pregnancy, which happens when a fertilised egg implants outside your uterus. I want to rule out this possibility so we can see that everything is normal and healthy. How are you feeling now?'

Molly wanted to burst into tears; she really didn't feel well. 'Not the best.' She sighed. 'In fact, I feel better when I lie down.'

'Okay, I want you to take the rest of the day off...'

'But the surgery?' interrupted Molly, who couldn't remember the last time she'd taken a day off.

'The surgery will still be there tomorrow,' insisted Dr

Sanders. 'I want you to avoid getting up quickly and don't stand for long periods of time. I want you to eat small meals throughout the day to keep your strength up. Avoid taking very hot baths or showers and drink more water. I know sometimes as soon as the water hits your stomach it will come back up, but you will keep some of it down. Oh, and another good tip is to wear loose clothing.'

'That may prove a little difficult; everything is feeling a lot more snug than usual.' Molly attempted to smile.

The back door opened, and Dr Sanders leant towards Molly and lowered his voice. 'There's two of you now and we need you both to be fit and healthy.'

Molly nodded her understanding.

'How are you?' asked Cam, sitting down on a nearby chair. 'Can I get you anything else?'

Dr Sanders looked towards Molly. 'I'll be in touch. Take the rest of the day off, stay out of the sun, and eat.'

'I need to go to the shops. I'm all out of food,' she confessed, thinking of the empty fridge back at home with a lump of mouldy cheese and a packet of multi-coloured peppers that she'd bought on a whim a couple of weeks ago. Molly couldn't remember the last time she'd done a proper food shop; there never seemed any point. With the late-night surgery she always stopped off and grabbed something on the way home, as there never seemed to be any time to cook for herself.

'You need to stay at home and rest today. Ring a

friend,' Dr Sanders insisted before heading towards the garden gate and disappearing down the path.

As soon as he was out of sight, Molly looked up towards Cam. 'I'm sorry about your plant pot. I can take it with me and…'

'Don't tell me you are going to rinse it and bring it back.' Cam laughed. 'I can live without a plant pot. Lucky this one didn't have holes in the bottom otherwise I'd dread to think…' He picked it up at arm's length and dropped it in the rubbish bin. 'It's as easy as that.'

Molly studied his face as she took a sip of her water. There were glimpses of the old Cam she'd met that night, the way he pushed her hair out of her face, the way he'd soothed her head, the look they'd given each other. The attraction was very much alive between them – she could feel it – but she couldn't help wondering what the hell was going on in his life to bring him back to Heartcross. And where exactly was his wife? Did he still have a wife? These were all questions that Molly wanted to blurt out, but she feared his whole demeanour would change, and she liked this kind, caring Cam more than the one she'd bumped into in the park.

'You heard the doctor, home and rest. Where is home? Glensheil, did you say?' asked Cam.

Molly was impressed. She'd told Cam where she lived the night they'd met in the hotel but now it seemed a little strange that he'd never mentioned he knew it well and had relatives living in the village next door.

'Yes,' she replied. 'Glensheil.'

'Okay, I'll go and get a pen and paper. You can make me a list of food you need and I'll drop it off for you.' He was up and out of his seat and headed inside, returning clutching a notepad and pen.

Molly was amazed, but welcomed the suggestion. She hadn't expected Cam to offer and go and do her shopping, especially as for the last forty-eight hours he'd given her the impression he couldn't stand the sight of her. 'I'm sure you have better things to do with your day?' she said, even though the last thing she wanted to do, feeling the way she did, was traipse around a supermarket.

'An afternoon of golf but time to kill this morning.'

'No work for you then, either?' she quizzed, wondering if he would open up about why he was back in Heartcross renting out his grandmother's cottage, which suggested to her it was going to be a long-term agreement.

Was it Molly's imagination or did Cam just bristle? For a second she thought she saw a flash of something in his eyes but wasn't sure if it was anger or sadness.

'A day off,' he replied, not explaining himself further, 'and this evening a lesson in beekeeping from Gabe, who's looking after the hives.' Cam glanced in their direction. 'I promised Grandma I'll make her up some jars of honey like Grandad used to do. He supplied many of the local farmers' shops with his honey and my uncle owned the bakery next door.'

'Yes, Dixie was telling me. She used the fruit from the orchard to make jams and chutneys.'

'They had a good thing going here – their livelihood, their love for each other.'

Once again Molly noticed a faraway look in Cam's eyes. Call it woman's intuition but something wasn't quite right.

'They had it made here. I mean, look at this place,' he added.

Molly couldn't agree more: the cottage was absolutely gorgeous and in a stunning location.

'I know Dixie is sad leaving all this behind,' she said. 'There's a lifetime of memories.'

'And I daren't tell her how frightened I am of bees.' Cam rolled his eyes.

'Get away! By all accounts your grandfather was the most famous maker of honey this side of Inverness.'

'And he made a decent living from it. Honestly, I can remember one summer when I was here with my cousin, we poked the hives with a stick, and I got four bee-stings within the space of a minute! As you can imagine I never went near those hives again. Tonight will be the first time since I was a little boy.'

'I can imagine you as a little boy, quite cute, always up to mischief.'

'Only quite cute?' Cam tilted his head at her and laughed.

'I suppose the moral of the story is not to go poking beehives with sticks.' Molly gave Cam a knowing look and he laughed.

'You may have a point there. It wasn't our finest moment.'

The atmosphere between them had seemed to soften. Molly could see why she had been attracted to Cam in the first place and that really hadn't changed. She wondered what sort of father he would make. Would he be hands-on, changing nappies, down on the floor giving piggyback rides the second he got home from work? She could picture them sitting around the table, laughing and joking, eating dinner, sharing their life together, but who was she kidding? Molly knew she was just torturing herself thinking about it. For all she knew he could possibly already have children. As curious as she was to discover more about his personal life, she really didn't want to face the answers just yet, especially if they weren't what she wanted to hear.

'I'll just have to man up and get on with it, and this time wear a suit. I'm doing this for Grandma. It's her eightieth birthday in a couple of weeks and would you believe it was my grandad's on the same day, but in a strange coincidence also the day they met.'

Molly brought her hands up to her heart. 'At the bandstand!'

Cam cocked an eyebrow. 'How would you even know that?'

'Because Grandma Dixie and I are like that … tight.' Molly crossed her fingers and watched for Cam's reaction. Obviously, she remembered Dixie telling her the night she visited her in the care home but if she knew little details like that, would Cam wonder what else she might know about him? Though it was actually very little.

All she could see was a flicker of surprise. She didn't know what she was expecting but he didn't seem worried about anything else.

'So the plan is I'm gathering all her family and friends for a surprise birthday party at the bandstand, with a stall selling Grandad's famous honey and Grandma's famous jams and chutneys. I've approached the council, spoken to Alfie, and he's giving me the go-ahead. I'm just waiting on a jazz band to confirm the date and I'll be set.'

'Cam, haven't you heard? Primrose Park has been destroyed.'

Cam's eyes widened. 'What do you mean? I was only there yesterday walking Maverick. It looked absolutely fine to me.'

'That's why I took my session on the green this morning. Someone has set fire to the trees; the bandstand has been completely destroyed, burnt to the ground. The fountain was destroyed and they've dug up the wildflower meadow. The police cordoned it off this morning, deeming it unsafe.'

Cam blew out a breath. 'That really isn't going to bode well with Grandma. She's been talking about her eightieth birthday party in Primrose Park for as long as I can remember. She's going to be so disappointed. Plan B, I suppose, is to have it here or on the green, but that won't be the same.'

Molly was impressed at the close relationship Cam seemed to have with his grandma. It was a good quality in a person. Thankfully, he seemed to have let his guard down with her a little too.

'How are you feeling now?' he asked tentatively.

'Still light-headed and queasy so I'm just going to go home and ring the surgery to make sure all my staff know they need to take over whilst I go and sleep it off.'

'It's probably just the sun and a twenty-four-hour bug all rolled into one.'

Molly knew this was the longest twenty-four-hour bug she was going to have but just nodded.

'Okay, a food list and your address and I'll nip and do you a quick shop before I go and play golf.' Cam was poised with the pen on the pad waiting for Molly to reel off her list.

'Thank you. Ginger biscuits, let's say three packets for now.'

Cam raised an eyebrow. 'Three?'

'I just like ginger biscuits,' she answered quickly,

brushing over any more questions by moving onto the next item on the list.

Once the list was finished, Molly stood up slowly, remembering what the doctor had said. 'And thank you for this.' She gestured towards the notepad.

'It's the least I can do when you faint on my path and throw up in one of my plant pots,' he grinned, his cool exterior now completely lifted.

'Darling, I've forgotten Darling!'

Cam opened the back door but this time he seemed to have lost his charisma. Darling bolted out barking, out of control and snapping at Cam's ankles.

'Come on, Darling, home.' Molly tried the firm voice like Cam had used before but Darling was having none of it.

'Home,' she repeated firmly.

Darling was jumping up at the back door, trying to pull down on the handle. 'I guess she thinks this is home, which technically it is. I could leave her with you.' Molly gave Cam a lopsided grin.

But Cam had taken his life into his own hands by clipping on Darling's lead and handing it over to Molly. 'Shopping is one thing but living life on a knife-edge waiting for the killer dog to jump at my throat is another, and I'm not sure Maverick looks too impressed. All we want is a quiet life, isn't that right, Maverick?'

'She's not that bad! Well…'

Molly slowly walked towards the van, leaving Cam at

the side gate. The van was stifling inside and Molly quickly wound down the window then started the engine to let the air circulate before shuffling Darling into her basket. She was still barking until she set eyes on Dixie's old blanket then, much to Molly's relief, finally lay down quietly.

Waiting for the inside of the van to cool, Molly took a breather and sat down on the old stone wall and rang the surgery to tell them she wouldn't be in. Her mind turned towards Rory, who'd been trying to convince her to go into partnership and bring the two surgeries together. In the past, Molly had enjoyed her independence, being her own boss, but in the current situation the offer was looking very appealing. Maybe she would talk to Rory and share her news with him; it could make things a little easier for her once the baby was born. But all she wanted to do now was climb back into bed and try and sleep the sickness off.

Two minutes later, sitting behind the wheel, Molly was just about to head up the road when she noticed a small red sports car slowly travelling down the road towards her. The car parked directly in front of her and she watched as a woman in a long, floaty floral dress climbed out of the car and pushed her sunglasses up on top of her short, sharp blonde bob. The woman Molly was staring at was the woman in Cam's profile picture on Facebook – his wife. With her window still down, Molly slowly reversed the van before indicating to pull out. She caught sight of Cam out of the corner of her eye. He was standing in front of the cottage and, judging by the look on his face, he wasn't expecting the woman's arrival. There was a muffled exchange of words before the woman stormed straight past Cam, heading around the side of the cottage towards the back garden. Molly was now staring – she couldn't help herself – and was embarrassed when Cam glanced towards her. Forcing a smile onto her face, she waved out of the window and drove away. As soon as she was out of sight she pulled over into a layby and burst into tears. She didn't even know what she was crying about. Was it the baby, was it Cam, was it because his wife had just turned up at the cottage? She knew it had been her choice to spend the night with Cam in the hotel without knowing anything about him, and now she had to face the consequences, but she had never banked on becoming pregnant and going it alone when she was still very much attracted to him. The worst part about it all was having to see Cam around if she couldn't be with him.

Molly dabbed her eyes with a tissue and was just about to set off home when her phone rang. It was the surgery, and as soon as the call connected she heard Dr Sanders's voice.

'Molly, I've chased up the scan and just so we can put everyone's mind at rest, they can fit you in on Friday. Is that good for you?'

'Yes, perfect,' she replied, and after a short

conversation about the details, Molly hung up the phone and headed towards home.

'So on Friday I get to see you for the very first time,' said Molly, talking to her stomach. Her emotions were a mixture of excitement and trepidation. It was all becoming very real, and even though Molly was carrying the baby, she felt very much alone. In the back of her mind there was still Cam... What was she going to do? Should she tell him? Should she not tell him? The answer wasn't clear-cut. The news could have a huge impact on his life, but the scan was on Friday and surely he should know?

A wave of fear descended over her just thinking about it. Would he reject her in anger? Would he think she'd trapped him and got pregnant on purpose? Or would he welcome the news with open arms? Whatever his reaction, Molly knew she was going to be in for an emotional ride. She exhaled. Her thoughts were continually batting through the two scenarios like a slow game of tennis, the emotional knot continually gripping her stomach. Molly didn't want him to miss out on the chance of becoming a dad, but she was in such a quandary.

'Who am I trying to kid? He has a wife,' she said out loud, pulling the van onto the drive next to her car.

Molly had to face facts. Cam had his own family and all she could do now was look after hers.

Chapter Twelve

M olly opened her eyes and glanced at the clock. It was late afternoon and she had been asleep for hours. The sun was beaming through the crack in the curtains and the sound of the neighbours chatting filtered through the open window. Outside was a perfect summer's day and she'd slept most of it away, but as soon as her head had hit the pillow she'd been out for the count. She smiled at Darling, who once again had dragged Dixie's old blanket up the stairs and was fast asleep by her side. It reminded Molly of herself and the teddy bear she dragged around with her for the whole of her childhood, her comfort toy she couldn't be without; that's exactly how Darling was with Dixie's blanket.

'I think we'd better at least try and enjoy what's left of the day.' Molly gently stroked Darling, who opened her eyes and was immediately up on her feet. 'But please can we try and keep the barking to a minimum? That would make me very happy.'

Darling jumped off the bed, wagging her tail, and waited for Molly as she swung her legs to the floor then pulled back the curtains. She stood for a moment and breathed in the fresh air before putting on her slippers and heading out to the landing with Darling hot on her heels.

The first thing Molly noticed was an envelope lying on the mat at the bottom of the stairs. She really must have been out of it, because she'd never heard the postman. Darling noticed the letter too and with a spurt she took off down the stairs and launched herself at it, seizing the envelope in her mouth.

'Darling, stop!' commanded Molly, hurrying down the stairs towards her.

Darling attempted to run off with the envelope but fortunately Molly's reactions were quicker and she scooped the little dog off the ground, taking her completely by surprise. Darling dropped the envelope.

'Thank you, I'll take that,' declared Molly firmly, giving Darling a look of disdain as she placed her back on the ground. Turning the envelope over in her hand, she saw it had been hand delivered, and she didn't recognise the writing on the envelope. She quickly tore it open.

I'm not sure if you will get this letter or whether Darling will get to it first! I knocked a couple of times but there was no answer so I'm assuming you are probably asleep.

I hope you're feeling better and I've left your shopping by the back door.

Cam x

The first thing Molly noticed was the kiss after his name and she immediately felt a warm, fuzzy feeling inside that thankfully this time wasn't nauseous. She rushed to the back door and looked down on the step. True to his word, Cam had delivered the food. There were two carrier bags full of supplies, but Molly's eyes were firmly fixed on the small bouquet of supermarket flowers lying on top – what a lovely surprise. Smiling, Molly picked up the flowers and inhaled the aroma like it was the first time she'd ever been bought flowers in her life. But this was different – Cam had bought her these and she wasn't sure what this meant. Was it just a goodwill gesture, a hope-you're-feeling-better gesture, or was there another meaning?

'Get a grip,' Molly told herself. 'They're just flowers. You weren't feeling well. It's simply a kind gesture.' But her lips were pressed together in a smile as her heart gave a tiny leap. It was only a couple of days ago that Cam didn't even want to speak to her. Molly had felt all doom and gloom. This was definitely a step in the right direction.

Molly lifted up the bags and put them on the kitchen table, then arranged the flowers in a vase and placed them in the middle of the coffee table in the living room before unpacking the food. Cam had excelled himself; there was more in the bags than what had been on the list and Molly could see fresh fruit and veg alongside pasta, chicken, and fish, giving her numerous meal options. She beamed as she took out three packets of ginger biscuits, and right at the bottom of the bag she discovered a box of chocolates.

'We have chocolates, Darling,' she said. 'Cam, you are a legend!' Cam's kindness had immediately brought tears to her eyes, and her emotions were once again out of control. Instantly craving a strawberry cream, Molly tore off the cellophane from the box and popped the chocolate in her mouth then savoured every moment. Maybe this pregnancy lark wasn't going to be that bad. If she could spend most of the day sleeping then eating chocolates, that really did sound like she was living her best life.

Once the shopping was put away, and after a quick shower, Molly was beginning to feel human again. Rummaging through her wardrobe she opted for a pair of shorts and a loose-fitting T-shirt. She pulled on her shorts and attempted to fasten them around her waist but it was proving near impossible. She breathed in and tried again but there was no chance these shorts were being fastened any time soon.

'Jeez! I have no clothes.'

Molly turned sideways and took a look at herself in the full-length mirror. She cupped her hands over her belly and posed like she'd seen celebrities do in magazines. She was beginning to notice a difference in her body shape – she had gained a small pot belly – and she wondered how long it would take for other people to notice the growing bump. Throwing the shorts back in the wardrobe, she pondered whether she would ever wear them again. She'd read lots of articles about women never losing their baby weight and hoped she wasn't going to be one of them, but eating a packet of biscuits every day was not going to help her get back into those shorts. Swiping the clothes on her rail, Molly found an elasticated pair of joggers – the only thing she found comfort in – but it was way too hot to be wearing those on a day like today.

'I know,' she said to Darling, as she reached for her sewing basket at the top of the wardrobe and retrieved a pair of scissors. Snipping off the legs, she'd instantly made herself a pair of comfy shorts. 'Perfect,' she said happily, looking at the reflection in the mirror, and made a mental note to go online shopping tonight for a few clothing essentials. After pulling a brush through her hair and adding a bit of blusher to her cheeks, she slipped her feet into her flip-flops and wandered downstairs. She felt like she was at a loose end, and after pouring herself a glass of juice she made herself comfy on the sofa and switched on the TV. With Darling keeping watch out of the window, Molly was flicking through the channels when she recognised the burnt-out bandstand from Primrose Park on her TV screen. The devastation was obvious and the news report was appealing for any information from the public that might lead to the arrest of the vandals.

Molly couldn't believe that only twenty-four hours ago she was there, surrounded by all of its beauty, and now the whole place was out of bounds until further notice. She knew that to recreate Primrose Park at its finest was going to take a long time. The cost of replacing all the shrubs and flowers would be hundreds of pounds, and the iconic bandstand was gone, now just a pile of ashes. It was so sad to see. Then Alfie, the local councillor, popped up on the screen, being interviewed in front of the vandalised wrought-iron gates.

'Unfortunately, Primrose Park will have to stay closed indefinitely,' he shared with the news reporter. 'We simply have no choice – everything is destroyed and with council funds already allocated elsewhere, there just isn't any more we can do at this present time.'

'Surely not,' replied Molly. She felt saddened by the scene she faced on the TV screen, but Alfie was right – trees would need to replanted, all the damaged areas dug up, and so on.

Molly thought back to her childhood, when she'd spent many an afternoon playing in the park with her dad and Willow the dog. They'd paddled in the fountain, picnicked by the bandstand, played hide and seek amongst the trees. It had been a place where she'd always felt a sense of calm, and she would miss taking a walk around the lake, even if she wasn't a huge fan of the fishing pond at the minute. Would her own child miss out on these happy memories?

Switching off the TV, she looked out of the window. The weather was still glorious and she decided to go out for a short walk – nothing too exhilarating. She looked at Darling, who sensed that Molly had moved, and they eyeballed each other. Molly was in two minds whether to take Darling with her but with the sun beating down she knew it wasn't ethical to drag her out in that heat.

Grabbing her bag and her sunglasses, Molly stepped outside into the sunshine, leaving Darling desperately barking at the window to try and get her attention. She found herself heading down towards the river, knowing that the trees along the river bank would provide the perfect shade. There was a sense of calm in walking by the water. Molly couldn't remember the last time she'd had a sleep in the day but she was certainly feeling better for it. The River Heart looked inviting, boats bobbing along the calm water, paddle boards and jet skis out in droves, and in the distance Carter's water taxi packed with diners heading out towards The Lake House. She stood for a moment, watching the eddies and whitecaps creating circular movement in the water, the leaf-dappled sunlight sparkling in some spots and boulders breaking the water's surface, causing white-water foam on the far side of the river.

Noticing a couple of children running up ahead holding ice-creams, Molly felt a sudden craving for a mint-choc-chip cone. It was a ten-minute walk to the ice-cream parlour on the edge of town and that's where she was heading. Soon she joined the line of customers excitedly discussing what they planned on getting as they looked at the chalkboard menu on the wall. Molly treated herself to an ice-cream and sat on the bench looking up at the clear blue sky, with hardly a cloud to be seen. Enjoying the cold smoothness of the ice-cream, she devoured it in seconds, before walking along the streets and making her way up the crest of the hill towards the cemetery where both her adopted parents were buried. They had been older than her friends' parents by around twenty years or so but it had never bothered Molly in the slightest; they'd chosen her to be a part of their family and she'd always been grateful, treasuring every second with them.

Feeling a wave of sadness, Molly walked through the impressive wrought-iron gate where two sun-blanched stone angels stood, one on either side. She followed the paved path winding between the well-tended lawns and decorative flower beds awash with colour, and cast an eye over the stone carvings of religious figures that were dotted about.

The flower seller had positioned himself under the shady branches of the enormous oak tree by the side of the church. Molly purchased two small bouquets and made her way over to the gravestones of her parents, who were buried next to each other. As she stood over their graves, a tear slipped down her cheek, knowing that they would have been so proud to be grandparents. Molly wished they were here to enjoy the arrival of her baby. She couldn't have had a happier childhood with them, and one thing she had learnt from her adoption was that spending quality time with your child was key – what you put into that relationship was what you got out. Life wasn't about materialistic things; it was about building memories, and Molly's memories were precious to her.

'You are going to be grandparents,' she whispered as she laid the blooms on the grave. 'And I'm going to make sure my child knows how wonderful you both were. You would have made the best grandparents.' Molly swallowed a lump in her throat. 'But it all seems a little bit of a mess and I wish you were here so you could advise me what to do.' Through watery eyes she stared at the headstones, talking to them as though they could hear every word.

After telling them she loved them both Molly started walking and within ten minutes she found herself standing outside Dixie's care home. She hadn't planned on visiting her today but now she was here and there was nowhere she needed to be, she pressed the buzzer and, as the door swung open, wandered inside. She headed towards Dixie's room but as she walked past the TV room she noticed her playing cards with a gentleman who looked very dapper, all dressed up in a suit. Dixie looked up and a huge smile spread across her face the second she laid eyes on Molly.

'What a lovely surprise!' she sang, patting the man's arm. 'Look, this is my friend, Molly!' Dixie seemed in good spirits. 'And this is Tom.'

'Lovely to meet you. Are you a resident here?' asked Molly, noticing that Dixie was in good spirits.

Tom stretched out his hand. 'I am, and I'm pleased to meet you.' He looked towards Dixie then back towards Molly. 'And I'm hoping you're here to save me from being slaughtered at cards because I don't know how this one does it but she's not lost a game yet.'

After shaking Molly's hand, Tom stood up. 'I will leave you to enjoy your company.'

As Tom left the room, Dixie gestured to the comfier-looking chairs in front of the TV. 'I'm so glad you called in. Your visit has made my day.' Dixie leant in. 'To be honest, it was getting a little boring winning again and again and the stakes weren't really very high – a couple of pennies. It wasn't worth my time.'

Molly gave a little chuckle as she sat down next to Dixie. She was such a loveable character.

'And you'd think my life was dull in here, wouldn't you? But this week alone I've had three marriage proposals.' Dixie raised a perfectly arched brow at Molly. 'But, I mean, what prospects do they have in here? It's not as though we can go punting on the lake or row down the river; they'd be lucky to still have a beating heart at the end of the day.'

'Dixie, you can't say that!'

'But it's true. Now, can I get you a drink? A cup of tea?' Dixie looked over towards the kettle.

'Honestly, I couldn't stomach a tea. Maybe just a glass of water, thank you,' replied Molly.

Dixie walked to the corner of the room where a drinks table was set out and returned holding two glasses of water, which she placed on the table in front them. The TV was on in the background – an antiques programme looking at old treasures.

'There's a few old treasures in here,' joked Dixie. 'In fact, more than a few. Now, why aren't you at work?' Dixie waggled her finger in front of Molly. 'And you have that chubbiness going on in your face. I know that look.' Dixie gave Molly a knowing look. 'And for a hot summer's day you are looking as pale as the folk in here and that isn't a good sign...' Dixie tilted her head to one side and didn't take her eyes off the flabbergasted Molly, who couldn't believe that Dixie might have guessed the predicament she was in.

'Why is it the older generation can say what they want and just get away with it?'

'You can change the subject all you want but I would still bet that you are expecting a baby. Now, am I right?'

'How would you even know that?' Molly couldn't believe that Dixie had come straight out with it.

'Years of life experience, my dear. Nothing gets past us old folk. People may think they can fool us most of the time, but we have special powers and know what's going on in the world. So why are you looking so glum about it? Is it the sickness?'

Molly nodded. 'It seems to be getting worse when every book or article I read is telling me it should be getting better. I can't stand it. My blood pressure is low, I couldn't go to work today, and I can't keep doing that.' Molly took a sip of her water.

'You must do what your body tells you,' said Dixie.

'I have no choice. It keeps telling me to be sick and today I've been asleep for most of the day.'

'And that is your body telling you that you need to rest. So listen to it and forget about work.'

'That's easier said than done when you own the business.'

'Then you must get some help. What about your partner? Does he help you out?'

Molly hesitated, knowing that Dixie was her child's

great-grandmother. She kept it simple. 'I'm no longer with the father.'

'And family?'

Molly shook her head. 'It's just me and my bump, but I do have a lot of good friends.'

'You need the support of good people around you. I was lucky I had my George. Even in those days he was a modern man, helping with the nappies and the feeds, and every Sunday without fail he used to take the children down to Primrose Park and push that pram for hours to give me a rest. You need a rest. Will the father be a part of your child's life? I'm being nosey, aren't I, but I'm allowed; I generally get away with most things now at my age.' Dixie gave a little giggle.

'That's half the problem. The father doesn't know,' admitted Molly. 'And I'm not quite sure what to do about that.'

'He doesn't know? Why doesn't he know?'

'It's complicated,' replied Molly.

'It always is,' replied Dixie. 'But he still deserves to know he's going to be a father.'

Molly was listening to Dixie and agreed with her. At this moment, Molly didn't dare to share that the father of her unborn child was Dixie's very own grandson. This kind of information could possibly destroy his family, if Cam was married, and Molly wasn't sure she could have that on her conscience.

'But having a baby isn't easy,' continued Dixie. 'I

remember it like it was yesterday. Sleep deprivation is the worst thing in the world, and it will be hard for you on your own. How complicated is it?'

'I've discovered there's a possibility he's married and now I don't know what to do. I don't want to cause any hurt to his family.'

'And I commend you for that, but this was his choice. You didn't do anything wrong. He must be in possession of all the facts. Being involved in the baby's life must be his choice and not one you can make for him by holding back the information. At least then you know you have been honest and up front and if that baby ever asks who its father is you haven't kept any secrets. And what's the worst that can happen? He doesn't want anything to do with the baby. And that means you are no worse off than you are now – going it alone.'

Molly's head was fighting her heart about the best thing to do but she knew that Dixie was talking sense. Of course, she didn't have to broadcast it to the world but if she told Cam about the baby it would be his decision whether he wanted to become a part of his baby's life. The only niggle that Molly had in the back of her mind was that if Cam did reject the baby, how was she going to feel bumping into him around the village? But worrying about something that hadn't happened yet wasn't going to help anyone.

'I think you're right, Dixie. I just need to be honest, and as long as I am, what will be will be.'

'Exactly that, but don't stress – you are all the baby has and you need to be the best you can be healthwise to look after it.'

Sipping on her drink, Molly had taken in everything that Dixie had said. She decided she had nothing to lose by telling Cam and that's exactly what she was going to do. What he did with the information was up to him.

'In other news,' chirped Dixie, 'my grandson has visited, he's demanded to see the paperwork and assessments, and there's hope he's going to get me out of here.'

'Is that why you're in a good mood?'

'I've just got to sit tight, he said, and not make a fuss. Stay calm. But believe me, that's difficult when you know there's some wrongdoing going on. I didn't think I'd be disowning a daughter at my age, but Birdie is leaving me no choice.' For a second Dixie seemed very teary. 'How could she do this to me?' Dixie gave herself a little shake.

Talking to Dixie, Molly was confident that the old woman had all her wits about her. Compared to the other residents, she seemed twenty years younger in age and spirit. 'I hope you are home very soon.'

'And I have my big event to look forward to – that's what I'm focusing on now. You must come and bring Darling, as she's part of my family. They don't allow animals here'—Dixie pulled a face—'but rules are meant to be broken.' She widened her eyes at Molly. 'You could sneak her in,' she whispered.

Molly knew that was not an option. There was no way on this earth Darling was going to be sneaked into the care home without being discovered. Molly was always up for a challenge, but that request was impossible.

'Tell me about your big event,' said Molly, but as soon as the words left her mouth she immediately thought about Primrose Park and realised that Dixie might not have a clue that it had been shut down by the council. But before Molly could say any more, Dixie gave a huge smile and sat upright, bursting to tell all.

'My grandson, Cameron, is arranging a garden party for my eightieth birthday at Primrose Park.' Dixie brought both her hands up to her chest. 'George and I planned this big birthday before he passed away as it was our next milestone birthday. Did you know we shared the same birthday and met on our actual birthday? The stars were aligned that night,' Dixie reminisced. 'It was a warm summer's evening, and Primrose Park was packed to the rafters. Everyone had tickets to see the Foster Brothers perform at the bandstand. They were the biggest band ever to grace the park and the tickets were sold in a matter of hours. I can remember that night clearly, like it was yesterday. I'd spotted George the moment he stepped inside Primrose Park. Dashing is how I would describe him, the most handsome man in town. I knew, the moment I saw him, I was in love. He was the one for me. There was something about him and I know it sounds daft, but I never believed in love at first sight until that moment. I knew nothing about this man, but I'd fallen head over heels.'

Molly didn't think that was daft at all; she knew that feeling well and had had that very same thought the second she'd laid eyes on Cam. Dixie was smiling, still head over heels for her man.

'We danced until midnight under the moonlit sky and shared our very first kiss that night, and that was that. We were inseparable from that moment on.' Dixie's voice wavered. 'Our love was a special love. I don't think many people get what we had in our lifetime. We both wanted to spend the afternoon at Primrose Park with our friends and family – a garden-party type event with champagne. I love a glass of champagne. We want deckchairs, a band performing on the bandstand, a stall selling our honey and chutneys. Cam has promised me he will step into his grandfather's shoes and make the honey.' Dixie paused. 'He's not a fan of bees though. I always thought that at least one of my grandsons would take the business over but they chose their own paths, which I know they are entitled to do.'

Listening to Dixie, Molly knew she would be devastated to discover the park had been vandalised. It was going to completely burst her bubble. Molly wondered whether she should share that news but maybe it was better if she heard it from Cam.

'Oh look!' Dixie pointed at the TV and reached across

for the remote control on the table in front of her. 'They are talking about Primrose Park; it's on the TV... How exciting.' Dixie turned up the sound. It was a repeat of the news report Molly had seen before she left the house.

Dixie was smiling when the news reporter began but then as the report played out she suddenly realised what had happened and was visibly upset. As the burnt-down trees, the vandalised fountain, and the ashes of the bandstand flickered across the screen Dixie's eyes brimmed with tears.

'What's happened? Why would somebody do that?' Dixie turned towards Molly, who passed her a tissue. 'That park is a special place for lots of people, especially me. I just don't understand.'

Molly wished she had the answers, but she didn't. 'I don't know,' replied Molly sadly. 'Mindless vandalism.'

'But my birthday... I planned to scatter George's ashes. Birdie has even granted permission to let me out of this place for the day under supervision. I'll tell you now, I was going to do a runner. I had a plan.' Dixie wept as Molly stood up and placed her arm around her shoulder. 'I don't want my birthday anywhere else and I want to get out of here.'

Molly could see that Dixie's memories meant the world to her. When you'd been looking forward to something, then it was suddenly taken away from you, it must be disappointing.

'Maybe you could have your birthday on the green

outside your cottage?' But as soon as the words had left Molly's mouth, she knew that was no consolation. Dixie had her heart set on Primrose Park.

'I need to tell Cam. He's been working hard to organise it and bring it all together. He's got enough on his plate at the minute without this extra hassle. Did you drop off the keys for me?'

'I did,' replied Molly, turning Dixie's words over her mind. Why was Cam having a hard time? Molly wanted to ask, but would questioning Dixie be unethical when Dixie didn't know the real reason Molly was asking? Molly's heart was battling her conscience; she wanted to know.

'He's very handsome, isn't he?' added Dixie. 'Such a lovely, kind boy. Always looked after me. That one has a heart of gold.'

Molly agreed that Cam was indeed handsome and it was comforting to hear he looked after his grandmother, but she couldn't quite work him out. His mood swings seemed to fluctuate from being very abrupt and distant to exactly how Dixie had just described him – kind.

'Very handsome. Is he married? Asking for a friend,' joked Molly, but already knowing the answer.

Dixie began to shake her head. 'He's had a terrible time of it of late. I don't want to speak out of school but he's going through a divorce. That's all I can say.' Dixie gave her a look that meant there was more going on, but she couldn't repeat any of it.

Molly had to do everything in her power to stop her jaw from hitting the floor. That was good to hear – for her, obviously, not for him.

'Hopefully, he's here to make a fresh start.' Dixie crossed her fingers. 'And to get me out of here.'

Molly didn't know what to feel. There was a tiny part of her that welcomed the news. Cam was going to be single, which made things a little bit easier, but then she didn't want to be happy about Cam having a difficult time. Maybe that's why he wasn't very welcoming when he first set eyes on her in Primrose Park. It was understandable if he was going through a break-up.

'Heartcross is the best place to make a fresh start,' said Molly, still giving the whole situation a lot of thought. After talking with Dixie she'd already made the decision to tell Cam and now she was feeling a little less guilty about him having a family, even though she really hadn't done anything wrong – and maybe he hadn't either.

On the walk home, Molly's thoughts turned towards Dixie. She was a remarkable woman, still devoted to George even though he had passed away. Their life together had been full of love and admiration. It seemed they had had the fairy-tale: Dixie had met her prince and they had lived happily ever after. This was exactly what Molly had dreamt about. Her adoptive parents had been a fantastic partnership, and she was in no doubt that they had loved each other, but it seemed a different kind of love to what Dixie spoke about. Molly wanted what Dixie had had.

'Bump! I've got an idea,' she whispered to her stomach and whipped out her phone from her bag. 'We are going to try and put things right for your great-granny.' Molly searched through her contacts and pressed Alfie's number. He picked up after a few rings.

'Alfie, it's Molly! I've got a question for you.' She took a breath. 'What's it going to take to get Primrose Park up and running in two weeks' time?'

'An absolute miracle!' came Alfie's reply without hesitation. 'Why do you ask?'

Molly explained about Dixie's birthday party and that she was keen for it to go ahead. Alfie thought she was biting off more than she could chew but agreed to look into the restoration of the park in more detail and get back to her.

Despite Alfie's reservations, Molly loved a challenge. All she could think about was the look of disappointment on Dixie's face, the tears in her eyes. Molly wanted to put a smile back on her face – not to mention the bonus of chatting with Cam about his grandmother's upcoming birthday party.

'Right, little one, if you can keep the dizziness and sickness under control for me that would help me out an awful lot whilst I try and make your great-grandma's birthday exactly how she'd planned it. Me and you are going to put Primrose Park back on the map where it belongs!'

Molly felt a spring in her step as she walked back along the river. The first thing she needed to do was to get the community together and singing from the same hymn sheet.

Chapter Thirteen

After Molly had prepared a delicious meal with the ingredients that Cam had dropped off for her, she spent a couple of hours with her feet propped up on the coffee table and her laptop balanced on her lap. Alfie had emailed her a document outlining the damage to Primrose Park and the estimated cost of putting it all right. Unfortunately, Alfie wasn't exaggerating, and trying to get Primrose Park up and running for Dixie's eightieth birthday party was going to be damn near impossible, but Molly wasn't going to let thousands of pounds stand in her way – not just yet, anyway. Surely, if the community all pulled together, they could try and tidy up the park, but deep down Molly knew that wasn't going to be enough. To repair the wrought-iron gates would cost hundreds, but it was the focal point of the park and they had to give it a go.

Taking the bull by the horns, Molly posted a message on to the Heartcross Community Facebook page:

Save Primrose Park! Please attend the meeting on the green tomorrow night at 6.30 p.m. Everyone welcome!

Immediately, the post was liked by numerous residents, which gave Molly a bit of hope that everyone would be on board. Numerous ideas were turning over in her head. What if everyone donated a plant from their garden? What if the boys at the farm built a new bandstand? They were always fixing fences and stuff – there must be ways around it. Apart from the cost, the only other two dilemmas that were standing in her way were time and, of course, Baby McKendrick. Only hours earlier Molly had slumped to the ground and the doctor had been called, and his advice was to stay at home and rest. However, Molly wasn't intending to dig up tree stumps or move vandalised fountains herself. She could organise everything. She could have her own little Ground Force going on; she could be the Alan Titchmarsh of the operation.

Hearing her phone ring, she saw that it was Allie calling. 'How are you feeling? Rory's just told me he popped into your surgery today, but you weren't working. Are you feeling under the weather?'

'Under the weather doesn't come close. I fainted at

Cam's feet at Bumblebee Cottage while Darling was again terrorising his dog through the gate.'

'And how did that go down after your run-in the other day?' asked Allie. 'Isla told us – she wasn't gossiping, just filling in the inner circle so we can all support you as much as possible.'

Molly knew that Isla wasn't a gossip. 'Actually, he was a little frosty at first but then looked after me very well. He's even dropped a bag of groceries off at my door along with flowers and chocolates.'

'That is a turnaround! Are you sure you didn't faint on purpose?'

'I can neither confirm nor deny,' said Molly with a laugh. 'Thankfully Dr Sanders didn't let it slip I was pregnant, but he's managed to organise the first scan…'

'And are you going to tell Cam before the scan?' probed Allie.

This was a question that Molly had been thinking about all day. Would it be too soon to tell? How was he going to react? What was he going to say? This was a huge deal. First, Molly had been thinking about trying to break the ice a little further with Cam. She'd witnessed his kind, loving side during her dizzy spell. He hadn't had to offer to go the shops for her, but he did, and he'd put himself out. If she tried to build up a relationship with him, it might not come as a huge shock.

But then again, would he see that as underhanded, because she hadn't been upfront in the first place? If she was in his shoes what would she want to happen? But Molly wasn't in his shoes; she'd had relationships that had broken up, but she'd always had her own house, her own financial independence. Cam's relationship was different; he'd committed to someone for the rest of his life. He'd married her, and now it seemed he was making a fresh start. What about his family home, his job? Divorce is one of the most stressful situations a person can find themselves in. They lose a friend, a partner, and have to adapt to living as a single person. Maybe Cam didn't want to put himself back into any sort of relationship, and here was Molly about to tell him she was pregnant and carrying his baby.

Molly faced up to Allie's question. Would she tell Cam? 'I think so. It's one of those special moments that will never be relived.' She knew the clock was ticking, and there wasn't much time left before the scan. 'Yes! I'm going to take the plunge!'

'And what are you hoping will happen?' quizzed Allie.

Molly was trying to be rational about the situation. Like Dixie had said, she wasn't going to be any worse off than she was now. She wasn't daft and was fully aware it had been a one-night stand, but in her eyes something good had come of it. Molly had no clue what Cam even thought about her and whether he was ready to jump straight into another relationship. It wouldn't be like what Molly had been used to before: boy meets girl, and they date for a time before finding out everything they need to know about each other. She and Cam would be thrown in at the deep end, with another human to look after. Their relationship would be all nappies, milk, prams, and extreme tiredness. If Cam even wanted that.

What was she hoping would happen? 'That he falls into my arms and we live happily ever after.' Molly wasn't holding back; she felt a connection with the utterly gorgeous Cam and even if he rejected her that wasn't going to change. 'And I know you're going to tell me I'm living in cloud-cuckoo-land,' she continued, but she knew deep down that if this didn't happen, she was still going to be okay.

'I'm not going to tell you anything, but don't they say things come in threes?' remarked Allie.

'What things?' asked Molly.

'A one-night stand, a baby, and Cam turning up… This was meant to happen!'

Molly laughed. 'When you put it like that, I've got everything crossed.'

'Me too,' added Allie. 'And on a work front, do you want me to tell Rory your news, keep him in the loop in case you need any further help over at your surgery?'

'That would probably be a good idea, but please tell him it's currently top secret.'

'Mum's the word,' joked Allie.

'And check the WhatsApp group. Try and get

everyone involved tomorrow. Operation Primrose Park is up and running.'

'Yes, I've seen it and I'll be there,' confirmed Allie. 'I won't let you down.'

Once Allie had hung up, Molly went through Alfie's email with a fine-tooth comb. She made a list of everything he'd highlighted that needed replacing and the estimated cost before splitting different jobs into different sections. All the burnt trees would need to be dug up and hopefully Drew and Fergus would be able to take care of that, but then, Molly thought with a sigh, the cost of replacing them was astronomical and how exactly was that cost going to be funded? Maybe Alfie was right and she had bitten off more than she could chew – but all Molly could think about was the joy it would bring to Dixie and the smile on her face

The following evening, Molly had parked the van at the pub car park then taken the short walk over to the green with Darling. Her day had gone very much like the day before: she'd woken up and spent nearly thirty minutes hovering near the toilet, praying the sickness would go away. Even the ginger biscuits didn't seem to be helping. She'd muddled through the dog behavioural class as best she could and had seen progress in the owners' techniques of rewarding for good behaviour. She only wished Darling had taken note. For the whole of the class the dog had spent the time barking uncontrollably in the direction of Bumblebee Cottage, but disappointingly Cam and Maverick were nowhere in sight. Molly was hoping to bump into him to at least thank him for the shopping.

Rona, from the teashop, waved at Molly as she walked onto the green. 'It's a lovely evening for it.'

'It is,' replied Molly, glad she was feeling a little better.

Rona looked her up and down, 'Are you feeling okay? You look kind of … I can't quite put my finger on it … exhausted.'

Molly was relieved that Rona's pregnancy radar was not as tuned in as Dixie's had been. 'I think the heat is wiping me out,' she replied with a smile.

'Just make sure you're drinking enough water throughout the day. Dehydration is a killer.'

Molly had tried her very best to sip water throughout the day, but her retching had been worse than usual.

'Drew and Fergus have loaded up the farm trailer, and they're bringing the chairs from the teashop and the long folding trestle table, with water and juice and today's leftovers from the teashop.'

'You are so kind.'

'In fact, here they are now.' Rona waved at the tractor pulling the trailer, which wasn't only carrying the chairs from the teashop, but what looked like half the village, who had clambered on board for a ride. Isla had her boys with her, Aggie and Martha were sitting on a couple of hay bales and Felicity waved back. Once Drew had parked up the tractor, he unclipped the back of the trailer and began to help everyone down.

'Dad, that was so much fun,' squealed Esme at Fergus as he swung her, giggling, off the back of the trailer and plonked her down in front of the grinning Felicity.

'Steady, Esme!' exclaimed Felicity, watching Esme and Finn stumble off towards the trees pretending to be dizzy.

'Got to love them,' said Isla with a smile, as she held onto Angus's hand.

'Save Primrose Park – with only two weeks to do it?' questioned Felicity, 'Firstly, are you mental and secondly, why only two weeks? What's the rush?'

Drew began unloading the chairs and everyone grabbed a couple and began to walk towards the shaded area of the trees.

'Dixie's eightieth birthday party,' explained Molly. 'And I know you're going to say, why doesn't she have the party here on the green opposite her cottage? But she's always planned to have a garden party at Primrose Park. Everything was going according to plan until the park was vandalised, and now somehow she's got bundled into a care home without her consent and can't escape.'

Felicity raised an eyebrow. 'You know what? It's

funny you should say that. Mum and Aggie were very surprised. There's no way Dixie is at the stage of her life where she's sitting with furry boots on her feet and a multi-coloured crochet blanket thrown over her knees, watching TV all day. She used to be up and out walking, and she popped into the teashop every day without fail.'

For the first time Molly had a nagging doubt – was Birdie actually telling the truth? 'Honestly, Flick, she was heartbroken when she saw the news. Dixie had her garden party all planned out and wanted to scatter George's ashes on the same day.'

'Okay, I get it but – don't take this the wrong way – why are you trying to sort everything out? Why not leave it to Birdie? If it was that important wouldn't they be rallying the troops? You have enough on your plate at the minute.'

'Because I feel I need to try and help. Dixie is going to be my baby's great-grandmother and I will talk to Birdie tonight and…'

'This is an opportunity to talk to Cam?' Felicity tilted her head to one side; she wasn't daft.

'Honestly, it's not just that. I genuinely want to do this. Primrose Park is a huge part of this village for everyone. I want to push a pram around the grounds, feed the ducks, play hide and seek in the woods and walk my dog – not technically my dog… ' Molly cast a glance over to Darling who fortunately was still lying down chomping at her chew.

'Okay, I get it. You want a family, with Dixie and preferably Cam. Building relationships is good but just be careful that when it all comes out about the baby they don't think you've tricked them into a friendship for your own reasons. Slowly does it. Honesty is the best policy.'

'I agree and if it's not what Cam wants in his life, surely I'm still allowed to build a relationship with my child's great-grandmother.' Molly shrugged but sounded hopeful.

'As long as that's what she wants with all cards laid out on the table,' replied Felicity, placing a chair down in the row under the shade of the tree before turning to hug her friend.

'I know, and I know when I share the news it isn't going to be plain sailing, but I will talk to Cam this week.'

'What's going on here? Why all the hugging?' Alfie appeared behind them with Polly holding a clipboard and looking very important.

'Just because we haven't seen each other for almost twenty-four hours,' joked Felicity. 'And how are you both?'

'This one works way too hard,' replied Polly, kissing Felicity on the cheek. 'Remember when I managed that pub back in London and you were telling me I was working way too many hours and was going to burn myself out? Well, that's nothing compared to the hours this one is putting in.' Polly gave Alfie a stern but good-humoured look.

'Primrose Park is a good cause; it's a part of Heartcross. If we can raise funds to build a bridge, this is going to be a walk in the park,' said Alfie. He grinned, just realising his choice of words.

Everyone was silent for a second before they burst out laughing.

'No pun intended! And here'—he handed Molly a microphone—'just flick the button and talk into this. It will save you shouting.'

Molly looked out over the green. Everyone was here, including Birdie, who was walking towards the row of chairs. Almost immediately, Darling spotted her and began her usual barking – she really didn't like Birdie, and Molly noticed that Birdie didn't even acknowledge her mother's dog, but just looked the other way.

'Can you excuse me?' Molly looked at her friends and began walking towards Birdie. She thought it best if Birdie understood that Molly's reason for trying to rectify Primrose Park was Dixie's upcoming birthday. Maybe Birdie would like to help in some way. Just as Molly was about to tap Birdie on her shoulder, she realised she was talking on the phone and hung back.

'Yes, it will be me that's doing the viewing for Bumblebee Cottage. If we can make it for 10.30 a.m. I will meet the prospective buyers outside.'

Molly looked over towards the cottage but didn't see

a 'for sale' sign. Maybe Birdie was trying to keep the sale low-key for some reason, but did this mean that Cam was moving on … already? She'd been under the impression that Cam was renting the property, but from what Birdie was suggesting, Bumblebee Cottage was going on the market. Molly was surprised and had an uneasy feeling in the pit of her stomach, but she wasn't sure why. Dixie hadn't said a word.

As soon as Birdie hung up the phone, Molly painted on a smile and called over to her, 'Birdie! Hi, how are you doing?'

For a second Birdie looked a little taken back then slipped her phone into her bag, 'Oh, I didn't see you there.'

'Sorry, I didn't mean to sneak up on you. Have you said hello to Darling?' asked Molly, knowing full well that Birdie had totally ignored the little dog. On one hand she couldn't blame her – Darling was sitting looking straight at Birdie and snarling away – whilst on the other hand you would think Birdie would attempt to say hello to her mother's dog.

'I haven't yet,' replied Birdie, giving Darling a half-hearted smile. 'What can I do for you?' Birdie's tone was a little matter-of-fact and, Molly felt, rather unfriendly.

'I've been to visit Dixie again today,' said Molly, watching the look on Birdie's face.

'Really, again?'

'She's a wonderful woman, isn't she? We really hit it off and you were right—'

'About what?' interrupted Birdie, watching Molly very carefully.

'She tried to convince me she shouldn't be in there. Very upset she was, and there are a few villagers surprised too, but I guess the assessors and doctors think she should be in there.'

Birdie looked uncomfortable and Molly noticed a tinge of crimson to her cheeks. 'What can I do for you?' Birdie was swerving the conversation at all costs. She waved across at Aggie and Martha, itching to get away.

'I wanted to catch you before I shared with the village the main reason we are here.'

Birdie cocked an eyebrow.

'This meeting is all about Dixie.'

Birdie narrowed her eyes, 'Mum – why?'

'Dixie has her heart set on having her birthday party in Primrose Park. She was devastated when she discovered it had been vandalised. As you know, the park means the world to her. So I'm enlisting everyone's help. Dixie and George were a huge part of this village for many years and I'm sure our wonderful community will pull together and do everything possible to get the park up and running again for Dixie's birthday. I'm sure Dixie will be over the moon.'

'I'm sure she will.' Birdie gave a forced smile.

'So any help of yours would be truly appreciated,'

sang Molly, noticing how very uncomfortable Birdie was looking.

'Of course,' replied Birdie without enthusiasm.

Molly was a little stunned by Birdie's response as she walked off to join her friends. It was like she couldn't really care less about her own mother's birthday. Birdie's reaction made Molly begin to wonder further about Dixie's situation. Dixie seemed to have all her faculties and was up on her feet with no problem too, looking like she could manage in the outside world perfectly.

Thinking further about her conversation with Dixie, Molly recalled her words: 'Apparently I have memory loss but the problem is I don't remember having memory loss.' Birdie had mentioned that her mum's memory had deteriorated rapidly and she was a danger in the cottage all by herself, but to Molly Dixie seemed as sharp as a pin.

Taking her place at the side of the stage, Molly tried to see past the bobbing heads and took a quick glance over towards Bumblebee Cottage. Cam's car wasn't on the drive and she assumed he wouldn't know about the meeting, but it didn't matter – depending on what happened in the next thirty minutes she could fill him in later.

Hearing a whoop from her friends as she took the microphone, and with Felicity, Isla and Allie giving her the thumbs-up from the front row, Molly stood in front of them all and took a sip from the glass of water that Rona had left on the table for her. She watched a few straggling villagers slip into the empty chairs and was thankful the heat of the day had ebbed to a comforting warmth. Molly was intrigued to see what the rest of the community would think. She noticed Julia and Flynn; surely Flynn with all his business connections would know of some local tradesmen? There was also Julia's right-hand woman at the B&B, Eleni – her boyfriend owned a building company. There had to be plenty of help out there but it depended on whether people could afford to give up their time for free and whether they could juggle their work commitments at such short notice.

Looking over the sea of faces, Molly took a breath and picked up the microphone. 'Thank you all for coming! You are probably wondering why I've gathered you all here this evening. I'm here to try and make someone's wish come true and I am hoping you guys are the people to help me make this happen!'

Almost immediately there was a buzz of excitement and Molly had everyone's attention. She continued, 'This last week, I adopted a dog, in the short term.' Molly didn't dare to look over in Birdie's direction just then. 'And the previous owner of Darling'—Molly took a glance over towards Darling, who was still busily chewing away—'has been a member of this community for the whole of her life. Yes, I'm talking about Dixie Bird.' Molly waved her arm towards Bumblebee Cottage. 'I believe Dixie and her husband were rather famous in this area for their homemade honey, jams, and chutneys.' Molly took another sip of water. 'The reason why I've gathered you here is not to give you all a history lesson but because in Heartcross we look after each other. I know I'm on the other side of the bridge but I grew up here, I spent my childhood here, and I am a part of this wonderful community.'

'Hear, hear!' shouted Isla, causing Molly to smile.

'Dixie was passionate about Primrose Park. She loved the meadow flowers, the woods, the lake, the fishing pond, and she even confessed to me she'd danced numerous times in the fountain on a late summer's evening, just like today.' Molly tilted her face up towards the sky and closed her eyes for a brief moment, feeling the warmth on her face, 'And now our beloved park has been vandalised. What seems to be enjoyment for some mindless petty criminals has spoilt all our enjoyment of Primrose Park.'

There was a muttering all around as everyone agreed with Molly.

'It's disgraceful,' shouted out Aggie. 'Has anyone been caught yet?'

Molly shook her head. 'I don't think so,' she replied regretfully. 'Dixie's eightieth birthday is in two weeks' time,' she continued. 'Dixie is one of our treasured residents and she's had this milestone birthday party planned to every last detail. She longs for a garden party held inside Primrose Park with all of her friends, enjoying her favourite tipple whilst dancing to the band playing on the bandstand just like she did in her youth. But more importantly, this was the day that Dixie wanted to scatter George's ashes, in the place they met, the place they fell in love. And this love story has another twist: they even share the same birthday, and it was that very day they met at the bandstand. So as you can imagine, there is nowhere else Dixie wants to celebrate her birthday. I was with Dixie when she discovered that Primrose Park had been closed and she was terribly upset, and this is why I'm asking for your help.' Molly searched for Alfie in the crowd and he held up a document in his hand. Molly walked towards him and took it from him before walking back towards the table.

'These vandals caused thousands of pounds' worth of damage and unfortunately, due to the cost, the council at this time has no extra funds and the park needs to remain shut. *But'*—Molly emphasised the word and everyone was looking in her direction—'but surely we can put Primrose Park back on the map in time for Dixie's birthday – with a little help from my friends? And this is where you all come in. Can we still give Dixie an eightieth birthday to remember?' Molly was looking hopefully over the sea of eyes looking back at her. 'I think we can.'

Molly noticed that Polly was nudging Alfie and after some gentle persuasion he stood up and began walking towards the stage. The villagers became silent as Alfie took the microphone. 'I agree with Molly; this could be doable if we all pull together.' Alfie gave Molly a reassuring smile, leaving Molly to let out a cheer and everyone applauded. 'Two weeks, you say?' He looked towards Molly to confirm then turned back towards the villagers. 'We will need the old tree stumps removing, the ground repaired, new trees planted, turf replaced and watered every day, especially in this heat; also, the meadow needs to be dug over and fresh flowers planted. Then there's the rebuilding of the bandstand. I'm not sure if we have any carpenters amongst us that can advise on this, but we want an exact replica of the old one. On top of that, we need to find a fountain specialist to fix and clean up the stone, and we need new gates.'

Molly crossed her fingers and took the microphone back from Alfie. 'Please raise your hand, if you have the time and the enthusiasm to help reopen Primrose Park.' Molly squeezed her eyes shut and held her hands in a prayer-like position, hoping when she opened them that everyone else's hands would be in the air.

'You can open your eyes now,' Alfie said, nudging her.

Molly gasped, 'Blimey!' From what she could see everyone's hand was in the air. Feeling overwhelmed, her emotions got the better of her and she burst into tears.

'You daft thing.' Alfie slipped his arm around her

shoulder and gave her a quick hug. 'This is what Heartcross is all about. Dixie will have her garden party.'

As Molly dabbed away her tears with the back of her hand, she heard the sound of a car engine and witnessed Cam's car pulling onto the drive of the cottage.

'I suggest you all get yourself some refreshments from the table while I try to compose myself and come up with a plan of action,' Molly said, swinging her arm towards the long trestle table that Rona and Felicity had set up at the edge of the green.

There were lots of questions that needed answering and Molly didn't have all the answers. Everyone could offer their time and labour for free but there were numerous other costs, and they were astronomical. 'I don't even know where to start,' whispered Molly to Alfie.

'You have started! You've got them all here and all willing to work for free – that's the hardest part done. Luckily, we have the weather on our side, sunlight every evening and a couple of weekends. But there's your man...'

Molly's eyes widened. How did Alfie know anything about her and Cam? She trusted the girls with her life, and they wouldn't have breathed a word. She felt herself trembling, 'What do you mean, there's my man?'

'Your man to help with all the flowers and plants for Primrose Park.'

Molly breathed a sigh of relief that Alfie wasn't thinking what Molly had thought he was thinking.

'You okay? Have I said something wrong?' Alfie narrowed his eyes. 'You look kind of pale.'

'No, not at all,' replied Molly, thinking her reaction must have looked strange. 'But what do you mean?'

'Doesn't his cousin own the biggest chain of garden centres in Scotland? If anyone can kit out Primrose Park with all new shrubbery and trees, that man definitely has the contacts, and it's all for a good cause – his very own grandmother.'

Molly lightly slapped Alfie on his chest then pointed at him. 'You are a bloody genius!'

'I know. You tell me all the time, don't you, Polly?' She'd appeared at their side and handed Alfie a drink.

'What's he blowing his own trumpet about now?' said Polly, laughing and rolling her eyes.

Molly and Alfie looked over in Cam's direction. 'Cam's cousin owns Birdvale, the biggest chain of garden centres,' Alfie told them.

Molly watched as Cam clambered out of the car in a white padded suit, and stifled a giggle – he reminded her of the marshmallow man in the film *Ghostbusters* as he began to stomp across his garden towards the front door of the cottage with Maverick close at his heels. Molly took the opportunity to shout over before he disappeared inside.

'Cam! Cam!' she bellowed the short distance across

the green. She was going to strike while the iron was hot. Surely Cam wasn't going to turn down the chance to help his grandmother have the garden party she deserved?

Cam looked over his shoulder and Molly waved, then gestured for him to come over. Alfie touched Molly's shoulder. 'I'm going to go and grab Drew and have a chat about the waste disposal from the park; he'll know what to do.'

'Good idea.' Molly nodded then turned her attention back to Cam.

He might look like the marshmallow man but my God, he was still handsome, and her heart gave a little flutter. She watched as he let Maverick into the cottage before shutting the door and walking towards her.

When he was within a few yards, he swept his hand down his beekeeper's suit. 'Just for the record, this isn't my usual attire.'

She couldn't help but flirt with him a little. 'I can confirm I know that for a fact,' she replied with a twinkle in her eye, causing Cam to smile.

'See, he does smile.' Molly looked amused, playfully nudging him with her elbow. 'I'm assuming you've been learning the fine art of beekeeping and have not just been for a drink in the pub looking like that.'

'And you would be right. How are you feeling today?' he asked, looking genuinely concerned before Darling spotted him and began frenziedly barking.

Cam wrinkled his brow. 'That dog really doesn't like me, does she?'

'I think it may be the suit. I wouldn't take it to heart. Thank you for the shopping, the flowers, and the chocolates.' Molly was watching him closely. 'They were a lovely surprise.' She tried to gauge his reaction.

'Don't get too excited – the chocolates were on offer and the flowers half-price,' he said with a straight face before laughing. 'And what's going on here?'

'All this is something you may be able to help the community with. Do you want to grab a drink?'

'I'm intrigued – tell me more.' They walked over towards the refreshment table and Molly caught Allie nudging Isla and Felicity the second she noticed Molly was talking to Cam.

'This meeting is all about trying to get Primrose Park back up and running in time for your grandmother's birthday party.'

Cam seemed amazed. 'Wow! All these people are here for my grandmother?'

'Exactly that,' replied Molly, passing him a drink, as they began to walk back towards the table at the front of the green. Thankfully, Isla had untied Darling and was walking her under the trees at the far end of the green, which meant she was occupied instead of barking at Cam. Molly made a mental note to ask Isla if she wanted to attend the dog behavioural classes as she seemed to be able to calm Darling in situations outside the home better than Molly could.

'Your grandparents have been a huge part of this community, and Primrose Park is iconic in the eyes of anyone that lives around these parts. We're all here to find a way to restore the park in the next couple of weeks so that Dixie has the garden party she deserves, and I'm trying my hardest to make it happen.'

Cam stood still, his hazel eyes boring into Molly's. 'And why would you do that?'

Feeling a twinge of guilt, Molly averted her gaze for a second, feeling a little anxious. She knew at the moment she was keeping a huge secret from him, and she wanted to tell the whole truth, but she also truly wanted Dixie to have the best birthday.

'Why wouldn't I? Primrose Park is a beautiful park; it means a lot to everyone.' Without thinking, Molly cradled her stomach. 'And sometimes it's all about making someone else happy. I'm rather fond of your grandmother; she is very charismatic.' Molly was at least telling the truth about this.

'Well, I'm impressed – vet-cum-dog trainer'—he cast a quick eye over towards Darling—'cum-Alan Titchmarsh.'

'But...' Molly took a deep breath, 'I think you may be able to help me too. I believe you know someone who may own a chain of very famous garden centres.' She tilted her head to one side and bit her lip, whilst holding Cam's gaze.

'You have done your homework, haven't you?'

'And if we are trying to get the park up and running in a couple of weeks we haven't got time to fundraise to pay for all the new plants and trees that are needed. The meadow needs kitting out and while Drew and Fergus can dig up all the burnt-out tree stumps, we need new trees to plant and that's—'

'Woah! Slow down, take a breath, otherwise you'll be fainting on me again.' Cam was grinning as he touched her elbow to steady her.

'Sorry, I'm just excited… Can you help?'

Cam nodded. 'Yes, I think I can. I have to be somewhere in the morning but if you're free tomorrow afternoon I can try and set up a meeting with Albie. You can attempt to sweet-talk him but lately he's had a huge soft spot for his grandmother.'

Technically Molly knew she should be covering the surgery tomorrow as long as Baby McKendrick was playing ball, but this meeting was an opportunity not to be missed.

'About two o'clock?' suggested Molly. 'Would that work for you?'

'Yes. Shall I swing by and pick you up as we need to head out your way?'

'Perfect,' she replied. 'Will you be wearing the suit?'

'I will not be wearing this hideous suit.' He cast a

look over himself. 'This is how far I will go to make my grandmother happy. But now I need to get changed before I actually melt. And meetings on the green – that's something I'm not used too. A very different life from the city.'

'And are you back off to the city soon?' Molly quizzed, wanting to know the answer.

'No plans as such. I've agreed to rent the cottage for twelve months.'

'That's good to hear,' she said, feeling herself blush slightly at her own enthusiasm, but she was slightly confused by the conversation she'd overheard earlier when Birdie was talking on the phone. Maybe Molly had got it wrong; maybe the cottage wasn't up for sale.

She watched as Cam headed back over the road and disappeared inside the cottage, then, wrapping her arms around herself, walked over towards Isla, who had tied Darling up under the shade of the trees.

'You look like the cat that's got the cream. You haven't told him, have you?' Isla took hold of Molly's arm and narrowed her eyes.

'Shh! Don't be daft. As if I'd blurt that out in front of an audience.'

'Yes, you're right, sorry. I just got excited there for a minute.'

'But tomorrow might be the ideal opportunity.' Molly's voice was low.

'Tell me more.' Isla leant in closer to her.

'As you know, Cam's cousin is the owner of Birdvale... Cam's agreed to set up a meeting tomorrow afternoon so I can negotiate plants and trees for the park, and he's going to pick me up. That means two car journeys together. I need to face facts; it's never going to be an ideal time to tell him, and the child will be eighteen before I know it—'

'Ha, they do grow up fast.'

'So I may as well get it over with sooner or later – tomorrow!'

Isla gave Molly a hug. 'It'll be okay – I've just got a feeling.' She gave her friend a warm smile.

'I wish I had your confidence.' Molly wasn't feeling as optimistic as Isla – in fact, she felt scared witless. This news was going to come out of the blue, but she'd made up her mind: tomorrow was the day she would tell Cam, and whatever the outcome she would worry about the consequences then.

'Let's get the park duties dished out and this show on the road,' said Molly, trying to push the thought of tomorrow out of her mind. There was no point worrying about it before it had happened.

Isla linked her arm through Molly's as they rejoined the rest of the villagers. There was a buzz of excitement all around and Molly could feel the enthusiasm.

'I think this is doable,' said Molly with a smile.

'I think it is,' agreed Isla, 'but make sure you don't

bite off more than you can chew. That little one comes first.'

'Absolutely, she does.'

'She?' Isla raised an eyebrow.

'It's just a feeling!'

Molly stepped back onto the stage and switched on the microphone. 'I have some news!' she announced, gaining everyone's attention. 'Tomorrow, I have a meeting with the owner of Birdvale Garden Centre, so fingers crossed I can persuade him to maybe donate some plants and trees!'

All the villagers began to clap and Molly felt on top of the world. Not only were they saving their treasured Primrose Park, but Dixie's birthday plans could still go ahead.

Molly quickly looked over towards Bumblebee Cottage. Cam was standing in the top window, now minus the beekeeper's suit. He caught her eye and waved before disappearing. Molly's heart gave a little flutter; even though they'd got off to a shaky start, she knew she was still very much attracted to him. She didn't regret the night they'd spent together and wouldn't change it for the world. All Molly could hope was that Cam would feel the same after she shared her news with him – tomorrow.

Chapter Fourteen

'Please, please not this morning.' Molly had spent the last thirty minutes retching over the toilet. She wanted to cry and really couldn't take much more. She'd been woken by the dawn chorus and as soon as her eyes were open the morning sickness had engulfed her. Every time she crawled back to bed, she found herself back cradling the toilet within no time at all.

'This is no fun,' she murmured to Darling, who followed her into the bathroom every time Molly moved. 'Why do women put themselves through this time and time again?' She wiped her face with a cold, wet cloth then curled back up under her duvet. First hot, then cold, she just couldn't get comfortable. She attempted to go back to sleep but baby McKendrick was just not letting her – the nausea still felt as bad when she closed her eyes. Trying to curb the sickness she reached for the packet of ginger biscuits and began to nibble one. She didn't even feel like a cup of tea.

At least she had a few hours before she was due at the green, followed by morning surgery. 'I want to cry, Darling. How do I get rid of this feeling?'

Molly didn't know how she was going to get through the day if this carried on. She tried sitting up in bed, then lying on her side curled up in a ball, but frankly nothing was working. Finally, she wandered downstairs and looked at the contents of her fridge, but there was just nothing she fancied. Pouring herself a glass of juice because she knew she needed to stay hydrated, she took tiny sips. She was sure she'd read somewhere that sniffing lemons could help reduce sickness and she was willing to give anything a go. She made a mental note to grab some as she passed Hamish's shop on the way to the green. 'I even smell like sick,' Molly said, sniffing her hair. She wrinkled her nose before climbing back up the stairs to take a shower.

As she let the water cascade over her Molly only had one thing on her mind: today was the day she was going to tell Cam. She couldn't put it off any longer, especially if he decided he wanted to come along to the first scan. So the question playing on her mind was: how exactly do you drop it into the conversation, and should she tell him on the first car journey or the second?

'Hey, remember the night we spent together? Guess what, I'm pregnant.' Molly was rehearsing the conversation in her mind and it didn't matter how she said it, it really didn't sound good.

'Ever thought of having a child? Well, guess what...'

Molly stepped out of the shower and took a deep breath. She had no clue what she was going to say so there was no point worrying about it now. She would just have to decide on the spot when the time was right.

After she'd dried herself and pulled a brush through her hair, she looked at her stomach in the mirror. Her body shape was definitely changing daily. Even she could see a roundness to her face, just like Dixie had said, and her waistline had disappeared a little more. Taking a swift look through her wardrobe, she found nothing suitable to wear; everything was way too tight for her stomach. She sighed. Isla had been kind and dropped off a bag of maternity clothes, and she had rummaged through it, but although the clothes were lovely, they were also huge. Maybe in a couple of months they would be more suitable. Just as she was about to give up, she noticed a pair of black joggers with an elasticated waist with a pull-in cord, and quickly tried them on. There was a lot of loose material gathered around the stomach, but if she wore a long T-shirt no one would notice. She had to face facts; she had nothing else to wear. This in-between stage was no fun; she wasn't fat but she was no longer thin. Was there going to be *any* fun stage to this pregnancy? Molly wasn't convinced.

A few hours later she was standing on the green,

having fortunately managed to get through the last hour without throwing up. She had a freshly cut lemon in her pocket wrapped up in kitchen towel, and any time she got a second when no one was looking she took a quick sniff, knowing how ridiculous it must look if anyone spotted her.

'And that's a wrap,' she said smiling at all the owners and their dogs standing in the semicircle in front of her. 'I can see a vast improvement in all the dogs this morning, even Darling!' Molly bent down and patted Darling's head. She had been on her best behaviour all morning; maybe she sensed that Molly wasn't feeling well. 'I will see you all tomorrow.'

As the owners and dogs began to disperse from the green, Molly looked at her watch. She had twenty minutes to make it to morning surgery on time. Once there was no one in sight, Molly took out the lemon and took a huge sniff. She wasn't sure whether it was all in her head but inhaling the aroma of the lemon was helping to settle the sickness.

'Actually, I don't care if it's all in my head, it seems to be helping me get through the morning,' she said, but Darling ignored her, too busy sniffing under the hedgerow. 'Come on, let's get to the surgery.'

Molly began walking towards the van, which was parked outside Bumblebee Cottage. She'd already noted that Cam's car had been gone since she'd arrived on the green and remembered he'd said he had some sort of meeting this morning. She wondered about his job. That day in the hotel he said he was a dentist, so had he taken some leave from work? She had no clue about his life at all, but maybe, spending a little time with him this afternoon, she would find out a little more. After she loaded Darling into the van she noticed the car parked straight in front of her was Birdie's, and there was another car blocking the drive. Hearing voices, she looked over towards the cottage and spotted Birdie walking around the side of the house with a young couple who were holding hands and who looked very much in love.

'Thank you for showing us round, we will be in touch,' said the man, shaking Birdie's hand before the couple walked towards their car.

Was the cottage up for sale, then? Thinking it was odd, as Cam was convinced he was renting it from Dixie for twelve months, Molly climbed inside the van and drove off towards her surgery over in Glensheil.

It was only a couple of minutes before she was driving down the track at the bottom of Love Heart Lane towards the bridge, thankful for the line of green foliage that provided some shade and shielded her eyes from the blinding sun that bounced off the windscreen. Once she was on the bridge she took a moment to admire the blue sky then glanced at the River Heart, the water glistening in the sunshine. There were droves of hikers walking across the bridge, heading towards the mountain, and children clutching their fishing nets and dangling them from the banks of the river.

Turning her head back towards the road, Molly sat up straight. There was Cam's car coming towards her across the bridge. She flashed her headlights and put her hand up to wave but immediately dropped it again and clutched the steering wheel. Cam wasn't on his own. Sitting in the passenger seat was the woman she'd seen at the cottage – his wife. They were driving into Heartcross. Cam's eyes were fixed on the road ahead and luckily he hadn't spotted her. Molly felt a little anxious, and couldn't help wandering what they were doing together. Deep down she didn't like it, even though she knew she had no control over what Cam did or who he saw.

'Don't panic. They probably just have a lot to sort out,' she murmured to herself, pulling into the surgery car park and parking in her favourite spot under the oak tree. But she *was* panicking; couples decided to get back together all the time. What if she was about to throw a huge spanner in the works?

Trying to calm her thoughts, she took another huge sniff at the lemon. All she had to do was get through the next few hours and then Cam would know her news – and in the meantime she prayed the surgery was going to be quiet this morning.

Just after midday, Molly arrived home, threw her keys into the bowl on the hallway table and risked a hesitant look in the mirror. There was nothing blooming about this pregnancy – her hair felt limp, her eyes dull, and her face pallid. She felt exhausted, which was ridiculous after only working a morning, but this must be one of the joys of pregnancy. She wondered whether she would ever feel herself again.

Pouring herself a glass of water and grabbing a chicken salad she'd prepared earlier from the fridge. Molly stepped outside into the garden. She didn't feel like eating at all but the last thing she needed was to faint again on Cam before she had a chance to tell him anything. Taking a moment, she closed her eyes, trying to conjure up Cam's presence that night in the hotel, and immediately her whole body erupted in goosebumps – the smile he'd given her in the car park, then at the bar, his gorgeous manly smell, the touch of his lips on hers... She wondered if that would ever happen again. Only time would tell. She wanted to know what he thought of her. Did he think about that night, or to him was it just one of those things? As she began to eat, she checked her emails on her phone and saw one had landed from Alfie.

He'd written down everything that had been agreed at the meeting. All the jobs had been allocated and work at Primrose Park was starting this evening. Drew and Fergus were heading on down there with the diggers, which meant hopefully that by the weekend all the tree stumps would be out and the meadow turned over ready for planting.

All the names of the volunteers were listed and the local pub and teashop were providing refreshments throughout the evening. 'I love it when a plan comes together!' remarked Molly, ruffling Darling's head. The dog was now lying down under the table in the shade. Molly couldn't wait to tell Dixie and see the smile on her face. This was really going to give her a boost.

After finishing her lunch, Molly freshened up and then made herself comfy on the settee. Cam would be here to pick her up in the next fifteen minutes but until then, she was going to close her eyes. Darling lay next to her, and rested her head gently on Molly's stomach. 'I think you know what's going on, don't you?' Molly said to her.

The peace and quiet were short-lived; the doorbell rang, setting Darling off barking in a frenzy. Molly bolted upright. 'You've got to stop doing that. You've made me jump out of my skin.'

But Darling wasn't listening. She was up on the arm of the chair barking out of the window at Cam, who was standing on the doorstep. 'You aren't going to make friends behaving like that,' Molly told her.

Molly managed to sneak out of the living room and close the door behind her before Darling could jump down from the chair. She opened the door to Cam, who was looking stunning and smelling gorgeous. He was dressed in a tight white T-shirt that enhanced his tan and a pair of blue tailored shorts to the knee. Molly's eyes discreetly looked him up and down. He looked like he should be walking the summer catwalks, while she was standing there looking dowdy, dressed in a pair of joggers that were pulled in around her waist and covered up with an oversized, baggy T-shirt, not exactly oozing fashion-icon but looking more like a sack of spuds.

'I thought I'd leave the beekeeper's suit at home but here, I've brought you a present: honey.'

'Did you just call me honey?' Molly grinned, teasing him.

'Honey!' Cam held up a jar of yellow stuff. 'I've made my first jar but I'm not sure it's as good as my grandad's.' He handed over the jar to Molly. 'Lemon? Is that your perfume I can smell?' He leant forward towards an embarrassed Molly then sniffed. 'That is unusual.'

Molly instantly felt herself blush. 'No, I've just been cutting up lemons. I'll just grab my bag and put Darling in the kitchen. Do you want to come in?'

He looked across at Darling who was still barking at him through the window. 'I kind of value my life, so I'll wait in the car and…' He looked down at Molly's joggers. 'Aren't you going to be too warm in those? It's roasting out here.'

Molly didn't want to say it was the only item of clothing that fitted at the moment. 'I'll be fine,' she said, and disappeared back inside to sort out Darling. On her way, she heard his phone ring.

As she slipped into the passenger seat next to Cam, he hung up the call and stared at the road ahead. Suddenly he seemed a little on edge and Molly sensed a slight tension in the air. 'Thank God for air con,' she exclaimed, breaking the silence. The temperature outside was a whopping twenty-eight degrees and there wasn't a single cloud in the sky. She took a sideward glance at him. His profile was just perfect. She remembered the night they'd spent together so clearly; he'd seemed so relaxed and full of fun, and a part of her wished she could turn back time to find out more about him.

'Indeed,' he replied, putting the car into gear and setting off through the town.

'Are you okay?' asked Molly, thinking she really did need to try and smooth the sudden tense atmosphere. 'Since you climbed into the car you seem kind of preoccupied.'

Cam turned his head towards her. 'It's just been a hell of a morning and I've got a couple of things on my mind.'

'Problem shared… Anything I can help with?' asked Molly gently. How the hell was she going to drop into the conversation, 'Guess what, I'm expecting your baby'? Was it ever going to be the right time?

'No, it's just life in general, but thank you.' He held

230

her gaze for a split second before focusing again on the road in front of him.

'I'm not even sure where we're heading,' said Molly, looking out of the passenger window at the striped awnings and colourful and welcoming window displays of the shops along the high street. They passed the post office, the library, and tree-lined pavements. The town was packed with tourists and the queue for the ice-cream vendor stretched right around the corner of the street. Suddenly Molly craved a mint-choc-chip ice-cream and looked longingly towards the cart as Cam stopped at the traffic lights.

'Not far,' he replied. 'Today my cousin is at the garden centre just on the edge of Glensheil. Do you know the one? Up by the roundabout before you hit the dual carriageway.'

Molly knew exactly the one. She loved a good mooch around the garden centre, and Birdvale was like a mini shopping centre – it had everything. 'Yes, it's one of my favourite places. Didn't you start off in business with your cousin? With a plant nursery behind The Old Bakehouse?'

Cam looked surprised. 'Gosh, you do know your stuff. That was a long time ago. How would you even know that?'

'Isla and Felicity mentioned it.'

'Have my ears been burning?'

'Maybe a little.' Molly wanted to say, 'Actually, an awful lot.'

'Albie was more into it than I was and when he first started out I couldn't see how we were going to make much profit, as believe me, it was difficult trying to keep the plants alive during summer never mind the winter. We invested in a rickety old greenhouse that blew down in the first storm we had, and that was when I'd had enough. Little did I know that Albie would take over the plant world then become the biggest garden centre chain in the UK – and it all began in the back garden of The Old Bakehouse.'

'I'm just surprised our paths never crossed at some point, but I suppose when you were coming here for your summer holidays I was off to my own grandparents' house – and we lived in Glensheil, not Heartcross.'

'I haven't been around much for the past few years. Mum went off to live in New Zealand with her new man and of course I'd pop in and see Grandmother when I had the time, usually a couple of times a month.'

'Did you notice your grandmother's health deteriorating?' asked Molly, intrigued to know Cam's opinion.

He shook his head. 'I haven't been around for a few months and it came as a huge shock. Albie messaged me and kept me updated; he said things were going from bad to worse and Aunt Birdie thought she was going to end up burning the place down. She had become quite forgetful and was lashing out at everyone. They sorted out a private assessment and drugs to calm down her erratic behaviour. It all happened pretty quickly... Right, here we are, my cousin's empire.' Cam turned off the main road and slowly followed the line of cars in front of them.

Molly couldn't believe they were here already. There hadn't been enough time to talk about anything much, but on the way home she still had every intention of sharing the news of the baby. Maybe she could invite him to talk; she would just have to play it by ear. Cam circled the car park twice before he found a vacant space and parked the car. Due to the glorious weather, everyone was out, pushing metal trolleys jammed full of beautiful coloured plants and trees.

'Do you know roughly what area of the park you need to cover with what?' asked Cam, switching off the engine and looking towards Molly, who was holding up a folder.

'Yes, Alfie has been a star and written down everything for me. Obviously, I don't expect to get everything for free,' Molly quickly added.

'If it's all for Grandma, I wouldn't worry about that. He would kit the world out for her. So I think you'll be onto a winner.'

They walked across the car park past the long row of shopping trolleys towards the grand entrance, which was stunning, a canopy of pink roses twisting around the green vines that clung onto the oak archway.

'How beautiful are those.' Molly stopped to admire the roses then reached up to inhale their aroma.

Cam had carried on walking but, sensing Molly wasn't with him, he turned and smiled as he spotted her standing on tiptoes sniffing the flowers. He walked back towards her.

'I can't smell anything.' She wrinkled her nose and tried again.

Cam leant forward. 'That's because they aren't real,' he whispered in her ear, leaving Molly feeling like an utter fool.

'I knew that – I was just testing,' she replied, with a grin on her face, hoping the red flush in her cheeks went unnoticed.

They walked through the automatic doors into a lavish foyer of water fountains. It was indeed one of the finest garden centres that Molly had ever seen. From the food emporium to the shelves packed with soft furnishings, vases and candles, this was a shopper's dream store – everything you ever wanted under one roof. They followed the one-way system to the outside area, where Molly stopped in her tracks. 'How beautiful. Look at those climbers.' They were spectacular, tumbling all around fake lampposts that also housed the most spectacular hanging baskets. 'I love a good clitoris,' exclaimed Molly, admiring the mass of small violet flowers.

A couple walking past burst into laughter and Molly looked at them with a puzzled expression. 'What did I say? All I said was—'

'Shh... Clematis, it's a clematis, not a...' Cam raised his eyebrows while he stifled his laughter, then shook his head. 'Bloody hell, Molly, I'm a man and even I know the difference!'

'OMG!' Molly brought her hand up to her mouth, completely mortified at her mistake.

'I suggest we go and get a cold drink whilst we wait for Albie but in the meantime if I was you, don't go smelling any more fake flowers or speaking too loudly.'

Molly laughed and saluted. 'I hear you!'

'But just for the record, I love a good cl—'

Molly swiped his arm before he could finish his sentence and Cam burst out laughing. Thankfully he now seemed a little more relaxed and Molly couldn't help but wonder whether he was flirting with her. They walked off towards the cosy café area, where Cam was greeted like a famous pop star. All the members of staff seemed to down tools and look over in his direction and wave. Molly even thought a couple of the girls were actually swooning.

'You've either got it or you haven't,' he said with a grin, accepting two bottles of water from a staff member.

'Shall we take a look outside? Albie shouldn't be too much longer.'

Cam led the way through the lavish gift section towards the outside area, which was just a mass of colour and immediately reminded Molly of the once beautiful meadow flowers of Primrose Park.

'These are real flowers, if you want to sniff these,' said Cam with a completely straight face before breaking into a smile.

'You are really not funny,' she replied, but as much as she pretended to protest, she was secretly pleased at the banter they were sharing. It took her back to that night when they'd joked and flirted.

'I disagree.' He grinned. 'Come on, there's a sheltered area at the back with benches under the canopy. This sun is roasting.'

Molly was thankful to head towards some shade; wearing the jogging bottoms was a big mistake and she felt like she was overheating. They weaved their way through the gorgeous-looking flowers and plants and Molly watched the assistants busy at work keeping the plants watered, which must have been a difficult task in this heat.

'That must take some doing, keeping the plants in tip-top condition until they are sold. I'm useless,' Molly admitted. 'I've had a couple of house plants in my time and both times they have curled up and died.'

'Maybe just get a plastic one next time,' joked Cam,

stepping aside as an assistant trundled down the aisle towards him with a wide trolley full of lavender plants.

'I'm not rising to it,' she said, pointing to the pots of pansies. 'Such pretty colours.'

'And very low maintenance,' he added as he began walking again and Molly followed.

But instead of watching where she was going Molly was looking across at a water fountain to her side and tripped over something on the ground. Letting out a scream, she grabbed a nearby post. Her face registered alarm and her eyebrows shot up. 'NO!'

Time slowed, as Molly watched a hosepipe uncoil itself like a snake and rise into the air, water gushing out straight at her. She tried to move out of the way, but it was too late. The water was ice-cold as it hit her body. Molly was soaked.

'For God's sake, why me?' she gasped, finally managing to move out of the way.

At first Cam looked genuinely shocked, as he reached out, grabbed the hose, and placed it back firmly amongst the plants where it belonged, but now he was trying to suppress his laughter. Molly was aware that everyone around her was staring in her direction. She looked up at Cam through her dripping wet fringe.

'It's not funny!' she exclaimed, feeling embarrassed, swiping the water from her arms and shaking her body from side to side like a dog that had just climbed out of a bath.

'It's a little funny… At least with this weather you're going to dry in no time at all.'

'Look at the state of me! I'm wringing wet.' Molly's oversized T-shirt clung to every part of her body, including her very tiny bump.

Cam took a step backwards and looked at her.

'I didn't mean "Look at me, look at me!", I meant it in general terms… Look at me.' Molly quickly pulled at the sodden T-shirt that was clinging to her breasts and stomach and tried to stretch it as much as she could. 'Will you stop looking at me!'

'Look at me, don't look at me. Typical woman, can't make up her mind!' Cam was still smiling but Molly was far from amused. Out of the corner of her eye, she noticed a figure walking towards them. The timing could not be worse. Albie approached and patted his cousin on the back.

'Good afternoon, long time no see, must have been our golf weekend.' Albie gave his cousin a bear hug then turned towards Molly, who had water dripping off the end of her nose.

'This is Molly. She's just had a fight with one of your hosepipes,' said Cam, grinning.

Albie gave him a puzzled look then turned back towards Molly. 'Oh no! Can I get you a towel or anything?'

Molly shook her head and was horrified to see water flick on to Albie's face. 'I'm so sorry!' She really wasn't off to a great start.

After Albie wiped away the droplets with the back of his hand he stared at Molly and held out his hand. 'As long as you aren't going to sue me.'

'Where's there's blame there's a claim,' she trilled nervously, aware Albie was still staring at her. Molly guessed that Albie was older than Cam. He resembled his cousin a little but his features were darker and he was a little taller, but not by much.

'Have we met before? I feel I know you from somewhere.' He narrowed his eyes and kept his eyes firmly fixed on Molly.

Was this her cue to blurt, 'I was your cousin's one-night stand at that hotel you went to when you last played golf, and guess what, there's going to be an extra family member popping along to see you in approximately six months' time'? But instead Molly shook her head. 'I'm a friend of your grandmother's and I'm really hoping you can help me.'

'Sounds intriguing, but I still think I know you from somewhere.'

'I don't think so, but I am a valued customer and I love your store.'

Cam cocked an eyebrow. 'Let's try not to make my cousin's ego any bigger than it already is. Shall we walk over to your office?'

'This way,' said Albie, leading them back into the store and then through a maze of corridors that was marked 'for staff only'. As they reached the door to his office Cam stepped back.

'I'll leave you in Albie's capable hands.'

'Are you not joining us?' Molly had assumed that Cam would be taking part in the meeting.

'This is your meeting. I'll leave you to sweet-talk my cousin. I need to make a few phone calls. Is it okay if I use the office next door?' Cam looked towards Albie.

'Of course.' Albie opened the door and gestured for Molly to take a seat. 'I won't be a second.' For a moment Albie stood out in the corridor with Cam.

Molly took a seat and looked up to see a bulletin board pinned to the wall holding various graphs and pie charts. She picked up the name plate on the desk and put it back down. It was a typical office with a computer, electrical cords dangling off the edge of the desk, a coffee mug, and a jumper draped over the back of the chair. Outside the office, Molly could hear their muffled voices.

'How did it go?' asked Albie.

'It was the worst morning of my life and that's saying something. Look, we can speak later but if I ever hear the word "baby" again in this lifetime it will be too damn soon,' replied Cam.

Molly couldn't believe what she'd just heard. She felt her heart thump faster. Had she just heard Cam right? What the hell did that mean? Molly didn't know what to think, but Cam's voice had sounded serious. Her thoughts were spinning and she didn't notice that Albie had re-entered the room and was sitting down opposite her.

'Penny for them?' Albie joked, bringing Molly back down to earth with a bump.

She looked up. 'Sorry, sorry, I was just in a little world of my own,' she admitted, sliding the folder over the desk towards him, though her mind was very firmly fixed on the conversation she'd just overheard, which had completely thrown her off track. 'I'm here because of—'

'Primrose Park and Grandmother's birthday party, I believe,' interrupted Albie.

Molly took a deep breath. 'Yes, that's right.'

'How long have you known my grandmother? She's recently gone into a home. Her health declined – overnight, it seemed – but she's great, isn't she? But just one piece of advice: never play cards with her. She will win every time. In the whole of my life, I have never known her to lose a game. That's a hell of a winning streak.'

Molly smiled. 'I'll remember that,' she replied, thinking how happy Dixie was when she had taken the pack of cards in for her. 'I only met Dixie for the first time not so long ago. I seemed to have been handpicked by Birdie to inherit her dog. I hope you don't mind me saying that Dixie was distressed about being in the home, and she wanted to escape.'

'It's always a difficult time adapting after you've been

in your own home for so long.' Albie was scrutinising Molly, 'I still think I've seen you somewhere before.' He was waggling his pen at her. 'I never forget a face... The hotel... The girl at the hotel with my cousin.'

Molly was embarrassed he'd remembered and wasn't sure why he was looking so smug about it. But she *was* the girl at the hotel and why should she feel embarrassed? She'd done nothing wrong.

'It was you, wasn't it?' Albie wouldn't take his eyes off her.

'Yes, that was me,' Molly finally admitted.

Albie exhaled. 'Wow! It is a small world!'

'It is indeed,' replied Molly, not knowing where this conversation was going next and immediately wanting to steer it in a different direction.

'What are the chances of that?' Albie was still staring at her in an unnerving way that made Molly feel a little uncomfortable. She watched him closely as he looked her up and down. Did he just do that? Molly was still aware that her T-shirt was damp and as she took a swift glance down she saw it clinging to her breasts and quickly pulled it forward. When she looked up again Albie was smirking.

'Take a look in the folder,' said Molly, not letting herself feel undermined by him. 'That is exactly what we need to get Primrose Park up and running in time for your grandmother's birthday party.' Her voice had suddenly become matter-of-fact. Already she wasn't a big fan of Albie but most probably she had to smile in the right places to get those plants to fill the meadow alongside the replacement trees. She watched as Albie took out a document from the folder and perused it.

Silence filled the room while Molly waited for him to say something. He finally put down the document on his desk and leant back in his leatherbound chair and rested his hands on his stomach. 'That's a hell of a lot of free plants and trees.'

'Approximately six thousand pounds all together and I appreciate it's a lot of money—'

'That it is,' interrupted Albie, still looking at Molly, who squirmed in her seat. 'And when exactly do you need all these plants and trees by?'

Molly took a deep breath. 'We are starting work at Primrose Park tonight. Most of us are working full-time so all we have are the evenings and this coming weekend, but everyone in the village is on board so I'm sure it will all come together.'

'And who is in charge of this project?'

'Me.' Molly held his gaze.

'I saw the news report. That's an awful lot of work to be done just to try and get the park reopened for my grandmother's birthday.'

'And your grandmother is worth it. I'm sure you already know how much this means to her. Primrose Park holds special memories for her and your grandfather and if we can all make this happen for her it will be a special birthday she'll never forget.'

Albie stood up and gestured towards the door as he walked around his desk, 'I'll take a look over this and maybe'—he hovered right next to Molly—'maybe we can meet up at a hotel, this weekend, and discuss this proposal a little more.'

Molly could see by the look on his face that he was undressing her with his eyes and she knew exactly what he was proposing – he had no intention of discussing plants or trees. He thought she was fair game, because she'd fallen into bed with his cousin at the drop of a hat, and now he thought it was his turn. The damn cheek of the man.

Feeling her body erupt in goosebumps for all the wrong reasons, she couldn't wait to get out of there and opened the office door wide. Out of the corner of her eye she was glad to see Cam striding up the corridor. Molly didn't know how she kept her composure, but she leant forward and whispered, 'Not a cat in hell's chance,' then forced a sickly smile on her face.

'But that's what you do, isn't it?' His darkened eyes stared into her.

'Only with people I like.' She looked at him with contempt then turned and smiled at Cam, who was now standing in the doorway. 'Great timing! We've just finished!'

'Did everything go to plan?' Cam looked at them.

'You just wouldn't believe how well our meeting went. Albie has been an absolute gentleman, haven't you, Albie? Do you know what Albie has suggested?' Molly was staring straight at an awkward-looking Albie who seemed to have a tinge of crimson to his cheeks. 'Albie has suggested that his wonderful company will absolutely provide all the trees and plants for the reopening of Primrose Park – and not only that, but as quickly as tomorrow. He and his team will drop off all the plants and trees at the park so everyone can get planting and watering. How fantastic is that?' Molly was beaming from one to the other and enjoying watching Albie squirm. She was playing him at his own game. 'And Dixie will have her birthday garden party. She will be so proud of you, Albie, for stepping up to the mark with no conditions. In fact, proud of you both. You were right, Cam; he'd do anything for Dixie.' Molly knew she was laying it on thick but underneath she was fuming at Albie's behaviour and she was not going to let him make her feel cheap. How dare he?

'I think that's more down to you than us.' Cam put his hand on the small of Molly's back as they walked out into the corridor. Molly stopped and turned towards Albie.

'Thank you, Albie, your kindness has been overwhelming,' she oozed before setting off down the corridor.

Albie looked like he was catching flies; his jaw had dropped to somewhere below his knees.

'I knew we could count on you. Thank you,' added Cam, patting Albie on his back.

Molly liked the way Cam had said 'we'. She knew it was just a figure of speech, but it made her feel all warm inside. 'You're smiling at me,' she said, holding Cam's gaze as she looked behind so he could catch up with her.

'I am. I'm impressed. You really are something, aren't you?' he said, giving her a look of admiration that made her heart flip. 'Usually he's a ruthless businessman and wouldn't do something for nothing, but it seems he may be mellowing in his old age.'

'Or maybe it's because it's for your grandma,' added Molly, knowing the truth.

'Maybe,' replied Cam, looking back at Albie, who was watching them from his office door. Cam waved as he disappeared around the corner.

Once they were back in the car park, Molly, thankful that she was no longer in Albie's company and feeling a sense of karma, gave a silent sigh of relief that that situation was over. But she was now faced with another situation on the journey home: she was about to drop the bombshell to Cam that she was carrying his baby, but she was wary after hearing the conversation between Cam and Albie earlier.

'Thank you for taking me,' she said, starting the

conversation whilst her mind was racing with what to say next.

'You're welcome. It's for the sake of Grandmother but the community too – they really do love their park.'

Molly bit her lip and took a deep breath. It was now or never. 'I did try and find you after that night, you know,' she said softly, daring to glimpse at Cam, whose eyes were fixed on the road in front.

She bit the bullet and carried on. 'And I was surprised that you just up and left without a word that morning.' Molly wasn't holding back but she was keeping it real. She was just saying how she felt and it had hurt. 'I honestly felt a connection towards you the moment I bumped into you in the car park and I thought you felt the same.' She didn't dare to take another look in his direction. 'I knew nothing about you except that your name was Cam and you said you were a dentist, so I only had one option, which was to google "handsome Cam dentist", but I couldn't find anything,' She gave a little chuckle to try and break the tense atmosphere, but Cam wasn't smiling. 'Did that night not mean anything to you?' Molly wasn't sure she wanted to know the answer as she swallowed down a lump in her throat and waited.

Complete silence. The atmosphere between them had somewhat plummeted.

'Are you really not going to say anything? The Cam I met that night in the hotel is a very different Cam to the man I met in Primrose Park, and to be honest I'm not exactly sure who you are... until I fainted and then I saw a glimpse of the Cam I thought I'd met that night. You became caring, rang the doctor, and bought me flowers and chocolates...'

'Anyone would have done the same,' he answered, finally.

'Would they though? You didn't have to offer to do my shopping and you didn't have to bring me here today. Deep down, I think you like me – I'm hoping you like me – and here's the thing: I like you.' There, she'd admitted it out loud. 'I couldn't believe it when you turned up. I was so excited to see you and your reaction towards me wasn't what I was expecting. We'd spent the night together.' Molly heard her voice crack, and she was determined to keep hold of her emotions.

'Look, it was just a night. These things happen.'

That wasn't what she wanted to hear... It was just a night...

Molly could feel her heart breaking. It seemed Cam didn't care about her the way she cared about him. He didn't care in the slightest.

'Do they? Well, not usually for me. I've never had a one-night stand in my life. I felt a connection towards you... I still do.' Molly looked out of the window and blinked back the tears. Cam didn't say anything.

'So is this what you usually do, go around picking up women at hotels and sneaking off in the morning?' Molly blurted before she could stop herself. She was hurting, and she willed him to say she meant more to him than just that, but Cam wasn't forthcoming at all. Molly could feel her heart being shattered into tiny pieces.

'Don't paint me in a bad light. You were more than willing and doing exactly the same.'

This just wasn't how Molly had expected the conversation to go.

'Was I though? Or is it because you have a wife, and you shouldn't have been doing it in the first place? Is that why you sneaked from my bed?' Molly knew she shouldn't have said that but she wanted to poke and prod him; she wanted to know what was going on in his life. But by the glare on his face as he looked towards her, she was going about it the wrong way.

'You have no clue about anything.'

'Then tell me,' insisted Molly.

Cam briefly closed his eyes. 'Look, I'm not good for anyone. I'm incapable of having a relationship and the only person I can look after at the moment is myself.' He raked a hand through his hair and as far as he was concerned that was the end of the conversation.

'So you didn't even like me?' Molly just wanted clarification even though she knew the answer was going to feel like she'd been stabbed through the heart.

Cam pulled up outside her house and kept the engine running. 'I can't have this conversation, Molly. I've come here to get away from...' He paused. 'Look, I'm glad you're all sorted with the plants and trees for Primrose Park.' He had totally swerved the question. 'I really am, but that's all I can offer you at the moment.'

'What's going on with you?'

'Just leave it – please.' Cam's tone was firm, and he really wasn't giving any more away, much to Molly's frustration.

Plucking up courage – it was now or never – she took a swig of warm water from the bottle in her bag and tried to calm her beating heart. 'You are going to have to talk about it at some point very soon because…'

He was staring straight at her. This wasn't the way she had ever imagined telling him the news. Molly had envisaged hearts and flowers, being swept up in his arms as he spun her round, overjoyed with the news. 'I'm pregnant. You are going to be a father.'

Silence.

Waiting for a reaction, Molly shuffled uncomfortably in her seat.

Cam looked perplexed, lost for words, and was shaking his head in disbelief.

'Well, say something,' insisted Molly, staring at him.

'I don't believe you. You can't be pregnant, and if you are I can't be the father.' Cam was adamant, his eyes wide.

'Why can't you be? Of course you are.'

'I really can't be.'

'I know we used something…'

'You don't understand. I *really* can't be.'

Molly couldn't believe it. Cam was in complete denial. 'Well, you were there that night, unless you're telling me I imagined the whole thing. My first scan is on Friday. Do you really think people faint for no reason?' She held his gaze. 'I'm pregnant and you are the father.' Molly couldn't spell it out any more clearly. She took a breath. 'I know this may be a shock,' she said, softening her tone, but Cam's face was emotionless as he stared out of the car window.

'You just need to go. I really can't do this.'

'What can't you do? I don't understand. This is real and this is happening. We need to talk about it.'

'I can't,' was the only explanation Cam offered.

'I don't sleep around, Cam, if that's what you're thinking.'

He remained silent.

'That is what you're thinking, isn't it? I don't believe this,' huffed Molly, close to tears. That was so far from the truth.

'Is it money you're after?' Cam looked her straight in the eye.

'Money? You are unbelievable. Is that what you think I want – money? I don't need anyone's money. This is my house and I have a very successful business. For your information, I felt a connection with you like I'd never felt before.' Even though Molly could feel the anger rising inside her she was still laying her heart on the line.

How dare he suggest she was after money? Who the hell did he think he was? 'You can't even take responsibility for your actions. That one-night stand has had lasting consequences and I will tell you now: whether you want anything to do with this baby or not, I will be bringing this baby into the world and I will love this baby.'

She didn't wait to hear any more.

'You know what, Cameron Bird?' She addressed him with his full name. 'If I could turn back time I would. I wish I'd never set eyes on you at that hotel.'

With a sick sinking feeling in her stomach, Molly climbed out of the car and, holding her head high, hurried towards her front door. She heard the car driving away, but she never looked back over her shoulder. Her whole world had come crashing down all around her. That conversation had not gone according to plan. Of course he might be in shock hearing the news, but claiming he couldn't be the father... As she shut the front door behind her, Darling ran towards her, wagging her tail. Molly scooped her up in her arms and buried her hot frustrated tears in her fur. 'What are we going to do now?' she murmured as Darling licked her face.

Damn Cameron Bird. Who the hell did he think he was?

'Stay calm,' she said. 'Deep breaths. You can do this on your own, you know you can.'

Carrying Darling into the living room she sat down on the settee and texted Isla.

Cam knows, but he's claiming the baby can't be his.

Almost immediately Isla texted back.

I'm on my way over.

Molly was thankful. Isla was a good friend and she'd help to put everything into perspective, but judging by Cam's reactions she was all alone in this pregnancy. At least she'd told him and had been honest; it was up to him what he did with that information. But she knew the truth: he was the father and if he didn't believe her it was him who would miss out, not her. One thing she knew was that Cam wasn't going to dip in and out of her child's life – he was either in or out.

Chapter Fifteen

Molly and Isla stood at the gates of Primrose Park. The whole place was a hive of activity. The community spirit was a given, and all the villagers were out in full force. Molly had never seen so many wheelbarrows and spades in one place. Drew and Fergus were hard at work tunnelling out the tree stumps with a digger, the burnt-out bandstand had completely disappeared, and the wrought-iron gates had been dismantled. The majority of the villagers were down in the flower meadow digging over the ground ready for the new plants that were arriving tomorrow.

The sun was still warm and Molly slipped off her cardigan and hung it on a post as they stood in the middle of the park and looked around. Alfie seemed to have everyone under control; he'd organised the villagers in different sections of the park.

'I tell you something though, this dizziness just won't go away,' confided Molly, taking a sip of water from her bottle.

'Here.' Isla reached in her pocket. 'You are looking a little pale.' She snapped a chocolate bar in two and handed half to Molly.

'Hurray for unhealthy food! You are a life-saver. Honestly, the only time I feel better is when I eat something I shouldn't.' A piece of chocolate was exactly what Molly was craving. 'And what else could a girl want? Chocolate and fresh air in my lungs.'

'You do whatever it takes to get you through your pregnancy and if that means eating what you fancy, just go with it. We can enjoy many evening walks with a pram to get the weight off so don't worry about that.'

Molly pulled at her baggy T-shirt. 'I know I'm not a fashion icon but I'm already feeling ugly and frumpy, and look...' Molly blew out her cheeks causing Isla to burst into a fit of giggles.

'What are you doing?'

'Look how chubby my cheeks have gone already. My face is just looking round.'

'It's just your imagination!'

'It isn't. Dixie knew I was pregnant the second she laid eyes on me. How soon do you start buying all the baby paraphernalia?'

'With Angus I had a lot of hand-me-downs from Finn, and by all means, if you can make use of anything, please

256

do. The pram is still in excellent condition, but I do know that sometimes you want stuff that's new.'

'Honestly, thank you. Let me know what you have. Two boys, how do you cope?'

Isla went to open her mouth and immediately closed it again, but Molly had already noticed. 'What were you going to say?'

Isla took a breath. 'I was about to say, "the support of a good husband".' She rolled her eyes. 'But that really isn't what you wanted to hear. I'm sorry, I didn't mean to—'

'It's okay,' interrupted Molly, 'I have to get used to the fact I'm on my own, and I don't want people walking on eggshells around me. Let's head over to the meadow,' she suggested, wondering how she was going to cope on her own with no immediate family.

They took the path around the side of the vandalised fountain and headed towards the vast wildflower meadow that only last week had danced with colourful blooms. Now there wasn't a plant in sight. The vandals had churned up the ground and it reminded Molly of a desolate third world country.

'What do you know about Albie?' asked Molly, waving at Allie and Rory, who were turning over the soil with their spades at the far end of the park.

'Drew isn't a fan of his – and Drew usually keeps his opinions to himself,' said Isla.

'Why's that?' asked Molly.

'He can't quite put his finger on it but there have been rumours in the past about dodgy underhand business deals. The small garden centre on the edge of Glensheil was forced to close its doors when Birdvale bought the land by the roundabout. They were doing really well but it seems their hand was forced, somehow.' Isla gave Molly a knowing look. 'Now it might not have anything to do with him but—'

'But it's a hell of a coincidence,' chipped in Molly. 'What do you know about Cam's parents?'

'Not much – they split up when we were children and he spent a lot of time with Dixie and George. Like I've said before, I heard that Cam's mother met someone else later in life and emigrated to New Zealand, but as far as Cam's father is concerned, I have no idea.'

'It's strange, isn't it, to think that the people we're talking about are going to be grandparents to my child and I have no clue what they look like or who they even are.'

'Cam was always a decent, kind human being.'

'Cam's not kind in my case,' added a despondent Molly. 'He thinks I sleep around and am after money. What does that make me? A hussy!'

Isla burst out laughing. 'Give over! Sorry for laughing but I've not heard that word for years. Don't be daft, you are not a hussy! He'll come round; give him time. It must have been a huge shock.'

'He wouldn't talk about it. Just clammed up. "No

good for anyone," he said.' The conversation still played on Molly's mind, and she wondered what he'd meant when he'd said that.

'Give it a couple of days for the news to sink in then go and see him again. I have to say, Albie has come good donating all these plants and trees. I really wasn't expecting that. Surely he wanted something in return.'

'That's another story, for another day.' Molly cocked an eyebrow as they joined the gang at the bottom of the meadow.

'Intrigued,' replied Isla, leaning forward and kissing Allie on both cheeks. 'Well, look at you all glammed up!'

Allie looked down at her soiled T-shirt. Her hair was tied back in a messy ponytail and her make-up was streaked from the sweat on her face.

'Some of us have been working hard, you know, unlike some that have just arrived,' teased Allie, wiping her sweaty hands down the sides of her shorts.

'And some of us are dying for a cold beer,' added Rory. 'Look how much soil we've turned over,' he said before pointing over towards to the duckpond. 'And Flynn and Julia have been having a ball out on the lake.'

There were two small rowing boats out on the pond. Julia and Flynn in one, Eleni and Jack in the other, both pairs of children holding large fishing nets. Julia looked wet through and she was shouting at Flynn to stop rocking the boat but by the look of mischief on his face he wasn't going to stop any time soon.

'I think the boys are having more fun than the girls by the looks on those faces,' said Molly, grinning. 'But it looks like they've cleared most of the rubbish out that the vandals tipped in.'

'They've been at it for a couple of hours, but they've done a brilliant job,' declared Rory, looking over towards the refreshment tent that Rona and Felicity were manning. 'Does anyone want a drink?'

'I'm thirsty. I'll come with you,' said Allie, handing her spade to Isla.

Watching Rory and Allie trundle off, Molly grabbed Rory's spade off the floor. 'As all this was my idea I should at least help a little,' she said, smiling and taking a discreet look around the park. She knew exactly who she was looking for, but Cam was nowhere to be seen.

'But don't you overdo it. Some of this soil is rock-hard due to the heat and I don't want you pulling a muscle or anything.' Isla looked at Molly's stomach.

'Don't worry, I'm not going to do anything daft.' Molly stood on the spade with one foot then two feet, but even with all of her weight it would just not cut through the soil. Wiping the sweat from her brow she began to jump up and down.

'Stop that! You're going to do yourself an injury,' whispered Isla under her breath. 'The last thing we need is Dr Sanders checking you over and a trip to the hospital.' Isla took hold of the spade handle and gave

Molly a look that meant 'get both feet back on the ground now'.

'And I second that.' Cam was standing directly behind Molly.

A surprised Molly spun round. Cam had appeared from nowhere. She cast a discreet but appreciative eye from his Timberland boots, past his multi-pocketed combat shorts, and up to the olive T-shirt that stretched across his broad chest. She was struck by how the earthy tones of his clothes suited his tanned skin, by his stubble glistening in the sunlight, and by his hazel eyes.

'For a moment there, it sounded like you cared.' Molly could have kicked herself, and cringed at the sound of her own words.

They stared straight at each other, leaving Isla standing at the side not quite knowing what to do.

'Lovely to see you again, Cam,' said Isla. 'I'll give you both a moment, shall I? Yes … yes, that seems like the best thing to do.' Isla pointed over towards the refreshment tent. 'I'll go and get us a drink.' She took a step back, but no one said a word. Isla quickly walked away, fully noting the tension in the air.

'Sorry, I didn't mean for that to sound so abrupt.' Molly did the decent thing and quickly apologised.

'It's okay. I probably deserved it,' admitted Cam. Neither averted their gaze and Molly's heart was beating nineteen to the dozen.

She was unsure what to do or say because, with the

whole village milling around, the last thing she needed was to draw unnecessary attention to them both. She lowered her voice and took a swift glance around her before turning back towards Cam. 'Whatever you may think, we do need to talk.' She took a breath. 'I'm telling you the truth, and yes, I get it, you don't know me from Adam, but this baby is yours. If you don't want anything to do with the baby or me, I can deal with that as long as I know that's the case and I can just get on with it – but I'm not having you dipping in and out of the baby's life if you happen to change your mind.'

Molly noticed that Cam was looking uncomfortable and staring at the ground.

'I just... I just can't...' He clammed up and raked a hand through his hair.

'You can't what?' chipped in Molly, frustrated, but kept her tone soft. 'Look, I know this is a shock and you probably wish you'd never set eyes on me again—'

'I don't wish that at all,' interrupted Cam, his hazel eyes boring into hers.

Molly held both her hands out, palms facing upwards. 'I don't know what to do or say here. I can feel this attraction between us. Surely you can feel it too?'

Cam didn't deny or confirm.

'Whether you believe me or not, this situation isn't going to go away and soon people are going to start to ask questions, not because they are nosey but out of curiosity because I do not have a partner, Cam. Do I lie? What do I say? I've no idea.'

Cam was giving out mixed messages. Molly just didn't understand any of it.

'Please just talk to me. Tell me what you're thinking.' She wanted answers even if it wasn't what she wanted to hear.

'It's not that easy. My life isn't that easy,' replied Cam. His mouth set in a hard line. 'I'm sorry, Molly, maybe I got carried away – you and I that night. You deserve better than what I can give you at this moment.'

Molly had thought about this man for three whole months, and now her heart was shattering like a glass being dropped onto the floor, pieces scattering far and wide.

'I don't believe you. You didn't get carried away and I didn't either. We both wanted it. Look at the way you look at me. I don't know why you're saying this… This thing between us is real, I can feel it. And isn't it up to me to decide whether I deserve what you can give me? Talk to me, let me understand,' pleaded Molly, noticing Cam suddenly looked distraught. His head hung low, his eyebrows were pinched together, and the pained expression on his face was a clear sign there was a lot more going on for him.

'This is just all too much for me right now,' he replied, not giving anything else away.

'This situation isn't going to go away. So am I right to

assume you don't want anything to do with me or the baby?' Molly knew she was pushing it but she wanted some sort of reaction; she didn't like not knowing. 'I heard you talking to Albie, in the corridor outside his office.'

Cam looked puzzled and shook his head, 'I don't know what you—'

'You said you never wanted to hear the word "baby" again in this lifetime, or something like that,' Molly replied, not remembering his exact words.

Cam's eyes widened, and he held up his hands. 'I really can't talk about this.' He turned and began to walk away.

'Cam, please wait. Don't walk away. Let me help you… Talk to me!' Molly was amazed to see Cam stop.

He turned back towards her. 'Molly, all of this, you are doing a fantastic job for Grandma. She will be amazed. Thank you.' And with that he carried on walking.

Molly let out a long sigh. 'Well, I suppose that's something. At least I got a thank-you,' she murmured under her breath. She was still puzzled by the whole situation. How was she going to get Cam to open up? She didn't know how to break down his barrier and get him talking. What really was going on there, and why didn't he want to hear the word 'baby' ever again? Molly was confused and none the wiser.

She walked back towards Isla with a sense that

nothing had been resolved and she really didn't know what to do next. Cam was guarding his private life keenly, which of course was his prerogative, but in this small community of Heartcross at some point soon her pregnancy was going to attract attention.

She caught up with Isla, who gave her a sympathetic look. 'How was the chat?'

Molly shrugged. 'At least we weren't shouting and screaming at each other but there's more to his denial that he's letting on.' She cast a glance in his direction. 'He said, that night he might have got carried away.' She heard her own voice falter and Isla touched her arm. 'I just feel useless. He won't talk to me and I feel like I'm in limbo,' admitted Molly.

'It's just a waiting game. Don't pressurise him. Let him come to you. You've given him the facts; he needs a little time to mull it over. Whatever is going on in his life is having a huge impact on his emotional state.' Isla was once again the voice of reason.

'I couldn't even persuade him to open up.'

'You will. Look at all this.' Isla swooped her arms wide open. 'You have a way of persuading people to go the extra mile and then some – you instigated all this. You are a kind and caring person, with more good qualities to boot. Cam will see that and at some point will open up. Just be there for him and I'll be there for you.'

'Thank God I have you,' replied Molly, giving her

friend a heart-warming smile then linking her arm through Isla's.

'It'll work out, just keep the faith,' reassured Isla.

Molly took a fleeting glance over her shoulder. Cam was chatting away to Rory, who'd returned, and they were both in sync as they turned over the soil.

'And, for the record, he didn't want you digging or jumping up and down on that spade... Baby steps – pardon the pun,' Isla added with a smile.

Of course Molly knew he would need time to mull over the news of the baby, but what next? What did she do now?

'I just don't like any type of uncertainty. You know me, I'm a workaholic and really organised. I don't like it when...' Molly flapped a hand in front of her eyes. 'I suppose I don't like it when I don't know what's going to happen. The not knowing makes me anxious.' She pushed back the tears that were blinding her eyes. She knew she hadn't planned for this to happen but now she was thinking it would have been so much easier with a sperm donor – at least then there would have been no feelings involved.

'Hold it together. We don't want anyone noticing you're upset, because it's not for very long that you can keep any kind of secret around here.'

'I know, I know.' Molly took a deep breath. 'Looking like this'—she pulled at her T-shirt—'people are going to realise, and then I will be the talk of the town when they try and work out who the father is.' Deep down Molly was worried; she thought back to the time in her childhood when she'd arrived at her new home with her adoptive parents. There had been many visitors to the house in the first few months – the authorities, social workers and her new parents' friends. Often Molly had heard whisperings behind closed doors, and she didn't like being the centre of attention for all the wrong reasons.

'It's no one's business,' reassured Isla.

'But that doesn't stop people talking, does it?'

'Let them talk. Your friends are here for you. Come on, this isn't like you. You're the one who had us all about to interview sperm donors. How would you have explained that one away?'

Molly's mouth creased in a small smile.

'That's better. Keep smiling. A happy mother means a happy baby.'

But Molly didn't feel happy. She wanted to talk to Cam; she wanted to know what was going on with him. All she wanted was a discussion with everything out in the open – surely that wasn't too much to ask? But she knew that couldn't happen here at the park.

'You will make a fantastic mother no matter what.'

Molly knew that Isla was right; she would embrace this situation. Under her breath she gave herself a pep-talk. No matter what happened she knew she was going to be okay.

'Come on, let's go and help shift the rubbish that they've bagged up from the lake and dispose of it in the skip. I feel I've done nothing yet to help.' Her thoughts about Cam were falling all over each other and she just wished she wasn't attracted to him the way she was, as that would make the whole situation a lot easier.

'Can we wave at Drew on the way? He's over in the diggers. I've had to tell him, you know, not because I can't keep a secret but just so he knew why he had to keep looking after the children at the drop of a hat.'

'That's absolutely fine.' Molly never wanted to put Isla in a situation where her husband was questioning why she kept disappearing. She had to face facts: everyone was going to find out sooner or later. Picking up a couple of lemonades from the refreshment tent as they passed, Molly followed Isla towards the diggers. Both Fergus and Drew had their children balancing on their laps, wearing yellow safety helmets that kept falling down over their eyes. They stood and watched as the digger arms dug underneath the tree stump and lifted it up in one swoop. Finn and Angus gave Isla a thumbs-up while Esme gave a cheeky smile. The kids were having the time of their lives.

'Look at them, both spending quality time with their fathers.'

Isla slipped her arm around Molly's shoulder and gave it a quick squeeze. 'And your child will have you to spend all the quality time with.'

'I know, but what if my child misses out on that father figure in their life?' One glance in Cam's direction confirmed her fears were valid, as his eyes met hers and he looked away once more. Molly thought back to her life before her adoptive parents. She could only remember small snippets – her father drinking heavily, her mother crying. There was lots of shouting, doors slamming, and Molly used to lie on the mattress in the corner of the living room with the duvet pulled over her head. She never remembered any quality time with them.

'He can't really believe I was after money.' Molly was still turning everything over in her mind.

'I'm sure that was said in the heat of the moment, the shock talking,' replied Isla.

The thought of money hadn't even crossed Molly's mind and she was disappointed that anyone would think she was after any sort of maintenance. Financially, she could manage perfectly by herself.

'Do you ever think he gave me a second thought after our night together?' Molly knew Isla wasn't a mind-reader and couldn't possibly know the answer.

'I'm sure he did,' replied Isla.

Knowing she'd never had a one-night stand before, Molly didn't class that night as anything sordid. In her eyes it had been perfect, a mutual emotional and physical attraction between two people. Molly could quite honestly say that since that night Cam had been in her thoughts every day. She'd imagined them as a proper couple, going on dates, romantic weekends, but that seemed so far out of reach now. Why couldn't everything just be simple?

'But in my opinion, for what it's worth,' continued Isla, 'let Cam come to you now. He's turned up here in Heartcross, renting Dixie's cottage. What has happened to his job and his wife? If Dixie's right and he's going through a separation, his emotions will be all over the place too. He won't know if he's coming or—'

'I saw him with his wife today, driving over the bridge towards Heartcross,' Molly interrupted.

'But that doesn't mean they're back together; they may just have a lot to sort out.'

'Isla, I've got this horrible anxious feeling swirling in the pit of my stomach and it just won't go away.'

'Please just try and relax and keep those stress levels to a bare minimum. It's easier said than done, I know.'

'If he doesn't want anything to do with me or the baby, how's that going to work? Do we ignore each other in the street, the pub…? I want us to be friends.' But was that doable? Molly knew her feelings for Cam ran a lot deeper than just friendship.

'Now you're worrying about something that we don't know yet.'

'I know it sounds daft, even cringeworthy at my age, but I've thought about this man for months. That night I believed in love at first sight.' Molly's face softened as she thought about the way he'd made her feel that night – like the only girl in the world.

'Come on, let's head down to the pond,' suggested Isla, saluting Drew and the kids before linking arms with Molly. 'Try and put it out of your mind for now.'

As they ambled towards the pond under the shady canopy of the trees, they said good evening to the villagers that were hard at work. Cam was still in Molly's line of vision. She watched him rub his suntanned face whilst he was chatting away to Rory, but he didn't look over.

Down at the pond Flynn and Julia were having the time of their lives, gently shoving each other playfully and throwing their heads back laughing. Molly felt a twinge of jealousy. That was exactly what she wanted in her life: laughter, the closeness of sharing a moment with someone special.

Flynn beckoned over to Molly. 'I think we're done. Can you spot any rubbish we've missed?'

They both took a swift glance over the water, but they had done a sterling job – every inch of the pond had been cleared of litter. Molly cupped her hands to her mouth. 'Not that we can see.'

Eleni and Jack gave her the thumbs-up and began rowing towards the tiny shallow area with the small wooden jetty. As they reached the edge of the pond, Flynn steadied the boat while Julia jumped out with a helping hand from Isla. As soon as she was on solid ground, Flynn followed suit and pulled the small rowing boat from the water before helping Eleni and Jack safely out of their boat.

Molly and Isla gave them a round of applause. 'It looks amazing!' exclaimed Molly. 'I've never seen it looking so clean. You've done wonders.'

'It looks more amazing than me,' said Julia, laughing though she was soaked to the skin. 'This one doesn't know the meaning of keeping the water in the pond. I think I'm wearing most of it and I absolutely stink.' She sniffed her T-shirt and wrinkled her nose. 'But look at all that.'

In front of them was a huge pile of rubbish ranging from Coke cans to a single boot, from cereal packets to paint tins. 'Those ducks look happy too.' Molly pointed to a proud mottled mallard that had slipped into the water followed by four ducklings.

'To be honest, I've had a great evening,' said Eleni. 'My sides are actually aching from laughing.' She slipped her arm through Jack's and he pressed a swift kiss to the tip of her nose. 'But we need to shift all this rubbish from the bank.'

'You don't need to do anything – you've all worked so hard. We'll get this shifted,' insisted Molly, reaching for a wheelbarrow that had been left nearby.

'Agreed,' added Isla. 'You lot go and get cleaned up and grab a drink. Meredith has even brought cold beers from the pub – they're in the coolers over at the tent.'

'That's me out of here,' said Flynn with a grin, 'but only if you're sure.'

Molly flapped her hand and as all four of them walked off chatting, she and Molly each pulled out a pair of rubber gloves from her bag.

'I'm quite happy to hide out here. I don't feel in the mood for mingling and making conversation,' Molly said as she began to scoop up the soggy findings from the river and drop them into the barrow.

'We can stay out of the way for as long as you want, but look at all those people – everyone busying themselves to get this park up and running. You did that.'

'I did, didn't I?' said Molly, reaching down. As she stood up quickly she felt light-headed and grabbed onto the side of the wheelbarrow. This was exactly how she'd felt the morning she'd fainted at Cam's.

Isla was merrily chatting away. 'Let me tell you about Martha – she's a new man in her life.'

'How did she meet him?' asked Molly, taking some deep breaths and thinking that Isla's grandma was having more luck than she was on the romance front.

'Tinder – she swears by it,' chuckled Isla. 'My grandma is definitely living her best life.'

Molly thought about Dixie, confined within the same four walls for most of the day in the care home, while Martha was out gallivanting most days, living life to the max. Surely there couldn't be much difference in their ages.

Isla continued, 'He's retired, obviously, was a successful businessman and, according to Gran, has numerous classic cars, a fantastic property on the water's edge and a cellar full of champagne. She's swaggering about dressed up to the nines with more energy than me, and being wined and dined in every five-star restaurant within fifty miles of here. The poor man doesn't know what he's letting himself in for. They broke the mould making my grandma. I'm only jealous.' Isla was still jabbering on. 'What with Drew's long days at the farm and his early-morning milking sessions, he's fit for nothing. Between you and me, I suggested another baby, but he's having none of it. I'm surrounded by boys and would love a little girl but I suppose there are no guarantees.'

Molly didn't answer. She couldn't focus, her eyesight was blurred, and she felt like she'd been whirled on a roundabout so fast that the whole park seemed to be spinning.

'Are you okay?' asked Isla, finally realising that Molly had stopped working.

'Isla, I feel faint and dizzy. I just want to feel normal again.' Molly blinked hard, trying to focus as she pulled off her rubber gloves then squeezed her eyes shut.

'It'll get better. The first trimester is hard going. But Molly, I want you to sit on the floor so you don't fall over. Don't panic. Take deep breaths. This is quite normal.'

'It doesn't feel normal. This feels far from normal. It's like my whole body has been taken over.'

Isla handed her a bottle of water from her bag. 'It has. Drink this; you have to keep those fluids up.'

Molly did as she was told and sipped the water.

'Look, don't panic. Dr Sanders is here somewhere – I saw him in the meadow earlier. Are you okay to wait there? I'll be as quick as I can and then between us we can get you home.'

'Yes, but please be discreet, I don't want to bring any attention to myself.'

Isla nodded her understanding and began to dash towards the meadow whilst Molly willed them to hurry up.

Apparently the gel they were about to put on Molly's stomach would be cold.

Standing next to her bed was Dr Sanders and nurse practitioner Mel, who belonged to the midwifery team over in Glensheil. Isla was sitting next to Molly's bed in a grey plush chair holding a glass of water whilst Mel took Molly's blood pressure then perched on the end of her bed.

'Okay, you've fainted again and just like the other day, Molly, when Dr Sanders took your blood pressure, it's still very low and this is what's causing your dizziness. There are so many hormones floating in your bloodstream at the moment, they can dilate your blood vessels and that's a cause of low blood pressure.'

Molly nodded and listened while she noticed Dr Sanders setting up some sort of equipment on the small table next to her bed.

'Molly, I need to ask you, have you any blood loss?'

Molly sounded stricken. 'I don't think so. Shall I go and check?'

'When was the last time you went to the toilet?'

'Just before I climbed into bed, but I didn't see anything.'

Isla squeezed her hand. 'When we get you through this first trimester, it will be plain sailing, you'll see.'

Molly was tearful. This was the unknown and she just wanted to feel well again. 'I really hope so.'

Dr Sanders turned towards Molly. 'We've got a Doppler here, and we will be able to listen to the baby's heartbeat just to make sure that everything is how it should be.'

Molly nodded; she'd never felt so scared in her life. Isla squeezed her hand and gave her a reassuring smile.

A few months ago, Molly would never have thought she'd be in this position. It felt so surreal. She watched as Dr Sanders sanitised his hands and asked Molly to roll her T-shirt up before he squirted the cold gel on to her stomach. Molly held her breath as Dr Sanders placed the

Doppler on the gel and began to move it around. 'Just try and relax,' he soothed.

'I can't hear anything.' Fear rose inside Molly and she tried to calm her beating heart.

'It can just take a moment.' Dr Sanders pressed a little more firmly then Molly felt Isla touch her shoulder.

'That sound gets me every time.' Isla had become emotional and flapped a hand in front of her eyes as they welled up with tears. 'And it's not even my baby.'

'That sound is your baby's heartbeat,' confirmed Dr Sanders, 'and it sounds very normal to me.' He gave Molly a reassuring smile.

No words could describe that magical moment when Molly realised that the sound like a train setting off down the tracks was her baby's heartbeat. Emotion engulfed her whole body and the tears flooded down her cheeks.

'That's my baby?'

'It sure is,' confirmed Mel. 'But we're taking no chances – your blood pressure is low, and we need you to rest, get your fluids up, and try and get this dizziness under control. If that means taking a week off, then that's what we need you to do. If you don't get any better we may have to admit you and put you on a drip to get fluids inside you.'

Molly was not going to argue. She had a fantastic team over at the surgery who would hold the fort until she returned, but it was true that while she was feeling like this she couldn't possibly operate at the surgery or stand on her feet for long periods of time. 'Does this mean I have to lie in bed?'

'You are going to do whatever helps you get through this. Eat often in small amounts and drink plenty of water. If you want to go for a walk, and you're feeling well enough, then take a short walk. If you need to lie down, lie down. You have to listen to your body.'

'I will, I promise.' Even though Molly was feeling exhausted and dizzy she couldn't stop smiling. The second she had heard her baby's heartbeat had changed everything for her.

She dropped her chin to her chest and placed both her hands on her heart before swiping at the happy tears rolling down her cheeks. She pressed her lips together to try and contain her emotion then shook her head in disbelief. 'I've actually got a life growing inside me, haven't I?' She was amazed. This was real – wonderful in fact – and she couldn't quite believe it. She had been so wrapped up in telling Cam, she'd forgotten to enjoy every moment, even when she was feeling poorly. It hit home that she was going to be a mum, and this was the most exciting thing that had ever happened to her. She had to believe and trust that everything was going to be okay, because she was no longer just Molly McKendrick, veterinary surgeon. She was Molly McKendrick, mum, which was the most important job in the world.

Chapter Sixteen

The next morning Molly opened her eyes after a good night's sleep and glanced over at the clock. Usually, at this time, she would be rushing to get herself ready for the dog behavioural class then straight over to the surgery, but thankfully her staff were taking care of everything for the next week. She wondered what the day would bring. So far the nausea was bearable and she hoped it stayed like that all day. Darling was curled up on Dixie's blanket right next to her and Molly realised she was beginning to become attached to the little pain in the arse. She gave Darling a quick ruffle of the head and the dog stood up, gave herself a little shake, circled around numerous times, and finally settled next to Molly's stomach.

'There's a baby growing in there,' whispered Molly. 'There's going to be a new member of the fam.' She smiled as Darling laid her head across Molly's stomach and looked up at her with wide eyes that then started to slowly close. 'Five more minutes won't hurt, will it?' Molly snuggled down under the duvet, her thoughts turning towards Dixie. The more she thought about it, the more things just didn't seem to add up. When she'd first met Birdie, she'd suggested that her mother was frail and couldn't cope with looking after herself in Bumblebee Cottage with Darling in tow, but Molly didn't get that impression at all. Dixie had her wits about her, her humour was sharp, her memory better than Molly's, and she had no trouble getting dressed or making herself a cup of tea. Maybe she was overthinking it but Molly had a gut feeling everything wasn't all that it seemed. With no firm plans and little on her to-do list today, she decided she'd go and visit Dixie and challenge her to a game of cards.

Thirty minutes later, Molly slowly rose out of bed just like the doctor instructed. So far so good – she was still standing on two feet and hadn't fainted just yet. She took a hesitant look in the mirror. Her hair was all over the place and yesterday's make-up was halfway down her cheeks but as soon as she'd managed some breakfast she climbed into the shower to freshen up. But then she had to face the same dilemma as yesterday: she didn't have much to wear that felt comfortable and at the moment she was all about the comfort. She scraped her hair back in a ponytail and pulled on the bobbly black jogging bottoms that looked as flea-bitten as the T-shirt she'd gone to bed in. She wouldn't be giving Kim Kardashian a run for her money in the glamour stakes. It really wasn't a good look.

Pulling back the curtains and pushing open the window she smiled; the blast of fresh air was a welcome breeze. The street below was already busy with people walking their dogs before temperatures hit a high, and cyclists enjoying the start of the day whilst people travelled to work. 'I wonder what today will bring,' murmured Molly, taking a sip of water from the glass on her bedside table before being alerted to the sound of a car screeching up the road.

Her smile evaporated instantly. Cam's car had just pulled up outside the house. She furrowed her brow and squinted. Cam looked visibly upset – shattered, even. What was going on? Her heart began to race. Maybe he was here to talk? The way he was driving the car seemed a little over-dramatic.

As she carried on watching from the window, a flustered-looking Cam jumped out of the car. She really hoped he wasn't here for any sort of confrontation, especially at this time in the morning. He must have sensed someone was watching him and looked up towards the bedroom. Within seconds her doorbell was ringing non-stop.

As Molly hurried downstairs, she reflected that the one value her mum had championed was to always keep an open mind and give people a second chance. She was going to do that with Cam. As usual, Darling hurtled down the stairs faster than Usain Bolt, barking at the top of her voice. Molly's hope for a peaceful morning had already shattered into little pieces.

At the bottom of the stairs Molly grabbed Darling by her collar, herded the unhappy dog into the living room, and shut the door firmly behind her.

Fumbling with the key, Molly opened the door to find a stricken-looking Cam standing in front of her. 'Whatever is the matter? Are you okay?' she asked, softly but engulfed in worry. She opened the door wide to invite him in.

'Molly, I need your help. I'm so sorry for turning up here, I just didn't know what to do.'

'My help?' Molly was perplexed. 'What's wrong?'

Cam looked pale, and there was a sudden urgency to his voice. 'It's Maverick. He's been unsteady on his legs since last night, and wasn't himself at all yesterday. His breathing is slow.' Cam was talking fast as he started backing towards the car. 'I've brought him straight here. I rang the surgery but you weren't there. I really didn't know what else to do. Please can you have a look at him?'

'Of course I can.' Immediately putting their differences aside, Molly took control, slipped her feet into her shoes at the foot of the stairs and followed Cam quickly towards his car.

'Thank you, thank you,' Cam was muttering. His voice wavered and he was on the verge of tears. 'He can't leave me yet; he's the only constant thing in my life.'

'I'll do my best,' replied Molly softly, noticing that Cam was shaking as he opened the boot of his car. She touched his arm and kept her voice calm. 'I'm going to go back inside and put Darling in the garden so she doesn't disturb us, then I'll move the coffee table. I need you to carry Maverick inside for me and lay him down on the floor in front of the fire facing the door. Got that?'

Cam nodded as Molly quickly disappeared back inside the house. Within minutes she was back by Cam's side. He was beside himself. 'I feel like I can't breathe,' he said, undoing his top button. 'He's not just a dog.' Cam looked lovingly at Maverick. 'He's my best friend.'

'Has his behaviour changed in the last few weeks?' asked Molly softly.

Cam nodded. 'He's been restless, he looks sad, lacks interest in most things, and he's incontinent.'

'Okay, talk to him, Cam – he needs to hear your voice. He's a good age for a dog,' she soothed.

'I know but it doesn't make it any easier. Why can't they just live for ever?'

As Molly set to work on the primary survey check, she shone a torch into Maverick's eyes to assess responses and pupil size. She knew by experience that Maverick only had moments left to live. He'd lost control of his tongue, there was severe muscle twitching, and his breathing was becoming shallow. Molly stroked his fur, the tears welling up in her eyes. As much as she loved being a vet, this was the hardest part of her job, and seeing Cam so utterly devastated made it ten times worse.

'I love you, buddy,' said Cam. 'I shouldn't be sad. We've been on so many adventures together. I just wish you were on this next journey with me.' Cam crumbled, in turmoil, the tears running down his face. Molly knew he was about to lose his best friend.

She turned towards him. 'I'm so sorry, Cam, he's gone.'

Cam lowered himself to the floor and hugged his best buddy. 'I knew this time would come but it doesn't make it any easier.' He kissed Maverick on the head and continued to stroke him.

It was breaking Molly's heart seeing him so sad. Cam turned towards her, unable to speak. His face was pallid, and tears slipped freely down his cheeks. He exhaled and kissed Maverick one more time.

Molly swallowed a lump in her throat.

'I knew it was his time but I just hoped there was something we could do. A magic potion to turn back time.'

'I wish there was something I could do too. I'm so sorry, Cam.'

They stared at each for a second before Molly opened her arms and Cam fell into them. She hugged him tight.

Chapter Seventeen

With his hands wrapped around a hot mug of tea, Cam sat on Molly's sofa staring into space. She'd organised the animal ambulance to come from the surgery and take Maverick away. Her cheeks stained with tears, she sat next to Cam on the settee in silence. Darling was curled up on Dixie's blanket on the chair by the window, thankfully fast asleep.

'Is there anything I can do for you?' asked Molly softly, breaking the silence.

Still in a state of shock, Cam placed his mug on the table next to him, picked up Maverick's collar and clutched it tightly. 'I just don't know what to do now. I feel so empty.' He could barely speak. 'This was a feeling I never ever wanted to feel again.'

'Again?' probed Molly gently. 'Have you lost another animal?'

Cam shook his head. His watery hazel eyes glanced down towards Molly's stomach.

Silence hung in the air.

'You've lost a child?' The words were out of Molly's mouth before she could stop them and she knew by the look on Cam's face there was some sort of truth in them. 'Cam, I'm so sorry. I don't know what to say.'

'Empty is how I feel, like a part of me has been ripped away.' Cam was too upset to say anything else.

Molly could clearly detect the pain in Cam's voice. She reached over and placed her hands over his. He looked up. 'Thank you for helping me today and just being there. It means a lot.'

'It's okay, you don't need to thank me.'

She watched as he stood up. 'I just want to go home, if that's okay?'

Molly nodded. 'Of course, but if you need anything, you call me.'

They walked towards the hallway. Cam opened the front door then for a second he turned back to face Molly and hovered. He leant forward and kissed her gently on the cheek. 'Thank you again.'

With a hand on her cheek, Molly watched him walk down the path and climb inside his car. As he started the engine, he glanced over and gave Molly a slight smile and a wave. She stood on the doorstep watching the car drive towards the end of the road. As soon as it was out of sight she stepped back inside and shut the front door.

Isla had been right – let him come to you – and that's what he'd done. The second he needed help he'd thought of her. Cam was beginning to open up and Molly didn't want to bombard him with questions in case he clammed up again. From the tiny snippet of information that Cam had shared, she couldn't imagine the trauma he'd been through. Here she was, excited about the new life growing inside her, and she'd never imagined that Cam had suffered such devastation. She knew it must have been hard for Cam to share that information, and realised that this was a tiny breakthrough in understanding what was going on for him.

———————

Hours later, Molly took a short stroll through the town and found herself walking through the entrance of the care home to visit Dixie. She couldn't wait to see the look on Dixie's face when she told her that her birthday party could go ahead as planned. Pressing the buzzer of the intercom, Molly waited until the door opened automatically, and she was greeted by Jan at the reception desk.

'I've come to visit Dixie. She's not expecting me,' said Molly, smiling as she signed the visitors log.

'I know we've met before but are you a family member or a friend?' asked Jan, smiling back.

Molly was just about to say 'a friend' when she

realised she was going to be some sort of family – it was just that Dixie didn't know that yet. 'Family,' she said, thinking about her baby.

'Well, I'm glad Dixie has got a visitor. She's been a little subdued in the last forty-eight hours and there was an incident in the night. We found her distressed, trying to escape. She thinks she's been tricked somehow into coming in here.'

Molly knew she was overstepping the mark but said, 'And what is your professional opinion on that? Surely there is paperwork, assessments and so on, by professional bodies outlining any health problems and recommendations.'

'The thing is, I've gone through the whole of the filing cabinet today with a fine-tooth comb and I can't seem to find Dixie's file. It seems to have been mislaid,' admitted Jan. 'I'm requesting copies today. I have mentioned it to Birdie, her daughter.'

Molly could tell by the tone of Jan's voice that she was concerned.

'And hopefully you can put a smile on Dixie's face,' added Jan.

'I'll see what I can do,' replied Molly, walking towards the TV room. She found Dixie sitting all by herself looking sad, but the second she looked up and saw Molly, a smile came to her face.

'Are you okay, Dixie? You look a little pensive,' asked

Molly pulling up a chair. 'I thought you'd be whupping someone's backside at a game of cards.'

'Thank God you're here, a normal person to talk to.' Dixie's voice was low and she kept looking towards the door.

'Has something happened?' asked Molly, touching Dixie's knee gently.

Dixie had a fixed look of concentration on her face, then, with a swift look towards the door, she said, 'I'm not entirely sure.'

'Do you want to tell me or shall I go and get Jan?' asked Molly, copying Dixie and keeping her voice low.

'No! Don't get anyone,' exclaimed Dixie immediately. 'Because I have no idea who I can trust.'

'You can trust me, Dixie. I promise whatever you tell me I won't breathe a word. I have no one to tell except this little one.' She patted her stomach. 'She won't tell anyone.'

'She? It's a he, mark my words,' announced Dixie, like she had some sort of superpower. 'But here's the thing. Apparently I'm in trouble.' Dixie's voice wavered, 'And I don't remember.'

'Who said you're in trouble?' asked Molly, noticing that Dixie was becoming visibly upset.

'Birdie. She said I hurt her, and I just don't remember. She showed me the bruise on her arm and said I had hit her in a temper.'

Molly was taken back. She was aware Birdie had told her that Dixie had begun to lash out but Molly had only ever seen evidence of a gentle, kind, loving woman. 'And why would you hit her?'

There was a long pause and Dixie shrugged. 'I've no idea. I don't remember even having cross words with her but she's telling me that I lost my temper and I lashed out. I've tried to remember but I just can't and then she's telling me I'm losing my memory, that's why I'm in here, so maybe I am? But I don't think I am. She's driving me mad. I think it's all a plan but no one will listen to me or help me.' Dixie finally took a breath.

Molly held both of Dixie's hands. 'Has Birdie told you what the argument was about?' she asked curiously, trying to understand the situation.

'She said she's told me a hundred times what the argument was about and she's not going over it again, but I still can't remember.'

Molly blew out a breath. None of this was making any sense to her. 'Did anyone witness this argument?'

Once again Dixie shrugged. 'I don't know because I don't remember the argument, but I overheard her talking to Jan. She said she was coming back this afternoon as I have some papers to sign.'

'What papers?' asked Molly.

'I have no idea, but Molly, I've got this uneasy feeling in my stomach and I don't like it. I just don't know what to do about any of it.'

Molly didn't like it either and talking to Dixie she could see she was genuinely upset.

'I don't think I'm forgetful'—Dixie gave a deep, heavy sigh—'but maybe I am, maybe I did hurt her... I just don't know.'

Molly had experience of dementia. Her grandma had developed the devastating disease and she'd spent a lot of time reading people's blogs in similar situations and absorbed all the information available to her. Dixie's behaviour was nothing like her own grandmother's and even though Molly knew the disease developed at different speeds and in different ways, she felt Dixie was in full control of her senses.

'What did you do yesterday?' asked Molly.

'Groundhog Day. I ate breakfast, sat in the garden, played cards, then had my lunch. Then last night I tried to escape but all the doors are locked and now they think I'm a troublemaker.'

'Can you remember what you had for your lunch?' quizzed Molly.

'Of course, I can – cheap rubber ham sandwiches on limp bread. The food isn't up to much in here. You can't beat a ham sandwich like the one from Bonnie's teashop. Now that's proper ham sourced from Foxglove Farm. Rona makes the best sandwich – granary bread, iceberg lettuce, ham, tomatoes smothered in piccalilli. Rona knows just how I like it. I'd do anything for a proper ham sandwich.'

The way Dixie had reeled off her day, there didn't seem any problem with her memory. Molly began to think, was something untoward going on here? What would Birdie gain by removing her from her home? It wasn't as though they lived together.

'And I miss my garden, my flowers and my bees. On days like this I'd spend the whole time in the garden and now all I have is a bench.'

'Dixie, when Birdie suggested you came to live here, did you object?'

'Of course I objected, that I do remember, but Birdie was having none of it. She says I lash out every time I see her and that I leave the oven on. Birdie says it's for my own good, otherwise I'm going to end up setting the cottage on fire. She said I left the open fire unattended and it's too dangerous, but I don't even remember lighting the fire. But there's where the problem lies; I just don't remember.'

Maybe Molly was overthinking it, but something wasn't sitting right with her. There were too many factors that just weren't adding up. Granted, she'd only known Dixie a short time, but in Molly's opinion Dixie wouldn't harm a fly.

'Dixie, are you selling Bumblebee Cottage?'

Dixie sat up straight. 'I will NEVER sell Bumblebee Cottage,' she replied emphatically. 'That place is my home and hopefully my grandson will live there on a permanent basis.'

'Cam?'

'Yes, I shouldn't say it and I know you shouldn't have your favourites but I do and he is mine.'

This conversation was ringing alarm bells loudly. If Dixie had no intention of selling the cottage why was Birdie showing a couple around it? What exactly was she up to? The question that was burning inside Molly was, was Birdie's assessment of Dixie true? Surely there would need to be medical reports. Molly's gut feeling was telling her there wasn't a scrap of truth in it. Had Birdie shipped Dixie off to the care home for her own gain? But what was that gain and what could Molly do about it? Maybe Birdie didn't want the responsibility of Dixie? Maybe Dixie had become too reliant on her?

'How often did you see Birdie when you were back at the cottage?' asked Molly, trying to figure out the truth.

Dixie puffed. 'Hardly ever – only when she remembered I was alive. And I'll tell you something for nothing – Darling didn't like her. I think that says a lot about a person if a dog doesn't like you.'

Molly agreed.

'Shall we have a drink? I'm such a bad host. There's fresh orange juice without the bits if you fancy a cold drink.'

'I can get it,' replied Molly.

'You will not.' Dixie was up on her feet and over at the drinks table within seconds. Molly admired how sprightly she was, and how easily she poured the drinks and carried them back towards her. As the sun gleamed through the open window Molly was mulling over the conversation from the last ten minutes when she suddenly sensed someone behind her.

Standing in the doorway was a rattled-looking Birdie carrying a file of papers. 'What are you two talking about? You look as thick as thieves.' She was staring straight at Molly. It was plain that Birdie didn't want her there.

Dixie let out a strangled sound and murmured, 'Don't leave me alone with her.' Molly saw how worried she looked.

'What did you say, Mother? I didn't quite catch it.' Birdie walked towards them and hovered by Dixie's chair.

'I said, how lovely to see you again. Since you've put me in this place you can't seem to stay away.'

'Mother, I visited you every single day at home. You've just forgotten and that's the reason why it's safer for you to be here. Mother's memory isn't what it used to be.' Birdie gave Molly a look then rolled her eyes. 'And I hear you've been causing quite a commotion in the night.'

Dixie opened her mouth to say something but thought better of it and remained silent.

'How are you?' asked Molly, trying to keep the conversation upbeat, knowing that the atmosphere had altered the second Birdie walked in.

'Busy,' came Birdie's short response. Birdie clearly wasn't looking impressed about Molly being there and in fact seemed quite hassled.

'That looks like a big stack of papers.' Molly nodded towards the file in Birdie's hand, knowing it was none of her business but unable to help herself.

'Probably more papers for me to sign,' replied Dixie, leaving Molly once again wondering what these papers were.

'Would you like to leave them so I can look over them with Dixie if you're … busy?' asked Molly, and waited for Birdie's reaction.

'Don't you worry, I wouldn't want to keep you,' replied Birdie, without elaborating any more. 'Are you just leaving? I'll take your chair.' She stared straight at Molly, who felt the hairs on the back of her neck stand up.

For some reason Birdie didn't want Molly there and she was doing her damnedest to make her feel uncomfortable, but Molly wasn't going to be intimidated by anyone and there was no way she was going anywhere. Birdie was showing a different side to her character from the one Molly had seen the morning she'd met her for the first time at Bumblebee Cottage. Then Birdie had been all sweetness and light, over-complimentary because she wanted rid of Darling. Molly stood her ground.

'Actually, I've only just arrived. Dixie and I are about

to play a game of cards,' replied Molly, bolder than she felt, considering Birdie was giving her a death stare. 'But do come and join us. We'd like that, wouldn't we, Dixie?'

Birdie was oblivious to the fact that Dixie had just winked at Molly, secretly chuffed that Molly wasn't going anywhere.

'Shall we move to the garden?' suggested Dixie, standing up. 'The outside table is free. I love a good game of cards.'

'Perfect plan.' Molly picked up her drink and began to follow her.

'There's no point me staying,' announced Birdie huffily. 'I may as well come back when you haven't got visitors.'

'Okay.' Dixie was not about argue. 'I'll see you tomorrow – again.'

Birdie paused, then walked away.

As soon as they were outside, Dixie asked, 'Has she gone?' pulling the pack of cards from her bra and making Molly laugh.

'I've never known anyone to keep a pack of cards in their bra. Yes, I think she's gone. Dixie, I don't mean to be nosy but what papers has Birdie had you signing?'

Dixie began to shuffle the cards then dealt them. 'She said legal stuff to do with my stay here, but she didn't give me time to read over the documents. She's always in a rush, that one.'

Molly was beginning to worry. What was Birdie up to? And why her sudden frostiness towards her? All she was doing was visiting Dixie.

Nine games later, Molly was well and truly whupped by Dixie. She was unbelievable; the cards fell in her favour every time. 'It's a good job I'm not a sore loser, isn't it?' mused Molly, looking at her watch. 'I'll have to go soon. Darling will be wanting some company and a walk.'

'Darling used to love going to Primrose Park with me. We would walk across the green, all the way up the coastal path, and loop round at the back of Starcross Manor and through the woodlands to the park. Do you know I'm not even allowed to go out for a walk without supervision? I can't be that forgetful – I always found my way home.'

'OMG! Dixie, I came here to tell you and it totally slipped my mind. The whole community has been out in force. We are all doing our very best to revamp Primrose Park in time for your birthday celebrations!'

Dixie's face looked like it was about to crumble. 'Oh Molly, you're such a darling. I can't believe this. Everyone is doing this for me?' Happy tears welled up in Dixie's eyes.

'Absolutely they are. All of the community has been working hard.'

Taking Molly by surprise, Dixie stood up and hugged

her tight. 'I can scatter my George's ashes on our birthday. This means the world to me. Thank you.'

'You can, and Dixie – I'm going to try and find out what's really going on here.'

'Thank you, thank you,' Dixie repeated. She held her hands to her heart, joyous at the garden party she was going to have.

Molly didn't want to leave Dixie but she was thankful that her spirits had lifted a little. They said goodbye and Molly headed out. Seeing Jan was on a call behind the reception desk, she waited for her to finish.

'I'm worried about Dixie,' Molly said. 'And I'm having difficulty understanding what's really going on. Have you noticed her becoming forgetful since she's been here?'

Jan shook her head. 'I've not been here long, just a few weeks. The last manager upped and left overnight with no warning. I'm reading over all the resident files to familiarise myself with each case, but in my opinion, and I've worked in a lot of homes, I would say Dixie has a better memory than I do. Off the record, I've just got off the phone from Peony Practice. Birdie didn't use the village doctor; they went private with the assessments to gain Dixie a place at this home. But I can't seem to find those reports – though I will.'

'Misfiled or missing? Are there any other residents' files missing?'

'I'm sorry, I can't comment on that – confidentiality and so on.'

Molly understood. 'Okay, but in Dixie's case do you think there is some sort of foul play going on here?'

'At this stage I wouldn't like to say, but I can promise you I will be locating those records and assessments today, come high or hell water.'

Molly nodded and gave Jan her business card. 'Please ring me if Dixie is upset. I'm only up the road.'

'I will,' confirmed Jan, taking the card from her.

Molly stepped outside into the sunshine. She couldn't believe how the promise of the day had turned into a morning of sadness and an afternoon of confusion. First the sad passing of Maverick and then the confusion surrounding Dixie's state of mind. Molly had taken on board everything that Dixie had told her. She knew the older generation needed to feel safe, surrounded by the people they knew, but Dixie *didn't* feel safe. Bumblebee Cottage was what Dixie knew. It was her security, and she had enjoyed her daily walk in Primrose Park with Darling. She had been keeping active and now she was confined to the care home.

Taking in the view along the river path, Molly had a gut feeling that things weren't quite right. She had no concrete evidence, but Birdie had looked and acted shiftily. What could Birdie's reason be for taking away Dixie's independence, and what could Molly do about it? The worry just wouldn't go away. Molly made the decision there and then to go and talk to Cam about what had just happened. Maybe he knew more about the situation and could put Molly's mind at rest. Even if he thought it was none of her business, at least she would have aired her concerns and tried for Dixie's sake.

Chapter Eighteen

For the rest of the day Molly had done exactly what the doctor had ordered and had taken it easy. She'd napped on the sofa, watched a movie, and prepared a chicken salad for tea. This afternoon all the plants should have been delivered to Primrose Park and the majority of the village was heading down there for a mass planting session.

Having a couple of hours to kill, she decided to drive over to the park and have a look at what Albie had delivered. On her return she would take the brave step of checking in on Cam to see how he was bearing up and if there was anything she could do. As soon as she picked up Darling's lead the dog was by her side, wagging her tail. 'Sit down,' commanded Molly and was amazed when Darling immediately sat.

'Good girl,' she praised, clipping on her lead and

giving her a treat. 'You are beginning to behave, aren't you?' Molly picked up her bag and car keys and headed towards the door. 'And let's hope the day ends on a high, eh?' She looked down at Darling waiting patiently by the front door with her front paws dancing.

As they walked up the path, Molly could hear her name being bellowed from down the street. She swung a glance to her left and there was Birdie striding towards her. Almost immediately Darling tugged at her lead and was up on her back legs barking in a frenzy. What the hell was going on? From the look on Birdie's face, Molly saw trouble ahead, but the last thing she needed was a confrontation in the middle of the street. Still, with Birdie fast approaching, she didn't have much choice except to paint a smile on her face and wait to see what this was all about.

'You are not a relative of my mother so why are you snooping about asking the care manager about my mother's wellbeing?' Birdie was straight to the point.

Molly's mouth fell open and for a moment she was rendered speechless.

Birdie's face looked like thunder.

'I'm not snooping, I asked an innocent question. Dixie is my friend and I care about her,' replied Molly, keeping her cool.

'Your friend? You barely know my mother. And why are you claiming to be a relative?'

'They just assumed I was.' Molly knew she'd told a

little white lie, but she didn't think this was the time or the place to announce that Dixie was Molly's unborn child's great-grandmother.

'Your visits upset her. I don't want you visiting my mother anymore. She's confused enough as it is.'

'Why would my visits upset Dixie?' Molly was standing her ground. 'We laugh and we play cards. Are you scared about what else she's telling me, Birdie?' Molly shortened Darling's lead. The dog was still barking at Birdie. 'And surely that's up to Dixie?' added Molly, holding eye contact with Birdie.

'My mother is getting confused, her memory is deteriorating, and she can be violent. You never know when she's going to lash out.'

'That really isn't the Dixie I've seen and I don't think she's even capable of lashing out.'

This discussion was getting heated.

'I am telling you to stay away and stop interfering in our family business.'

'Interfering? Your mum is a wonderful woman – why wouldn't you want to embrace that? Why are you keeping her cooped up, Birdie? In this weather she should be enjoying the garden at Bumblebee Cottage, enjoying walks with her friends. You've taken everything away from her and are isolating her, and yes – people tend to go downhill fast in that situation and give up. Dixie told me she has no intention of selling Bumblebee Cottage, but I saw you showing prospective buyers around.' Molly widened her eyes. 'What papers are you asking Dixie to sign?' She'd overstepped the mark, but she was fighting Dixie's corner.

'My family business is none of yours and I suggest you keep your nose out of it.'

'I can see I've touched a nerve about something.' Molly wasn't to be silenced. Birdie was rattled and Dixie's welfare was at stake here.

'And for God's sake, shut that dog up.' Birdie curled her lip and gave a scathing look towards Darling who hadn't stopped barking.

'Dogs are a good judge of character, Birdie. I don't think Darling likes you much.'

Birdie snorted in contempt then turned and stomped off down the street, leaving Molly only more determined to find out what the hell Birdie was up to.

A couple of minutes later Molly drove to Primrose Park and spotted Cam's car parked outside the entrance. She pulled up in front of it. She wasn't expecting him to be here, but this gave her the perfect opportunity to bump into him and check he was okay and maybe discuss the situation with Dixie.

Taking Darling out of her basket, Molly looked at her sternly. 'I need you to be on your best behaviour, no barking or snarling. Do you hear me?'

Darling gave a little whimper and nudged Molly's nose softly.

'Now don't go getting all cutesy on me.' Molly

lowered Darling to the ground and walked into the park. The bent wrought-iron gates had been removed and a pile of wood was stacked up where the bandstand was going to be rebuilt. As they approached the meadow, Molly stood and stared. The view took her breath away. 'Wow, someone's been busy,' she exclaimed.

Birdvale had dropped off all the trees and plants but to her astonishment they hadn't just been left by the entrance to the park as she'd imagined. They'd been arranged over the cultivated ground in the meadow, organised by height and colour. There was a smattering of clover, sunflowers, lavender, marigolds, and blazing stars amongst the flowers Molly recognised. The leaves glistened with water droplets in the sunshine and Molly saw that a water butt and watering cans had been left on a brand-new meandering walkway of stepping stones through the bursts of colour. She inhaled the sweet flower perfume. It all looked truly wonderful. Someone had been hard at work.

She and Darling took the path at the side of the meadow where rolls of turf were stacked up by the pond for the area of grass that had been scorched. She knew that a lot of water was going to be needed to keep all the plants and grass hydrated, and Drew up at the farm had come up with the perfect solution. They'd filled large milk churns with water from the river and were transporting them here on the back of the wagon. Jessica, the local primary school teacher, had arranged for each class to come and water the plants at different time slots during the day. Everyone was getting on board to restore Primrose Park and it would all be worth it to witness the joy on Dixie's face.

Cam was nowhere in sight. Maybe he wasn't here after all. Molly knew he would be in turmoil, trying to cope with the loss of Maverick. She began to walk down the path towards the fishing pond, where it would be cool and shady for Darling. Cam was very much on her mind. Perhaps his initial gruffness towards her had merely been because his personal life was in such a mess? Molly knew that the break-up of a marriage was supposed to be one of the most stressful things a person ever went through. And then, soon after, he'd had to come to terms with the news of her pregnancy.

Molly was aware they couldn't just pick up from where they'd left off the morning after their night together; it wasn't as simple as that. The only thing she could do was be there for him. He had a lot on his mind and she wasn't going to put any pressure on him. He needed to be a part of the baby's life because he wanted to, not because he felt an obligation. Molly knew all she could be was herself. If Cam wanted to be a part of their life, they could work on the next steps together – and if he didn't, she knew she was going to be okay.

Admiring the sun shining through the branches of the trees, Molly carried on walking around the pond. Then she noticed a lonely figure sitting on an old fallen tree that had been turned into a makeshift bench at the end of the small wooden jetty. Cam was holding a fishing rod and looking deep in thought. He obviously had a deep passion for nature and the great outdoors; he looked just the picture of calm.

The ground was uneven, with fallen branches covered in moss, and the pond was completely still, not a ripple on its sun-dappled surface. Molly could hear the humming of the dragonflies, and the birds in the trees above, as she walked towards Cam. He looked like he'd set up home for the night with his one-man tent. Next to him lay a pile of chopped firewood and a man-made firepit. A small plastic picnic table was piled with plastic cups and plates, hot dog buns, and a small camping stove. On the ground was a food cooler with a couple of cans of beer balanced on top.

At the sound of a twig snapping Cam glanced up towards her. He looked awful, his face puffy, his eyes sad.

'Hey.' Molly's tone was soft.

'Hey,' he replied, casting his rod in the water.

'I wasn't expecting to find you here. You haven't been evicted, have you?' asked Molly, nodding towards the tent, thinking she wouldn't put anything past Birdie.

He shook his head. 'I just needed some space, time to think.' He looked out across the water. 'This is one of my favourite places in the whole world. I spent a lot of time down here with Grandad. He taught me to fish and when I was older'—he took a breath—'this is where I'd come with Maverick to hide from real life. We spent a lot of time cooped up in this tent and we barely caught a thing, but it was our time – me, Maverick, and the great outdoors.' His voice quivered.

'Do you want to be alone? I can go,' said Molly softly, looking out over the water as Cam reeled in his fishing line.

He shook his head. 'No, it's fine.'

'If you're sure?'

'I'm sure.'

'Have you been here all day?'

Cam shook his head. 'Only this afternoon. I took delivery of the plants and trees and spent the last few hours sorting them out in the meadow, but feel free to move them around.'

'That was you?' Molly was amazed at Cam's overwhelming kindness. That must have been some hard physical labour.

'I just needed to keep myself occupied, because every time I stop—' His voice cracked. 'I miss him so much already, it's like my right arm has been cut off.'

Molly nodded and touched his arm gently. 'Losing your best friend is heartbreaking.'

Cam pushed his fringe from his eyes and swallowed before turning back to look at Molly.

'What am I going to do without him?'

Molly gave him a soft look of reassurance. 'Treasure those memories. He had a wonderful life with you.'

'You expect them to go on for ever, don't you?'

'You do, and Maverick would have been so grateful to have a best buddy that took just the best care of him.'

Cam was lost in his thoughts for a moment, his eyes welling up with tears. 'I've never been on my own before; he's always been there. And what have you done to *her* – drugged her?' Cam gave a surprised look at Darling, who hadn't uttered one tiny growl. She'd sat down at the opening of the tent, looking like she was on guard. 'That's where Maverick always sat.'

'I told her she needed to be on her best behaviour and for once I think she knew it was non-negotiable.' Molly gave her an adoring look; she was sure Darling had some sort of sixth sense.

'They don't call you the dog whisperer for nothing, do they?' Cam managed a smile.

There was sadness in the air and Molly knew that making light-hearted jokes was helping to take the edge off it.

'Are the fish biting? I'm assuming the stick needs to be in the water.' Molly gave him a cheeky smile.

'That stick is a rod, and at some point, yes, it needs to be in the water.' He rolled his eyes. 'I was just about to cook up a gourmet meal.'

Molly looked at the frying pan on top of the camping

stove. It was packed with sausages. 'Gourmet, you say.' She raised an eyebrow.

'Extremely gourmet. I can even stretch to fried onions, a bread roll, and a bottle of brown sauce.'

'Brown sauce is definitely my favourite.'

'I have enough for two.'

'That would be perfect,' said Molly.

He offered her the camping chair at the side of the tent, then lit the stove. There was a sense of calm and peace as the sizzle of the sausages and the amazing aroma began to make Molly feel ravenous.

'Are you going to put that stick thingy in the water then?' she asked.

'It's generally how it works if I want to catch something.' He smiled at her.

'And there are actual fish in that water?' Molly wasn't convinced; she'd never seen fish in the pond before.

'What do you mean? Actual fish as opposed to pretend ones?' he teased.

Molly rolled her eyes. 'You know what I mean. This is meant to be relaxing, right?'

'It is – there's nothing better than sitting by the water passing away the time. Do you want to have a go?'

Molly looked up and smiled. 'I thought you were never going to ask. Of course I do!'

'All right! I can show you.'

He picked up the rod. 'This is a rod.' He gave her a cheeky smile. She was now standing close by his side.

'Okay, see this thing here, you have to take off this catch, and that's going to let the line run free.'

Molly was watching closely what Cam was doing. Their faces were centimetres apart.

'So give me your hand.' Cam placed Molly's hand on the rod and cupped it with his. Feeling his touch and his presence so close, Molly felt her stomach give a little flip. 'Take your finger – you want to hold the line into the rod here,' said Cam, looking deeply into her eyes. 'Right there, look.'

Molly did what Cam had told her to do.

'Then bring back the rod and look out for the trees and bushes, like this.' Cam's hands were still cupped over Molly's. 'Then you're going to whip it forward, obviously in that direction, towards the water.'

'I'm not totally stupid,' Molly protested.

'And as soon as it's to the left of you, let go of your finger.'

'Here goes! Woah! I did it!' Molly watched as the line reeled out into the air and landed in the pond.

'That's it, now you are fishing!' Cam opened his arms wide with a smile on his face. 'Now all you have to do is sit and relax whilst I serve up our gourmet feast.'

'That was easy.' Molly sat on the chair holding the rod and feeling chuffed. 'And all I need now is a bite. You know what this means, right? If I can learn how to fish, you maybe can learn how to be friends with Darling.' She grinned.

'Casting a line is a lot easier than trying to impress Darling.'

'It's only fair,' Molly insisted.

'Are you sure about that?'

They both glanced over towards the tent. Darling had curled up on top of Cam's sleeping bag, her eyes firmly shut and her front paw twitching.

'I've never known her sleep anywhere else except on Dixie's blanket. She drags that blanket around the house like her life depends on it,' said Molly. 'And are you staying out here tonight?'

'I am. It'll be perfect under the stars,' replied Cam, serving up the sausages and onions on the buns with a squirt of brown sauce on top. 'Here you go.'

Molly hadn't been expecting a fishing lesson, never mind food, but there was a sense of calm between them as Cam boiled a pan of water to make a cup of tea. 'This is the life, isn't it?' Molly looked out over the water. 'Back to basics.'

Cam handed her a mug of tea, sat on his fishing box next to Molly, and began to tuck into his food. 'There's something about the simple things in life. As a boy my grandfather would bring me to this very spot. Albie wasn't into fishing – he couldn't sit still long enough – and used to be quite disruptive. I was secretly pleased to get some time with Grandad all by myself. Look…'

He pointed to the trunk of a nearby tree. Molly turned around and saw, carved into it, the initials CB and a date.

'That was the date of my very first fishing trip with my grandad. He told me I'd get the bug and he was right.'

'Wow, you must have been aged around five or six,' said Molly, taking a sip of her tea.

'And I loved school holidays at my grandparents'.'

'Mmm, these sausages are delicious… Foxglove Farm sausages?' asked Molly, closing her eyes and savouring the flavour.

'There are no other sausages.' Cam pointed to Molly's chin. 'You've got some sauce…' He handed her a tissue and she wiped her mouth.

Hearing Darling snore loudly they both spun round and laughed. Molly felt relaxed in Cam's company and liked the fact that he was opening up and telling her about the time with his grandfather. 'I've never known her be so well behaved,' she remarked, genuinely surprised that Darling had curled up and gone to sleep. 'She's your grandmother's pride and joy. Talking of Dixie… I'm worried about her.'

'Why?' he asked, putting his empty mug on the ground.

'I don't want you to think I'm interfering. I've already felt the wrath of Birdie today.'

Cam raised his eyebrow. 'What do you mean?'

'I know this is nothing to do with me and I need you to know I'm sharing this with you for all the right reasons. If it turns out I'm wrong I'll be the first one eating humble pie, but I believe Dixie.'

With a fleeting look of worry on his face, Cam sat up straight. 'Believe my grandmother about what? Go on.'

Molly relayed everything she knew about Birdie's accusations of violence. 'My grandmother has never lashed out at anyone in her life,' Cam said, taken aback. 'This doesn't sound right at all. I was told by Auntie Birdie that Dixie was getting forgetful and nearly burnt down the cottage and she was incapable of looking after herself.'

'And there's the missing paperwork – your Auntie Birdie was furious with me because I've been speaking with Jan, the manager, about the situation. I claimed I was a family member... and she informed me that Dixie's paperwork wasn't in order and Birdie had used a private doctor for the assessments.'

Cam looked pensive. 'Auntie Birdie called a family meeting, claiming Grandmother was a danger to herself, and Albie agreed. He said he'd seen it first-hand too.'

'Do you have any evidence of anything? Have you seen your grandmother lashing out or forgetting anything?'

'Absolutely none,' he confirmed.

'And there are the papers that Birdie wants Dixie to sign.'

'Papers? What papers?' Cam now sounded alarmed.

'I honestly don't know. Legal documents, maybe for the sale of the cottage.'

'That can't be right. My grandmother would never

sell Bumblebee Cottage or The Old Bakehouse. The cottage is not for sale and I know that for a fact because we've come to an agreement – I'm renting it for twelve months until I've got some things in my personal life sorted, and then I plan to buy it off her. We've already talked about it. All this is ringing alarm bells. That cottage will always be in the family.'

Molly took a breath. 'It sounds like you have a lot on your plate, Cam, but I have to tell you: your Auntie Birdie showed around some prospective buyers the other morning, while you were out.'

Cam raised both eyebrows. 'What? I've been so caught up in what was going on in my own life, I haven't even questioned what's been happening…'

'You can't beat yourself up over that. It sounds to me like you have a lot going on in your life. And after all, Birdie is your family, someone who should be trustworthy.' Molly took a sip of her tea. 'I saw you with your wife yesterday.' The words slipped out of her mouth without thinking. She carried on staring at the rod in front of her, waiting to see if Cam would provide an explanation.

For a second he remained silent. 'I bet you think I'm a rat, don't you? But I promise we weren't together when I spent the night with you.'

Molly could see from his face that he was telling the truth and willing her to believe him.

'I think usually I'm a good judge of character…' she replied, hopefully encouraging him to talk.

'Yes, you did see me with my wife. We had papers of our own to sign.' Cam took a deep breath. 'We met at university, where I escaped to after my failed attempt at growing plants for a living, which I pretty much hated from the start.' His look of frustration made Molly laugh. 'I was absolutely rubbish at it. Hannah and I both studied dentistry together and after we qualified and worked a couple of jobs for different practices, we decided to open our own private practice, which was extremely successful. We got married and bought a house. As time went on, living and working together became very strained.'

'Yes, that's understandable, home and work life just roll into one,' Molly contributed.

Cam looked pensive. Molly didn't want to push for more information, but he went on, 'Then Hannah wanted to start a family. If I'm truly honest I was quite surprised at the time because she loved her work and was very career-minded, and every time I talked about having a family, she brushed it off. Then all of a sudden our whole life became only about one thing – trying to get pregnant.' Cam took a breath. 'And that's when things started to change.'

Still listening, Molly didn't interrupt.

'Hannah wasn't getting pregnant. She became obsessed with our diet, the amount of coffee we were allowed to drink, and alcohol was out… I spent the next six months eating salad and drinking water. I used to make excuses that I had to run errands after work, so on the odd occasion I could nip into the pub for a quick pint, but then afterwards I felt so guilty that I'd let her down. After twelve months still nothing happened. We'd bought the ovulating kits, and if I'm honest'—he blew out a breath—'things started to become mechanical. There was no more laughter, no more cuddling up on the settee; Sunday afternoons films with a glass of wine became a no-no. It was like Hannah's watch was set to certain times and I had to perform on the spot. It became soul-destroying and still no baby. We went for tests and it all came down to me, a low sperm count, and that's the one of the reasons that when you said you were pregnant, I doubted you… I'm sorry.' Cam sounded heartbroken and his voice wavered. Molly could see he'd been through a very traumatic time.

'It's okay, don't be sorry.' Molly could absolutely see why Cam had reacted to her news the way he did. She'd assumed he'd lost a baby but maybe the truth was they just couldn't have kids and the pressure had spelled the demise of their marriage.

'It's me who's sorry – and I am, Molly, for reacting that way that morning in the park. Even though she and I have been separated for a while we've lived in the same house. I'd arrived that morning in Heartcross after a huge row with Hannah over splitting our assets and the financial settlement. Thankfully, that's all been sorted now, and we just need to sign the legal papers.'

Before Cam could say any more, Molly unexpectedly jumped up off the chair, her plate and cup toppling to the floor. Waving eagerly, she pointed at the rod and rushed to pick it up. 'Eek! We have a bite! I've never caught a fish before.'

Cam was up on his feet. 'You won't now if you don't stay quiet.' He was grinning in amusement at Molly who was about to burst with excitement.

'What do I do?' Come on, show me!' enthused Molly.

'Look, like this.' Cam stood behind her and wrapped his arms around her, his hands on hers. Feeling his body so close to hers, Molly held her breath. Every time, there was that spark of electricity. She looked over her shoulder and he was smiling straight back at her. The fish was frantically thrashing about in the water as Cam helped Molly to reel in the tiniest fish she had ever set eyes on.

'Is that it?' exclaimed Molly, amazed that such a tiny fish could create so much havoc in the water.

'I've seen bigger fish in a tin of sardines,' he teased, and as soon as the fish was in reach he unhooked and handed it over to Molly to let it loose back into the pond.

'Ew, no!' she exclaimed, wrinkling her nose and holding her hands up in the air in protest.

'Go on, it's your first fish,' encouraged Cam. 'Memories!'

He began to walk towards the pond with Molly by his side and they hovered at the edge of the water. He held the fish towards Molly who once more scrunched up her eyes and held her hands out.

'Okay, I'll give it a go,' she finally agreed.

'Be careful, and don't drop it!'

'Of course I'm not going to drop it.' Carefully taking the fish from Cam she bent down and gently released it back into the water. With a huge proud beam on her face she stood up and watched the fish swim away. 'My very first fish... There's something therapeutic about this fishing lark, isn't there?'

'Well, I think so. It's a good place to come and escape and get lost in your thoughts. The calmness of the water always helps.'

Their eyes stayed locked for a moment until Molly heard rustling behind them and spun round to see Darling's tail sticking out of Cam's cool bag. Whilst they were occupied with letting the fish loose in the water Darling had discovered rashers of streaky bacon and devoured them in seconds.

'My breakfast for tomorrow!' Cam was shaking his head but thankfully saw the funny side.

'Darling! NO!' Molly raised her voice, but it was too late – all that was left was the tinfoil that had been wrapped around the bacon. 'I'm so sorry!'

Cam laughed. 'Looks like I'll need to catch my breakfast in the morning!'

Looking pleased with herself, Darling sat down and licked her lips.

'We better head off before this one causes any more trouble.'

'At least she's not trying to savage me for a change!'

'That's very true,' replied Molly, looking at her watch. 'All the villagers will be heading up to the park very soon and I want to avoid questions about why I'm not at work.' Molly paused and looked directly at Cam. 'Thank you for teaching me how to fish ... and for what it's worth, I'm so sorry about Maverick. I really am.'

Cam nodded his appreciation.

Molly had turned and was walking away with Darling when Cam called her name. She turned around again.

He was looking straight at her. 'And for what it's worth, I didn't think you were after money at all. I'm sorry... And, Molly, when did you say the first scan was?'

Molly's heart gave a tiny leap. Was Cam asking about the first scan because he wanted to go?

'It's Friday, a cancellation appointment, even though I'm overdue a scan, as I had a scare.'

'A scare?' Cam was up on his feet. 'What do you mean, a scare? Why didn't you tell me?'

'It's okay, Dr Sanders listened in on the baby at home with some sort of machine.' Molly couldn't help herself and came over all emotional. She flapped a hand in front of her face. 'Don't mind me, it just gets me thinking about it... I heard the baby's heartbeat for the first time and it was...' Molly didn't finish her sentence.

Cam blew out a breath and raked a hand through his hair. He was beaming. 'You've heard the heartbeat?'

'Yes,' said Molly, and, taking the bull by the horns, 'Do you want to come on Friday?'

Cam was nodding. 'Yes, if that's okay with you.'

Molly rummaged quickly inside her bag and pulled out a business card. 'Here, take this. My number ... just in case you need it. Text me and I'll give you all the details.'

Molly turned and walked away with a huge smile on her face. This was the first time Cam had asked questions about the baby. Again, she reflected that Isla had been right: take things slow and let him come to you. This was the first positive step towards his becoming involved in their lives. Molly felt weightless and headed towards her van with a spring in her step.

Hearing her phone ping, she glanced at the screen. It was a number she didn't recognise. As she opened the text message she beamed.

Here's my number, just in case you need it. Cam x

The first thing that Molly noticed was the kiss. She felt all warm and fuzzy inside as she stored the number safely in her phone.

Chapter Nineteen

The next morning Molly only suffered an hour of queasiness before she began to feel human again. Mornings had mainly consisted of stuffing her face with ginger biscuits but today she was winning at life after managing to keep down a whole bowl of sugary Weetabix.

She was sitting outside in the garden with her feet propped up on the chair and her face tilted up to the sun, her eyes closed. Today was going to be another hot day with the temperatures hitting a whopping twenty-nine degrees. Molly was glad that yesterday she had ordered numerous loose-fitting outfits, which had arrived, saving her from the elasticated bobbly jogging bottoms.

'Come on, Darling, let's go and choose an outfit,' she said, placing her dirty breakfast dishes in the sink before climbing up the stairs. All the clothes were laid out on the bed. There were a couple of dresses, which Molly had already tried on, but as she always wore trousers she felt a little self-conscious.

'What do you think of this one?' She held the dress against her body while looking in the mirror.

Darling was sitting perfectly still and watching her.

'You don't look too impressed. What about this one?'

Darling gave a tiny bark.

Molly raised an eyebrow. 'Was that just a coincidence or do you actually prefer this one?'

Darling barked again.

'This one it is then!'

Molly slipped the dress over her head. It hung just above her ankles – the perfect maxi dress for this weather – but she immediately noticed that her bump was starting to become a little more obvious. She knew as soon as word got out everyone would be intrigued to know who the father was, and she hadn't quite decided what she was going to say. This was something else she needed to have a conversation with Cam about sooner rather than later.

With a squirt of perfume, Molly slipped her feet into comfy ballet shoes and declared herself ready. Yesterday, she'd taken a few photographs of the flowers and trees that had been delivered to Primrose Park, and she thought Dixie might like to see them. This afternoon all the wood was being delivered and tonight Drew and Fergus were testing their carpentry skills as they started work on the replica bandstand. Thankfully, she hadn't heard from Albie and the only time she would have to face him again would be at Dixie's birthday party, where there would be lots of people to talk to, helping her to avoid him.

Ten minutes later she was on her way to visit Dixie. She wondered if she would win at least one game of cards today, but she wasn't holding out much hope. On her walk towards the care home she began to think about life in general. Even though she wasn't feeling one hundred per cent she was actually beginning to enjoy her time off work. She liked being successful in her job, owning her own company, and being the boss to all her staff, but since hearing the baby's heartbeat her priorities were beginning to shift. In the past when she'd thought about having a family, Molly had had visions of dropping her baby off at nursery and picking them up after the early surgery. She'd thought her life would carry on as normal but now she couldn't stand the idea of that. She didn't want to miss any milestones or magical moments. Molly never thought she would have considered this but she was seriously thinking about taking a career break and leaving her chief member of staff in charge.

At the care home, Jan was on the reception desk again and gave Molly a huge smile.

'How's Dixie today?' asked Molly, filling in the arrival log.

'Top form – no word of a lie, she's fleeced another resident, Wilf, out of fifty pounds this morning in a mammoth card game that lasted approximately two hours. Wilf didn't want to give up, but Dixie wasn't playing for nothing. She is a card shark that one,' chuckled Jan.

'A winning streak that's lasted a lifetime.' Molly was impressed. Dixie should have considered being a professional card player back in the day. 'Is Dixie in the TV room?' asked Molly, about to head down the corridor.

'Her daughter arrived about fifteen minutes ago, so maybe the garden or Dixie's room.'

'How is everything?' quizzed Molly, noticing that Jan suddenly looked uncomfortable.

'I'm so sorry, I'm not allowed to discuss anything with you. Dixie's next of kin—'

'Don't worry, I understand,' interrupted Molly, not wanting to put Jan on the spot but knowing she'd probably had her knuckles rapped by Birdie.

'All I can say is that Dixie is my main priority.'

'Thank you, that's all I needed to hear.'

With Birdie already at the home, Molly didn't want to cause another scene. She knew that Birdie would not be happy to see her. She considered going home and coming back later but then, as she thought about it, she realised Dixie would probably be relieved by her arrival. They were nowhere to be seen in the TV room or the garden so cautiously Molly headed towards

Dixie's bedroom and stopped a couple of metres from the door. She could hear Birdie's voice, raised in frustration.

'Why can't things just be straightforward with you? Why do you have to question everything?'

Molly stood and listened.

'Just do it; I haven't got all day. I've got better things to be doing than sorting all this out.' Birdie was sounding desperate.

'I don't need you to sort out anything and I am not signing those papers until I've talked to Cam about it first. You are rushing me.' Dixie sounded fraught.

'You told me to sort all this and now you're changing your mind.' Birdie was insistent.

'I did not, and I want to get out of here. I want to go home.'

'This is your home now. You can't look after yourself.'

'Yes, I can. I don't know what you've told people but I'm not any of the things you say I am.'

'Oh yes, you are. Look at these bruises, you did that to me.'

'I did not.' Dixie was adamant. 'I want to talk to Cam. And why has my phone disappeared? Have you taken my phone?'

'Always your favourite, wasn't he? Even when he was a child you favoured him more than your other grandson.'

'At least Cam is kind and looks out for what's best for

me, and he's not out for everything he can get like some others I can mention.'

'How dare you!' exclaimed an annoyed Birdie. 'Just sign the papers.'

'NO!' came Dixie's reply. 'I want you to leave.'

'Not until you've signed the papers. You've always been defiant.'

Molly was horrified to hear some sort of kerfuffle. The conversation was getting too heated for her liking.

Anguish surged through Molly's body as she heard Dixie give a yelp like a wounded animal. Immediately, Molly flung open the bedroom door to witness a horrific sight. A distressed Dixie was shielding her face, Birdie's hand inches from her cheek.

'What the hell are you doing?' Molly was staring straight at Birdie as she rushed towards Dixie and put her arm around her shoulder. 'Please tell me you haven't just slapped your own mother.' She didn't wait for an answer but leant forward and pressed the alarm buzzer by the bed that rang through to reception. 'You should be ashamed of yourself.'

Birdie didn't even have the grace to look a little sheepish. 'It's nothing to do with you, interfering again.' Birdie gave Molly a death stare which made the whole of Molly's body tremble.

'She's trying to make me sign those papers.' Dixie looked petrified, and her voice quivered.

As Molly reached forward to grab the papers, so did Birdie.

'This has nothing to do with you.'

'Hitting your mother has everything to do with everybody,' retaliated Molly. 'This is a matter for the authorities.'

'For your information I didn't hit my own mother. She went to hit me, and I tried to stop her. But I don't need to explain myself to you.' Birdie's cheeks were blazing as Jan appeared in the doorway.

'I'm so sorry, I need to leave, Jan. My mother is making up stories again.' With that, Birdie flounced out of the room, the papers safely in her possession.

'It's just not true. I haven't done anything.' Dixie was visibly upset, her whole body shaking. 'And I haven't been taking those tablets either.'

'Tablets?' chorused Molly and Jan in unison.

'Birdie tries to make me take them.' Dixie lifted up her mattress to reveal numerous packets of tablets, which Jan scooped up.

'I think Dixie is telling the truth,' urged Molly. 'From what I saw then, it wasn't Dixie who lashed out.'

Jan nodded. 'Are you okay, Dixie? Can you tell me what just happened?'

After Dixie broke down in tears and told them what had just happened Jan walked to the door. 'I'm calling Dr Sanders, just to come and check you over.'

'And what about the police?' suggested Molly, looking from Dixie to Jan.

'No police, please,' replied Dixie, who began to cry. 'I just want to go home.'

'I'm not sure I have much choice, Dixie,' replied Jan softly, sitting down on the bed next to her. She took Dixie's hands in hers. 'After Dr Sanders has checked you over, we can talk about what has just happened. But I don't want you to worry about a thing,' soothed Jan. Dixie nodded.

Molly slipped an arm around Dixie's shoulder. 'I'm going to make you a cup of tea and then I'm going to ring Cam and we're going to sort this mess out.'

'You do believe me, don't you? I haven't hurt anyone.' Dixie dabbed her eyes with a tissue.

'Of course I believe you, Dixie,' replied Molly without hesitation. 'Let Jan talk to Dr Sanders and even though I can't make any promises, let's see if we can get you home.'

Dixie cupped her hands around Molly's. 'You are a treasure.'

'And so are you. Now, I'm just going to make you that cup of tea.' Molly stood up.

'In that drawer.' Dixie waved towards it. 'Open that drawer.'

Molly did as she was asked and pulled out the drawer. Lying on top of Dixie's clothes was a bottle of port alongside a wad of ten-pound notes.

'Pour me a small tipple of the hard stuff to settle my nerves and please take the cash and put it somewhere safe. Thank God Birdie didn't find it.'

'Dixie, where have you got all this money from? There must be around—'

'Six hundred pounds,' interrupted Dixie with a smile. 'I've started to run a secret port and poker club. I've not lost a game yet.' She tipped Molly a wink. 'Those are my winnings.'

'You are a dark horse,' said Molly admiringly, pouring Dixie a small glass of port.

'I had to make my own fun in here somehow.'

Molly smiled. 'I'm just going to check up on Jan. Will you be okay for a second?'

'I will, thank you,' replied Dixie. Sitting on a chair by the window, she looked out over the small garden outside and sighed. 'How have I ended up in here?' she murmured under her breath.

As Molly stepped out the door, she wondered exactly the same and immediately rang Cam but the call went straight to voicemail.

'Cam, it's me, Molly. Ring me as soon as you get this – it's urgent.'

Chapter Twenty

I t was early evening when Molly opened her eyes. She must have dozed off on the sofa. She quickly cast a glance over her phone, which was lying on the coffee table in front of her, but there was still no word from Cam. She was surprised but thought maybe he had been caught up with something or Jan had managed to speak to him directly.

She stretched out her arms then swung her feet to the floor. 'This pregnancy malarkey really does make you tired. I've never napped so much in my life,' she said to Darling, who had been dozing next to her. 'Let's check for the post.'

She stood up slowly, walked into the hallway and picked up a small parcel and some letters from the mat. 'It's here!' she exclaimed excitedly, ripping open the padded envelope to reveal a baby name book. She quickly flicked through and was amazed at all the names. How was she ever going to choose?

'Let's make a drink and we can sit down and have a proper look.' She laughed at herself – she was always talking to Darling as if she was a person.

As they walked towards the kitchen, Molly stopped dead in her tracks.

BANG… BANG… BANG…

Barking, Darling ran towards the back door and began to sniff frantically at the bottom. What the hell was going on? Who would be hammering on the door like that, as if it was a matter of urgency?

Without thinking, Molly walked towards the back door and unlocked it. She was stunned to find a furious-looking Albie there. By the look on his face he wasn't there for a friendly chat or to pass the time of day.

'Have you never heard of a front door? What are you doing in my back garden?' Molly was perplexed.

'Have you never thought to mind your own business?' He stared coldly at her, making her bristle.

She could see that Albie was spoiling for a fight and she could only assume that it had something to do with Birdie.

'Go away, Albie. If this has anything to do with Dixie then I have nothing to say to you.'

'Isn't that a shame, as I've got a hell of a lot to say to you.'

Molly went to shut the door but a furious Albie put his hand on it and one foot inside Molly's kitchen.

'Take your foot out of the door! Are you insane?' She was beginning to panic.

Darling took the opportunity to take hold of the bottom of Albie's trousers with her teeth and began to growl.

'Get that mutt off me,' Albie yelled, trying to shake his leg.

'She's very choosy about who comes into our house. I'm asking you again to leave.'

With a huge kick forward Albie hurled Darling into the air and she yelped.

'How bloody dare you! So you go around kicking animals now, do you?' Molly attempted to slam the back door, but Albie was too strong for her and forced his way into the kitchen. 'I'm going to call the police.'

Albie laughed menacingly.

Now Molly felt threatened. She didn't like the dark look in his eyes at all. His face was flushed, his tie askew, and the sweat marks under his armpits were rapidly spreading down the sides of his shirt and his sleeves. Her eyes narrowed. Her heart was thumping and inside she felt fear but there was no way she was going to let Albie know that.

Albie had an axe to grind and it didn't look like he was leaving anytime soon.

'Please leave, Albie.' Molly stared coldly into his

bulging, bloodshot eyes, sure she had just got a whiff of alcohol.

'That's not very welcoming, after I've just parted with thousands of pounds' worth of plants for you.'

'For your grandmother's birthday garden party,' corrected Molly, sounding braver than she felt.

'The least you can do is offer me a drink.' He glanced swiftly at the kettle. 'In fact, maybe something a little stronger.'

Molly didn't answer. The last thing she wanted to do was make Albie a drink.

'And why are you interfering in my grandmother's life?'

'I thought you would be happy that someone is looking out for your grandmother, especially after your own mother is trying to drug and abuse her.'

'That is a very strong word to use.' Albie looked amused.

'But the absolute truth.' Molly was holding her own but felt sick to her stomach with the uncertainty of how this was going to pan out. Albie was now leaning against the cooker with his arms folded, looking her up and down. She shuddered, feeling threatened by his presence.

'My grandmother is in that home because that's the best place for her to be.' Albie held Molly's gaze.

'In whose opinion? I don't believe you. Your

grandmother is a strong, independent woman in control of all her faculties.'

'Do you think we care what you think?'

Molly took a breath. 'I'll tell you exactly what I think. I think you and your mother have concocted a plan to make your own grandmother believe she is being forgetful in order to get her to sign Bumblebee Cottage and The Old Bakehouse over to you – just so you can make a few quid.'

'Those properties are my inheritance.'

'Not just yours, though, are they? You are manipulating your own grandmother and trying to trick her into cutting others out of the will. It's daylight robbery. You and Birdie should be ashamed of yourselves and I've rung Cam to tell him everything.' Molly could kick herself for answering back. She needed to get rid of Albie, not antagonise him further.

'Aw, my cousin, the man who can't even keep his family together. You were just another notch on his bedpost – one of many.'

Albie leant forward and stroked his finger down Molly's cheek.

Frozen to the spot, she shuddered.

'In fact,' Albie looked through to the living room and the settee. His whole manner was disturbing. 'We don't need a hotel room. And you owe me.'

Molly felt like she couldn't breathe; her throat was getting tighter and tighter, as if someone was choking her. All she could think about was her baby – but if she made a run for it the baby could get hurt. Molly didn't know what to do. She needed him out of there and fast.

She glanced at her watch and tried to take control of the situation. 'Is that the time? Sorry, Albie, I have my friends coming round in a minute,' she said in a matter-of-fact tone. 'I need to get ready.'

'Nice try.' He laughed, not believing a word she'd said.

Molly remained silent, her heart racing. She had never experienced anything like this before. She prayed for someone to knock on the door or ring the bell. The more she thought about making a run for it, the more terrified she felt. Her eyes brimmed with tears and the pulse thumped in the side of her head. She took a step back and snagged a glance towards her phone lying on the worktop. If she could somehow grab it and run to the bathroom, if she managed to lock the door she could ring for help.

Albie's face was smouldering with rage. He moved closer towards her. 'So tell me, what are you doing with a loser like my cousin? We got all the details on the way home, you know. He didn't even say goodbye, did he?' Albie gave a chuckle. 'We laughed, the moment you saw him in the car park we had bets and his was a dead cert. He knew he was going to have you the moment you looked in his direction.'

Molly felt sickened. Was this true? Had they really

been laughing at her and taking bets? She didn't know what to believe.

'I am not with your cousin.' Molly began to move slowly around the kitchen table, edging her way towards her phone. Albie began to mirror her movements; it was like a slow game of cat and mouse. Molly heard the sound of his breathing change. It was now or never – she had to take the plunge. She bolted as fast as she could to reach for her phone. Albie grabbed her and she let out a high-pitched scream. Darling sounded distressed, down on her front paws and barking continuously. The touch of Albie's grubby hands on her made her feel nauseous. 'Get the hell off me.'

'Cam wouldn't mind sharing you, you know. It wouldn't be the first time.' His sadistic smile glinted in the sunlight that shone through the back door. He held her wrists even tighter.

'Get off me, I'm pregnant,' she screamed in fear.

Molly's inner strength took over as Albie was distracted by a noise outside the back door. She took her chance and brought up her knee swiftly, leaving Albie muttering expletives under his breath.

'You cow.' Albie lifted his arm up and went to strike, but from out of nowhere Molly heard Cam's voice.

'Molly! Molly!' Disbelief written all over his face, Cam rushed through the door and pushed his cousin out of the way. 'What the hell are you doing? Get off her.' He grabbed hold of Albie's arm. His cousin narrowed his eyes then wholeheartedly laughed.

'Go home, Albie, you've been drinking,' ordered Cam, who was staring at his cousin with contempt. 'You're an absolute disgrace.'

'And what are you doing here?' Albie raised an eyebrow.

Molly knew exactly why he was here. She'd left him a voicemail telling him to ring her as it was urgent. She'd wanted to tell him about what she'd witnessed between Birdie and Dixie.

'OMG!' Albie looked between the pair of them. 'She's pregnant with your baby, isn't she?'

Neither Molly nor Cam answered.

Albie threw his head back and let out another peal of laughter, 'Well, well, well, this is a turn up for the books. Especially after—'

'Shut up, Albie.' Cam was staring straight at his cousin.

'Do you know how many babies this one has made this year?'

Molly's eyes widened. What the hell was that meant to mean? She didn't understand. Was this what Cam did? Breeze from hotel to hotel picking up women? Molly felt like she could vomit on the spot.

'The tangled web you weave. I know someone that's going to want to hear this information.'

'Don't,' replied Cam. 'I'm warning you.'

'Warning me? You're a joke. You always were.' Albie was on a roll. 'You couldn't even hack hard work, never wanted to get your hands dirty, but all you had to do was flutter your eyelashes at Grandma and Grandad and you got everything. But now your halo has well and truly slipped, hasn't it?' he sneered. 'In fact'—he looked at his watch—'I may just head over there now. You'll never guess what dear Molly—'

'Molly knows that Hannah and I have separated,' interrupted Cam.

'You couldn't even give your wife what she wanted and here you are, impregnating the tart you picked up from the hotel.'

But Albie didn't have time to say any more because without warning Cam hit him square on his jaw, making him stumble backwards and grab onto the worktop.

'You'll regret that,' snarled Albie, bringing his hand up to his jaw. 'I promise you that.'

'You know what, I should have done that a long time ago. Now, just go.'

Molly was relieved as she watched Cam throw Albie out of the house and firmly close the door. A thud followed as Albie kicked the backdoor but then there was silence.

Molly breathed a huge sigh of relief.

'I'm so sorry.' Cam took a step forward, but Molly put up her hand to stop him coming any closer.

Her eyes were fixed on his. 'What the hell did he

mean? Exactly how many babies have you made this year?' Molly's voice rose as she cradled her stomach.

'It's not what you think,' replied Cam.

'How many?' insisted Molly.

'Three, but it's still not what you think,' swore Cam.

But Molly wasn't up to listening to any more. She was confused. She'd been under the impression he'd lost a baby and now she didn't know what to think – all her thoughts were tripping over each other.

'Oh my God, so there is some truth in what Albie was saying?' Molly swung her arm and pointed after him. 'You even had bets that you'd have sex with me. You are unbelievable.' Distraught, Molly blew out a breath. 'Just get out.' Molly opened the back door, her eyes wide.

Cam walked towards her. 'It's not what you think and it wasn't like that at all.'

But Molly was too angry to even listen, and as soon as Cam stepped outside she slammed the door behind him and immediately locked it. Slumping to her knees, she scooped up Darling, who gently licked her tears. She hugged Darling with all her might and cried like she had never cried before. She had never been so terrified as when Albie wouldn't leave, and she was grateful that Cam had turned up when he did, because she didn't even want to think about what could have happened – but now the only thing on her mind was the argument she'd just had with Cam. Was she just another notch on his bedpost? Had they truly laughed and taken bets?

Standing up, and putting Darling down on the floor, she splashed water on her face then patted it dry with the towel. Glancing out of the window, she saw the sky had blackened and the trees were swaying in the breeze. The weather was about to break after the continuous sweltering heat that seemed to have lasted weeks. A storm was coming.

'Come on, let's get you out for a quick walk before the rain comes. I could do with the fresh air.'

Immediately, Darling recognised the word 'walk' and began to dance on her paws and wag her tail. Checking that the back door was locked, Molly clipped on Darling's lead and headed outside.

As she pounded the pavements, all Molly could think about was the last twenty minutes and Albie's words. Was this the reason Cam had split up with his wife, because she just couldn't take any more? Molly knew she shouldn't guess but she just didn't know what to think.

To calm her beating heart, and hoping the fresh air would lift her mood, she walked over the bridge from Glensheil into Heartcross. She made her way along the rough gravel track towards Love Heart Lane and headed to Bonnie's teashop. With the dark clouds looming overhead, all the customers had moved inside, and Molly could see a queue at the counter. Enjoying the smell of freshly brewed coffee in the air, Molly waved at Felicity through the window and decided she would take the path around the foot of Heartcross Mountain and call in at the teashop on the way back for a hearty chicken sandwich with a zing of mayo.

She climbed over the stile and the mossy rocks gave way to a meandering trail passing through purple heather and bracken. The views were breathtaking, tree roots crisscrossing the path covered in wildflowers and berry bushes. Birds were flying overhead. Molly looked up at the mountain. With the fells rising on each side, it was stunning. A handful of hikers were heading her way and Molly stepped to one side to let them pass.

'You aren't heading up the mountain, are you? The rain is coming,' said a man, nodding towards the black clouds above. 'Don't go getting yourself stranded.'

'I won't,' replied Molly with a smile. 'I'm only walking up to the hut then back to the teashop. I'm just waiting for the queue to go down.'

The man waved his hiking pole above his head in acknowledgement, as the gang of hikers began to clamber over the stile and into Love Heart Lane.

'Let's put our recall skills to the test.' Molly looked down at Darling, who was sniffing under a bush. 'Darling,' she called and rattled a bag of treats. Immediately Darling's ears pricked up and she looked hopefully up at Molly.

'Sit,' commanded Molly and to her amazement Darling did just that.

'Good girl,' Molly praised, handing her a treat. 'Are you and I finally bonding? I'm beginning to see what

Dixie saw in you,' she chuckled. 'Okay, here's the deal. I'm going to let you off the lead but you come back when I say, as that rain is going to be here very soon.' Molly bent down and unclipped Darling's lead, but to her surprise the dog stayed close. Each time Darling was distracted Molly would call her back and each time Darling was at her heels in seconds. 'If you carry on behaving we're going to need to watch your weight with all these treats,' she joked, watching as Darling ran off once again in front of her.

With Darling behaving, Molly was glad she'd escaped into the fresh air to clear her head. All she could think about was Albie and Cam. Albie seemed bitter about Cam. Maybe it had stemmed from their childhood? They were, after all, two totally different characters. Her impression of Albie was that he was an unsavoury character. Molly hoped that the care home and Dr Sanders would look into what had been going on with Dixie. Her initial impression of Cam, of course, had been that he was drop-dead gorgeous, with a smile to die for, and she could still remember that he'd made her feel like a million dollars that night, so loving and caring…

But the question now that she was turning over and over in her mind was, how genuine was he? Her gut feeling was telling her that what Albie was saying wasn't true … or was it simply that Molly didn't want to believe it? For purely selfish reasons Molly wanted to know. She felt choked up just thinking about it, and hoped she wasn't just another notch on Cam's bedpost, but at the moment that seemed very likely. Feeling crushed, she let out a sigh. She didn't know what to believe. All she knew was that one night had changed her life for ever and very soon she was going to be in charge of another human. She prayed she was going to be enough and would never let them down.

Even though the weather was about to break, it was still extremely warm. Molly swung Darling's lead and began walking along the mountain pass. This was a place Molly hadn't walked in many years. The last time, if she remembered rightly, was with her father before she went off to university. Off the beaten track, untouched by time, amidst the mountainscape, it still all felt familiar to her. The view from up here was one of outstanding beauty, and the further up the mountain pass you climbed, the further you could see – for miles and miles. Molly breathed in the fresh air and smiled at Darling, who was having the time of her life ferreting amongst the clumps of purple heather.

Molly noticed a large bush up ahead and was heading that way when she turned around. There was a rustle in the bushes, and a movement, which Darling spotted at the same time. Without warning and with her nose to the ground, Darling took off faster than a high-speed train. Within seconds she was out of sight.

'You're kidding me, right? Darling, get back here!'

Molly shouted, her heart beginning to hammer against her chest.

'Darling!' Molly continued to shout. She was beginning to feel panicky; there were some steep drops off the side of the mountain and she wasn't sure if the pass was familiar to Darling. She couldn't imagine Dixie walking her up here. Pressing forwards, Molly felt huge drops of rain begin to fall. The timing couldn't be any worse. As she stumbled along the rocky terrain, the rain worsened and Molly was soaked to her skin in seconds. Still there was no sign of Darling. For a moment Molly thought about turning around but she couldn't just leave her. Frantically calling out her name and rattling the bag of treats, she continued to follow the path.

'Darling!' she shouted again, cupping her hands around her mouth. Then she felt a tiny discomfort in her stomach. She stood still and took some deep breaths. Then the pain worsened.

Clutching her stomach and in a blind panic, Molly screamed for help at the top of her voice, but no one came. All the hikers had headed off the mountain as soon as the weather began to change. As the pain worsened, Molly knew she had to make the decision to leave Darling – she couldn't carry on. In distress she shouted to her once more. Then she was just about to turn round when she remembered the little brick hut on the side of the mountain. It couldn't be far away. The pain was worsening by the second and Molly knew this couldn't be normal. Tears stung her eyes as she realised there was a possibility she was losing the baby.

'No, no, please no.' The words turned over in her mind. At first the pain was intermittent and her back ached dully, then the pain came faster and faster. She couldn't believe this was happening to her. With relief, as she turned a corner she saw the hut and pushed open the creaky old door. There was litter strewn all over the floor and an old battered sofa that stank to high heaven but Molly didn't care – she just needed to sit down. Perching on the edge of the sofa she frantically rummaged inside her bag, looking for her phone.

'No, please no,' she mumbled.

Damn.

Her phone was lying on the worktop in the kitchen. She'd forgotten it.

Throwing her bag onto the settee in frustration, and with tears stinging her eyes, she brought her knees up to her chest then lay down on the damp settee, resting her head on her bag. The pain seemed to lessen slightly when she lay in this position. She knew she couldn't have walked another step. Her mind was in turmoil. What was she going to do?

'Stay with me, little one,' she murmured, still clutching her stomach. She was engulfed with a feeling of nausea. She closed her eyes and willed everything to be okay.

Then the door creaked and a sodden, forlorn Darling

appeared in the doorway. 'You rascal, come here,' said Molly. Darling shook her coat and droplets of water sprayed everywhere. She jumped up onto the settee and began to nudge Molly with her nose and whimper. 'You know, something isn't quite right. This is a long shot, Darling'—Molly blinked back the tears—'but you need to go and get help.' She remembered how, when she'd fainted at Bumblebee Cottage, every time she said the word 'home' Darling would jump up at the back door. Darling thought of the cottage as home.

It was a long shot but Molly had to try. 'Darling... Home ... home...'

The word 'home' triggered Darling to sit up straight and prick up her ears.

'Good girl, Darling. GO HOME.'

Darling barked and immediately ran towards the door. She stopped and looked back at Molly, who was curled up in a ball. 'Home, Darling, home.'

Darling ran out into the torrential rain. All Molly could do was pray and hope that Darling would raise the alarm.

Chapter Twenty-One

C am was furious. He'd thought his escape to Heartcross was going to be drama-free and how wrong could he have been. Standing in the window, watching the rain hit the windowpane like bullets, he took a breath. This year was not panning out as he'd thought it would. He'd separated from his wife, lost his job and, if the truth be told, it had felt like a huge weight had been lifted off his shoulders when he'd arrived in Heartcross hoping for some respite. Never in a million years had he thought the gorgeous woman he'd spotted that day at the hotel would be carrying his baby.

He looked at his watch. Dr Sanders was due to arrive in the next five minutes along with the manager of the care home. Cam didn't know what to expect. After arriving back from Molly's he'd swigged a large glass of whisky. He didn't think his day could get any worse until he sat and listened to the answering-machine messages. What the hell had Auntie Birdie been up to now?

Hearing a car door slam, Cam glanced out towards the road and breathed a sigh. It had completely slipped his mind that Hannah was coming over to pick up the signed legal papers that transferred their business to her. No doubt, thanks to Albie, she was furious and striding up the path on a mission. He knew exactly what that mission was, and he braced himself.

Closing his eyes for a second he walked towards the front door but Hannah had beaten him to it. It swung wide open and she slapped him right across the face.

'Albie's told me. How the hell could you do this to me?' Her eyes were blurred. 'Don't you think I've been humiliated enough?'

Cam's hand was cradling his stinging cheek. 'Thanks, Albie,' he murmured under his breath.

Hannah pushed him in the chest. 'Were you ever going to tell me that you're having a baby with some tart you picked up in a hotel room?'

'Molly is not a tart,' Cam sighed.

'And you're together?' Hannah's voice faltered. She didn't take her eyes off Cam and he knew she was hurting.

'No, we are not together and yes, she has told me she is pregnant with my baby. Of course I was going to come and tell you at some point, but I've only just found out myself. Hannah, we're getting a divorce. We haven't been together for nearly six months.'

'And you got over me that quickly that you jumped into bed with a complete stranger.'

Cam wasn't going to get into an argument about that now. He looked over her shoulder. The front door was wide open and rain was still lashing down. Dr Sanders should be arriving any minute and the last thing Cam wanted was him walking into World War Three.

'Are you waiting for someone? Is she coming here?' Hannah mirrored his actions and looked out onto the lane.

'No, she isn't,' he replied, shutting the door. 'And I know this is hard for you, just as it's difficult for me. I've given you everything – the house, the dental business. I've walked away with nothing, absolutely nothing. I'm starting from scratch. I don't even have a job because it's too difficult to work alongside each other now.'

'You've given me everything? Everything except a baby! But you've managed to give the one thing I wanted in the whole wide world to someone you barely know.' With the tears streaming down her face, Hannah began to hammer her fists hard against Cam's chest until he grabbed both of her hands.

'Stop, please, Hannah. This isn't doing either of us any good. I can't do this anymore.'

'Do you know how much I hate you right now?' Hannah's voice cracked. 'All I ever wanted was a baby.'

'Hannah, we tried and tried to have a baby until it stripped us both of our love for each other.'

'But we could have kept trying.' Hannah stopped struggling to free her hands and stared at him.

'Hannah, we've had more IVF attempts than the average couple. We were working ourselves into the ground to afford it financially.' He took a deep breath. 'We couldn't carry on. Our life became about one thing and we lost each other along the way. You were always enough for me but I just wasn't enough for you.'

'I can't believe this is happening,' she cried.

'Look…' Cam took a breath. 'We've been through the mill and back and you will always hold a special place in my heart—'

'But…' Hannah interrupted.

'We couldn't carry on. How could we keep trying for a baby when we were barely speaking to each other?'

Hannah let out a long shuddering breath. 'And now you're going on that journey with someone else. Not me.'

'It's not quite the same journey.'

'But you're going to have a child.'

'I am.' This was the first time Cam had admitted it out loud. He had never thought it would be to his soon-to-be-ex-wife. 'What's happened has happened and I'm truly sorry you are hurt, I really am…'

'But…'

'But you will meet someone and it will work out for you. You will be happy again. It's just not going to be with me. We stopped being happy a long time ago.' Cam took a breath. 'And for what it's worth, I'm truly sorry you found out this way. I would have told you when... Anyway, it doesn't matter now.' Cam picked up the legal documents, which were in a file on top of the dresser. 'Here, they're all signed. Take care of that business. It was bloody hard work building it up to the success it's become.'

Hannah's face seemed to soften as she took the papers from him and exhaled. 'Very bloody hard,' she agreed. 'Thank you. What are you going to do now?'

Cam shrugged. 'I'm not quite sure,' he replied, even though he had a few ideas whirling around inside his head.

They stared at each other for a moment, knowing they'd been through the mill together but this was the end; this was the moment when they went their separate ways, living without each other.

'For what it's worth, you will make a fantastic dad. I'm just heartbroken we never got our baby.' With that, Hannah stepped out into the rain.

Cam swallowed a lump in his throat and watched her leave. Each IVF attempt had appeared to be successful. Cam could only liken the emotions they both went through to a fast rollercoaster ride, full of highs and lows, but each attempt had resulted in a miscarriage, leaving them devastated and dealing with the loss, each in their own way.

As Cam shut the door, he let himself sob. With his head in his hands he sat down on the armchair in the living room. All he could think about was the last few years, and then Molly. He'd tried everything to keep his marriage with Hannah together, he'd supported her as best he could, and of course he'd been devastated when it all fell apart. Hannah's need for a baby was the factor that had broken the marriage. He just wasn't enough for her by himself. He felt like a failure. They'd just grown so far apart, and each of them was hurting with the pain of each and every loss. Deep down he was scared that the situation with Molly was history repeating itself.

His thoughts turned towards Molly. He knew she must be feeling upset and confused, and he didn't want her consumed with anxiety whilst carrying a baby. He'd seen the devastating effects of that before. He made the decision to go over and see her as soon as he heard what Dr Sanders had to say. Albie had twisted the truth and Cam wasn't leaving until he'd explained the whole situation to Molly.

The second he'd set eyes on her he'd been captivated by her smile and her sparkling eyes. Everything about her had been perfect, even the way they had banged heads. He'd never expected to be swept off his feet again but he had been, in an instant. The immediate connection had taken him completely by surprise. He had felt a twinge of guilt, leaving the hotel that morning without saying a word, but he was scared; he'd tried so hard to make things work between him and Hannah and couldn't face the rejection if Molly thought he'd been a mistake. He'd been selfish, he could see that now, and all he could do was ask Molly for her forgiveness. He didn't have a clue what she wanted from him but she needed to know he would be there for the baby. Somehow they needed to figure it all out between them the best way they could. He'd always wanted to be a dad. Admittedly, these were very different circumstances from anything he'd ever imagined, but there was a life growing inside Molly, his baby, and he was going to do everything in his power to be the best father he could.

Dr Sanders was nowhere in sight, so Cam walked into the kitchen and switched on the kettle. He rehearsed in his head exactly what he was going to say to Molly when he saw her. He looked out of the window over the orchards of Bumblebee Cottage and smiled. He had fond memories of growing up here, playing hide and seek and running wild over the lush green grass. Already he could imagine his son and daughter enjoying the outdoors just like he had, and it gave him a warm feeling inside. He urged Dr Sanders to hurry up because he really wanted to go and see Molly.

The rain had eased a little and over the mountain top there was a glimmer of sunshine trying to break through. All this rain would have done wonders for all the freshly planted trees and plants up at Primrose Park. He'd called in to see Rona on the way back from his fishing trip and she'd agreed to make Dixie a magnificent cake for her eightieth birthday, a cake of Primrose Park, featuring figures of his grandma and grandad holding hands by the bandstand. He was so grateful to Molly for proposing to the community that if they all pulled together they could restore the park to its former glory. The more he thought about Molly, the more he admired her drive and determination. Without question he was attracted to her, he had been the moment he set eyes on her, but with the way things were, could they risk any sort of romantic relationship? They were parents first.

As the kettle boiled, Cam heard a weird scratching noise. He stood still, trying to make out where it was coming from, then jumped out of his skin when the back door handle was pushed down. He moved quickly towards it to discover Darling, soaked through, jumping up on her hind legs and pulling down on the handle.

'What the heck?' he muttered..

Darling began barking then took hold of the bottom of Cam's jeans and began to tug, trying to drag him outside.

'What are you doing? Get off me!'

But Darling took no notice; she let go for a second and began to bark, then raced towards the gate. Cam was perplexed. Where was Molly? He poked his head around the door to see if she was on her way but now Darling was running back and forth between him and the gate, barking continuously, and again the dog took hold of his jeans and pulled.

Cam narrowed his eyes. 'Do you want me to follow you?' Darling was off again towards the gate. Grabbing his coat and his keys and stuffing his phone in a back pocket, Cam headed out in the rain to the front of the cottage. Darling was off over the green but kept stopping and barking, making sure Cam was following. As he quickly followed her, Cam didn't know what to think. Molly was nowhere in sight, so he supposed that Darling must have escaped somehow – but where was she off to now? Pulling out his phone, he rang Molly's number but she didn't pick up.

Within minutes Cam found himself at the top of Love Heart Lane. Darling's behaviour was becoming weirder by the second. Where the hell was she going now? She crawled under the stile on her belly and waited patiently on the other side for Cam to catch up.

'I'm not climbing mountains in this weather. Darling, get back here!' Cam demanded with authority but it fell on deaf ears. She carried on running, leaving Cam no choice but to follow.

'I'll be in Molly's bad books if I don't get you home, Darling!' Cam looked down at his brand-new white trainers, which were not going to be white for very much longer, as he launched himself over the stile on the now muddy rocky terrain.

Darling was out in front. 'I really need to work on my

personal fitness,' Cam mumbled, stopping for a second to get his breath back, but Darling was back by his side pulling at his trousers. He swooped down to try and pick her up but she was too quick and was back on the track. As they turned a corner, Cam pushed his wet hair out of his eyes, glad to see that Darling had stopped by the door to the hut.

'You wait there, you little monkey. I'm getting fed up with this game,' Cam said, as Darling pushed her nose into the gap of the door, nudged it open and disappeared inside.

Water was dripping from Cam's coat and trousers, his trainers were sodden, and his hair wet against his forehead. 'At least you aren't going anywhere now,' he said, flinging the door open – to find a sight he wasn't expecting: Molly curled up in a ball on the old battered settee.

'Oh my God.' Cam was down on his knees by her side. 'What's wrong? What are you doing here?' His eyes were wide as he gently tucked her hair behind her ears and wiped away her tears with his damp sleeve.

'It's the baby… I think I'm losing the baby.'

Cam blew out a breath. 'Okay, Mol, try and stay calm. Take deep breaths. I'm going to get you to hospital.' He held her hand as he reached into his back pocket for his phone, which suddenly began to ring. He was surprised he had a signal and immediately accepted the call.

'I can't believe this is you – sorry I'm not home but

it's an emergency. Dr Sanders, we need an ambulance, Heartcross Mountain. It's Molly – she thinks she's losing the baby. We're in the hut.'

He hung up the call and once again sank to his knees. 'That was lucky. Dr Sanders was at the cottage.'

'Why is he at the cottage?' asked Molly, still clutching her stomach.

'He was coming to see me about my grandmother. Jan's discovered wrongdoing, fraudulent paperwork and assessments, but let's not worry about that now. Help is on the way.'

Cam rubbed Molly's arm gently whilst she closed her eyes to block out the pain.

'I was going to come and find you once Dr Sanders had been. I'm so sorry about before.'

Molly opened her eyes and looked at him. 'It's okay.'

'It really isn't okay. I'm sorry about Albie, there's no excuse for him, but I need to talk to you about what he said. I do have some explaining to do but it isn't what you think.'

Molly closed her eyes again. She had so many questions and wanted to listen to his explanations, but right now all she could concentrate on was the baby.

'I just need you to know there weren't any other women and I certainly haven't fathered numerous children here, there, and everywhere. I ... we had numerous IVF attempts, and each was successful but then... I know this isn't the right time but—'

Molly looked up. 'It's okay, I understand. I'm sorry for not letting you explain.'

'I want you to know, I'm here for you and the baby, whatever you need.' Cam took off his coat and laid it gently over her. 'I won't let you down.' He gave her hand a little squeeze. 'And I have to tell you this – I think my opinion of your annoying dog has changed. Darling is one intelligent hound.'

Darling was sitting behind Molly and resting her head across her leg.

Molly attempted a smile. 'She's done all right, hasn't she?'

'I didn't know what to think when I found her jumping up at my door handle. How did she manage to navigate her way back to the cottage? I'm seriously impressed.'

'Because I'm the dog whisperer and I told her to go home. That's where she thinks home is – which is a bit gutting, if I'm honest, because I've kind of got used to having her around,' replied Molly. She clutched her stomach again and whimpered, then grabbed Cam's hand and held it tight. 'I wish they would hurry up.'

Cam was up on his feet looking out of the door but there was still no sign of the ambulance. 'They won't be much longer,' he reassured her.

'Please don't let me lose the baby, please don't let me lose the baby,' Molly was muttering over and over.

Cam watched in horror as Molly's face crumpled and all the colour drained from her skin. She began to sob.

At the sound of sirens in the distance, Cam felt relieved and stood up. 'The ambulance is here now. Are you okay if I go outside and let them know where we are?'

Molly nodded. 'The baby is going to be all right because it has to be.' She forced a brightness into her voice that she wasn't feeling, but she hoped and prayed with all her might.

Stepping outside on the edge of the mountain pass, Cam began to wave his arms frantically to alert the paramedics. The rain had eased off and the sun shone through, creating a most spectacular rainbow over Heartcross Mountain. Dr Sanders had followed the ambulance in his car along with Jan. The siren stopped but the blue light still whirled as the ambulance door swung open and they began the ascent up the mountain pass with a stretcher.

As soon as they were within earshot, Cam called out, 'She's pregnant but in pain,' and held the door open. Dr Sanders, carrying his medical bag, followed the paramedics into the hut.

'Please help me,' Molly sobbed.

'You're in the best possible hands,' Dr Sanders reassured her, 'and we're going to get you to hospital. Now, take deep breaths.'

Molly looked straight at Cam. 'Please will you come with me?'

Cam looked towards Darling. He wasn't sure they were going to welcome a dog into the hospital and he couldn't just leave her on the mountain.

Jan came to his rescue. 'I'll take Darling. I think I might have someone who would love to spend the evening with her. No animals are allowed in the care home but on this occasion I'll turn a blind eye.' She smiled. 'I'll wait in the car, give you all some privacy.' With Darling on her lead, Jan ambled back down the path towards the car.

'Thank you,' replied Cam, taking Molly's hand. 'Yes, of course I'm coming with you.' He bent down and tenderly placed a soft kiss on Molly's head. 'Try not to worry.'

Dr Sander's manner was calm as he asked Molly a series of questions, before the paramedics took her blood pressure then lifted her carefully and strapped her onto the stretcher.

'We have to get you down the mountain path, which is going to be a little bumpy. If you need us to stop for a second just shout, but the sooner we can get you to hospital...' said Dr Sanders.

Feeling helpless Cam watched, standing at the side of the stretcher and blinking back the tears. He was willing them both to be okay, but he'd been in this situation so many times before with Hannah and so far he'd never got the happy ending.

When they finally reached the bottom of the pass, they transferred Molly to the trolley in the back of the ambulance. Cam sat next to her and held her hand. The ambulance door was slammed shut and they sped off towards the hospital, sirens blaring.

Chapter Twenty-Two

As soon as they arrived at the hospital, they whisked Molly off up the corridor. She'd spent the whole journey with her eyes shut tight, praying with all her might that it was going to be okay, and hadn't spoken a word. Cam didn't let go of her hand until they arrived at the hospital.

They immediately transferred Molly to a bed and began to wheel her down the corridor. 'How's the pain now?' asked Dr Sanders.

'Subsided a little,' confirmed Molly.

Feeling helpless, Cam hovered at the side of the bed.

'First things first: we need to check what's going on in there and I want you to stay as calm as you can.'

A tear ran down Molly's cheek. 'What could it be?'

'I'm hopeful now the pain has subsided. I don't want

to second guess. Let's have a look what's going on, then we can deal with facts.'

As they reached the scan room, Dr Sanders turned towards Cam. 'If you would like to wait in the waiting room, there's a vending machine if you want to grab a coffee.'

Cam looked towards Molly then back towards Dr Sanders. 'I would like to be with Molly. I'm the baby's father.'

Hearing those words coming from Cam's mouth gave Molly all the reassurance she needed; Cam was true to his word. He was going to be there for them both. She reached out for his hand and he took her hand in his and gave her a heart-warming smile.

The revelation took Dr Sanders by surprise. 'I'm so sorry, I didn't realise. Let's get you both inside then.'

Molly was helped from the bed then onto another one inside the tiny room. The sonographer, Emily, began to set up the equipment and checked over Molly's details.

'When was the last time you drank and went to the toilet?' she asked, her manner soft and kind.

'A couple of hours ago and I'm actually dying to go to the toilet.'

'That's a good thing if you have a full bladder. And what about food? When was the last time you ate?'

'Around midday,' replied Molly, nervously looking at the screen.

'You're booked in for a scan on Friday, I see,' said

Emily, taking Molly's blood pressure again. 'It's a little on the low side,' she commented and looked over to Dr Sanders.

'Yes, Molly has suffered with dizziness and sickness and has been resting this week.'

'Though I'm not sure how getting stranded on a mountain is resting,' Cam said, and rolled his eyes.

'Sometimes we think we can take on the world,' said Emily with a warm smile. 'We're ready to go.' She angled the monitor towards herself then took a blanket from the corner cupboard. 'Can I just ask you gentlemen to avert your eyes... Molly, I need to lift up your dress but I'll cover you up with a blanket and put some tissue in the top of your pants. Then I need to squeeze some jelly on your stomach, which may feel a little cold.'

Molly nodded and Emily did exactly what she'd said she was going to do.

'The scan itself won't hurt – it just may feel a little uncomfortable if I press hard, and you may need the loo. Are you ready?'

Feeling claustrophobic, Molly took some deep breaths.

'Just try and relax,' soothed Emily.

Silence filled the room as Emily guided the probe over Molly's stomach. Dr Sanders stood behind Emily. It felt like ages before anyone spoke.

'Please tell me – is everything okay?' Molly's voice faltered – this was taking longer than she'd expected.

Emily smiled at her and Cam. 'I can tell you exactly that.' She turned the screen towards them both and turned the sound up. 'That is the sound of your baby's heartbeat'—then Emily pointed to the screen—'and here is your baby.'

Molly gasped and covered her mouth with a trembling hand, 'Look at me, I'm shaking.' She reached out towards Cam, whose eyes were full of happy tears, and he cradled her hand in his.

Molly felt a sudden lightness as she let the relief sink in and briefly closed her eyes before looking back at the screen. 'It's just so surreal and magical.'

'And can you hear that?' asked Emily.

They fell silent.

'That is the whoosh of the blood flow towards your baby.'

Molly couldn't stop the tsunami of tears flowing down her face and Dr Sanders passed her a tissue.

'And are you sure everything is okay? What caused the pain?'

Dr Sanders perched on the edge of the bed. 'Your body is going through huge changes. Your uterus is expanding, which means your organs are shifting and your ligaments must stretch to adjust to these changes.'

'And if that's not enough, let's not forget morning sickness, heartburn, often leg cramps, puffiness around your eyes, and often cramping,' chipped in Emily with a smile. 'We women have to put up with a lot.'

'But you will get familiar with the changes in your body,' added Dr Sanders reassuringly. 'Some degree of abdominal pain is perfectly normal during pregnancy but if you're worried at any time all you have to do is pick up the phone or come into the hospital. But if it's accompanied by other symptoms, such as fever, discharge, or bleeding, you need to be checked out immediately. However, in this case your baby looks healthy. So let's hope Baby McKendrick makes a safe appearance into the world on around 5th February.'

'Baby Bird,' corrected Cam, causing everyone to smile.

Molly raised an eyebrow. 'Baby McKendrick!'

'Okay, we can talk about that,' said Cam with a smile. 'But don't you think Baby Bird has a better ring to it?' He looked towards Dr Sanders who put his hands up in the air.

'I couldn't possibly get involved in that discussion.'

Cam exhaled and touched Molly's arm. 'The 5th February – that's Maverick's birthday.'

Emily began to wipe the gel off Molly's stomach then lowered her dress before removing the blanket.

'And here you go, I thought you might like these.' Emily passed over a selection of images. 'Your baby scan.'

Molly was overwhelmed with emotion and brought her hand up to her heart; she couldn't believe this was happening. 'Just look at those.' She took them from

Emily and handed one to Cam. 'That's our baby.' Her voice choked with tears; she leant her head against Cam's shoulder and traced the tiny peanut shape with her finger.

'It is so,' replied Cam, smiling proudly at Molly.

'We're just going to leave you for a second,' cut in Dr Sanders. 'There's some paperwork I need to fill in and Emily here is going to organise your next appointment with the consultant and midwife. But I still want you to take it easy. Your blood pressure is very much on the low side, though hopefully this will improve as we move along with the pregnancy.'

'I'm not going to be lifting a finger,' confirmed Molly. After this scare she was going to make sure she looked after herself and the baby.

As the others left the room Molly and Cam were still looking at the scan pictures. 'I'm glad you're here,' she said. 'And thank you. I thought my heart was going to pound out of my chest when they turned the monitor the other way.'

'I know exactly what you mean but I need to thank you for letting me be here.'

'You're the father and I know we aren't *together* together, but we are on this journey together.'

Cam looked at Molly in a way that made her heart give a little leap.

'Would you like to come back to the cottage?' asked Cam hopefully. 'I'll make us some food.'

'That would be lovely. It's a date,' replied Molly. As soon as the words left her mouth, 'I didn't mean it's a *date* date.'

Cam was smiling. 'I know what you meant. I'm sorry about the past few weeks.'

'It's okay. I'm beginning to understand why this was a complete shock... You can keep that one.' Molly pointed to the picture Cam was holding in his hand.

'Are you sure?'

'Absolutely I'm sure. I'm just glad you're here.'

The wide grin that spread across Cam's face didn't go unnoticed.

'I'm just glad you gave me another chance. This was the one shot I had at showing up for my kid. I'm not going to miss that.' He squeezed Molly's hand. 'You aren't going to be alone in this. I will be here for you both. I'm going to be a father, after everything... I can't quite believe it.'

Molly squeezed his arm. 'Exactly that. You're going to have a child that you love more than anything in the world and they're going to love you. This baby is going to be one lucky child with us for parents.'

Cam then smiled. 'And let's face it, with my looks and my brains this baby is going to be a superstar!'

'You mean *my* looks and brains,' said Molly, swiping his arm playfully as Dr Sanders walked back into the room, clutching Molly's medical records in his hand.

'I just need to check – how is the pain now, Molly?' he

asked.

'Honestly, I'm feeling fine,' she replied, feeling like a weight had been lifted off her shoulders.

'Are you sure? Because if you'd rather, you can stay in hospital. We can admit you for the night and keep a close eye on you.'

Molly shook her head. 'No, honestly, I just want to go home.' Dr Sanders popped his head back around the door and spoke to someone before turning towards them again. 'I can give you both a lift home – it's on my way.'

'Thank you,' replied Cam. 'Maybe we can chat in the car about your findings regarding my grandmother?'

Dr Sanders looked towards Molly then back at Cam.

'It's okay – anything you need to say can be said in front of Molly.'

Dr Sanders smiled as he held the door open for them both.

Molly swung her legs slowly down from the table and Cam helped her to stand up straight.

'Any dizziness?' he asked, bending down to retrieve her bag.

'Only with excitement.'

Molly knew this was the first step in them coming together as a parents. The situation they were in wasn't going to be easy, but she felt they'd come a long way in a short time. They couldn't just fall into a relationship – they needed to discover each other – but she hoped that this was the start of something good.

Chapter Twenty-Three

'I 'll sit in the back,' insisted Cam, as Molly opened the back door of Dr Sanders's car.

'Honestly, I'm fine in the back,' said Molly, 'and it will give you a chance to talk to Dr Sanders about Dixie.'

'And can I make a suggestion? Please just call me Ben. Calling me Dr Sanders makes me feel really old and I'm probably the same age as both of you,' he insisted. 'And if you're free any time for a pint in the pub,' he said, turning to Cam, 'I could do with being introduced to the villagers on a personal level, not just in a professional capacity.'

'Anytime,' replied Cam. 'I've only just moved to the village, so a drinking buddy is most welcome. You don't by any chance play golf, do you?'

'I do. I played a quick nine holes up at Starcross Manor at the weekend.'

'That's very good to know,' replied Cam cheerfully.

Ben started the engine, drove towards the barrier of the car park, and slowed down. He entered a code on the keypad and the barrier lifted. They sped off along the bypass before Ben turned towards Cam and said, 'About Dixie, there's good news and bad news.'

Molly noticed that his tone had turned solemn.

With a look of concern on his face, Cam said, 'Go on.'

Ben slowed down at the traffic lights and indicated right. 'In a nutshell, there is evidence that Dixie's medical assessments were falsified.'

'I don't get it. Why would anyone want to do that?'

'The assessment has been signed by a doctor who has been under investigation, but nothing has actually been pinned on him yet.'

'And what is he under investigation for?' asked Cam, not taking his eyes off Ben.

'Off the record, falsifying medical records in exchange for a payoff.'

'What?' Cam was trying to process this information. 'So you're telling me that Aunt Birdie has paid someone to pretend my grandma is forgetful. How does that happen when my grandma would know she hadn't even had the assessments?' Cam was mystified.

Molly leant forward. 'Exactly that. Birdie would have engineered the situation so Dixie would think she had forgotten that she'd taken the tests, even though she hasn't.'

'And they would do this because?' The puzzled Cam looked over his shoulder at Molly.

'To trick your grandmother into signing over her properties to them because she isn't of sound mind, and they can have all the money.'

'But surely, if you go into care you would have to sell your home to pay for it?' Cam looked at Ben, trying to understand the situation.

'Usually, but there's also care that's fully funded by the NHS – it covers personal care, healthcare, and care-home fees, including board and accommodation. It's available to people who are assessed as having a primary health need that's significant. This is where this scam has developed: the doctor has falsified the records and tests in exchange for payment. Which means the care home is paid for.'

'And your Aunt Birdie sells the properties, Bumblebee Cottage and The Old Bakehouse, pocketing a substantial amount of money, and cuts you out of the will,' added Molly.

'But didn't the care home think the assessment didn't match what they could see of Grandmother?'

Ben raised an eyebrow. 'Here's where the plot thickens. The manager of the care home is married to the doctor. She was in on the scam too.'

Cam restrained the urge to swear. He could feel his blood boiling. He looked between the two of them. His stomach turned over. How could they do this to his grandmother? 'This is outrageous!' he exclaimed, raking his hand through his hair. 'And Aunt Birdie has engineered all this just for money? She terrified her own mother in exchange for a few quid? I was also paying my rent money straight to Aunt Birdie to help out with the cost of the home, and she was pocketing that too... She was quids in.'

Even as he spoke, Molly knew how awful it sounded. The dismay on his face said it all.

Cam let out a long, shuddering breath, 'And who is this doctor?'

'Dr Ethan Jones, and his wife is Zara. Nothing has been proved but I think charges have been brought against them.'

Cam looked over his shoulder at Molly. 'Ethan! That's Albie's best friend from school. He lives in that huge mansion on the river – drives around in his Aston Martin.'

'Zara Jones left the care home just after Ethan was taken in for questioning, maybe feeling that they were getting closer to uncovering the scam – who knows?' said Ben. 'But when Jan took over, there was a lot of paperwork missing, including your grandmother's, which made Jan wonder what was going on, since your grandmother's care was being paid for. But I will tell you Jan has had to report this to the police, and your Aunt Birdie – and possibly Albie, by the sound of it – will be investigated and possibly charged.'

'And rightly so.' Cam's eyes were wide. He was devastated. 'They need to throw away the bloody key. I can't believe this.' He was beside himself. 'My poor grandmother. Did you say good news? Can there be any good news after that revelation?'

'Your grandmother isn't forgetful or violent,' Molly said softly. 'That's good news.'

'And Dixie doesn't need to be in a care home. She can go home,' Ben said with a smile. 'The police are going to see her in the morning to talk to her, and she will need to make a statement. It might be better if you're with her.'

'I'll be there, and I hope they find them all bloody guilty. Family – who needs bloody enemies? I'm fuming. All this just for money? I've got a good mind go straight over—'

Molly put a firm hand on Cam's shoulder. 'You are going nowhere. The last thing we need is for you to get into another fight with Albie and be arrested. We have responsibilities now.' She looked down at her stomach. 'No stress, no anxiety – that's what's needed. Dixie is safe and that's all that matters.'

'I know you're right, but they tried to swindle their own flesh and blood, someone who has been nothing but kind to them. It's making my blood boil just thinking about it.'

Molly agreed wholeheartedly, 'People do strange things for money,' she added softly.

'I'm sure Dixie will glad to go home,' said Ben,

adding with a grin, 'and no doubt the rest of the residents will be over the moon.'

'And why's that?' asked Molly.

'Because Dixie keeps fleecing them all of their weekly pension. She's one good card-shark, that one. Even I lost three games on the run.'

Ben's touch of light-hearted humour made them laugh as he pulled up outside Bumblebee Cottage. They thanked him for the lift and Molly promised to take care of herself.

Cam paused outside on the pavement and looked towards The Old Bakehouse.

'Don't even think about it,' Molly said, gently pushing him up the path to the cottage.

'I'm in need of a serious caffeine hit. This has been a hell of a day of high and lows, this one.' He waggled the scan photo in the air. Later he would fix it to the front of the fridge with a magnet in the shape of a jar of honey.

'Tea or coffee?' he asked, switching on the kettle.

'Tea for me, please,' replied Molly, staring wide-eyed around the kitchen. 'Wow! You have been busy.' Molly walked over to the table. There were jars and more jars of honey lined up. 'Have you made all these?'

Cam smiled proudly. 'I have but with my fat fingers I can't get the labels straight on the jars or tie the tartan ribbon around the lids. It's driving me insane,' he admitted, handing Molly a cup of tea. 'There's sugar in the pot on the table if you want some.'

'The Bee's Knees homemade honey – very fetching!' said Molly picking up the labels. 'Dixie is going to be so chuffed when she sees all these.' She placed a label squarely on the jar, then tied the tartan ribbon around the neck. She held it up for Cam to see. 'Ta-dah!'

'Well, just look at that. It looks good enough to be on the supermarket shelves,' said Cam admiringly, taking the jar from Molly. 'You have this one, the first official pot.'

Molly smiled. 'Aww, thank you. It looks too good to eat – and what a brilliant name!'

Cam chuckled. 'The name of the business took a whole weekend to come up with. When Grandma told Grandad he was the bee's knees, that was it, the name just stuck. I have to admit it was very therapeutic making all this – stress-free, unlike my usual job.'

'And are you going to go back to your job? What's happening there?' asked Molly, spooning sugar in her tea and taking a sip.

'Technically, I don't have a job.' He pulled out a chair and looked at her. 'I thought my life was a mess but sometimes you have no clue what's around the corner.'

'Is that a good thing or a bad thing?' Molly bit her lip and waited for Cam to answer, while strategically placing the labels in the centres of the jars.

'A good thing.' He sat down opposite her. 'And today, when I saw you in that hut, my heart sank. I was coming to find you, because I didn't want you to be upset and made anxious by Albie's words, which were so far from the truth.'

'I know that now and I'm so sorry, Cam. Yours is such a sad story.' Molly was genuinely upset by the trauma and the emotional journey that Cam had been on. It really couldn't have been easy for either him or his wife at the time.

'It was all Hannah would talk about – babies. After the miscarriages, the next thing I knew, leaflets appeared on the kitchen table regarding adoption. She wanted a decision there and then, and I couldn't give her the answer she was pushing for. I just needed a break from it all. That's why Maverick and I went fishing a lot – I needed some time out. I wasn't allowed to say no, that wasn't an option for Hannah. She issued an ultimatum and I wasn't ready. I was still grieving for the babies we'd lost.'

'And that's why you didn't want to hear the word "baby" anytime soon?'

Cam nodded. 'I didn't believe I could possibly get anyone naturally pregnant after everything I'd been through. But then I checked with a consultant and the bottom line is – he said it was indeed possible.'

'Honestly, Cam, there has been no one else since that night…' Molly reassured him.

Molly was a little lost for words. Cam had bared his heart and soul to her and all she wanted to do was stand up and wrap her arms around him.

But,' he continued, 'the day I bumped into you, I felt a spark. I'd never met anyone like you before.'

'What do you mean?' asked Molly, her body giving a little shiver.

'Your smile, those eyes, the dress – and of course my boxer shorts lying on the floor.' He rolled his eyes and smiled. 'I couldn't stop thinking about you. I dragged Albie to the bar before the golf game just in case I got a glimpse of you.' He held Molly's gaze and she felt a warm fuzzy feeling inside. She really wasn't expecting this. 'And then when our rooms were next door … it was just meant to be.'

Molly swallowed. She had a question burning inside and wanted to know the answer. '"Just meant to be"?' she repeated. 'So why did you run? There was no message next to my pillow, no address, absolutely nothing. Do you know how that made me feel?' Molly heard her own voice crack with emotion.

'I'm so sorry. Maybe I felt guilty that I'd had the best time, maybe scared in case you rejected me. But as time went on I thought about you every day, and I felt terrible that I'd upped and left. I knew our paths would cross again at some point because I was coming to Heartcross and you said you owned the vet's practice in Glensheil. I would have come to see you and explain but I couldn't have dragged you into my personal life at the time. The morning in the park'—Cam moved the honey jars on the table to one side and reached across for Molly's hands

—'I'd just had a huge row with Hannah over all the financial stuff and I was trying to clear my head. You caught me off-guard and I'm sorry for my reaction. I'd actually planned our first meeting over and over in my head.'

'Oh, had you now?' Molly smiled.

'I had'—he grinned—'and it didn't involve pesky dogs trying to take my leg off in the park.'

Molly bit her lip to try and stifle her chuckle. 'You've got to love Darling!'

'And I am deeply sorry about my reaction when you told me you were pregnant. Our night together had been about us, our connection, and then, when those words left your mouth, I felt like I was back on the same rollercoaster that I'd just got off.'

'It's okay,' said Molly softly, 'I do understand.'

They finished their drinks in silence, Molly mulling over everything that Cam had just shared with her.

'The second I saw you, I told Albie I'd bumped into a gorgeous girl in the car park, but before I could point you out he spotted you in the bar. He'd taken a shine to you – until I told him you were the girl in the car park. He was miffed, to say the least.' Cam shook his head. 'I can only apologise for his behaviour but I think he and Auntie Birdie are going to have more things to worry about now.' He raised an eyebrow. 'Now here's the thing.'

'Go on.' Molly was intrigued. What was Cam going to say next?

'Come with me tomorrow. I'm bringing Grandmother home no matter what...' Cam paused. 'Shall we share the news that at last she is going to be a great-grandmother? That'll boost her spirits, and give her something to look forward to. Take her mind a little off what's happened. But it's up to you. I'm not sure when you want to start telling people about the baby.'

'Are you sure? Once it's out there people are going to start asking questions. Are you ready for that? Are we ready for that?' Molly looked across the table at Cam. He didn't hesitate with his answer.

'I'm completely ready. I know we have a lot of things to sort out and I've no idea what you actually think of me...' Cam tilted his head to the side. 'And I know we're on this mad journey together but...' He gave Molly the most gorgeous smile. 'So here's the thing – would you like to go out on a date with me?'

Molly felt a smile spread across her face. 'That would be lovely,' she replied, feeling on top of the world. 'And just for the record, I'm glad we're on this mad journey together.'

They both stared at each other with goofy grins until they were interrupted by Molly's phone pinging. 'It's a text from Alfie. Asking me to phone him when I'm free. Do you mind?' she asked Cam, who shook his head.

'Hi, Alfie! Yes, I'm with Cam now.'

Cam gave her a quizzical look.

'Yes, we can come over now.' Molly hung up the

phone. 'Alfie wants us to head over to Primrose Park. He's got something he wants to show us.'

'How are you feeling? Are you sure you want to traipse over to the park?' asked Cam with concern. 'You should be resting.'

'Honestly, I'm feeling fine, just a little tired, and Alfie seemed very excited. Come on, let's not burst his bubble. He's worked so hard to get the park up and running again. And then maybe we can grab some food?'

'Sounds like a plan. Come on, I'll drive.'

Molly and Cam stepped outside the cottage and as Cam opened the car door for her, he noticed in the corner of his eye a blue flashing light. Immediately they looked over in the direction of The Old Bakehouse. Molly couldn't help but stand and stare as they witnessed Birdie being escorted from the property and helped into the back of the police car. She looked as if someone had just slapped her hard in the face. She turned her head towards Cam and Molly and gave an unnerving sly smirk, which made Molly shudder.

'How do you feel about that?' she asked hesitantly as they watched the police car drive off down the lane.

'I hope they throw the book at her – at them both. How could you ever treat your own mother that way? It beggars belief.'

'Dixie is going to be just fine as soon as she's back home. She'll be right back on track by tomorrow.'

'I hope so. I'm quite looking forward to having the

company. It's too quiet without Maverick. I keep looking for him and it's going to take some getting used to. At least Grandmother will take my mind off things.'

Five minutes later, they arrived at Primrose Park. The wrought-iron gates were back in pride of place and beautifully framed the entrance to the park. The flowers and trees swayed in the light breeze as they walked under the row of oaks that flanked the path to the bandstand, where Alfie had asked them to meet him. At the sound of their footsteps Alfie swung around with a huge beam on his face. 'Ta-dah!' He gestured towards the bandstand.

'Oh my God! Wow!' exclaimed Molly, staring at the circular structure in front of her. She couldn't believe her eyes. Drew and Fergus had done a magnificent job. The simple construction was an exact replica of the bandstand that had been destroyed, and was painted in the same colours. 'Look at that!' Molly looked over at Cam, who stood and stared. His beautiful eyes were full of emotion and for a second he was unable to speak. Molly touched his arm.

'Grandmother is going to be made up,' he finally managed to say. 'I can't thank you all enough for pulling this off.'

'This is one hell of a community,' replied Alfie, walking up the steps and standing in the centre of the bandstand. 'And have you heard the news?'

Molly shook her head, 'What news?'

'The police have arrested the youths responsible – apparently teenagers with a lack of respect for public property and time on their hands.'

'I hope their punishment fits the crime,' said Cam.

'Me too,' replied Alfie. 'But now for the reason I've brought you here… there's just one thing that's missing.' Alfie gave Molly a quick wink.

They watched as Alfie picked up a long rectangular object, wrapped in brown paper, that was propped against the bandstand.

'What have you there?' asked Cam, stepping up on to the bandstand.

Alfie handed the package to him. 'Go on, open it.' He smiled at Molly.

'What's going on?' asked Cam in wonderment as he noticed the look between them. Then he began to tear open the paper.

'Just look at that.' Cam's voice cracked as he stared at the plaque that he was holding in his hand. '"For George and Dixie, who danced all night and for the rest of their lives together". Did you do this?' asked Cam, wide-eyed, looking at Alfie, who shook his head then nodded towards Molly.

'You have Molly to thank for this.'

Cam turned towards Molly. 'You organised this?'

She gave Cam a warm smile. 'I did. This is Dixie and George's place and I hope all those future couples who meet and dance here are just as happy and in love as your grandparents were.'

Cam looked stunned. 'Thank you. Grandmother is going to love this.'

Alfie pointed to a spot on the the roof of the bandstand. 'It's going right up there so anyone who steps up here will see it straightaway.'

'I can't thank you enough. It's the perfect dedication and inscription. Every time I come here I will think of them both.'

Alfie placed his hand on Cam's shoulder before stepping down from the bandstand. 'I'll leave you both.'

'Thanks, Alfie,' said Molly, watching him as he walked back towards the entrance of Primrose Park and drove away. Then she turned to Cam. 'From what Dixie has told me, she and George had a wonderful life together – and there's no better place for this plaque. They met here and fell in love here and I'd say they had a special kind of love that not everyone in this life experiences.'

'Come here.' Cam held out his arms and Molly immediately stepped into them and hugged him tight. The familiarity of being wrapped in his arms sent a shiver down her spine.

'I know we don't know what is going to happen with us'—Cam tilted Molly's face towards him—'but I know you're going to be in my life for a long time and I like that feeling.' He gave her a look that melted her heart, then pulled her back against his chest and rested his head on hers. 'And standing here is the best place to start that journey together.' He pressed a soft kiss to the top of Molly's head. Her eyes welled up with tears, and she didn't dare look up. Her heart thumped as she closed her eyes. She felt like the luckiest girl in the world.

Chapter Twenty-Four

It was Thursday and a beautiful day. The sky was perfectly blue and the early morning sun blazed through the bedroom window. Molly lay in bed and automatically reached out for Darling – who wasn't there. Darling had been allowed to stay with Dixie for the night and even though Molly was happy that they were going to be reunited, she felt bereft. She'd bonded with Darling and was going to miss her being around the place. Throwing back the duvet, Molly sat up and for the first time since being pregnant felt relatively normal, with no dizziness or sickness. Long might that continue.

It was just a little after ten o'clock when Molly checked her phone to see a text from Cam on the screen.

Just off to the care home. Come over around eleven. X

Last night, after leaving Primrose Park, they'd headed back to Bumblebee Cottage and as promised Cam had organised some food. After bigging up his own culinary skills it hadn't taken too much effort to get the fish and chips from the chippy van that stopped outside the cottage every week, carry them inside, and dish them out onto plates.

Molly couldn't help but smile remembering how Cam had fussed all around her after they finished their food. He wouldn't let her help wash up but ushered her into the living room, where he plumped up the cushions on the settee and propped her legs up on a stool. She secretly enjoyed every second of the attention. Cam sat next to her and the conversation and banter flowed so naturally. She felt at ease in his company. They laughed when Cam came up with the worst baby names she'd ever heard. He looked wounded when Molly turned down all of his ridiculous suggestions.

'Look,' he said, taking a photo album from the dresser, 'this is my grandparents' wedding photo album.'

As Molly carefully turned the pages both Dixie and George looked like they had just walked off a film set in Hollywood. It was the height of summer when they'd married and Dixie looked stunning, wearing an ivory dress that hung just below her knee whilst holding a parasol above them both. 'You can see the love in their eyes. The pair of them ooze so much admiration for each other.' Molly looked up to see Cam watching her. 'You're staring at me.'

'Your nose wrinkles at the top when you concentrate. It's kind of cute,' he replied, giving her a lopsided grin.

When he dropped her back home later that evening, like a true gentleman he opened the car door for her and walked her to the front door. As Molly put the key in the lock she turned to face him.

'You gave me a heart attack, you know,' Cam said, 'when I found you in the hut. I just want you to know the baby is exactly what I want.' He looked like he was about to say something else but hesitated. Her gaze dropped to his lips then back up to his eyes. She willed him to kiss her.

'It's exactly what I want too,' she murmured as Cam leant forward and placed a tender kiss on her cheek. As he turned and walked away, Molly's heart gave a flip, and she touched her face with her hand.

As she got up and wandered downstairs, Molly's thoughts turned back to Dixie, who would most probably know that her own daughter and grandson had tried to contrive a plan to get her out of the way for their own monetary gain. Thank God she'd followed her instincts, otherwise goodness knows what Birdie and Albie would have got away with; it didn't even bear thinking about. Molly hoped that Birdie had spent an uncomfortable night in a police cell. It was unbelievable that she could treat her own family that way – but fortunately Dixie now had Cam looking out for her, and Molly couldn't wait to share the news that Dixie was going to become a great-grandmother.

After a bite to eat and a quick shower, Molly flicked through the new clothes in her wardrobe, pulled out a maternity dress, and slipped it over her head. The dress floated over the top of her bump and she twirled around, looking at her reflection in the mirror. After drying her hair and dabbing on a little lipgloss, Molly observed that she'd caught the sun on her face and there were tiny freckles dotted across her cheeks. She felt radiant. There was definitely a glow about her skin today.

As soon as she was ready she set off on the short walk along the river towards the care home. The water was alive with boats and kayaks and there were a couple of swans bobbing along by the banks. When she arrived, Molly was greeted by Jan on reception with a smile. Jan immediately put down what she was doing to talk to her.

'How is Dixie?' asked Molly.

'Relieved that she isn't going mad but angry that she was nearly duped out of her properties. She is currently whupping Cam's backside at cards and I think he's already handed over a lot of cash.'

Molly gave a little chuckle. 'Is she allowed home today?'

'Dixie is already packed, and Darling has been an absolute darling. We bent the rules last night having her here, but after what Dixie has been through, if anyone had complained they would have had me to deal with.'

'Thank you, Jan.' Molly touched her arm before heading down the hallway towards the living room. Dixie's laughter was ringing out from the far corner and for a few moments Molly watched her and Cam playing cards. With a pensive look on his face Cam played his next card. They both looked up as Molly walked into the room.

'I'm being thrashed again,' said Cam, laughing and giving Molly a warm smile. 'How are you feeling?'

'Funnily enough it's the first morning I actually feel human,' she replied, breezing into the room and pulling up a chair next to him. 'And how are you, Dixie? I really don't know what to say about any of this.'

Dixie grinned as she lifted up the cardigan that was draped across her lap to reveal a sleeping Darling. 'We've been reunited and I can't wait to get her home.' The beam on Dixie's face said it all, yet Molly felt a little wave of sadness, knowing that Darling's company would be missing from her life.

'Reunited.' Molly leant forwards and gently stroked Darling, who opened one eye then nuzzled Molly's hand.

'And in other news, I'm not going mad.' Dixie raised an eyebrow, 'Black sheep of the family, those two. They'd better pray they don't cross my path anytime soon.'

Dixie's smile had given way to a serious look of horror. 'They could have walked away with the lot but now they won't have anything.'

'Grandmother is chucking Birdie out of The Old Bakehouse.'

'That I am. I don't care if she is my flesh and blood. What do they expect? Trying to make me believe that I'm forgetful and going barking mad – the cheek of them.' Dixie tutted. 'I want them out by the weekend.'

'Where will they go?' asked Molly, looking between the two of them.

Cam shrugged.

'Who knows, but that is no longer my problem.' Dixie leant over and patted Cam's hand. 'Go on, tell Molly your news.' The beam returned to Dixie's face.

'Oooh, what's going on?' asked Molly. 'You both look like the cat that's got the cream.'

Dixie pointed at Cam. 'This grandson of mine has made my day. He's out of a job—'

'So I've decided I've going to re-open The Old Bakehouse alongside my grandfather's business,' said Cam. 'I'm going to get those jars of honey and chutney back on the shelves, and freshly baked bread back in the bakery. Don't worry, I've already spoken to Rona and I'll be concentrating more on fresh bread. I may already have a contract lined up with Starcross Manor and The Lake House.'

'Wow, I wasn't expecting that. That is brilliant!' said

Molly. Cam bent down and picked up a book that was in a bag at the side of the table, and passed it to Molly. 'Take a look.'

The book was full of handwritten recipes. 'What's this?' asked Molly.

'The secret to my grandfather's and great uncle's success – their recipes for all the produce I'm going to make and sell…' Cam delved once more into the bag and pulled out a white baker's hat and an apron. 'My uncle's. I really am stepping into their footsteps.'

'Look at those – you are a proper baker. Do you actually know how to bake?' asked Molly.

'I've got a few sessions booked in up at Starcross Manor with Andrew the chef. Apparently he does the bread baking masterclasses. All I can do is give it a go. I've got nothing to lose.'

'I think you'll become the best baker in Heartcross,' added Dixie.

'That's because I'll be the only baker in Heartcross,' replied Cam with a grin.

Everyone laughed.

'There's nothing like a freshly baked loaf and I'm sure you will do your grandad and Uncle Ted proud,' said Dixie encouragingly, placing the next card on the table. 'Your turn. Remember, this game is winner takes all.'

'How could I forget?' Cam looked towards Molly then pointed to the wad of cash that was stashed under Dixie's mug.

CHRISTIE BARLOW

Dixie was looking very pleased with herself. 'Once this game is finished, hopefully Jan will tell me it's time to go home.' Dixie looked towards the door whilst Cam discreetly knocked his knee against Molly's and raised an eyebrow.

Molly knew exactly what that look was for and nodded, giving Cam permission to tell Dixie about the baby. Dixie was pondering which card to play next.

'Grandmother, we have something to tell you.'

Molly couldn't help but notice the excitement in Cam's voice as Dixie looked from one of them to the other.

'And don't worry, it's good news – in fact, just the best news,' continued Cam. 'Do you know how you've always wanted to be a great-grandmother?'

Dixie scrunched up her face. 'Have you been drinking?'

Cam laughed. 'No, I haven't, but I'm going to be a father.'

'You've definitely been drinking. I don't understand,' replied Dixie, looking perplexed.

Cam slid the scan photo across the table. Dixie went to pick it up and without thinking laid a card on the table.

'Winner!' exclaimed Cam. 'That's the card I needed! I've won! For the first time in my life! Come on, hand over the money. Winner takes all, you said!'

Darling sat up on Dixie's lap wondering what all the

commotion was about, then jumped onto Molly's knee. Dixie's hand was shaking as she picked up the scan photo and stared at the image. 'Is this really real? How? When? Who? Did you go back to—'

'No,' interrupted Cam, placing the money back on the table. 'And it's most definitely real.' He reached across for Molly's hand and Dixie's mouth fell open.

Molly was smiling. 'My baby is Cam's baby. It's a very long story...'

Without a word Dixie stood up, her eyes teeming with tears, and threw her arms around Molly. 'This is the best news, just the best news. Are you two...?'

'We are kind of just coming to terms with being parents and are working on everything else,' added Cam, giving Molly a look that melted her heart. 'But our next date is your birthday, because from what I know, Primrose Park holds the magic for long-lasting, loving relationships.'

Dixie held the scan photo to her chest. 'After all the upset in the last twenty-four hours this news has made my day. But I think I was duped – that card game is null and void. I lost my concentration,' declared Dixie, looking at the wad of cash Cam was slipping inside his wallet.

'Not a chance. I will remember this moment for ever.' Cam tipped Dixie a wink just as Jan arrived in the doorway holding a huge cake in a box and a bouquet of beautiful blooms.

'We will be sorry to see you go, Dixie, even though all the residents will have a better chance of keeping hold of their cash once you've left,' she teased.

'I'm going to be a great-grandmother,' blurted Dixie. 'Look!' she said, holding up the scan picture. 'I just can't believe it.'

Jan turned towards Molly and Cam. 'Congratulations!'

'Thank you,' Molly and Cam replied in unison.

Molly knew their news would spread around Heartcross in no time at all. Everything was coming together: Dixie was going back home, Cam was resurrecting the family business, and Molly was going to become a mother. Feeling all warm and fuzzy inside, Molly was truly happy. She ruffled Darling's head and she snuggled into Molly's chest. 'If I'm honest, Dixie, I'm really going to miss this one but I'm so glad I can see her most days.'

'Anytime, because you are family – my family. I knew the first time I set eyes on you, you were special.' Dixie meant every word.

'And so did I,' whispered Cam, making Molly's heart leap.

'And how did you pair meet? I want to know everything,' urged Dixie.

'I think that may have to wait,' cut in Jan. 'We have everyone waiting to say goodbye.' She handed the cake and the flowers to Cam then helped Dixie to her feet. 'I will miss you and you're more than welcome to visit anytime. Just don't bring the cards,' Jan whispered in jest.

As Dixie stepped out into the hallway, tears sprang to her eyes. The residents had lined the hallway with their arms in the air, providing an archway for Dixie to walk under. With her hand on her heart and Darling by her side, an emotional Dixie walked under the arms of all the friends she had made. Standing at the entrance of the care home, lost for words, she turned back towards the sea of faces smiling at her, and the residents began to give her three cheers. Cam juggled the cake in one hand, grabbed a surprised Molly's hand with the other, then pulled her under the sea of arms too. They took a moment to take in the sight before Dixie saluted and walked out of the building.

'I'm going home, thanks to you two,' murmured Dixie. 'I'm going home.' She handed Darling to Molly whilst Cam opened the car door and helped her inside.

'You are indeed,' replied Molly, placing Darling on Dixie's knee. 'I'm going to walk home,' she added, touching Dixie's shoulder. 'I'm going to take advantage of not feeling dizzy or nauseous.' Ruffling the fur on top of Darling's head Molly swallowed a lump in the throat. She really was attached to her.

'Are you sure?' asked Cam, carefully placing the flowers and the cake in the boot of the car. 'I can easily drop you home.'

'Yes, it's only a short walk along the river. Honestly, you go and get Dixie settled back in at home and we can catch up later.'

'Okay, but ring me later. Promise?' Cam was looking down at her and neither of them moved. They stared at each other and Molly was certain Cam was thinking about kissing her. For a second the air was charged with possibility, then Cam began to fidget with his car keys. The moment hung in the air.

'I best go.' Molly pointed to the pathway and took a step back. 'And yes, I promise.'

Feeling a spring in her step, Molly waved at Dixie, who had wound down her window. Darling was now standing on her lap with her head poking out, sniffing the fresh air.

Cam climbed in the car and as Molly walked slowly away she overheard Dixie say to him, 'You've landed on your feet there. Molly is a lovely girl. I knew getting you back to Heartcross would be the making of you.'

'And I wholeheartedly agree,' came Cam's reply. The smile on Molly's face widened, and, glowing inside, she ambled up the path towards the river.

Chapter Twenty-Five

I t was early evening when Molly heard a knock on the front door and was met by Cam's lopsided grin. 'I need to be rescued, for a few hours at least.'

Molly quirked an eyebrow and opened the door wide. 'Tell me more.'

'The cottage is overrun with villagers! Well, when I say overrun... Martha, Aggie, and Rona are sipping sherry and enjoying a card game with my grandmother whilst they hear all about the fall of Aunt Birdie and Albie...' He paused. 'Not to mention the fact that she's going to be a great-grandmother.'

'Ha, the news is out then? I wondered how long it would take.'

Cam stepped inside and followed Molly into the living room. 'Honestly, I'm exhausted. Question after question I've had fired at me – those women should think about changing their career to police interrogation. They would have criminals admitting to crimes within seconds.'

'Talking of criminals, any news on Birdie and Albie?' asked Molly, plonking herself down on the settee next to Cam and swinging her legs over his knees to make herself more comfortable.

'Apparently they've been charged with fraud and deception and, as we speak, are grudgingly moving out of The Old Bakehouse.'

'And where is she moving to?' asked Molly, surprised that Birdie hadn't put up more of a fight.

'Goodness only knows, but she's been back to the cottage today pleading forgiveness. She tried to spin a tale that Albie had been blackmailing her, but Grandmother didn't entertain any of it. She gave her her marching orders and told her she hoped they threw away the key. Aunt Birdie did shout some profanity in my direction, but I just waved at her. I really don't know what she was expecting. Grandmother was never going to welcome her back with open arms, nor Albie. They made their bed...'

'I agree,' Molly replied, noticing that Cam had rested his hands on her legs.

'Once this hits the news – and it will – my gut feeling is that Albie's businesses will be in trouble. He's going to lose contracts left, right, and centre,' said Cam.

Molly looked alarmed. 'Surely they won't have the

nerve to turn up at Primrose Park tomorrow for the garden party, will they?'

'I hope not, for Grandmother's sake. She's been looking forward to this day for so long.'

'And you becoming the village baker! It's all change for you,' exclaimed Molly. 'Dixie was so chuffed.'

'From dentist to baker.' He grinned. 'And as long as you're going to be my chief label sticker, all will be good in the world.'

'Can you imagine if our daughter—'

'Son, according to Grandmother,' corrected Cam.

'I was going to say, if our daughter or son followed in either of our footsteps – vet, dentist, baker – it would be so cool.'

'They aren't going to be short of a Saturday job in the future. I wonder who they're going to look like?' Cam's eyes were wide, thinking about it. 'It's going to be a huge change.'

'It is, and I can't wait to meet him or her.' Molly felt excited; everything was coming together and even though at one point it had looked as if she would have to take this journey by herself, she was pleased she and Cam were in it together.

'I don't suppose you have any spare cardboard boxes?' asked Cam, with a swift change of subject.

'There are quite a few knocking around at the surgery. What do you want them for?'

'I'm moving house. Much as I love my grandmother,

she'll bankrupt me in no time if we live under the same roof. She'll have me playing cards morning, noon, and night if I let her,' he said with a chuckle.

Molly was stunned. Cam had only just arrived in Heartcross – surely he couldn't think about moving on already? What about her and the baby? 'Where are you going?' She was glad her voice didn't falter, though her heart was beating nineteen to the dozen, waiting for Cam to answer. 'It's not going to be too far away, is it?'

She saw a beam stretch across Cam's face. 'Don't be daft. As they say around here, once Heartcross gets its hooks into you, you never escape.' He squeezed her leg. 'Grandmother has suggested that I move into The Old Bakehouse, which means that I'll be on the premises for work, and still close by. Everything is coming together.' He looked adoringly at Molly, and gave her legs another little squeeze. 'I know this is early days for us and we've been thrown in at the deep end, and I don't know what's going to happen between us...'

'What do you want to happen between us?' asked Molly softly, not taking her eyes off him.

'I would like to give it a go, a proper go.'

'Me too,' she replied, a smile spreading across her face.

'I did know, the very first moment I set eyes on you, you know. There was just something about you.' Cam stretched out his arms towards Molly and she snuggled into his embrace. 'I know this isn't going to be plain sailing but I think you're amazing – not to mention beautiful.' He gently pushed a stray hair behind her ear.

Molly looked up and met his gaze, her heart swelling with happiness, and willed him to kiss her. It was like he'd read her mind. Cam dipped his head and softly brushed his lips against hers. Molly felt so right being with him. He flashed her the most gorgeous smile. She stood up and, holding his hand, led him slowly upstairs and into her bedroom. The moment they lay on the bed, they began kissing, slowly at first but then with urgency. Cam's kisses left Molly wanting more.

'You are perfect,' he whispered, kissing her neck and making her gasp.

'Stop talking,' she murmured, pulling him closer.

It was ten o'clock in the morning when Molly opened her eyes. She sat bolt upright in bed with an anxious feeling – the bed was empty, and Cam was gone. She listened and was relieved to hear movement in the kitchen and smell the aroma of sizzling sausages.

'Phew,' she murmured to herself, knowing that Cam hadn't run out on her a second time.

A moment later she heard footsteps padding up the stairs and with the most gorgeous smile Cam appeared in the doorway holding two mugs of tea.

'There she is, finally awake.' He placed the mugs on

the bedside cabinet and slipped back into bed, wrapping his strong arms around her. An overwhelming feeling of happiness gushed through Molly's body as she nestled into Cam's chest.

'A cup of tea in bed – and is that breakfast I can smell cooking? A girl could get used to this, you know.' She leant upwards and pressed a soft kiss to Cam's lips.

'I should think so too. You deserve to be spoilt.' He passed Molly her mug of tea. 'Now drink that. Breakfast is ready in five, but I'll have to go soon after as I've a busy day ahead.'

Molly nodded and sipped her tea. It was all hands to the pump this morning. Most of the villagers were meeting at Primrose Park just after eleven. There were marquees to erect, bunting to hang and the buffet to be laid out. Dixie's eightieth birthday garden party would begin at two o'clock and Molly would have the pleasure of escorting her there.

As Cam disappeared back downstairs Molly threw back the duvet, pulled on her old faithful sloppy cardigan and looked directly in the mirror.

'Jeez, McKendrick,' Molly said out loud, smoothing down her wild hair and quickly wiping the smudged mascara from under her eyes before following the aroma downstairs towards the kitchen.

The table was set, and Cam was standing at the cooker looking utterly gorgeous and about to serve up a full Scottish. Molly was impressed. She wandered up to him and wrapped her arms around his waist, squeezing him tight, thinking about the day ahead. The whole community had worked so hard turning Primrose Park back into its former glory. Dixie had settled back into Bumblebee Cottage where she belonged, with Darling. Thinking again about the ordeal that Birdie and Albie had put her through, Molly became a little teary.

'Hey, what's up?' asked Cam, noticing that Molly had suddenly gone quiet.

'I was just thinking about Dixie.'

'It makes me angry every time I think about it,' replied Cam, placing the breakfast on the table. 'But she's safe now and we're going to give her the special day she always wanted.'

Molly nodded. 'This all looks very impressive. And the good thing is that Dixie is back where she belongs.'

'She is, and not only that, but my dear grandmother wants to work in the bakery for a couple of mornings a week,' said Cam. 'And who am I to argue? I'm thankful she trusts me enough to carry on the family business. It's really got me out of a sticky situation.' He smiled. 'At least I've got a job out of it. I just hope I do them proud.'

'Of course you will… Shhh… Listen.' Molly tapped Cam's hand then stood up quickly and turned up the volume on the radio. They both listened to the newsreader share the news report that the owner and director of Birdvale Garden Centre had been arrested for fraud and deception in connection with falsifying reports.

Cam blew out a breath. 'I've got a feeling once the police start digging they'll uncover more and more cases.'

'It makes me shudder just thinking about what they've done.'

'Today is all about my grandmother and your one job is to get Dixie there on time!'

'And I will.' Molly gazed at him across the table. 'Thank you for spoiling me. This breakfast is amazing.'

'I will spoil you at every opportunity – and that's a promise.'

They tucked into the hearty breakfast and afterwards cleared the dishes away. Molly was looking forward to today. Everyone would be out in full force to celebrate Dixie's birthday and there was nothing better than the whole community coming together.

Just before he left, Cam hovered on the doorstep and pressed a kiss to Molly's forehead. 'I'm missing you already,' he said, holding out his arms for Molly to step into them. 'I'm glad you came into my life,' he whispered softly.

Molly snuggled in close, feeling safe and content in his arms. 'Back atcha,' she said, smiling and tilting her face upwards. Cam kissed her so tenderly, it sent shivers down her spine. Her heart was bursting with happiness.

Cam looked down at his watch. 'Have we got time for

—?' He tipped Molly a cheeky wink.

'Er no.' She swiped his arm playfully. 'There's so much to do – the tables and chairs need to be set up, the band needs to do a soundcheck, and all the refreshments have to be transported to Primrose Park. As much as I would love to climb back into bed with you, there is no time!'

Cam gave her a lopsided smile. 'There's always time!'

'I'll make it up to you later,' she said with a grin, 'but I need a shower, and I need to get ready and pick up Dixie.'

Cam pulled a wounded face.

'Don't give me that look.' Molly couldn't resist him – he was gorgeous. She pulled him back inside and, like giggling teenagers, they ran upstairs. Another thirty minutes wouldn't hurt.

———————————

Just a little after half past one Molly parked her car near Primrose Park then wandered across the green towards Bumblebee Cottage. The weather was perfect, the sun was shining, and only a few clouds dotted the cobalt sky. She rapped on the door and waited. Immediately she heard Darling sniffing on the other side, then Dixie's footsteps. As the door opened wide, Darling was wagging her tail and weaving in and out of Molly's legs.

'Wow! Look at you, Dixie,' exclaimed Molly.

Dixie was standing in front of her with a dash of make-up, her hair just so, and the most perfect long cream floaty dress with a matching parasol.

'It doesn't look too old-fashioned, does it?' asked Dixie, looking down at herself. 'I wasn't sure.'

'Dixie, you look incredible. It's the perfect dress for a perfect day.'

Dixie reached out and took Molly's hand, and Molly saw that Dixie's eyes were beginning to water. 'Oh no, what have I said?' she asked nervously.

'It's all right, dear,' replied Dixie with a smile. 'This was the dress I wore when I met my George and he said exactly the same thing.'

'And he'd be right,' replied Molly, giving Dixie the warmest of smiles.

'I know today is meant to be a celebration, but I would like you to come with me to scatter George's ashes before the party. I'm not sad,' Dixie confirmed. 'I just want him floating free in the place where we loved to walk the most ¬ Primrose Park.'

'Of course, I will,' said Molly. 'It will be my honour.'

'Thank you,' replied Dixie, ushering Darling to the kitchen. 'Now, you stay there and I'll be back before you know it.'

Immediately Darling did as she was told.

Dixie linked arms with Molly as they walked over the green. 'I can't thank you enough,' said Dixie. 'This is the first time I've seen Cam smile in a long while.'

'And long may that continue,' replied Molly. 'Because he certainly puts a smile on my face too.' She gave Dixie's arm a little squeeze.

'You never did tell me how you two met.' Dixie looked at Molly with enquiring eyes.

'I bumped into him in a car park and knocked his underpants clean out of his hand.'

Dixie looked puzzled, making Molly laugh. 'Let's save that story for later.'

Arriving at Primrose Park, they saw coloured bunting woven through the wrought-iron fence that enclosed the park. A huge sign hung from the gates – 'Welcome to Dixie's 80th birthday' – with a photo of Dixie and George on the night they met.

Molly never ceased to be conscious of how beautiful Primrose Park was. It had been designed to make a statement and impress visitors, and today was no different. It had been restored to its former glory, if not better. Molly felt a thrill of victory.

'He was a handsome bugger, wasn't he?' Dixie nodded to the photograph of George.

'He was,' replied Molly.

'And all this for me?'

'All for you, Dixie.'

'George would have loved all this. He was always the life and soul of the party ... and he would have loved being a great-grandfather too.'

'Do you want to scatter the ashes first?' asked Molly,

noticing Cam coming towards them.

'Yes, please,' answered Dixie. 'Down by the fishing pond. George loved that place.'

Cam planted a huge kiss on his grandmother's cheek. 'Happy birthday! The park looks amazing, and that's thanks to your organisational skills,' he added, turning towards Molly and taking her hand. 'The park is heaving and everyone's waiting for your arrival,' he said, turning back towards his grandmother.

'We're just going to wander down to the fishing pond to scatter your grandfather's ashes,' said Molly gently.

The three of them linked arms and slowly walked down the path which led to the fishing pond. For a second Dixie was lost in her own thoughts, then she gave a chuckle. 'You know what? In the whole of George's life he never beat me at cards either. He used to get quite frustrated about that.'

Dixie walked towards the huge willow tree and perched on the wooden bench underneath it, clutching the urn. She passed her parasol to Molly, who noticed that Cam's eyes had welled up. It was the perfect day to lay George to rest. Everywhere was peaceful, the colourful wild blooms dancing in the light breeze by the water's edge, the mallards swimming across the pond barely making a ripple. Molly dabbed her eyes with a tissue.

They watched as Dixie, head bowed, stood up under

the graceful foliage of the arching branches and walked towards the water.

Nobody spoke as they all stared out across the tranquil water of the lake. Dixie was lost in her memories. The she said, 'I was a very lucky lady to meet you on this day all those years ago. The love we shared was so special. Thank you for falling across my path, George Bird.'

Molly's eyes glistened with tears and Cam slipped his arm around her shoulders.

Dixie unscrewed the lid of the urn and scatted George's ashes into the air. 'Happy birthday, dear George, my George.'

Molly looked up at Cam and whispered, 'Wouldn't that be the perfect name for our baby?'

Cam's face lit up. 'Perfect for a boy, Georgina for a girl.' He kissed her lightly on the lips. They stared at each other for a moment and Molly knew she'd fallen head over heels in love with Cam.

'You two promise me one thing.' Dixie looked between them. 'Never go to bed on an argument and always look after each other.'

'We promise,' Cam and Molly chorused.

As they all walked back towards the main entrance of Primrose Park, they heard the band begin to play. The park looked amazing. Long trestle tables with crisp white tablecloths held a magnificent buffet. Clusters of colourful balloons were tied to every tree. Excited children were running in every direction. Some of the villagers were sprawled out on picnic rugs at the side of the bandstand while others were dancing to the music. There were jugglers, stilt-walkers, and a stall that was overflowing with honey and jams that Cam himself had made.

They carried on walking towards the bandstand, enjoying the jovial atmosphere. 'Oh my! Look!' exclaimed Dixie, spotting the plaque on top of the bandstand. She dabbed her eyes. 'Such a fitting tribute.'

'You have Molly to thank for that,' replied Cam proudly.

'I feel so lucky to have you both. Thank you! But before I get accosted by everyone, please could I borrow Cam?' asked Dixie.

'Of course,' replied Molly, gesturing towards him. 'Be my guest.'

'Cam, I met your grandad right here and we danced all night.' Dixie held out her hand, 'Please would you have my first birthday dance with me?'

A huge smile spread across Cam's face as he led his grandmother to the front of the bandstand and everyone around them burst into rapturous applause.

As Molly whipped out her phone to video the dance she was joined by Felicity and Isla, who were sipping champagne.

'And how's life in the land of Molly?' asked Felicity, handing her a soft drink.

'Pretty damn good,' she replied with a smile on her face. 'And Drew and Fergus have done an amazing job of the bandstand. This party was exactly how Dixie had planned it.'

When the band finished playing that song, Dixie joined Martha and Aggie by the marquee whilst Cam looked over towards where he'd left Molly and gestured for her to join him for a dance.

'How romantic. The only time I can get Drew to dance with me is if he's had a few too many, which won't be too long by the look of him.' Isla rolled her eyes in Drew's direction. He was trying to persuade the juggler to give him a go.

Molly placed her drink on a nearby table and propped up Dixie's parasol next to it before joining Cam on the grass in front of the bandstand.

As the band struck up the next song, Cam slipped his arm around her waist and pulled her slowly towards him. 'You are gorgeous,' he whispered. His touch sent electricity flying through every nerve in her body. The heat of his breath tickled her ear and her whole body erupted in goosebumps.

'Oh my,' murmured Molly, 'we seem to be the only ones dancing.'

All eyes were on them.

At first she felt a little self-conscious but once they began to dance, she enjoyed every second of it. Cam's eyes were locked with hers, glistening with love. His strong arms held her tight and she savoured every touch.

'This is where the magic happened for my grandparents,' he said. 'They met on this day, on their birthday, and lived happily ever after.'

They stood hand in hand looking up at the plaque on the bandstand. Cam squeezed her hand and looked adoringly at her. He looked like he was about to say something and her heart thumped with excitement.

'Woah!' Molly's eyes widened as she clutched her stomach. 'Cam! Oh God, Cam!'

Cam looked stricken. 'What is it? Are you okay? Do I need to find Ben?'

Her voice quivered with excitement. 'I don't think I need a doctor, and I'm more than okay.'

'Huh?' Cam raised his eyebrows.

Molly grabbed his hand and placed it on her stomach. Beaming up at him, she gasped, 'There it is again. Can you feel it? I think I'm shaking and I know my heart's thumping.' Her eyes danced with delight as she held her breath. 'I've just felt a flutter, a flutter like no other flutter. Yes! There it is again! I felt our baby move for the first time!'

'Really?' Cam gave a big grin, his hand still pressed firmly on Molly's stomach. 'Yikes!' He picked her up off the ground and spun her around a couple of times, causing her to throw her head back and let out a peal of laughter. As he put her safely back on the ground, Cam took both her hands in his and gave her a look that was full of love.

'What does it feel like? Tell me!'

'Magical, wonderful, like I'm dreaming!' exclaimed Molly.

'I feel like I'm going to burst,' declared Cam, putting his arm around Molly's shoulder and pulling her in close. 'This is a good sign.' He pointed towards the plaque attached to the bandstand. 'I think this park and bandstand have some sort of special power, and if we are half as happy as my grandparents were, we are still going to be the happiest couple ever.'

'Are you getting all soppy on me?' Molly had a twinkle in her eye. She was overcome with happiness.

He turned her towards him. 'Nothing could be more romantic than feeling our baby move for the very first time right here on this spot.'

'I agree,' she replied, blinking away the happy tears.

Cam wrapped his arms round her. 'This is a moment I'll never forget! This is us, this is our family. Our plaque will be up there one day.'

'I love being a part of this family,' whispered Molly, tilting her face towards Cam's and kissing him tenderly on the lips.

'Me too,' he murmured.

Molly was truly happy.

Acknowledgments

It's thank you time, which is exciting because it means I have managed to write my thirteenth book!

First up, I could never have written *Primrose Park* without the support of my brilliant publisher, One More Chapter, HarperCollins UK. Writing a book is a huge team effort and even though my name might be on the cover a lot of hard work goes on behind the scenes. As always thank you to the brilliant supportive cast, Melanie Price, Bethan Morgan and Claire Fenby. A huge shout-out to the legend who is Charlotte Ledger. Without a doubt Charlotte is the most wonderful person you could ever have the pleasure of meeting in the publishing world. From the outset Charlotte believed in my writing and supported my career every step of the way – I'm so grateful to Charlotte for turning my stories into books – you are the best!

Thank you to my fabulous editor Emily Ruston, who in the most amazing way makes my books the best they can be. You rock!

Thank you to Charlie Redmayne, an encouraging and inspiring CEO. You captain a great ship!

I want to send a massive thank you to my children, Emily, Jack, Ruby and Tilly. They are my greatest achievement with my books coming a close second!

Much love to Woody (my mad Cocker Spaniel) and Nell (my bonkers Labradoodle), you are both my writing partners-in-crime and are always by my side.

In our lifetime, we make a number of friends, some stay for a short duration, some for long and some we forget. But then there are friends who stay forever, with whom we share an extreme comfort zone and they become your best mate in the world ever, resulting in an epic friendship. Much love to Anita Redfern, who is that epic friend, a friend like you is like no other friend. A friend like you is having no worries in my life. Thank you for putting up with me for nearly thirty years!

A special mention to Nicola Rickus and Molly McKendrick. Nicola has been a friend of mine for many years and works at the local vet's. When I was writing *Clover Cottage* she introduced me to Molly McKendrick, the local veterinary surgeon, who I fired many research questions at in connection with the Love Heart Lane series. Little did I know when my writing partner-in-crime Woody took a turn for the worse last year it was

Molly who treated him and had him back by my side as soon as possible. So who better to name the main character in this novel after? Obviously the storyline is completely fictional and doesn't bear any resemblance to Molly's personal life, except her name is Molly and she is a veterinary surgeon!

High fives to a lovely bunch of authors who support each other daily: Glynis Peters, Deborah Carr, Terri Nixon and Bella Osborne. Writing can be a lonely job but all of you bring a smile to my face on a regular basis – thank you.

A virtual group hug to all my readers, bloggers, reviewers, retailers, librarians and fellow authors who have supported me throughout my career. Authors would be so lost without you, and I'm so grateful for your support.

I have without a doubt enjoyed writing every second of this book and I really hope you enjoy hanging out at Primrose Park with Molly and Cam. Please do let me know!

Warm wishes,

Christie xx

ONE MORE CHAPTER

YOUR NUMBER ONE STOP FOR PAGETURNING BOOKS

One More Chapter is an award-winning global division of HarperCollins.

Sign up to our newsletter to get our latest eBook deals and stay up to date with our weekly Book Club!
<u>Subscribe here.</u>

Meet the team at
<u>www.onemorechapter.com</u>

Follow us!

 @OneMoreChapter_

 @OneMoreChapter

 @onemorechapterhc

Do you write unputdownable fiction?
We love to hear from new voices.
Find out how to submit your novel at
<u>www.onemorechapter.com/submissions</u>

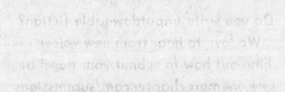